True Radio Confessions

Sex, Drugs & Rock 'n Roll

Dwight C. Douglas

Dedication

"I don't know why you people seem to think this is magic. It's just this little chromium switch here."

This one goes out to the Firesign Theatre and all those other extra-large radio personalities who understood the medium and contributed their talent, thoughts and care to make broadcasting dynamic and entertaining.

Table of Contents

Forward (Into the Past)

This work is a dramatization inspired by true happenings. However, various scenes, names, businesses, incidents, locations, characters, times and events have been fictionalized for dramatic purposes.

But don't let this "forward" fool you into thinking that none of this happened. Most of it did.

1. The Cold Reality

I hate the cold. You know... that penetrating atmospheric iciness which seeps deeply into the marrow of your bones sending bitter, almost painful, sensations to your brain. Coldness is a pointed reminder of why many humans migrated to Earth's warm spots. Those who stayed behind just huddled together more closely, attempting to fight nature's chill. Somehow, they held on and managed to stay alive, but were always envious of the smart, the wise or the eager who left for the glorious sunshine of another place. Those merry gypsies played their guitars and danced in warmth every day and night, moving from one toasty town to another and basking in the glow of a perfect station in life elusive to most others.

Let us begin this story toward the end, but just when you think it's over, the magical needle in the turntable tonearm hits the runout groove of the record, lifts, swings to its left and then realigns before slowly and gently settling into the first groove and the album side plays yet again. It's like the way we often repeat things we heard, saw or felt. For me, repetition is a means to process and understand the happenings of my life. Repetition, rotation and radio waves became indispensable ingredients of my existence.

Human beings have developed a sense of security based on repetition. When listening to a song we gravitate toward "the hook," the catchiest, most memorable part. A song's construct follows a format. The verse tells the story which leads to the chorus, and in this related and repeated refrain we often find the song title. Then, like the unpredictable moments in our lives, a major modulation or change takes place in that strange, contrasting section called "the bridge." It pulls us away from the redundancy, but never for too long or far before taking us back to the familiar, repeated parts of the tune, which make us all sing along. Isn't a song a bit like life?

It was a frigid night in December — the kind where the snowfall looks like fairy dust and the wind toys with its light, fluffy buoyancy, blowing the minuscule flakes this way and that. We were descending from the clouds at three thousand feet, and as we made our left turn over Kentucky, I could see the bright blue marker lights outlining the runway below. We hit a wind shear on descent, but the capable pilot quickly righted the aircraft. Having acquired and conquered a fear of flying earlier in life, I was comfortable, so much so that I had to stifle a chuckle as I wondered why it was necessary to land in Kentucky for my Cincinnati, Ohio destination.

It was nice of my cherished broadcasting buddies from years past to send a limo for me. I was the survivor of a magical myriad of radio stations scattered across the United States, and maybe they thought I had earned a free ride. Some of these guys stayed in Ohio and made their livings working in local radio while I was bad and nationwide, as ZZ Top would have sung. I had finally retired and moved to Florida, which eliminated most of the cold, but the warmth never melted the feeling that I was lucky. Sure, I knew the old maxim about *radio eating its young*, and there were times I found myself in the jaws of the corporate monsters and liars who inhabit the broadcasting business, but radio had been very, very good to me.

The gathering in Cincinnati was a homecoming of sorts. You see, I was born and grew up in Dayton, Ohio, only a little more than fifty miles up I-75. I hadn't been back to my hometown for years because I was busy with my radio career and most of my family had either moved away or sauntered off to that "better place" people sometimes talk about.

There was a time when Dayton was a booming city with well-kept sidewalks and a wealthy class of old money. The town was named for Jonathan Dayton, an American Founding Father and Revolutionary War veteran. The city's early settlers were inventors, and it wasn't long before some of them formed the National Cash Register Company. NCR made Dayton famous for not only that positive ringing sound, but also for the company's many other inventions and patents. Aviation was born in Dayton, with the Wright Brothers building their first aircraft in the "Gem City."

I remember older townsfolk bragging about the Winters National Bank and sharing the myth about Jonathan Winters' family members and bankers standing in front of the building smoking cigars and telling jokes. Who knows, maybe that fable was invented after Jonathan became famous. I don't know if it was because of or despite his local notoriety, but Jonathan Winters became one of my favorite comedians. I also remember him briefly being a disc jockey on WING Radio. I was just a kid back then, constantly listening to the radio and collecting 45 RPM records of my favorite songs. RPM means "revolutions per minute," and it describes how fast a record player must spin to properly play the recording. Yeah, sorry, I've been diverting a bit here, but you should probably get used to that.

I snatched my single bag from the luggage carousel and turned to look for what would most likely be a man, probably wearing a threadbare black suit and holding a poorly made sign displaying my name. That practice always seemed like an invasion of privacy to me. Suddenly I spied a large piece of white cardboard with *McPherson*, my radio name, scrawled upon it in large but uneven block letters. I greeted my driver and we walked toward the automatic doors. The moment I stepped outside; cold moisture danced on my face.

It's certain my parents weren't thinking about giving me a radio-ready name when I was born. The good news is they didn't opt for a "junior." I am the son of Otto and Ida Klotenfelder. Being of Dutch and German heritage you might wonder why my family didn't stay in Pennsylvania where they first landed. Well, most of my father's family were clock workers back in the old country, and his mechanical skills and aptitude suited him perfectly for a design and fabrication position at National Cash Register, thus Dayton.

I was christened Herbert Augustus Klotenfelder, which never fit on any form and surely wasn't a radio name. On this night in Cincinnati, however, my friends would be using the only name they knew for me, Sonny Joe McPherson.

The limo arrived at an immense, silvery building in a suburb of Cincy. The large, blue letters against a silver background of the Channel One Communication sign hovering above the top floor graphically worked in unison with the clean, balanced C1C logo on their left, implanting an image of technology, power and flair. The limo driver handed me my small overnight bag and I exchanged it for the tip in my left hand. As I slapped the straps of the bag across my shoulder, I thought about the thousands of trips I had made around the country chasing my radio dreams. I learned a lot along the way, and over time I was well-rewarded for my skills. In the here and now I was preparing for an emotional gathering. Some of my radio friends were suffering with ill-health in their advancing years, but a greater sadness would come from missing those who had gone to meet their maker, or maybe they just punched up their show-closing jingles before falling into that black abyss of dead air.

I stepped into the elevator, hit the tenth-floor button and unfastened my overcoat. It smelled of mothballs, the fate of most winter wear stashed away in a Florida closet. The elevator whizzed to the top floor and its doors smoothly and silently opened. Just then came a thunderous blast of melodic audio in the form of one of my old radio jingles, "SONNY JOE MCPHERSON, DISCO 99! <WHOOSH>"

Next came applause from those familiar yet aging faces standing around a huge Altec Lansing Voice of the Theater loudspeaker system,

"What the fuck guys, you almost gave me a heart attack!"

They all laughed and up stepped Sam "the Man" Richardson who yelled,

"As sure as I'm the Man that was the goddamn plan, Sonny boy!"

All of us in the group reached out and were soon a single knot of shaking hands and eager hugs. Buck Morrow, the C1C VP of Engineering, broke things up saying he wanted to give me a tour of the "plant." You see, this wasn't just a single radio station. The sprawling building housed the C1C corporate headquarters, the company's nine Cincinnati radio stations plus additional studios which were used to record the eighteen national network formats the company forced upon many of their owned stations in smaller markets. This was extremely far removed from the little radio stations of the past, sitting in single, one-story buildings with blinking towers out back.

As we walked down the hall, I saw each station's on-air studio through thick, double-paned glass windows. Suddenly, there was Q102, the major market station that had programmed a Top 40 format longer than any other United States FM station. We'll get into the details of Top 40 soon. Propped in a chair where the DJ would normally sit was an obscene blow-up doll. All the stations were running "voice tracks," disc jockey patter pre-recorded a day or two before by a star performer who would be heard on multiple stations across the country. As we got to the window of one of the most famous rock stations in America, I turned to Buck,

"Why is there a stripper's pole on that stage in the middle of the studio?"

Buck laughed, "Well, that was for the morning show when it used to be live, kind of a Howard Stern thing."

"Wait, the morning show isn't live anymore?"

"Nope, budget cuts. We're now running a syndicated morning show out of Dallas." Buck paused, rubbed his chin, then said,

"Hey, I heard Billy was going to be here tonight."

"I couldn't get him to come back to Ohio for anything. He loves that sizzling dry Arizona climate and the scorpions, not the band, the arachnids."

As we walked down the long corridor each studio was dark and empty, but I saw various lights winking and blinking on the control board and other gear in each room, indicating the stations were on the air while audio was switched automatically.

At the end of the hall, we faced a large studio door with an oversized *ON THE AIR* light above. It was just like the many I had opened and entered throughout my radio career.

"Buck, where does this lead?"

"That's the portal to my pride and joy, a complete broadcast and recording studio for visiting artists and bands. We've recorded and aired some incredible performances and un-plugged concerts in this room."

Buck swung open the heavy, six-inch-thick soundproofed door and we walked into a large, well-appointed audio studio. Two expensive Neumann microphones were mounted on stands tucked under the open lid of an immense, shiny-black Steinway D-274 grand piano, and a large, open cabinet on the back wall stored hundreds more mics. I saw boxes of Sennheiser, RØDE, Shure, AKG, Audio-Technica and other professional microphone brands. Off to the right was a large, double-paned window allowing visual contact between those here in the studio and folks in the control room on the other side of the glass, where all the audio processing, recording and broadcasting gear was housed.

As my friends entered the studio, I slipped off my coat and threw it on the Steinway bench. William W. Walker, a guy I hadn't seen in over twenty years, waved me to a table set up with food and beverages. "Hey Sonny, get the fuck over here. They have your favorite, Macallan 12!"

Time had swept away the movie star appearance of my old friend, but oh my God that voice. What a set of pipes, sonorous and resonant as ever! Years ago, he was a radio companion for teenagers but W3, as we called him, was now raking in the cash recording voiceovers for movie trailers and commercials for top national brands.

As more of the old gang joined the gathering, I was thinking how they all knew the stories. Ah, the stories! An industry populated with the kind of creative, free-wheeling and immensely talented people who worked in radio was bound to have tales. My friends held their own versions of what happened in each one, but there wouldn't be enough time during this one night to sort them all out.

I was pleasantly surprised to see Vanessa Smithgaard, who had adopted the "nom de radio" Vickie Vanguard and was now the music director of World Famous KROQ in Los Angeles. She was on her way to New York to interview Dave Grohl of the Foo Fighters. Lucky girl!

It wasn't long before Lady Glenda, the Night Dream, walked into the comfy studio dressed just like Stevie Nicks would have in the 1980s. She used to be one of the most well-known radio personalities but today, like the rest of us, she had as many wrinkles as she had miles.

I walked up and gave a her a big hug, "Glenda it's so good to see you."

She pushed me away, "You bastard!"

There was an extended pause while my face asked why.

"You got me un-hired, fired and rehired at more stations than I can count, remember?"

"Glenda, I'm so sorry but all that happened years ago."

She then burst out laughing. "Sonny, boychick, I'm just fucking with you."

The Cold Reality

I grabbed her arm as we cracked up together, strolling to the bar where we made drinks, which couldn't legally be called doubles or even triples. Maybe they were homeruns.

So early in the gathering, yet it was already shaping up to be a fabulous night with timeworn but dear, precious colleagues.

2. Drinking With Friends

I have an old radio saying, "When your ratings are great, you drink with friends, but when the numbers are terrible, you drink alone." Our reunion night was part wonderful and part stressful. All of us laughed, some cried and there were those who were still carrying grudges and laments about crap that happened years ago. The radio business is filled with remarkably gifted and artistic people, but some of them have astonishingly poor social and people skills. When such a person rises to a managerial level, as often happens, their actions and interactions can inflict serious pain on those they lead. Some hold feelings of injustice and anger about such folks and often repeat their stories, even after the person who once wronged them was long gone. I listened politely to several of those tales as the night wore on and was reminded and relieved at the way I had somehow escaped many of the worst people and situations, which are an inherent part of the radio business. More than anything else, I chalk my fortune up to dumb luck.

Late in the evening, Buck the engineer racked up some old tapes of what we in the business call "airchecks," recordings of on-air disc jockey shows with the music and commercials removed. These were known as "telescoped" recordings and were primarily used for review in meetings with the DJ's boss, the program director, also known as the PD. They also played roles in training, job applications and sometimes legal situations, like proving or disproving an allegation of a disc jockey slandering someone in the community. Many stations installed a tape cassette recorder that began recording when the studio mic was switched on and stopped recording when the mic was switched off. Such a device eventually became known as a "skimmer." It automated the task of recording airchecks, and the name was perfect because everything except the disc jockey breaks was skimmed away.

Buck pushed the play button on an old Ampex reel-to-reel tape deck which held my aircheck, and I was immediately apprehensive. It's all too easy to believe you sound godawful on an old recording, when you actually sound much better than you think. Remarkably, a few of my breaks were funny and others near perfect. Some in the room heartily laughed while others mustered slight smiles through the alcoholic haze.

At one point in the evening, Glenda strode up to me and asked the name of the hotel where I was staying. I laughed, and said,

"Let's not start something I can't finish these days."

"Oh, boy, another rebuff from Sonny Joe, just like that terse rejection letter you sent me when I applied for work at KTFM."

I shook my head. Glenda was an amazing radio legend who remembered every station, all the faders, buttons and switches on every control board she ever touched, as well as the many career incidents that dented her ego. However, she was totally out of touch with her real life. You might think that after five husbands she had learned her lesson in love, but she was a radio gal. I know that probably sounds a bit out of fashion, maybe even politically incorrect in these days, but women in the male-dominated broadcasting business have always been unique. They could be "one of the guys" when needed, but never missed an opportunity to turn on the charm or release a well-timed tear to attain their goals around the radio station.

Glenda confided in me that she was suffering from stage four breast cancer, and this was going to be her last rodeo. Pain settled in my heart, and I felt a lump rise in my throat. Glenda noticed, hugged me, kissed my forehead and whispered,

"Don't you worry about me, you old son of a bitch. You're not only a great broadcaster, you're also a talented writer. Why don't you author a book, a true and honest account of the radio business with all those crazy stories we always recall? It would certainly be a hit with broadcasters, but it could also provide great insight to radio listeners who have no idea about all the challenging work, technology, insanity and exuberance making those amazing songs and sounds blast out of their radio speakers."

The words just popped out of my mouth without me realizing their insensitivity,

"I should wait 'til all the people die so I don't get sued."

Glenda laughed,

"Listen you goofball, that would be way too late. Write it now, so our kids will be able to understand the things we did, why we did them and, fuck, how all of that put them through college."

"Wait, you have kids?"

"See what I mean? We are people, almost like real humans, and all that radio shit we went through should be memorialized in context."

"Maybe it's the scotch but I have no idea what you are talking about, Glenda."

She kissed me again, gave me a tight bear hug and reached around to grab my butt. Then off she went to jump into another conversation, knowing that news of her health calamity was safe with me.

It was hard breaking away from the group. I don't travel as well as I did in my youth and the five or six, who's counting, whiskies were messing with my equilibrium.

When I returned to the limousine, the driver asked about my bag. I then did my own walk of shame back into the building to retrieve it. Sitting in the warm limo heading downtown to the Cincinnati Netherland Plaza Hotel, I couldn't help but feel the gravity of the evening. Like most broadcasters, I knew that commercial radio had been around since 1920 when Dr. Frank Conrad first cranked up a transmitter located in the top floor of his two-story garage in Wilkinsburg, Pennsylvania, a suburb of Pittsburgh. The radio business today is vastly different from what transpired during its hundred-year history. I began to wonder if the marvelous aspect of American life called radio could be on its deathbed, about to be done in by streaming services like Spotify, YouTube and Pandora. I had to urge my brain to stop with the negative thinking.

As I unpacked in the hotel room, I thought about what Glenda had suggested. A few of my friends in the biz, so-called "radio people," had authored books about broadcasting. Some shared detailed stories about the mob paying radio guys to play certain records while others regurgitated all their grievances with tales of unwanted corporate oversight, former abusive bosses and the overbearing city fathers in those places where their voices flowed through the ether.

I grew up in a Catholic home, but my father was not inclined to get up early on a Sunday to go anywhere. He used to say, "It's there if you need it, son." On the other hand, every Sunday my mother would meet up with her Polish and Russian women friends and walk the few blocks to attend Mass at St. Mary's Church. Donned in their babushkas, they would huddle over the multi-tiered rack of candles in the vestibule, lighting some and praying for those family members and friends they believed could use a little pick-me-up from God. As for confession, well that may have been useful to those who carried the guilt planted in them by an overzealous nun with a wooden ruler, but for me a confession was personal. Should I be inclined to ask my maker for his forgiveness I will do so directly. Okay, enough of this religious excursion. We now rejoin our regularly scheduled story, which is already in progress.

There were many glamorously amazing, demonically bizarre, unexplainably immoral and downright unbelievable events I heard about, witnessed or took part in during my fifty years in the radio business. As I sat on the edge of the hotel bed, plugging in all my electronic devices and setting an alarm for the morning, I was asking myself why I flew from balmy Florida to frosty Ohio in December to see a bunch of old broadcasting buddies. I could have just said no and stayed on the beach. Now there's an interesting phrase. "On the beach" is a radio euphemism for being out of work, which happened all too regularly in the wild and tumultuous world of broadcasting.

I certainly had lots of stuff to do back home — clean the patio, kill the ghost ants, put up the Christmas tree, wrap presents and, well, you know, things. It was almost as if I was drawn to an old flame, like the moth seeking the warmth of a candle. The light is so bright the little bug can only imagine all the grand things waiting there, but in the end flies directly into his own death.

During the first couple years of my retirement I avoided even listening to my local radio stations. I didn't want to be mentally critiquing what I heard. I spent time with satellite music channels with no DJs and that was absolutely better for me. I got a few random calls from former associates asking if I wanted a short radio consulting gig, but I always declined. The money, the light from the candle and the warmth of some kind of temporary flame just weren't worth it.

I slipped into the big bed in this grand dame hotel and pulled the plush covers up to my chin, I reached over to turn off the light, but quickly grabbed my phone and did one last Google search for the day. I typed in, "radio confessions" and up popped, "*Confessions* is a popular feature which first appeared on the BBC Radio 1 weekday breakfast show in the early 1990s, devised by its host, Simon Mayo." I thought, okay, so this is already a thing. I wondered if someone else had already authored a book packed with true confessions containing the stories that most radio people knew. If they had, perhaps my amplified details would add more drama and flair to the old tales. Would anyone outside of the industry even want to read such stories? Well, no reason not to try, right? What's to lose?

I thought about my childhood days in the confessional when the priest would sit and soak up my acknowledgements of misdeeds before quietly dishing out my penance to gain God's forgiveness and release any dirty, sinful guilt that had built up inside me. Like many things that tend to pressurize inside a human, the idea of staying silent and taking my radio stories to the grave was comforting, perhaps even compelling, but that's not the path for me. It's time to get them out.

I took several aspirins to lessen the effects of all that alcohol. One of my drinking buddies in the old days claimed drinking as much water as alcohol would prevent a hangover. That was good advice back then when my "DJ bladder" could last through an entire four-hour on-air shift without me needing to drain the main vein. Tonight, however, my old man bladder would be ringing the bell every two hours.

I turned off the light and settled in for a good night's rest. As I was slowly descending into dreamland, I thought about what might have happened had I followed my father's footsteps and gotten a job at NCR. Then again, my mother was a substitute teacher at the elementary school. What if I had become an educator? I can no longer talk to them about any of this because they now live in the great cash register in the sky. That might sound a bit disrespectful, but my dad would laugh. His humorous encouragement was one of the reasons why I got into radio. Then that old saying *things happen for a reason* popped into my mind, but what's a person to think if their life turns out to be a turd?

I heard the fan of the heating unit in my hotel room whirling up each time the temperature dropped enough to tickle the thermostat. I turned the light back on, jumped out of bed, walked to the wall control and flicked the switch from Automatic to Fan, knowing that would keep the rumble consistent throughout the night. You see, radio people have this thing about sound. We are trained to hear everything, particularly those nuances most "normal" folks would never perceive. There's actually a name for this skill, it's called "critical listening." Broadcasters use it to hear distortion and cure it or to grimace at a bad edit and fix it. To geeks like me, sound is God.

Back in bed, my mind could wander again. Just as I was about to drift into sleep, an image of my childhood bedroom back in Dayton came into focus. There I was, pulling the covers up to my neck and looking over at the small shelf where that dull-beige GE radio sat. It was on, but the volume was so low I could barely hear it, and certainly my parents couldn't hear it at all. The glow of the vacuum tubes sent a wash of golden-orange light against the wall in the pattern of the ventilation holes in the radio's fiberboard back.

I fell into a dream, traveling back to the past, reliving the genesis of my love affair with radio.

3. The Awakening

The radio clicked on, and I looked over at the clock. It was 6:59 as the morning DJ yelled out his catch phrase, "Good Morning, Orville and Wilbur, get your lazy bums out of bed! It's time to fly!" That was followed by a recording of the legal station identification. Over the years, broadcasters have shortened that awkward phrase to "legal ID." The word legal is there because it's part of the laws of the Federal Communications Commission, the United States governing body best known as the FCC, which regulates broadcasting. One of their laws requires every radio and television station to broadcast a station identification announcement, consisting of the station's call letters and city of license, during the natural break closest to the top of the hour.

"You're listening to the Flying WING, W-I-N-G, Dayton." A jingle singing the station's call letters came next, followed by the song *Can't Get Used to Losing You* pulsating its way through my little radio speaker. That tune is by Andy Williams who's not one of my favorite artists, but the staccato violin notes caught me instantly the first time I heard them. To this very day I still love their haunting sound. On the other hand, the schmaltzy chorus reminded me that this was more my mom's style of music, but it was only the winter of 1962 and Andy hadn't even introduced us to the Osmond Brothers yet. I jumped out of bed and opened my door to see if I could get into my home's single bathroom.

It wasn't long before I would be taking the short walk to Rike's, an amazing seven story department store, to gaze at the hundreds of shiny 45 RPM records stuffed in colorful sleeves and sitting in the wooden bins of the store's music department. When I wanted a more obscure rhythm and blues or soul record, back then known as "race records," I would hit Gold Circle, an establishment that was not only the place for all the cool cats but also for a nerdy little-boy music lover just like me. And of course, it wouldn't be Dayton if I didn't mention the

Forest, the hippy hangout, or Dingleberries, a vinyl store that opened after I left town. Yes, that was its name.

A dance called the twist had just hit the scene, and everyone was cashing in on that craze. Hank Ballard and the Midnighters recorded the original version of *The Twist,* but Chubby Checker's adaptation became the massive hit. Later Mr. Checker sang *Let's Twist Again,* Dee Dee Sharp was *Slow Twistin'* while Sam Cook was joyously *Twistin' the Night Away.* Joey Dee and the Starliters released the speedy *Peppermint Twist,* a 45 single I purchased for seventy-nine cents. I became fairly good at doing the twist which, coupled with the endurance gained by hopping around on my pogo stick, allowed me to enter and win the ninth-grade twist contest with Sharon Hillman, who was the girlfriend of my best buddy Eddie. The twist was a dance that didn't involve touching a girl, so I could get into it.

As my 45 RPM record collection grew, I gained a parallel interest in electronics which developed into a bit of a hobby. I had a natural curiosity about technical things. When my father came back from World War II, he brought home two German Leica Rangefinder cameras, which I had assumed were merely "borrowed" from their original owner. That led me to spending time in my makeshift darkroom developing film. Now there's an interest few kids my age had.

One Christmas my mom and dad gifted me a Webcor tape recorder. The idea of storing and reproducing sound on magnetic tape fascinated me, and I loved watching the round tube with its green light opening and closing in cadence with the sounds picked up by the microphone. It was an early type of volume meter and marvelously magical, which is exactly why it was known as a magic eye tube.

I remember the day a friend told me I could build a radio station in my house, probably not realizing he had just suggested a perfect landing spot for a kid with a heavy interest in both music and technology. My jaw dropped when I found an article in Popular Electronics magazine describing two amateur radio transmitters then on the market. One was sold by the Heath Company under their Heathkit brand, and the other was developed by the Allied Radio company in Chicago and marketed as the Knight Kit Radio Broadcaster, a vacuum tube device which transmitted in the standard AM radio band. The Knight Kit came with instructions on how to assemble the metallic blue chassis and wire all the capacitors, resisters, tube sockets and connectors to give me quick entry into the radio business. Three electronic vacuum tubes powered the little transmitter, one 12AX7 amplified the audio input signal, one 50C5 served as the oscillator and another 50C5 was the modulator.

There were two connectors on the front of the Knight Kit, one labelled "XTAL PHONO MIKE" and the other "MAG PHONO MIKE." Now as any proper radio enthusiast will tell you, they are "mics," not "mikes," but the inventors of this little transmitter weren't radio guys. You could set the unit to broadcast on any frequency within the commercial AM radio band from 600 to 1600 kilohertz (kHz), which was good because you wouldn't want to be trying to overpower one of those stations that beamed in at night from distant cities all over the country.

Certain AM stations in the US, technically known as clear channel stations, do not share their broadcast frequency with any other station. When the Earth's atmosphere cools at night, the ionospheric layers shift, and the signals of AM stations are reflected back to Earth in ways that differ from their daytime propagation, causing reception at locations geographically distant from their point of origin. A high-powered AM clear channel signal can bounce quite far and still be received because there are no other stations broadcasting on that frequency. The clear channel station closest to me was WLW in Cincinnati, which broadcast with 50,000 watts at 700 on the AM dial. I picked 990 kHz for my little homebrew station because it was a "quiet" frequency in Dayton.

I'll take a short pause here to explain the terms AM and FM, the two transmission methods US commercial radio stations employ to propel audio to radio receivers. There are two axes of a radio waveform, horizontal (width) and vertical (height). An oscilloscope is an electronic device that allows one to "see" an otherwise invisible radio wave. If you were to look at the waveforms of an AM and FM radio station on oscilloscopes, you would see the waveform of the AM station bouncing up and down while that of the FM station would be bouncing left to right. For AM transmission, the height (amplitude) of the waveform varies (modulates) according to the sound being transmitted. This is called amplitude modulation or AM. With FM transmission, the width (frequency) of the waveform varies. This is known as frequency modulation or FM. In both cases, the variances of the waveforms are detected in the radio receiver and reconverted to sound. The difference between AM and FM is technical, but FM transmission provides fuller fidelity and less noisy reception as compared to AM, which can become almost unlistenable during an electrical storm. Okay, let's get back to the Herbie Show in Dayton.

It didn't take long for me to figure out I could plug my Webcor mic into the tape deck, set the machine to record, and send the output of the tape recorder to the little Knight Kit transmitter. Next, I took the output of my small 45 record player and fed it into the phono input of the transmitter, BAM, I had myself a music radio station! The instructions said to use a small length of copper wire as an antenna but, thinking big, I bought fifty feet of copper cable and ran it out of my bedroom window and up into the Bing cherry tree in the backyard.

I studied broadcasting in books and attended electronics classes in middle school, so I suspected this long antenna meant my transmitter was operating somewhat illegally, but I wanted to get as much coverage as possible. My friend spread the word in the neighborhood that we would be on the air Monday night. We recorded a thirty-minute show on the Webcor, and as it played back, we walked around the neighborhood listening to our handywork on my small, red-plastic Japanese transistor radio. Much to our chagrin, we were only about a block away before our little radio station faded away. Radio lesson number one, get the biggest signal you can.

There was no fame because there was no audience. Potential listeners must be able to hear you, and should they be listening you'd better be giving them something they want. I had all the hit records the girls loved, but our squeaky immature voices turned them off, and us as well. I called my great new station Radio Rudy, in honor of the University of Dayton mascot, but most of my neighbors were unaware of its existence while listening to the local commercial stations. I started to become disinterested in my low-power project and moved it a little to the side, focusing on school, homework and parents, the important ingredients of a kid's life.

I kept buying records though, and someone suggested I contact the committee that ran the Sunday after-church dances at the community center. Their DJ had gone off to college and the music stopped as of the previous Sunday. When I made a cold call and announced my interest in the gig, I was hired on the spot. In the center dancehall, which was adorned with large black and white pictures of Tommy Dorsey and Glenn Miller, I found an old, hundred-watt Bogen P.A. amplifier connected to giant speakers in the four corners of the room. For my first gig I brought my little 45 RPM turntable along with a large box of 45s, and it wasn't long before the ladies who ran the dance were telling me to "TURN THAT MUSIC DOWN!"

Every Sunday afternoon I was front and center at the hop, standing on an elevated stage next to a shiny, chrome Electro-Voice microphone at the ready. The mic was used only by me to make "You left your headlights on" messages or to announce, "Betsy Lou please call home now." I would clear my throat trying to make my voice sound deeper but understood I would have to wait for Mother Nature to eventually install that desired upgrade.

People were talking about my DJ stint, winning the twist dance contest and my little radio station. At some point kids started calling me

Radio Rudy. Even though my little radio station was not that well known or successful, it led into one of my more awkward childhood moments.

One afternoon, a guy I knew about but had never seen in the flesh came knocking. He was an older lad, about two hundred pounds of pure bully, wearing an old T-shirt stained with mustard from his five-hotdog lunch. His name was, and I am not making this up, Harry Barber. This guy was already intimidating, and his long, unruly hair didn't help. I swung open the door and Barber said,

"So, this is where Radio Rudy lives?"

I was surprised he knew about my station. His house was too far away to hear the tiny signal, so how did he know about my radio hobby? A smug grin was plastered across his face as he said,

"Do you know that an FCC truck is going around trying to find pirate radio stations? Do you know how the government deals with unlicensed broadcasters?"

My heart stopped. Most Daytonians are law abiding citizens and my father always emphasized that I must never do anything that would embarrass the family. This sounded serious. Barber picked something from his nose, flicked it away, then continued,

"If they find you, they'll come to your house and take all your records, your tape recorder, your mic, and the transmitter."

"But I thought it was legal…"

"Well, your signal is way better than most low-power stations. What is your secret?"

I clammed up. He kept going,

"I'll give you twenty bucks cash for that transmitter. You need to lay low for a while."

I looked down, as if the answer was written on the floorboards of my porch. I would be lost if the FCC confiscated all my 45s. I certainly couldn't give up that tape recorder because it cost my parents lots of money, but I had paid only twelve dollars for the Knight Kit Broadcaster, so I would be making money by accepting Barber's deal. I told him to wait at the door. After grabbing a paper bag from the kitchen, I started climbing the stairs to my bedroom when I heard my mother call out,

"What are you doing, Herbie?"

And just as any self-respecting kid would do, I replied,

"Nothing."

Once in my room I disconnected all the wires from the transmitter, put it into the brown paper bag, and marched back to the front door. I handed the bagged transmitter to Barber, and he produced a twenty-dollar bill saying,

"You'll thank me for this later."

He walked away and I went back to my bedroom, folded up all the wires and packed away the Webcor. I was still nervous, and my hands were shaking a bit.

Flush with cash, I told my mother I was going to Cassano's for pizza with the guys and she replied,

"Okay but only one piece, Herbert. You don't want to ruin your dinner."

After parking my bike, I walked into the pizza place in Kettering and there were a few of my school friends. I sat down and Roger Demering looked over and laughed at me. I responded,

"Roger, you're a dickface. What's so funny?"

"Well, I understand you got conned out of your radio station today."

I waved to the server and looked back at Roger,

"What are you talking about?"

I ordered a pepperoni slice along with a Coke then shook my head,

"Boy, you guys are like old ladies with the gossip."

Roger leaned forward and said in a lower voice,

"There is no FCC truck. Fat-ass Barber was jealous and just wanted to get you off the air."

I sat there, munching that delicious pizza and trying to control my appearance while gazing out the window. I hoped my face wasn't becoming crimson with embarrassment. I realized I had just learned another radio lesson I would carry for life — if you can't beat them, you buy them out. Yes, I was taken by a manipulating malefactor, but I still had my weekend DJ gig and, of course, I held onto that dream of working at a real radio station someday.

The sun was starting to go down, which meant it was time to get on my bike and head back home. As I passed the five and dime store, the small speaker over the door was playing, *"He went away, and you hung around, and bothered me, every night. And when I wouldn't go out with you, you said things that weren't very nice!"* It was the Angels' song *My Boyfriend's Back.* I was thinking to myself that's a solid hit and I need to pick up that record.

At this point, I decided to just play music for myself and concentrate on school. I was out of the radio business and thinking that playing football or being in a rock band were other potential high school diversions.

Radio Rudy taught me how to construct a device that could send an electrical waveform through the air that listeners could receive to hear both music and voices coming out of their radio. That little boy magic of radio had now infused my soul, but I didn't yet realize how so much fun could become a job, a career, a lifetime. For now, I was just a kid with a dream and a radio in a room, my room, a place where I could go and tell my secrets to.

Over the next several years, the Beach Boys, Motown, and those great Brill Building hits bounced off the walls of my small bedroom. The music coming out of my plastic radio kept *me* from bouncing off the walls and helped to keep some wild hormones in check. DJs were mysterious forms to me. I knew them only by their voices, but when they made me laugh, I wanted to be just like them.

I was happy my new radio had a sleep timer, so I could now count sheep while my favorite station was playing the countdown every night. One announcer would constantly scream, "This is your LEADER!" Man, I thought, now there's a slogan! I just couldn't stop listening and imagining that maybe one day the voice coming out of everyone's radio would be mine.

4. Rush to College

There was a time when many Americans believed we needed a boogeyman, an enemy, to help people focus and unite under a single cause. I grew up in an age where "Commies" were bad and we were the good guys, the men wearing white hats while riding white horses. But while fears of the atomic bomb forced us into school day drills of duck and cover, I had no desire to live my life looking at my classmates from underneath a desk, which was absolutely no protection as far as I was concerned. All that stuff seemed silly by the time I was ready for college.

In those days, us kids were running around with long hair, bell bottom jeans and Navy peacoats to fit in with the emerging trends of our youthful society, but we were also uniting under another banner. Peace signs were everywhere, and the tide was turning against the Vietnam war. While my mother and father were not anti-war, they were not at all mesmerized by the patriotic fervor that led other parents to send their kids off into foreign jungles to die for a vague notion known as the "Domino Theory."

Military types in the Pentagon, fresh off World War II and the Korean "conflict," preached that if one country fell to communism then, just like dominos, many others would also fall. Our presidents, from Eisenhower through Kennedy and Johnson then onto Nixon, believed if we bombed North Vietnam "back to the Stone Age" it would halt the spread of communism.

This kid saw some of his friends' older brothers going off to war in that faraway land. Some never came back. Others were shipped home in wooden boxes. Too many returned to their homeland with large chunks of their bodies damaged, especially their brains. Guys who left as boys came back as men, men who were addicted to hard drugs or suffering from PTSD. Nothing about any of it seemed good to me. I was happy to learn over the next couple of years the government would give anyone enrolled in college a deferment from serving. Sign me up!

I was late out the gate applying to institutions of higher learning. I sat for the S.A.T. last-minute, so there was no chance of taking it again. My score was extremely low, which meant I didn't prepare properly. I had a reasonably high I.Q., but I was never good at test taking. My applications to Ohio State University in Columbus and Case Western Reserve in Cleveland were rejected, and my father suggested I apply to the University of Dayton so I could live at home, which would help keep the family expenses in order.

It was the last week before registration when the acceptance letter came. I wouldn't be going to Vietnam, instead I would be attending classes at the downtown college near my home, the University of Dayton. I would elect a major in Communication and a minor in Marketing. I didn't know exactly what I wanted to do with my life, radio broadcasting was merely a dream right now, and I figured those classes would help orient me. My parents were so happy that I would remain home they had little care about what I studied.

I was in the registration line standing behind a young woman who looked as nervous as I felt. She turned around and asked in a sheepish voice,

"How does this work?"

"I have no idea, I'm new."

She laughed and said,

"Of course, but what if you can't get into a class?"

"I don't know, I guess you should be ready to pick something else. Hey, I'm Herbie, what's your name?"

"Sarah Lee…"

I started to laugh, but then remembered a schoolmate from elementary school named Helen Keller,

"I'm sorry, the name…"

"Too bad you couldn't wait. My last name is Kelly."

We both grinned and later learned that we were in the same 8 a.m. Psychology I class, which had to be taken by all students enrolled in a liberal arts program. I came to enjoy that class because it was the beginning of my understanding about why all those mental capsules would ooze through my brain when certain "cause and effect" events took place. I sometimes would think, yep, that's why my mother or father did this or that.

Perhaps a time marker will help here. This was 1968, and college students basically lived in one of five extremely different boxes. There were the full-on Greek frat boys with their attendant sorority sisters. We had the freaks, or as they were called by the US President, the hippies. Then there were the artsy, creative theater types with their flamboyant ways of dressing and acting. Our school had a terrific dance program, and I would sit in class with tall, fit men dressed in leotards and carrying duffel bags full of their costume changes and dancing shoes. I considered the dancers, both male and female, part of the theater group. Then there were the business majors with their three-piece suits and ties. Who were those guys? Finally, there were the YAF-ers. Young Americans for Freedom was a coalition of traditional conservatives and libertarians with a presence on many college campuses back then, and there was just something about them I didn't like, especially when they walked around constantly quoting William F. Buckley.

I couldn't fully relate to any of those groups, and I was starting to feel like an outsider who didn't fit in. At some point during my second week at school I was walking down Kiefaber Street when I spied a small sign to my left, *WVUD, Student Radio Station.* I stepped up to the entrance, swung open the front door and walked in.

Standing in the lobby I was looking through a window into a radio studio which was in total disarray. Turntables had been lifted out of their cabinet next to a control board and turned upside down. Two guys with long hair and smoking cigarettes were looking into "the board." Its top had been removed and was now leaning against a wall next to a giant rack of unknown devices, some with steady or blinking lights and others dark. I saw a strange panel that almost looked like snakes were swarming over it but would later learn it was a "patch panel" with many jacks. Wires with plugs could be inserted into the panel to connect various jacks together, and that directed audio and control pulses among the station's three studios. This was certainly a huge step up from Radio Rudy! One of the geeky guys came out to greet me.

"What do you want, man?"

"So, how does one get a job here?"

The guy laughed and now the other guy tripped over a cable while walking toward us,

"The radio station is a school activity. Anyone can sign up for it."

"Okay, where can I do that?"

He handed me a clipboard and I saw about fifty kids had signed up before me. I printed my name and student ID on the form and passed the clipboard back,

"So, when will I be contacted?"

"Man, you are pushy, maybe you should work in sales. Don't worry, we'll find you but there is no guarantee you'll get an air shift."

I shook my head in agreement of sorts and walked out. I wondered why the station wasn't already up and running. Perhaps the engineering guys weren't ready to go live because they let too much time slip by. Maybe the station needed someone to bring everyone and everything together. I could see myself in such a role, but my confidence and perspective were probably overblown. I realized I had no clue about how broadcasting actually worked, but I was hoping I could become a radio guy at this student run "activity."

After I got seated for my 8 a.m. Psych I class, in walked the coffeecake girl, Sarah Lee, smiling and slipping into the seat right next to me. I greeted her with a nod and a good morning, and she handed me a mimeographed memo,

"I see you signed up for WVUD."

"Yeah, how would you know that?"

"They put me in charge of communication."

"Really?"

"You should attend this meeting if you want to get an assignment at the station.

"Wow, thanks. I'll be there."

It was a glorious, sunny Friday afternoon, not exactly a suitable time for the radio station to be having its first meeting of the semester. Lots of kids go home for the weekend after Friday classes, but it wasn't long before it became apparent the timing of this meeting was on purpose. A round man with tons of energy and a flat top haircut stood on top of the reception desk in the lobby of the student radio station,

"Okay all you radio rookies, I'm a senior here at WVUD. My name is Brady Cook and if you all would just shut up, we'll get this meeting started."

The room quickly sucked into silence. I looked over at Sarah Lee and saw she was full-on attentive while clutching a pen and notebook. I also noticed a tall, thin guy with long, straight hair. He was extremely alert and seemed to be studying everyone in the room, looking first this way, then that. I would later learn his "air name," the name he used as a DJ rather than his legal name, was "Brewster Billy." That strange moniker was derived from his town of origin, Brewster, Ohio, and not his prowess of downing massive quantities of beer. The little Village of Brewster is located sixteen miles southwest of Canton, and its main attraction is the Dolly Madison Museum. All that said, Billy didn't come off like a small-town hick.

Brady began outlining the station rules, the primary ones being if you didn't show up for your shift you would not be getting another, no equipment was to be taken out of the radio station, and you had to fill out a discrepancy form for any device that failed to operate properly. I glanced at Sarah Lee who was now writing furiously in her notebook. Boy, she assumed power quickly. The meeting took a sudden turn when an older student asked about Greg McManus,

"Why are we having this meeting without Greg?"

The long-haired thin guy took a sip of coffee that colored his slight moustache, and then he answered,

"Well, he went home to Chicago for the weekend."

"Okay, but our station's faculty sponsor appointed Greg to be our general manager, the GM, so he should be here"

"Right, and he isn't, so fuck him."

The room erupted in laughter and that impressed me. It was obvious this Brewster Billy guy didn't pull punches, said exactly what he meant and knew how to be funny.

Brady pointed at another student, a guy whom I had already seen around campus with blonde hair styled very much like a girl's page boy. He wore a freshly pressed, flowery shirt and cream-colored jeans. I couldn't help noticing he kept kneading and massaging his crotch. His pants were noticeably worn in that area presumably due to the constant rubbing. Brady, who came off like the station drill sergeant, looked around the room and shouted an order,

"Skip, tell everyone here what's going on."

Crotch boy ran his tongue over his front teeth and began,

"Ladies and gentlemen, we have to save the radio station. Our general manager is inept. His failure to have us on air the first day of classes is just one of the many things he's done, or in this case, hasn't done. Our radio station is falling apart!"

There I was at the very first station meeting and slowly realizing all of us were stepping into the middle of a potential coup. I hadn't yet met this Greg guy, but I heard his father was a famous radio announcer in Chicago and his son was running home every weekend to ask daddy what he should do with our small campus station. Greg strived to run WVUD like Chicago's powerhouse WGN, but the students were revolting. I read one of his arrogant memos on the wall and wondered if I wanted to get in the middle of this insanity. Maybe I picked the wrong college.

Us newbies were taken into a studio and one of those engineering guys began instructing about recording audio using one of the new tape cartridge machines the station had just purchased. The three Gates ATC "cart machines" in the air studio were playback only, but there was a unit that both recorded and played back here in the production studio.

Tape cartridges, "carts" as they were known in the biz, have a fascinating history in radio. For over thirty years, they were the primary means of audio playback at most radio stations. Their introduction fundamentally changed the way the entire radio broadcasting business operated on a technical level.

In began in 1952, when a sound engineer named Bernard A. Cousino came up with the idea of an endless loop of recording tape. It was mostly used in retail stores and business conventions with a constantly repeating message which described a product or process. Since the tape was in a loop, it played endlessly.

In 1954, an associate of Cousino named George Eash developed the Fidelipac tape cartridge. It was a small, gray, plastic case that held an endless loop of tape. Specialized Fidelipac players soon followed, making it easy to quickly switch messages by exchanging cartridges.

This innovative technology caught the eye of General Manager Verne Nolte at WJBC Radio in Bloomington, Illinois. He asked his engineers to build a prototype player for use in broadcasting, which they did. Their device began playback immediately at the press of a button, and when the audio ended the tape was back to its starting point, the cart machine automatically stopped, and the cart was ready to be played again. This technology was perfect for the fast-paced Top 40 format with many short audio elements clustered together.

The radio engineers formed a business they called Automatic Tape Control, ATC in shortened form, and made a marketing deal with Collins Radio. That broadcast equipment company introduced their Collins/ATC cart machine at the 1959 National Association of Broadcasters convention in Chicago. Those machines were the hit of the show, and forty-five radio stations placed immediate orders. Gates Radio later bought the ATC design, made significant improvements, and released their Gates ATC machines, which became the workhorse of the industry.

It's interesting that four-track and eight-track tape cartridge players eventually found their way to American cars. The broadcasting industry had created a monster that was replacing radio listening in a considerable number of automobiles.

Initially, all radio station commercials, jingles, promotional announcements (promos) and news snippets (actualities) were played on the air from carts. Early machines had some issues with audio quality, but as those were resolved it became common for stations to also record songs onto tape cartridges. This technology was utterly fascinating to me, and I thought it was good that all the folks at the station, regardless of their role, were learning this aspect of radio.

Looking around the studio, I noticed a picture of Greg McManus hanging on a wall. Someone had drawn a Hitler mustache on him and added a caption, "I saw nothing!" Just then it hit me. I remembered seeing McManus at a table in the student union urging people to join YAF. I was curious what led him to become the general manager of the radio station. People like him were the furthest from the mindset and political persuasions of most kids pursuing radio, an occupation open to just about anyone with a reasonably good voice, the gift of gab and decent motor skills.

Greg returned the next week, and my neutral opinion changed after I met him. He was a serious lad who had preconceived notions about how radio should be formatted and executed, and if you didn't do things his way, *you* would be executed! To be honest, I was intimidated by anyone having more radio knowledge than I did. One lesson I learned quickly was regardless of your side in the "let's get rid of this guy" campaign, Greg treated all newcomers like young pledges. He would criticize and poke fun at trainees who were learning how to do a radio show. I didn't like the guy.

GM Greg held a meeting and announced the station would not go back on the air until all the new students were trained and ready. Well, that triggered an almost-mutiny. Within minutes a petition was circulated that demanded we go back on the air immediately. It was signed by every member of the radio station, except Greg, and delivered to the station's Faculty Sponsor, Paul Spineki.

I'll never forget the day Spineki, an English professor at the university, strutted into the radio station. He looked more like a student than a faculty member. Long-matted curls of red and brown hair tumbled to his shoulders. He wore a bright purple shirt over colorfully striped bell bottom pants, which swung about the tops of his giant clodhopper boots as he walked. After his flamboyant entry, Paul pulled Greg McManus into the small, soundproofed news studio.

They talked for several minutes as a group of us watched through the window. I could see Greg's face getting fiery red, and he was obviously raising his voice while gesticulating furiously to make points to this "boss" the little general didn't know he had. It wasn't long before Spineki stood, shook Greg's hand, and then abruptly left the booth. Everyone watched Paul stride through the lobby. Before walking out the door he threw us all a peace sign and blew a creepy kiss to one of the girls.

Not long after, Greg came out of the little studio and said, "Okay, even though we aren't ready, let's fire up this station. Please, everyone, follow the Wednesday schedule. We're going to put this baby on the air, right now!"

There were claps and cheers as Brewster Billy made his way to the control board. One of the disheveled engineer geeks walked over to the equipment rack, flipped up a little switch on a panel, then pointed a finger directly at Billy who pushed a button to fire off the legal ID cart,

"This is W-V-U-D, Dayton, the voice of the University of Dayton, with music and more!"

Billy flipped a switch to roll a turntable, and a song began playing. It was the 1968 hit by the Lemon Pipers named *Green Tambourine*. The electronic harpsichord of the song's introduction, it's "intro," blasted forth loudly and in amazing fidelity from all the speakers throughout the station and I got goosebumps. Man, this was fun; this was exciting! Despite the politics and controversy, I knew this was exactly where I wanted to be, where I belonged.

In this breathtaking moment, the lyrics made great sense, *"Drop your silver in my tambourine, Help a poor man build a pretty dream, Give me pennies, I'll take anything..."*

In fact, I would do anything to get a DJ shift on the station, but was I ready? Maybe this poor man needs a pretty dream.

5. The Way It Is

College can be quite the challenge to an immature teenage mind. On one hand, you've been sent away, and your parents expect you to function as a productive student. Many times, the investment by each of your family members is substantial. On the other hand, you are free to do whatever you want, and this new reality will now be fundamental throughout the rest of your life. I was living at home and commuting to school each day in my puke-yellow, beat-up, overheating Volkswagen Beetle. I would occasionally sleep over at the dormitory using the excuse of "study groups" for my non-return to home. Problem was, my parents weren't dumb and if I was doing so much studying with the guys then why were my grades so poor?

Learning and doing at the college radio station was incredibly addictive. I would skip many classes so I could hang and work with my friends there. This might be good place to pause and share some insight with my non-radio reader about where things sat in 1968.

Back in the sixties, American college stations were little learning labs where kids could soak up radio knowledge and experience, and the tried-and-true Top 40 commercial music radio format was a great teaching tool. Just like the culture around it, myths and half-truths tend to dominate the radio business. One of those stories involves a guy name Todd Storz. He is often credited with inventing the Top 40 format, which many historians claim began at his family-owned radio station KOWH in Omaha, Nebraska. The legend goes that in the early 1950s Storz observed the waitresses in his favorite diner playing the same jukebox songs again and again. This became the motivation for broadcasting a select group of about forty popular songs in continuous rotation on a radio station. The format became known as Top 40, and it was phenomenally successful.

But I must point out that in a kind of spontaneous creation, many other stations around the country began airing the same format at the same time. I knew a radio guy named John Tyler who used to say, "There are no original ideas; we all live in the same atmosphere."

I'd like to get another bit of radio arcana out of the way here. Call letters for US radio stations were first regulated by the Department of Commerce when they assigned each commercial radio station a three-letter or four-letter name. In later years, rules were codified in the Communications Act of 1934. It mandated the call letters of all broadcast stations in the USA west of the Mississippi would begin with the letter K, while those stations east of that river would begin with W. There are some exceptions, such as WEW in St. Louis and KDKA in Pittsburgh, because their call letters were in place before the Communications Act came along. By the way, that Act was part of an international agreement under which Mexican station call letters would begin with the letter X and Canadian radio call letters would start with a C.

As for college radio stations, many of them operated with power low enough the federal government had no interest in regulating them. WVUD was one such station. Other college stations with higher power transmitters had to apply to the FCC for a license and call letters, which were typically granted, provided they were not already in use and no other station complained about the application. Some of those stations became fixtures in their communities, playing avant-garde music or broadcasting educational content.

In the late sixties, a commercial FM Classical Music station in Cincinnati started to play rock songs at night because the owner's son wanted to experiment with the new Free Form non-format that was popping up in major cities across America. The lad used the air name Dr. Michael Bo Xanadu and called his program "WEBN's Jelly Pudding Show." As is true in most businesses, money talks in the radio trade. The Jelly Pudding Show became so successful the station converted to full-time rock, except for Sunday morning when the son stepped aside while his father hosted a classical music show.

Most of the Ohio students in the dorms at the University of Dayton knew about WEBN, but the out-of-town kids had grown up on the Top 40 stations in their home markets. Yes, in the radio business a city is known as a market, mostly because radio advertisers in areas outside the city proper bought commercials on the most powerful and highly rated stations in that nearby city. The reach and impact of a station typically exceeds its city limits, so measuring ratings and ad sales within a broader geographical area yielded more accurate results.

Us college kids were free to do what we wanted at school, and our discipline regarding class work was much less than the effort we put into exploring life, partying and, certainly at the top of the list, "playing radio." Despite those nighttime sexual romps in our darkened studios, WVUD was a functioning radio station, deploying the mechanics of a radio format along with schedules of "air shifts," which is an inside term for the time period of a radio show.

While WVUD's general manager was hanging onto his power by a thin thread, upper classmen who had put years into the station decided on a Top 40 format with some album tracks sprinkled into the mix, which was wildly accepted by our listeners and perfectly fine for most of us. We just wanted to be on the air practicing our DJ skills and spinning vinyl records on turntables.

Most radio listeners have no idea about how a radio station's format is constructed and executed. There's a common belief that disc jockeys just play whatever songs they want, whenever they want. Well, that's exactly how it *doesn't* work! A radio station's program director decides which songs to play and how frequently to play them, and the specifics change from week to week. A fundamental concept of a music radio format is song rotation, the process of repeating the airplay of songs at controlled intervals depending on popularity. Highly favored songs rotate more frequently than songs with less appeal. Songs are classified by their popularity and appeal to the audience, and then placed into a category with other songs having the same appeal.

Radio stations have pet names for their song categories, and in many cases the biggest and best hits were called Powers or As, although I know of one station that named them Gorillas. These would rotate every two hours or so. Then there were the up and comers and once hugely popular songs now losing their appeal, and those were assigned to a category often called Secondaries or Bs. Such songs rotated twice as long as the As, meaning they played half as often. New songs might be in a category named N which played much less frequently. In a typical week maybe one or two new songs would be added to a station's playlist and received much less prominent exposure than the big hits. Perhaps it's self-evident, but a station's "playlist" contains all the songs in rotation.

Part of managing song categories and rotation is a notion of turnover, the length of time it takes for all the songs in a given category to play. The goal of categorization is having the same turnover for each of its songs. Turnover is a function of the number of songs in a category and the number of times in an hour a song from that category is played. So, if Category A has nine songs, and one is played four times an hour, roughly every fifteen minutes a listener will hear a power hit, and all the power songs will repeat every two hours and fifteen minutes. A new song might be played once every four hours and thirty minutes, allowing it to gradually become familiar to the audience who would eventually decide they loved it, and one day it would move to Category A, or they hated it so much it would be pulled from the playlist.

Note our example category turnovers are "skewed" with respect to the clock. A Category A song that plays at 9:15 will next play at 11:30 then again at 1:45. This is intentional because it eliminates the possibility of a listener always hearing a given song playing on, say, the half hour. I referred to the "mechanics" of a radio format earlier, and these are just a few pieces of the Top 40 mechanism. I had no idea math was part a format's formula, and as I became exposed to this and other programming concepts in college radio it made me understand I had a lot to learn. There was much more to this craft beyond the songs.

Some of the younger, hip college students from big cities like New York, Chicago, Boston and San Francisco were preaching the gospel of "jelly pudding," but the kids from smaller towns wanted the Top 40 hits. It was the beginning of a kind of divide within popular music. The Top 40 stations were playing little records with big holes (45 RPM singles) and the new Album Rock stations were playing tracks from big records with little holes (33-and-a-third RPM albums).

This ideological/musical divide would affect radio over the next decade. One of the motivations for the explosion of FM stations was a new ruling from the FCC saying that broadcasters owning an AM and FM station in the same market must have different programming on each. In the past, most AM/FM broadcasters aired the same programming on both stations, a practice known as simulcasting. Some rightfully pointed out that radio signals are in the "public domain" and declared broadcasters should be providing separate programming on their AM and FM signals.

The FM Non-Duplication Rule was adopted by the FCC in 1964. It stipulated that a holder of both AM and FM licenses in cities with a population of a hundred thousand or more could simulcast no more than fifty percent of their AM programming on their FM signal. This was gradually increased to seventy-five percent after the rule was challenged and then resolved by the Supreme Court. Yes, station owners had to put non-duplicated programming on their FM signals because Chief Justice Earl Warren said so.

Song repetition is one of the biggest radio listener complaints, yet it's a fundamental necessity for a successful music station. As Top 40 stations became increasingly popular, more and more listeners were asking, "Why do they play the same records over and over again?" Well, it would be easy for me to say, "That's just the way it is," but that would be an irresponsible and incorrect answer. You see, rotations occur at every level of life. Without these repetitive occurrences, caterpillars wouldn't turn into beautiful butterflies and people wouldn't make babies. However, there's another dynamic in play with radio.

At the risk of being too obscure, I'll present it this way. The idea of a space-time continuum originated with the groundbreaking work of Albert Einstein, who concluded that space and time are interwoven rather than being separate and unrelated. Let's think of time as, well, time. You only have so much time to listen to the radio. We don't know when you will drop in and give us a few quarter-hours of listening. I say quarter-hours because for years radio ratings have measured the number of listeners to each station per quarter-hour. So, when you tune in, Mr. or Ms. Listener, how long can I keep you? If within ten minutes I deliver one of your favorite power hits, you may keep listening knowing another one is not too far behind. So, and here I go stretching this metaphor, the "space" between those big hits must not be too long a "time." Okay, I know that was a leap, but we both landed safely on the other side.

I'll expose the concept of song rotation with one simple question. Is it better to play a song a lot of people like rather than a song a lot of people hate? Seems obvious, right? When a radio station plays the most popular songs in frequent rotation, chances are when a listener turns on their radio, they will be hearing a tune they really like and will not feel tempted to dial around in search of a better one. This illustrates a fundamental factor of effective radio programming.

A good radio format eliminates negatives, like too much chatter by loquacious DJs, long commercial breaks and bad songs. By the way, the art of commercial zapping didn't start with your VCR or DVR, it began with the push buttons on Twentieth Century car radios. If there were two popular stations in your town, you could punch back and forth between them to find that monster hit your girlfriend wanted to hear. It also meant that should you punch out of one of her favorite hits, she might punch *you* out when attempting to reach second base.

There is a lengthy list of radio terminology known to those in the biz but not to a typical listener. How about a "talk-up," where the last word spoken by a DJ over the instrumental opening of a song ends exactly when the song's vocal begins. Some artistically inclined disc jockeys could not only consistently and seamlessly "hit the vocal" every time, but also "pot up" the song briefly at each "post" of the intro. What the hell, pots and posts? The volume controls on a radio station's audio console, also known as an audio desk, a control board or board, are called "pots," a shortened form of the word potentiometer, which is a sliding or rotating electronic mechanism that adjusts volume level. A post is a musical accent during the instrumental beginning of a song. It can be wonderful hearing an experienced DJ time his delivery and accent his words by quickly and precisely "potting up" each post in a song's intro. And here you thought I was out on a limb with that Einstein reference! If you're starting to think there's more to radio than what meets the ear, you would be correct.

Us radio freaks at WVUD learned early on the worst of all radio sins is "dead air," which is absolute silence — no music, no disc jockey, no jingle, no commercial, just... nothing. When dead air happened, all eyes in the radio station would turn to the panicked on-air DJ. Upper classmen would sometimes pull a dirty trick on a youngun' by cutting off their studio speakers but not taking the station off the air. It was rich entertainment to watch the horror in the eyes of the newbie disc jockey, hearing that ominous silence but being unable to correct it. Because the negativity of dead air was so strong, it wouldn't be long until a freshly indoctrinated DJ would begin to have *The Dream*, a recurring nightmare in which they are behind the control board, the song is ending, and they have nothing ready to play and no idea what to say or do next. Most on-air radio people have this dead-air dream, which often ends with a jarring awakening in a cold sweat.

As much as those radio nightmares were a major negative for us young radio announcers, they were also part of the joy, the magic. The feeling experienced by a circus tightrope walker is akin to that of running a radio show. Not having the next song ready is like a fear of falling off the wire. Broadcasting is a physical and mental balancing act. You first must think of something relevant to share with your listeners, then punch up that next song while concocting concise language on the fly to convey that thought in those thirteen seconds before the vocal comes in. Oh, you might slip on the tightrope by "stepping on the vocal," and that's okay. Just make sure there's always something on the air, but never, ever, any of the seven dirty words we'll speak about later. Uttering any of those could kill your career, and it's just one of the many aspects of radio that make it a fun and challenging business and artform.

6. Put Salt on Its Tail

Most of the people I've met in radio have a strong connection to music, far deeper than a typical listener. There have been times I've said some program directors love music so much it gets in the way of successfully programming their radio stations. What I mean is it's almost certain disaster when a program director follows their own feelings about music rather than those of the listeners. There comes a time during the early learning phase of most broadcasters when they realize their personal taste in music is vastly different from the audience they are trying to build or serve. Back in the late 1960s, however, broadcasters and listeners alike were experiencing a musical renaissance beyond anyone's imagination.

Starting in 1967, new, progressive artists like Jimi Hendrix, Janis Joplin, the Doors and Cream began their careers. Then, the Beatles and the Rolling Stones began morphing their sounds to the burgeoning progressive era with the albums *Sgt. Pepper's Lonely Hearts Club Band* and *Their Satanic Majesties Request*. Top 40 radio responded by playing songs like *All Along the Watchtower* and *White Room*, but for the most part pop and R&B (rhythm and blues) songs received far greater airplay on those stations.

Us young radio students at the University of Dayton understood we needed to acquire the skills needed by radio stations around the country so we would be ready for those "high paying" jobs as disc jockeys when we graduated. Few of us thought about radio management positions. After all, we weren't business majors; we were studying journalism, communication or speech. Some theater majors drifted into our student station at times, but they were more interested in scripted content rather than DJ shifts. Yes, being a radio announcer meant there were times you would read text you or another had written, as in news reporting and voicing recorded promotional announcements, but most of the talk you hear tumbling out your radio is adlibbed bits of disc jockey chatter. The style and creativity of some individual's patter gave them a way to stand far above the rest.

The famous Woodstock Music and Art Fair, now simply known as Woodstock, took place in 1969 from August 15 to 18, and the myths of who attended began almost immediately once the music ended. Although there were approximately four hundred thousand attendees, it seemed like just about everyone you knew claimed to have been there. The movie *Woodstock* wouldn't be released until the spring of 1970, but there was a palpable buzz about all the artists who played at that famous outdoor musical gathering. One group's Woodstock appearance happened in the middle of the night. Crosby, Stills and Nash were billed as a "super group" with Stephen Stills coming from Buffalo Springfield, David Crosby formerly of the Byrds and Graham Nash who was the high harmony voice of the Hollies.

Crosby Stills and Nash were going to stage a concert in Cleveland and that became a major buzz on campus. Lots of kids were excited about the show and tried to get tickets. Cleveland is a bit over two hundred miles from Dayton, slightly more than a three-hour drive. The show was scheduled for December 12, 1969, and the band would be performing at Public Hall, an old downtown venue built in the 1920s. It had three performance areas, a little theater that held six hundred people, a music hall that held three thousand and a large arena that could seat ten thousand.

Now here comes a bit of a confession. There was a guy on campus who was like a character straight out of a Cheech and Chong movie. His name, and I am not making this up, was Jacky Paradise. He looked a little like Lowell George of the band Little Feat, and always wore this huge bear-skin coat, even when the weather turned warmer. He had pulled that fur sheath, which dated back to the Roaring Twenties, from his grandfather's closet. That garment had kept the elder Paradise warm during his college days. In one pocket Jacky carried a wad of cash and in the other were baggies of every drug imaginable. Yes, he was a crazy-beyond-belief drug dealer. One of the big hits by Steppenwolf was *Born to be Wild*, featured in the movie *Easy Rider*. Fittingly, they were Jacky's favorite rock band and movie.

One day, Jacky walked into the radio station, high as a kite, demanding to speak with the DJ, yours truly. He showed me four tickets to the CS&N Cleveland concert and said if I immediately played *The Pusher* by Steppenwolf, he would give me the tickets.

Now in case you don't know, *The Pusher* is actually an anti-drug song. Some people would have you believe the song glorifies drug use but that's incorrect. Here are the song's opening lyrics, *"You know I've smoked a lot of grass, O' Lord, I've popped a lot of pills, But I've never touched nothin' That my spirit could kill. You know, I've seen a lot of people walkin' 'round, With tombstones in their eyes, But the pusher don't care, Ah, if you live or if you die — God damn, The Pusher, God damn, I say The Pusher, I said God damn, God damn The Pusher man."*

This song was not on WVUD's playlist, and I had to scramble to locate the album before I could even consider the possibility of granting Mr. Paradise his bribe-laden wish. I found the record in the production studio, brought it into the air studio and cued up the track. I turned to Jacky,

"You sure you want to give up those tickets?"

He shook his head in the affirmative and just seconds later I cracked open the mic,

"Okay my friends that was *These Eyes* by the Guess Who and I'm sure you'll try to guess the artist of this next song, which I'm playing on WVUD by special request."

I flicked a switch on the console to roll the turntable and the subdued strumming guitar intro began. I quickly jumped back in and spoke in a soft voice,

"Here's *The Pusher...* by Steppenwolf... on WVUD."

It was at that point, I realized the song had a runtime of five minutes and forty-three seconds, way too long for our format during "afternoon drive time," whatever that term could possibly mean to college radio listeners. I imagined John Kaye's chorus of "God damn, God damn!" over and over on a Catholic university radio station would get some attention, and it certainly did. It was only about two minutes into the song when Greg McManus poked his head into the studio,

"What the hell are you doing, Klotenfelder? That is not an approved song! It's not on the playlist!"

His face was as red as a chili pepper, and while pulling the studio door closed, he added,

"You need to come see me immediately when you are off the air!"

My radio career imploded in my mind while Jacky smiled and handed me the tickets. They were in the twelfth row, holy crap what a catch! It was then I remembered the discussion about payola in one of my communication classes, and here I was taking a bribe to play a song. Suddenly I wished my shift would never end.

The meeting with McManus didn't go well. Brewster Billy, who had been appointed program director a few weeks earlier, stood up for me but that didn't help. I took a severe scolding from the GM and was told I must never again play any song that wasn't on the station's playlist. McManus put me on probation saying I would be allowed to work only overnight shifts. Radio is the one business that schedules workers to terrible time periods in order to punish them or make them seek a new job. So, I was demoted but at least I wasn't fired. That piece of crap upper classman Greg McManus knew I would do anything to stay on the air, and he also understood how hard it was to find students to work overnight. My reassignment solved a problem for him, not me. Would I ever sleep again? Greg most likely promoted Billy to program director under the old maxim of keeping your enemies inside the tent rather than outside pissing into your command post. Billy offered some comfort,

"Don't worry, that jerk will forget this happened in a few days. He's not that bright."

I didn't work the overnight shift on December 12th, which was a Friday. I got my friend Geoffrey Gordoni to cover my radio show, knowing he would probably invite his several girlfriends into the station with him for free fellatio; he was just that kind of guy. I "convinced" Billy, Brady and Sarah to go with me to the CS&N Cleveland concert. Billy loved Crosby, Stills and Nash and used to famously interrupt the song *Suite: Judy Blue Eyes* when he played it on the radio. Right after the band sang the line, *"How can you catch the sparrow?"* Billy would flip open the mic and scream, *"Put salt on its tail!"* which I am almost certain no one got. I asked him to please not do that at the concert. Brady was from Cleveland, so he would know where to park and get us to the venue. I asked Sarah to come because we needed transportation and she had her father's immense 1967 Chrysler Imperial at school. That was an easy sell because she thought David Crosby was cute. Takes all kinds.

After Friday morning classes, we stopped at the UD Deli to get some sandwiches for the road. Even though the trip would be short, we wanted to save money by not eating at a restaurant. Public Hall is located at 500 Lakeside Avenue East, and I remembered the Cleveland Rosenblums basketball team used to play there. My father talked about how Max Rosenblum owned department stores and the team, joking that if he owned a basketball team he certainly wouldn't have named them the Dayton Klotenfelders.

We listened to AM radio because that's all that was available in Sarah's car. As we got close to the city, we tuned into Cleveland's leading Top 40 station, WIXY 1260. Dick "Wilde Childe" Kemp was on the air with frantic enthusiasm and tons of reverberation, a tactic of many stations in those times used to make them sound larger than life. One of the Wilde Childe's catch phrases was, "Jam up, jelly tight and peanut butter thick." None of us in the car knew what that meant, but we all had a good laugh.

When we arrived in Cleveland, we were greeted by a little kiss from the lake. The wind was blowing, and it was a nippy thirty-five degrees, going down to twenty-five that night. We huddled in the Imperial, but the thing sucked up so much gasoline that Sarah Lee would start the engine so we could get warm, then shut if off to conserve gas. It was only five o'clock and we couldn't wait to get into the hall and our seats. We wondered why we left Dayton so early.

When you're a witness to history, you never forget. All the hippies and freaks at the concert were bathed in that year's Woodstock glow. When the band took the stage, we were surprised to see four. Buffalo Springfield's Neil Young had joined the group. Music artists usually save their best song for last in the concert, so we were shocked when the band opened with their massive hit, *Suite: Judy Blue Eyes*. That turned out to be a great decision, however, because the song erupted into a massive singalong, which pulled the entire audience into the show. Those guys played and sang flawlessly, and their vocal harmonies were unbelievably precise and perfect. It was a fantastic performance, our seats were amazing, and I was hoping no one would ever find out exactly how I got those tickets.

During the rockin' Neil Young song *Sea of Madness*, the smell of marijuana was everywhere and a guy behind me tapped my shoulder and handed me a lighted joint. I took a large puff and looked over at Sarah who shot a stern look that said, "No way you're driving us back later."

As we walked to the car after the show, I was thinking how great those songs were and believed all of them should be played full length on the radio, not just the shortened singles. We listened to WKYC on the way back home and heard the fastest talking disc jockey ever, Jackson W. Armstrong. One of his gimmicks was a gorilla as a sidekick. Jackson called his deep-voiced alter ego Gorilla, and he seamlessly bounced back and forth between his patter and voicing Gorilla without a gap. He also called himself, "Your leader," the same tagline I heard Jim Quinn use on WING in Dayton. Gee, do radio people copy each other?

At one point during the ride home I noticed a billboard advertising a brand-new Cleveland FM station named WMMS, but since there was no FM radio in the car, I would try to find an aircheck later. We arrived back in Dayton after 2 a.m., and not wanting to wake up my old man I crashed in Brady's dorm room. This had been one of the most memorable nights of my college life, but regretful events were on the horizon.

The ongoing fight between Greg McManus and most of the student staff of radio wannabees at WVUD was getting out of hand. Brewster Billy played the album version of *Does Anybody Really Know What Time It Is*, a hit song by the group Chicago Transit Authority. McManus got his knickers in a knot, which triggered his famous beet red face and tormented high voice. To be fair to Billy, the runtimes of the different versions of the song didn't vary by much. The album version was 4:36, the jukebox single version ran 3:20 and the radio edit clocked in at 2:54. Regardless, Greg, being the pedantic jerk he was, came down hard on Program Director Billy by firing him. The entire WVUD staff appreciated the irony of the song lyrics, *"Does anybody really know what time it is, Does anybody really care?"*

So, the most beloved member of the WVUD staff was canned over one minute and forty-two seconds of music, the difference in length between the album and radio edit versions of the song. Billy then went legal on McManus' ass and took his firing to the President of the University of Dayton Law School, a well-known former lawyer from the famous Ohio firm of Taft Stettinius & Hollister. Yes, that Taft.

It was determined that one student could not legally fire another from a university activity, so Billy was back and focused on making Greg's life shitty. Meanwhile, Billy and I had struck a solid friendship. I liked his confidence, directness and overall knowledge of the radio business. He seemed to like my ideas just as much as my sense of humor and constant joking. I made him laugh… a lot. But there was something else, a mutual respect and synergy. We each had acquired our radio knowledge in different and diverse ways, but when we talked about things at WVUD or fantasized about a future in radio, our ideas merged and coalesced. It was like we filled little gaps in each other that made our schemes and dreams feel solid and attainable.

The war between the not so straight-shooting general manager and the clique of WVUD veterans led to graffiti on the walls of the radio station and, eventually, an air studio fist fight between Greg and Brady. Station staffers had been constantly complaining to the Dean of Student Affairs about the overbearing McManus and things blew up. Meanwhile, the station was devolving into disobedience, and those DJs who wanted to play unapproved album cuts brazenly did so. They desired the Vietnam War to end just as much as they craved freedom on the air, and battle lines were being drawn. It wasn't long before the college administration dropped napalm on our radio station's little war.

We received a memo from the Dean stating we were to vacate the studios at the end of classes before the winter holidays of 1969. The station would be shut down and the university would build a new facility in a different location. We were heartbroken. The major reason most of us stayed in school was to learn radio, and the most frustrating academic aspect of our university was the communication classes were mostly focused on television and print, not radio. The campus station was a bone the administration threw to students years ago, and now it was dark, silent, off the air.

One light shined through the sadness, however. Greg McManus transferred to a bigger school so he could wreak havoc on some other unlucky student body. We had a meeting and pledged to all work together to build a new radio station. Paul Spineki asked Brewster Billy and me to head the project. I have no idea why he picked me, but Billy had great engineering chops and he and I had developed a solid friendship and worked well together so it made sense. I was also skilled at soldering.

Our new facility would be much larger with two additional studios, so we needed gear. We met with the Dean of Student Affairs who gave us a budget, then we were called to another meeting in the Vice President's office, where, strangely enough, we were given another budget. I looked at Billy and winked. When we got out into the hall outside of the VP's office, Billy turned to me,

"Are you turning gay? Why did you wink at me?"

"Brewster boy you're a dumb shit. Don't you see the one hand doesn't know what the other hand is doing?"

"Meaning?"

"Meaning we now have a second budget. We can draw from both and build an amazing radio station."

"But what if they figure it out?"

"Don't worry, by the time these assholes understand what happened we'll be gone; well, at least you'll be gone."

7. Caught in the Act

Billy and I worked over the holidays, ordering state-of-the-art professional radio equipment from broadcasting manufacturers, which all seemed to be located in Illinois. We came to school every day and collected the new gear which had been delivered to the student bookstore with the quirky name Rudy Reads. Because it was open year-round, the bookstore was the drop-off location for all campus deliveries. It was great fun loading a hand-truck with packages containing our new broadcasting hardware. We'd wheel them over to the new studios of WVUD and enjoy the process of unboxing or uncrating then deciding where each piece should go.

We were following our plan, buying equipment first from one budget then the other. Since we needed signatures on any expenditure over two hundred dollars, we were constantly dashing between the dean's and vice president's offices.

Some students who had jobs on campus, like running the bowling alley, the swimming pool or the bookstore, were allowed to stay in a dorm room over the holidays. One of those kids was Jacky Paradise, who worked in the mailroom and had once bribed an aspiring disc jockey. I was never sure why he was given permission to stay, but it certainly didn't turn out well for him.

As Billy and I were returning from the radio station to the bookstore to check for more hardware deliveries, we saw an ambulance parked in front of Founder's Hall, one of the oldest dormitories on campus. The vehicle's lights were turning and blinking as two men in blue EMT jumpsuits rolled out a gurney with a white sheet completely covering what was obviously a body. I looked at Billy,

"Holy shit, who do you suppose that is?"

It didn't take but a second to learn the answer. A Dayton city cop strode out of Founder's carrying that infamous bear-skin coat, which perhaps was now evidence of some sort. I shook my head knowing that Paradise probably overdosed on his own merchandise. Billy whispered,

"Well, there goes the pusher. God damn the pusher."

We both chuckled, enjoying that dark and sarcastic sense of humor we shared.

We hustled some newly arrived boxes back to the radio station which, aside from office furniture, was tremendously coming together. We tore open the crates to get at the well-crafted custom racks that would hold the station's records and tapes. They were fabricated by a guy named John Grinnan who built high quality shelving in his Minerva, Ohio woodshop. We also positioned freshly arrived Formica cabinetry which would house each studio's control board, mic stands, turntables and cart machines. The large glass window in our new air studio looked out onto the student union, which gave off the vibe of a big city radio station. Every now and then a curious passer-by would stop and peer inside to see our new facility taking shape.

Not too long ago, Billy and I had taken a day to trip to Pittsburgh, Pennsylvania to see KQV, the city's highly popular Top 40 station. Yes, it was another K-station east of the Mississippi. KQV had these fabulous street-level studios where you could stand at a metal railing in front of a huge window and watch the DJs broadcasting. We talked about perhaps one day working on the other side of that glass.

All of the KQV disc jockeys wore suits and ties as if they were going to church. I thought radio announcers should be trendier and hipper, but at this ABC-owned station all the jocks looked like bankers. After about an hour we were tired of standing and decided to get something to eat. We crossed a street where a cop was directing traffic using hilarious dance moves. We asked if he knew a good place to grab a bite, and he directed us to a nearby chicken joint named George Aikens. Then the cop did a chicken dance right in the middle of Liberty Avenue. Funny! Lunch was delicious and Billy and I agreed that place had the best rotisserie chicken we'd ever eaten, golden, crunchy skin and tender, juicy meat just bursting with flavor. I told my mother it was better than hers and she bopped me over the head with a wooden spoon.

Meanwhile, we were racing against the clock but rounding the bend getting the university's brand-new radio station ready for our student listeners who would be returning the second week in January. Hands flew as we feverishly wired-up gear to the consoles and equipment racks, hung large studio speakers and hustled the station's records, carts and reel-to-reel tapes out of storage and into the new shelving. Suddenly there was hard, loud knocking at the door of the station. I looked at Billy,

"Who the hell could that be?"

I opened the door and one of the president's "boys" with signature slicked-back hair was standing there in his three-piece suit and a superior look plastered across his face. Our college president back then was Reverend Roger Ray, but as a sign of our humble disrespect we often called him Rev Ray. I couldn't help but wonder what was up,

"Uh, can I help you?"

"Yes, Father Ray wants a meeting."

"Which one of us does he want to see?"

"Both of you! Now!"

And with that, the officious little prick briskly turned and walked away.

We came to a stopping point in our studio work, adjusted our T-shirts and dirty jeans and headed to St. Mary's Hall where Rev Ray's office was located. The University of Dayton is one of three Marianist universities in the nation and the second-largest private university in Ohio, so it's quite a prestigious place of the uptight, religious variety. I looked at Billy as we crossed the campus while mentally crossing ourselves,

"This couldn't be about…"

"Well, I'm thinking this might be confession time. I'm glad we're both Catholic."

Mrs. Johansen sat in front of Father Ray's door as the final filter keeping unwanted visitors away from the president. She had a pleasant smile, but she also could be stern and forthright — like a nun,

"You two gentlemen do have wills, yes?"

"Please?"

She reached for the intercom switch and changed to a more serious voice,

"The radio guys are here, Father."

There was a muted, unintelligible response, then Mrs. Johansen looked up at us and put on her smile,

"He'll see you now."

Billy and I walked into the office. The walls were filled with awards, trophies and framed photographs. One of them showed Father Ray shaking hands with John F. Kennedy. A smaller photo captured a moment of our university president standing with Dwight Eisenhower and Richard Nixon. Centered on the wall behind his desk was a huge, ornate frame holding a photo of Father Ray with the Pope himself.

The office's fluorescent lighting cast a harsh radiance across the red and blue colors of various school bric-a-brac scattered throughout the spacious but intimidating room. There was a Latin phrase handsomely printed on little wall hangings splattered here and there — *Pro Deo Et Patria* — which we learned at orientation meant *For God and*

Country. The president asked us to sit down. Two overstuffed chairs faced the enormous, carved wooden desk where Rev Ray was seated. Billy walked over to the chair on the left and I sank into the one on the right. Father Ray tapped his silver pen three times as we sat. He was completely silent as his piercing, beady eyes drilled little holes into each of our skulls.

The wrinkled flesh of Father Ray's face showed he held most of life's frustrations and stress inside. His expression clearly indicated he was particularly unhappy in the current moment. We sat for what seemed like hours but was probably only three minutes, still a long time to be waiting in silence. Eventually, Father Roger opened his dry lips and then forcefully slammed his pen onto the desk,

"Are you aware that we had a death on campus?"

We both nodded our heads, acknowledging that terrible tragedy but wondering what it had to do with us. He continued,

"I assume you went to the chapel since you are here working at the radio station?"

Billy spoke first,

"Not yet, Father, but we will. You do know that Paradise was a drug pusher, right?"

Father Ray raised his voice,

"Mr. Kalpolski, that is **not** true. There are no drugs on this campus."

"Oh, we thought...."

Billy's voice faded for lack of words. You could have cut the tension in the room with a knife, which I was thinking might be a good thing to have right about now. The president was clearly ready to address the topic of the meeting. He stood up from his chair and walked behind us, standing exactly midway between our two chairs. Rev Ray put his right hand on my left shoulder, not in a kindly-warm priestly manner but rather in a creepy-feely priestly way,

"How long did the two of you think you could get away with it?"

I felt the need to provide an answer without giving anything up,

"What do you mean, Father?"

"What I mean is, you do know it's a sin to lie, right?"

Billy jumped in,

"Are you talking about the radio station?"

"Yes, I know you guys have been ordering equipment from two different budgets, essentially doubling the amount of what you were supposed to spend. We caught you red handed."

I side-glanced at Billy, who was pointedly staring at Rev Ray's hand kneading my shoulder and each of us had to stifle a giggle. Father Roger then delivered our sentence,

"Okay, that's it, NO MORE MONEY!"

"We aren't business majors we are communication majors. We just assumed the VP and Dean knew what they were doing."

Rev Ray inched close to me,

"I won't mention this to your father, Mr. Klotenstein."

"It's 'felder, Father, Kloten*felder*."

"Well, I'll certainly remember that name. Now you boys cancel all the orders that haven't come in yet and build your radio station with what you already have. The game is over, and you're cut off. You may see your own way out now."

We rushed over to the bookstore, hoping some new shipments had arrived. After all, Father Ray had said, "… that haven't come in yet." We were sad to discover there were no boxes waiting there for us. After returning to the station, we jumped on the phone to cancel orders, well, those orders that didn't have a restocking fee. We surely didn't want the school to pay out money it didn't need to. While we didn't get everything we wanted, our double-dipping had already provided enough gear to build an amazing radio station. As for that lack of office furniture, Billy and I made a late-night trip to the administration building and "borrowed" some desks and chairs.

We pulled a week of all-nighters breaking in our ill-gotten furnishings while talking about how we would launch our new station. We could have made the brand-new studios our focus at sign-on, but we wanted a splashy theme. Billy said something about a marathon. I asked,

"Like Jerry Lewis?"

He laughed, and then I suggested we do the launch around a theme named, get ready, *The Marijuanathon*,

"How long can you stay on? How long can we stay on… MARIJUANA?"

There it was again, that synchronous sense of whacked-out humor we shared. I laughed so hard snot shot out my nose. Billy said,

"You know, this might get us thrown out of school?"

I agreed, and then we headed straight for our new production studio number two to record sweepers. In radio, a sweeper is not a vacuum cleaner. It's a recorded station promotional element that plays between two songs, sweeping the listener from one piece of music to the next. Our new sweepers would allow the jocks to get back into the swing of things after being away from the radio station over the winter break. The DJs would just run the board and punch up the records and promos without the performance stress of voicing live breaks.

Soon WVUD was back on the air and *The Marijuanathon* was quite a success. The administration was so concerned with keeping the Jacky Paradise story out of the newspaper they didn't disrupt our provocative programming, although it was alleged that Rev Ray said he couldn't wait for those two radio guys to graduate.

When we launched our new radio station in January 1970, one of the biggest albums was the Beatles' late 1969 release *Abbey Road*. Billy, being a crafty tape editor adept with magnetic tape and a razor blade, recorded the album's medleys onto a reel-to-reel tape, edited them into individual songs, then recorded them on separate tape cartridges to make it easier for the DJs. Our student listeners gave us positive comments and encouragement. Things were going well!

Girls came down to the student union and pulled the sofas up in front of our window to study while listening to music. Some scribbled requests on scraps of paper and slapped them against the glass. We did it! We brought our station back and made it even better, but more importantly we united and energized the team. We were having fun doing what we loved. When my grades in a particular class became poor, I just cancelled it. At that rate it could take me five hundred years to graduate, but it surely would be an entertaining ride.

There were times I thought about my foolishness of not studying harder in high school to get better grades and achieve a decent S.A.T. score. I could have gone to Ohio University or even the liberal, free-thinking state school in Kent, but here I was in dinky Dayton.

Walking to my car to head home I was thinking about how Billy and I had built new and impressive studios for WUVD and righted the radio station's legacy. Our programming was compelling and innovative. Students were listening and responding, and we were profoundly proud of all we did. But I had a problem. I was impatient, which has always been both a gift and a curse to me, and I no longer wanted to be in school. I was ready to ditch the classes and books and begin working in radio. As if on cue, Billy ran up behind me. Before he spoke a word, I popped this on him,

"I've been thinking, and I don't know if I want to stay here, Billy. Maybe I'll send out some airchecks and try to get a job at a real radio station."

Billy looked dumbfounded,

"Why would you leave now Herbie? You haven't graduated yet and things are going so great."

"Hey, life is short brother, and it's time for me to get on with mine."

A look of reflective sadness crossed Billy's face,

"Okay, I can understand that. But let me help you put together your audition aircheck and a resume."

"What's a resume?"

8. Leaving the Nest

There comes a time in life when one must decide what is most important. I was wondering whether to continue formal study of my broadcasting craft or dive directly into what I wanted most. Some college football players face a conundrum trying to figure out whether to stay in school and get a degree or, as they say, "come out" and get into the NFL draft.

I'm not saying I was ready for prime time in radio, but I was worried if I stayed in school any longer, I would run out of money and be slow out of the career gate. Billy helped me put together a resume and two airchecks, neither of which sounded nearly as good as my in-person rap touting my radio skills and music knowledge. I was a walking-talking encyclopedia of rock music information. I had read every Rolling Stone magazine, and the back cover of just about every rock album, so I could talk the talk. My board work was excellent and my "sense of segue," blending the end of one song into the beginning of the next, was superb. Now there's a topic worth exploring a bit.

Top 40 radio is all about energy and what's known as "forward momentum.". The DJ must maintain the audio flow by hitting the start buttons in such a way that every successive element is seamlessly and quickly delivered to the air. A Top 40 format involved talking up the song intros and jumping in at the perfect moment of the outros, not too soon and never too late. Some songs have a "cold start," meaning there's no instrumental introduction; a vocal, with or without accompaniment opens the song. Think of *Somebody to Love* by the Jefferson Airplane. For such songs, the disc jockey must punch up the song immediately after the patter, jingle or recorded promo that precedes it. A song having a "cold ending" is one that doesn't fade-out but ends abruptly or with a sustained chord. Think of *Honky Tonk Women* by the Rolling Stones. For those kinds of songs, the disc jockey must fire the next element, be it talk, a jingle or a promo, with precise timing to the beat of the music, which makes the two of them blend flawlessly together.

Leaving the Nest

The new Free Form non-format was extremely different. For one thing, announcers never talked over a song intro because purists perceived it to be an important part of the song which shouldn't be obscured by disc jockey chatter. A good Free Form DJ blended two songs together in a pleasing way. The art of the segue was a staple of this new programming style. Doing a great, ear-tickling segue, like playing the beginning of the Who's *Won't Get Fooled Again* on top of the long, sustained final note of the Beatles' *A Day in the Life*, blew listeners' minds, especially if they were high on marijuana. When a jock, shortened term for disc jockey, did a jarring segue it was referred to as a "train wreck," not a good thing.

I recorded two airchecks for radio job applications, one tailored for Top 40 stations and another for Free Form FMs. By the way, Underground was a nickname for Free Form, but that un-format didn't last awfully long. To increase ratings, many rock stations began tightening their playlists, deployed music categories and implemented primitive rotations. The name Progressive Rock was used for these kinds of rock stations. Progressive Rock eventually faded away as stations shortened their playlists once again and blended in even more song rotation techniques of the Top 40 format. This variant of the format became known as Album Oriented Rock.

I was scouring Billboard and other trade magazines in search of an on-air job. I found an opening in Ashtabula, Ohio, a small town situated east of Cleveland near the border of New York. The station was licensed to Ashtabula, which was part of the Cleveland Metropolitan Area. I figured if I could land a job there, some Cleveland radio programmer might hear me on that suburban station, be impressed with my work and look into hiring me. I had learned by observation that radio was an elaborate game of luck-driven ladder-climbing, hoping each new gig would lead to a bigger city, a more prestigious station and, of course, a higher salary. I knew going in that a disc jockey job in such a small town would pay by the hour and maybe net me about sixty-two dollars a week, but one must start somewhere.

The potential job I found was at 107.5 WBAT-FM, and the station's name didn't seem odd to me. After all, there was WJET in Erie, Pennsylvania and the combo WRED and WHOT in Youngstown, Ohio, curiously all owned by the same guy. WBAT-FM was the sister station of WBAT-AM and fell under the FCC rule that at least fifty percent of its broadcast day couldn't be simulcast. WBAT-FM had a Class A FM license, meaning their maximum power was three thousand watts and the height of their antenna could not exceed three hundred twenty-eight feet above average terrain. FM radio signals travel along a straight path, referred to as line of sight, so the higher the antenna the farther the signal will travel. Ohio is flat, and radio signals travel farther there than they do in hilly or mountainous regions. When a broadcaster applied to the FCC for an FM license, they were required to submit an engineering study showing how their intended power and antenna height would not interfere with any other station.

The FCC classified FM stations into three types. There was Class A, which stipulated that three-thousand-watt limit, Class B which allowed up to fifty thousand watts and Class C, which in some markets operated at a hundred-thousand watts. Most of the Class Cs were located in the south where cities were separated by large distances. Landing a job at WBAT-FM would mean I'd be far enough away from Dayton so any embarrassing breaks wouldn't be heard by my family or friends back home.

There is another tidbit I should mention here. WBAT-AM is what's known as a "daytimer" in the radio business. The FCC had carved out a group of licenses for lower power AM stations that were licensed to broadcast only between local sunup and sundown. You see, cooler night temperatures cause shifts in the ionosphere, which changes the way AM radio waves spread. If transmitting at night, a daytimer would interfere with other radio signals on those same frequencies but located elsewhere. In the winter months, when the sun went down early, a daytimer's broadcast day ended during afternoon drive time.

I sent the station a letter introducing myself and included the five-inch reel-to-reel tape of my Free Form aircheck. I had no idea what to expect and was surprised a few days later when the station's program director, a guy named Skinny Kenny Reeves, called and asked if I would come to Ashtabula the following Saturday morning for an interview. I did my best to sound cool and collected on the phone, but after hanging up I practically jumped over the desk in the WVUD studios where I took the call. That was particularly eventful because it let Reeves know I was at an actual radio station, even though it was just a college facility.

I arrived in Ashtabula on Friday night. My VW Beetle didn't overheat, and I decided to splurge for a motel room at a Holiday Inn near the station. My new transistor radio had an FM band, and it was about 8 p.m. when I tuned into WBAT-FM. I was surprised to hear jazz music, but at 9 p.m. PD Kenny Reeves came on the air playing album rock songs. He used the name Brother Love on his show and sounded like an old-school hippy-dippy DJ, complete with worn out cliches and antiquated references. Kenny's show opening was completely dated with, "Good evening groovy guys and chicks, you're in the arms of Brother Kenny Love." I cringed hearing him call the singer of one of the tunes he played "a cool cat," and he continuously used the word "baby" when referring to his listeners. I thought about checking out and driving back to Dayton.

I fell asleep after a while, and when I woke up at 4 a.m. WBAT-FM was playing Gospel music. I checked the dial, but it was still tuned to 107.5 FM, meaning the station was doing "block programming," a radio biz term for broadcasting different formats throughout a day or week. Sure enough, when I woke up in the morning to get ready for my interview at the station, WBAT-FM was playing R&B. This was something I hadn't expected. My little college station with its round-the-clock Top 40 format was far more together and professional than this.

When I drove into the station's parking lot only three other cars were there. The tower behind the brick building was about three hundred feet tall. The tower itself transmitted the AM signal and I saw the FM antenna mounted on the side of the tower near the top. It had two "bays," circular extrusions on one side of the antenna, which conducted the radio signal into the air. Most high-powered FM antennas would have six or even eight bays.

I arrived at the station's main glass door entrance right at 9 a.m. and peering inside saw no one in the lobby. A little button was mounted to the right side of the door next to a sign, "After Hours Ring Bell," so, guess what I did. After several other short button presses and maybe five minutes of waiting, a lanky man in his late forties appeared on the other side of the windowed door. He was smoking a thin Tiparillo cigar and sporting a goatee, corduroy bell bottom pants and a flowered shirt. His receding hairline was greased back and around his neck was a string of hippy beads made of Hawaiian shells. Oh boy, he looked like a 1950s beatnik. He opened the door and shook my hand,

"So, Mister Herbie, welcome to the BAT!"

"Thanks, love the facility."

I was not trying to patronize the guy, but hey, I never had an interview for a job before, well, I mean an interview for a "big time" radio job. Kenny led me through a dim, narrow hallway covered by cheap, game room paneling. Pictures of music stars Louie Armstrong, Ike and Tina Turner and others were unevenly tacked to the walls. It was obvious they were cut from magazines and placed in cheap frames. I felt like I was in a different world. So far, everything was way below the level of professionalism I had expected.

We passed what I assumed to be the AM on-air studio, a sizeable room in the middle of the building with glass windows present on three of its four walls. I saw a rack-mounted Scully tape recorder playing a 10½-inch reel of tape, spinning at what appeared to be 7 ½ IPS (inches per second). Typically, that's an hour's worth of audio and I speculated there was no live announcer on duty and at least this portion of the station's Saturday morning programming was prerecorded. As we got closer to the studio, I saw a young Black kid sitting behind the console and he waved as we walked by. A few steps later we reached Kenny's office. He stepped aside, waved me in, and said in a friendly voice, "Go ahead and have a seat." Kenny settled in behind his desk,

"So, your family lives in Dayton?"

"Yeah, my father works at NCR and my mom is a teacher."

"Why didn't you go to a bigger school and escape the town?"

I laughed at the word, "escape" and then answered,

"Yeah, well, I guess I applied at the last minute and… well my father…"

"That's okay, I get it. Let me explain what we are trying to do here at the BAT FM."

"Yeah, I do have some questions about the programming."

"Okay, I'll get to that, but you do realize that every time you talk you start with the word 'yeah,' right?"

"Yeah, ah, I mean, sorry."

"Okay, I'll bottom line it. The owner of the station would like to increase the ratings and sell more commercials. This whole rock thing is exploding. Woodstock was such a groovy event and there's been lots of favorable response to my nighttime show. I play LP cuts and read some poetry and the kids are digging it. We get tons of calls and letters from listeners as far away as Jamestown and Chautauqua, in New York."

Now I was, as they say, green and wet behind the ears, but I believed I had figured it out. Lucille Ball was from Jamestown, which was eighty miles away. Cleveland was only sixty miles away in the other direction. I was thinking the BAT's intention was being a big fish in a small pond, programming and selling ads to the smaller Ashtabula market rather than going up against the sharks in Cleveland. My marketing classes were paying off. I spoke up,

"Are you going to stay with block programming?"

Mr. Reeves seemed engaged by my lingo and leaned in, lowering his voice as if he was about to tell me some secret shit,

"Our plan is adding more and more rock programming until we have a full-time slate of hip guys playing the progressive, underground sounds." Mentally, my eyes rolled up,

"Where do you see me fitting in?"

"Well, we have two rock music shifts open, 1 p.m. to 4 p.m. and 12 midnight to 4 a.m."

"Why wouldn't that overnight shift go until 6 a.m.?"

I was not only trying to understand his plan for WBAT-FM, but figured they paid by the hour and more hours meant more money.

"Well, it's until six Saturday night into Sunday, but why aren't you interested in the daytime shift?"

He didn't really answer my question, but I answered his,

"Yeah, I'm just starting out and hoping to try some ideas and work on my style. I think I would feel more comfortable being on the air much later than afternoon drive time."

"That's cool, that's cool. I'm talking with a kid from Cleveland named Jimmy, but he likes to be called Jimmer. He wants to use the name Captain America on the air. You know, like *Easy Rider*? If I slot him into the daytime shift, you can have the overnight show. Your tape was good, and I feel comfortable after meeting you, so the job is yours if you want it."

"Great! When can I start?"

"We plan to launch Radio Free Ashtabula next week. Can you be here and ready next Monday night at midnight?"

"Sure!"

Next, he led me to a spacious studio-theater at the back of the building, explaining the station has been tight with a few local Gospel music groups for years and the studio was used for live concert broadcasts. A rich benefactor gave them money to keep the Gospel show on from 4 a.m. to 6 a.m. on weekdays and from 6 a.m. to 2 p.m. on Sundays, so there was the reason for that shortened all-night show. The station feared alienating the local church groups if they changed the format too quickly, which was a tiny, dark cloud that would all too soon explode into a severe thunderstorm.

We walked onto the raised stage together and Kenny showed me several large, wooden cabinets. He unlocked and opened the doors to reveal hundreds of rock albums stored in alphabetical order. I was amazed at such a complete collection for a station that broadcast only a few hours of rock songs during the week. My beatnik boss was tight with the local record promoters and there were frequent deliveries of new releases. He took the Tiparillo out of his mouth, smiled at me and said,

"Okay, Mister Herbie, you can play any song from this library. You make the playlist for your show. It's all in your hands."

"Any song? Wow, far-out."

"Except one."

"One song? What is it?"

"*The Pusher.*"

9. One Room Walkup

It all seems so easy, until it's time to do it. The first thing on my to-do list was a drive back to Dayton for a sit-down with my mother and father. I needed to explain why I was dropping out of college and taking a job almost three hundred miles away from home for the same money I could earn working at our local Kroger grocery store. The next thing on my list was finding an apartment for much less than the two hundred and fifty dollars I would be bringing in each month.

The talk with my parents went much better than I expected. My father made me promise I would consider this a one-term sabbatical from school to see if I really liked the radio business. He said he would continue to pay for my education should I decide to reenter school in the fall, then he handed me five hundred dollars for my moving expenses. Mom was okay with me leaving town but made me promise I would come home to visit on as many Sundays, my day off, as I could. She was also relieved I received number 311 in the draft lottery, which meant I didn't need a college deferment to stay out of Vietnam. With my promises made, I had to get back to Ashtabula and find a place to live.

I made a stop at WVUD to say goodbye to the guys, and I encountered two broad and opposite reactions from my radio student friends. One was heartfelt congratulations, almost as if I was graduating. The other was a kind of cold envy. Skip was a downright prick when he spoke out of the side of his mouth,

"Ashtabula, is that like market number nine thousand?"

"It's only sixty miles from Cleveland, Skip."

"Sure kid, call me when you get to Cleveland. Good luck and don't get no ash on you."

Billy, of course, was positive,

"Wow, that's really great man! Hey, let me know when you get settled in and I'll come up and we'll go out for Big Boys."

Parting ways with my college radio station was a bittersweet experience. I would repeat the drama of leaving a radio station many times again during my career, but the great memories of WVUD and my friends there stayed with me over the years. I have since learned many radio people carry an almost mythical remembrance of their first station, and I am no different. To this day I know WVUD was the best in so many ways, and no other station will ever top my experiences there. After fifty years, that college station still has a great reputation, and I am proud of the small role I played in its continuing success.

I bought copies of the Cleveland Plain Dealer and Cleveland Press newspapers and searched for an apartment to rent. I found a place near the station and grabbed it quickly. It was on the top floor of an old three-story house in a quiet neighborhood off Bunker Hill Road. The building was owned by a retired lady in her eighties who lived on the ground floor. She explained a single woman named Marilyn Ford occupied the second-floor apartment, and she was the librarian at the Ashtabula Public Library.

The top walkup flat was mine. It was a cozy, furnished, one-room place with a small bathroom and a single window facing west. That was perfect because I would be sleeping during the day and the sun wouldn't be intruding. Also, the lady on the second floor would be gone all day so the top-floor guy could get some daytime sleep. A long stairway attached to the back of the house provided a private entry to each of the two apartments. I considered those stairs might be a tough climb after freezing rain or a snowstorm, but hey, I was young and from Ohio.

My new program director, Kenny Reeves called me to discuss my name. I had used "Herbie da K" at WVUD, an homage to New York's Murray the K, a disc jockey known as "the fifth Beatle." Reeves was not at all down with the name, saying I should concoct a name based on astrology, which he said was the "hip thing" with "the kids" as he called his listeners. I couldn't help wondering if they are "the kids" then who the hell am I? He asked me my astrological sign, and I admitted that I didn't know. So, as happens with many radio people, my boss picked a name for me,

"Okay, Herbie, you're gonna be Gemini... and, you know, read some listener horoscopes and work some other hippy stuff like that in."

Who was I to argue? He was the PD. Obviously, the station wouldn't promote my show around the clock because each shift featured a different blend of music for a dissimilar audience. I did listen to Brother Kenny's show, however, and heard him talking about Gemini coming to the BAT on Monday at the stroke of midnight. It was thrilling hearing my name, even though it wasn't really my name, coming out of my radio through the magic of the invisible airwaves beamed from a commercial radio station!

After moving into my new place that Friday afternoon, I ran into Miss Ford, the lady on the second floor, who stated in clear terms she was to be called Marilyn, not Miss. She was in her early thirties and wore a long, beautifully flowered pattern dress with peace signs scattered between the petals. The dress had an empire waist that emphasized her ample breasts, and I was careful not to gaze lower than her eyes. She had long blonde hair, and I do mean long because it flowed down to her waist. We made our introductions, then I asked,

"Ah, hey Marilyn, is the library open tomorrow?"

"Only from 9 a.m. to noon. Is there something in particular you need?"

I explained the predicament with my new DJ name and needing to talk about astrology on the radio without knowing a lick about it. She snickered and smiled,

"Well, aren't you lucky, It just so happens that astrology is my thing and I consider myself an expert. Why don't you come to my place tomorrow for dinner? I'll walk you through the basics and help you plan a suitable approach for your radio show."

I agreed and felt so relieved. After another few trips unloading the meager possessions from my car, I sat at my apartment's small kitchen table, plugged in my AM/FM clock radio, and dialed around to get acquainted with the local stations. Because I was up on the top floor, all the Cleveland stations were loud and clear. I spent a few hours listening to WMMS and was both amazed at how good it sounded but also intimidated. A company named MetroMedia owned the radio station and its call letters stood for MetroMedia stereo. One of their disc jockeys was named Billy Bass and I thought about my buddy Billy back in Dayton. This Cleveland guy sounded more Top 40 than most of the other Progressive FM jocks I had heard, but Cleveland was a big city. What did I know?

Late afternoon the next day, I made my way down to the second floor of my new home away from home and knocked on Miss Ford's door. I heard Indian sitar music playing inside the apartment. She came and opened the door quickly, her hair wound into what looked like a macrame weave. She was wearing a bright red silk shirt untucked over blue jeans and no shoes. She waved me in while talking on her phone tethered to a tangled twenty-five-foot cord. Of course, I heard only her side of the conversation,

"Look, I know you thought this was something else, but man, let's just be friends. I need a break and you need some time to work on your problems. Seriously, we'll be much better off without each other. You'll see."

There was a pause, she gestured me over to the couch and then walked to the kitchen to check on a boiling pot.

"Yes, I truly do think you need a shrink, Larry. Okay, okay, this has gone on long enough. I have a guest, dinner's on the stove and I gotta run now. Look, no hard feelings and I honestly think this is a perfect move for both of us. Let's talk another time. Catch ya later. Bye."

She lowered the stove's burner and shook her head,

"I'm so sorry about that."

"None of my business, but that sounded like a tough call."

She turned around, smiled and answered,

"No, that was an easy call. Next, Next, Next!"

I looked around the room and admired an excellent collection of psychedelic concert posters from both the Fillmore East and the Fillmore West. Unlike my one room apartment, Marilyn's unit had a bedroom. Its door was open, and I saw the room was bathed in black light.

I was thinking I need to be careful here. It's best to not get involved with someone where you live. My new neighbor was more than ten years older than me, but on the other side of that coin she certainly was a free spirit with no big sister vibe at all.

"Marilyn, this is an amazing collection of posters. Where did you get them?"

"Oh, there's a wonderful little shop in Cleveland that has some great stuff. I wish I had a bigger place to hang more like them."

I asked if I could use her restroom, and when I entered the unmistakable odor of kitty litter hit me. When I came out, I asked,

"So, you have a cat?"

"Three. Oh, I forgot to ask, are you allergic?"

"Not that I know of, but where are they?"

"They are probably sleeping in my bedroom closet. They're finicky and usually hide from strangers."

"What are their names?"

"Curly, Moe and Joe."

I laughed and thought, man what a hip librarian. She had prepared a fabulous spaghetti dinner with a big salad and garlic toast. After the delicious meal I helped with the dishes and then we returned to the cleared table. Marilyn brought out a thick, large book with gilded pages and handed me a brand-new notebook along with a pen. She said I should take notes.

She asked for my city of birth, my birthdate and whether I knew the time I was born. My mother always made a big deal about me being a night owl because I waited until 4:13 a.m. to arrive. Marilyn flipped through her voluminous reference book and then exclaimed,

"You're not a fucking Gemini, Herbie, you're a Taurus. Had you been born three minutes later then you would be a Gemini."

"I take it you don't like Geminis."

"Well, they're great at creativity but inconsistent. You never know which twin you're going to get."

We mapped out some hypothetical charts and she taught me how to present the information — Pluto in Capricorn, Neptune in Pisces, and so on. I thanked Marilyn for her help and asked if I owed her anything for the guidance and the notebook, adding that she could keep the pen. She laughed and said that I owed her a dinner sometime. I agreed to those terms, said goodnight and made my way up to my room at the top of the world.

My first WBAT-FM show on Monday went off without any technical problems or missteps. I played some of my favorite rock tunes, Van Morrison, the Beatles, the Stones, and a new band that everyone was loving, Led Zeppelin. I read horoscopes and predicted how each sign's day would unfold after the sun came up. I concentrated on my content and delivery, and every time I cracked the mic to speak, I imagined the air all across Ashtabula pulsating in cadence with my voice. After Radio Rudy and WVUD, it was incredibly thrilling hosting a show on a "real" radio station.

All night I was drinking bottles of Coke while working, and when I got home it took quite a while to unwind and get to sleep. I remember briefly stirring when the sun came up, thinking I had finally made it to the big time, and with that I turned over and snoozed again.

I woke up at 3 p.m. remembering Kenny Reeves had asked me to call him at the station. I didn't have a phone, so I walked to a small grocery store further down Bunker Hill and used the pay phone there. It took a while for the receptionist to find him,

"Hey Gemini, smooth show last night. Very groovy, but I do have one suggestion."

"Sure, of course. What's up?"

"Kid, that horoscope thing isn't working. Dump it."

"What about my name?"

"No, Gemini stays, but just play the tunes and add your discography, you know the music tidbits."

"Yeah, sure."

"Okay, have a great show tonight, Mr. Gemini."

I hung up the phone and had an empty, rumbling feeling in my stomach. It occurred to me that some food might be good at this point but there was great news; I was standing right in front of a small grocery store. I went in and bought some stuff for my small apartment fridge.

After just one day into my professional broadcasting career, I had already learned a valuable lesson. Radio required flexibility because things could change in a second. I felt badly that Marilyn Ford had done so much astrology training for nothing, but as I traveled through the radio maze, I would always remember a great Three Stooges line. All three are in a single bed and Larry is loudly snoring, so Moe slaps his face and yells,

"Wake up and go to sleep!"

I thought to myself that I'll sleep once I'm dead or fired.

10. Protestors in the Night

I find that when things are going well it helps to keep a little dark space in the back of my mind as a reminder that failure can jump into a life at any moment. When my program director decided the horoscope thing was shit, I was left with no gimmick, no tagline. People would meet me and say, "So, you're a Gemini. Well, my little brother is one too, and he's an asshole!" That's not exactly a wonderful opening to a new friendship. When I admitted to women that I wasn't really a Gemini and told them my real name, most would just walk away. No self-respecting female wanted to be with a Herbie.

During my first break after midnight on one of my early shows I teased my listeners with an announcement that a brand-new feature would be coming up at 1 a.m. and they should keep listening. I had no idea what that bit would be, but I had fifty minutes to concoct something. While a long song was playing, I went into the production studio and recorded a two-minute improv comedy routine using vocal impressions and sound effects. I layered some music behind it and decided to call it a "radio movie." I was thinking it was a sure-fire way to get the stoners off.

While in college, I became hooked on a group from Los Angeles named The Firesign Theatre. They were a four-man comedy troupe with a background in radio, broadcasting a late-sixties series of shows titled *Radio Free Oz* on KRLA. I became familiar with the group when Columbia Records signed them to a five-year record contract, and they released albums containing hilarious parodies of old radio plays. Their quirky sense of humor, accented by their over-the-top production technique, was weirdly cool and very West Coast. My 1 a.m. feature on the BAT was a humble attempt to honor them. I wasn't at all sure that eastern Ohio and far western New York would get the humor of those radio playwrights from California, but I took my best shot at imitating them or, as they characterized it years later during a phone conversation with me, "ripping them off."

My very first radio movie wasn't all that special. It was off the cuff and perhaps more spacey than funny, despite that the phone lines lit up,

"Hey far-out man! What the fuck was that? Can you do that again?"

I explained this was a new feature I would be doing every night at 1 a.m. Then I got to wondering if I should say every night or every morning. If I used the word night, it might not resonate with those working late shifts. To them, it's the middle of the day. But if I used the word morning, it could remind some people it was time to shut off the radio and get into bed.

I always followed my nightly radio movie with a long song so I could answer the phone calls and judge the reaction to my latest creation. I began to take more care when writing them and stepped up the production, doing my best to make my radio movies just as compelling as Firesign Theatre recordings.

The next night I followed the feature with Iron Butterfly's song *In-A-Gadda-Da-Vida*, which was seventeen minutes and two seconds long. Years later I learned the story behind the unusual song title. Doug Ingle was the band's vocalist, and one night he wrote the song while drinking way too much wine. He asked another band member to write out the lyrics but slurred his words so badly that when he tried to say *In the Garden of Eden*, it came out and got written as *In-A-Gadda-Da-Vida*. That mistake was good enough to sell a million copies of the song!

The reaction to my radio movies was gratifying and they became a focus of my show, but I worried about my boss terminating the feature. About ten days into running the radio movies, Kenny Reeves called on what is known in the radio business as the "hotline." It's a studio telephone with a non-published number known only by management. That phone doesn't ring, instead a bright, blinking light signals an incoming call. All too often it was used to ream out a DJ's ass for something they said or did on the air, but this night my program director sounded upbeat and maybe just a bit tipsy,

"Hey, Gemini, Brother Kenny here. What's the radio movie for tonight? I'm here with some friends and we all really love that thing."

I was blown away. He not only listened to my show but liked the bit I created! Wow, I had no idea. Later that month, he asked if the radio movie should play earlier, but I argued that it's appealing and we should continue to make listeners wait to hear it, you know, keep them listening longer. He quickly agreed. It wasn't difficult to come up with inventive ideas at this unsophisticated, almost amateur, radio station.

One night, a college caller told me her friend kept her radio playing under her bed to help her fall asleep. I played this up on the air with a long, slow mantra of, "You are tired, your eyelids are getting heavy, drooping now, almost closing. You are getting sleepy, very sleepy, sleepier and sleepier." I ended this bit of nonsense by having the radio heave an irritatingly long and loud belch and asking why he had to live under the bed. It was simple, playful fun.

Now what I'm about to share rarely happens in radio, but it's an important part of my story. One night I was exceptionally tired and barely able to stay awake. Falling asleep on the air could end my short career, so I went to the station's vending machine. Once there, I remembered I had used the last of my money earlier in the night to gas up the Beetle, so I knelt on the floor next to the machine, reached up inside and dislodged a Twix bar. I felt guilty, but I rationalized that keeping the station on the air justified this tiny bit of thievery. The sugar burst kept me going that night, but obtaining it wasn't my only bad boy behavior during the shift.

Not long after finishing the Twix bar, I got a call from a lady with an incredibly sexy voice asking if I could play *The Pusher* by Steppenwolf. The station had a specialized taping device named Metrotech, which recorded everything going out over the air. This was a defensive mechanism should evidence be needed to fight a legal claim made about the station's programming. Of course, I knew the rule against playing the song, but damn, I wanted to please my listener. Without a great deal of thought, I pushed the Stop button on the Metrotech machine and restarted it right after the song finished. A week later my boss asked me if I had played that forbidden song,

"Nope, never played it. Check the Metrotech."

I have no clue what prompted his question, but my answer kept the wolf away for the moment. A few nights later however, something happened that I am sure was karmic payback for the candy pilfering and Metrotech caper. It was about 3 a.m. and I had just cued up my next song. I looked up and saw a motley crew of eight young folks about my age staring intently at me. It was a frightening scene. I segued into the next song and then, making sure the mic was off, I demanded,

"How the fuck did you get in here?"

They explained they saw an old Black guy walk in the front door who didn't pull it completely closed behind him. I figured that was Walter, who hosted the WBAT-FM Gospel show when my shift ended at 4 a.m. He was an older gentleman and a bit hard of hearing, so I am sure he never knew others entered the open door behind him. I pressed my onlookers,

"Who are you? Why are you here? What do you want?"

One of the guys explained they were from Chautauqua, New York, a lake resort community in the northwest area of the state, and they were arrested during a demonstration at the home of their county's draft board director. They had gathered in the director's front yard, chanting war protest lines and burning their draft cards. I asked again,

"Okay, but why are you here?"

One of the ladies spoke up,

"We want to go on the air and tell the story about what happened to us in the court room."

They alleged they were taken to magistrate court, someone turned off the lights in the courtroom, and state cops beat the shit out of them with their nightsticks. I cued up the next song while listening, took a deep breath, and attempted to calm the situation,

"Okay, that is certainly terrible and, yes, a total injustice, but why would you want to go on a three-thousand-watt station in the middle of the night when the fewest number of people will hear your story? Besides that, any attempt to take over a US broadcast station is a federal offense. If the police came here and found you doing this, they would be legally justified in shooting you. Knowing how poorly they fire their weapons they would probably kill me too. After all, I look just like you."

After raising a slight chuckle from them, I handed over the business card of our news director and suggested they call him at 10 a.m. tomorrow, which was actually today, and get a slot on his 5 p.m. *BAT News You Can Use* program. They agreed and peacefully left the radio station.

I learned later their story was true and the Chautauqua Eight, surely not as famous as the Chicago Seven, ended up fighting in court for years. Eventually they received an apology from the Governor of New York, but never obtained compensation for their wounds and violated rights. As we'll soon see, another small Ohio town had a dark cloud hovering above it which was ready to burst and change the world.

Being the disc jockey of a Free Form radio show, I felt the need to connect with my audience. After hearing that story, I played this set of songs, *For What It's Worth* by the Buffalo Springfield, *Blowin' in the Wind* by Bob Dylan, *Universal Soldier* by Buffy Sainte-Marie and *Fortunate Son* by Creedence Clearwater Revival. That finished my radio program for the night. I walked back to the studio-theater to refile the records, and I heard Walter open his 4 a.m. show with *Oh Happy Day* by the Edwin Hawkins Singers. Man, what a great song!

I felt satisfied knowing I diverted some anger and produced a solution to a would-be disaster that could have hurt those kids, and possibly me. More than that, I was wondering what would happen next in America. African Americans were angry, college students were angry and the reaction to anti-war protests had escalated to a dangerous degree and divided the nation. Where was our country headed? Protest songs sounded great on Free Form radio, but could they get us out of Vietnam? Top 40 radio stayed away from controversies. They had no reason to upset their big advertisers like Coca-Cola, McDonald's and Wrigley's Spearmint Gum.

From my vantage point, WBAT-FM was doing well. I was playing more commercials each week, but something was coming, something significantly bigger than this DJ from Dayton. What happened next would teach me a lesson about the power of the people, the *true* power of the people.

11. We Shall Overcome

My mother insists everything happens for a reason but, truth is, there are times happenings have no discernable purpose. Such a conflict might ignite a deep, late-night discussion among philosophy majors, but my small brain separates the facts of reality from the platitudes and cliches of my fellow men and women. More on happenings and reasons shortly, but for now I want to talk about food.

Kraft Macaroni and Cheese dinners have always been packaged in a distinctive blue box with the red and white Kraft logo top and center. This image is burned into my brain because I bought ten of them at a time and lined them up on the shelf above the sink in my small apartment. They cost nineteen cents a box back then, so I could afford to buy a bunch at once. I gobbled mac and cheese at just about every dinner, which was actually a late afternoon breakfast for this overnight disc jockey.

Sometimes, when I was feeling wild and creative, I would add a can of tuna for protein, and that's how I became a master chef. Most of the radio people I knew back then consumed pounds of fast food because of their hurrying impatience, but I preferred my blue-box meals and, damn, they tasted great. While I was occupied keeping myself alive on sixty-two dollars a week, I was oblivious to some dark clouds gathering over Radio Free Ashtabula.

Many FM stations were moving to new formats because of the FCC mandate to end simulcasting their AM and FM signals. Some stations launched new formats while others changed incrementally. I heard about WCOL-FM in Columbus, Ohio playing Christian and Gospel music from 6 a.m. to 6 p.m. then running a rock format starting at 6 p.m. The young DJ was a guy named Jim Roach, real name, and he kicked off his show one night with the hit song *Fire* by the Crazy World of Arthur Brown. Here are the opening lyrics, which began with ten words spoken in a strident, commanding voice, *"I am the god of hellfire and I bring you, Fire, I'll take you to burn, Fire, I'll take you to learn, I'll see you burn!"*

Not long after the song began playing, there was loud banging on the front door of the radio station. Roach peered out a window and saw a large man standing there, holding an axe, fully prepared to take back his station. Passion and radio listening used to go hand to hand. The disc jockey called the cops, and with their encouragement the axman left.

When you make a promise to people, they will remember it. Ashtabula was sixty miles from Cleveland, which in 1970 had an African American population of thirty-nine percent. WBAT-FM was a radio station licensed by the FCC, meaning its owners had to be careful with operating and programming it. It will help if you have some insight about the way radio licenses are obtained and maintained to best understand the tale I am about to share.

Unlike totalitarian countries, here in the United States "We the people" own the radio airwaves; they're in the public domain. We codified a principal that a private or public business or organization had to prove they were worthy of the privilege to transmit a signal through our atmosphere. Some said that "privilege" was a right to print money because most radio stations sold advertising and made healthy profits, but that's the nature of capitalism. At the dawn of radio broadcasting, when there were fewer radio stations than newspapers, broadcast advertising revenue was far less than print, but as time went on radio, and eventually television, captured ever growing pieces of the advertising pie. This is one of the reasons the FCC mandated that a single entity could not own a newspaper, an AM station, an FM station and a TV station in the same market. Another rule stipulated a single owner could have a maximum of seven AM stations, seven FM stations and seven television stations across the whole country.

Those were good rules, intended to prevent a media conglomerate from controlling the opinions of one city, much less the entire nation. Since major broadcasters could not extend their reach in a single town, they bought up stations in what are known as "major markets" such as New York, Los Angeles and Chicago.

Ashtabula was not a major market, it was a dinky small town, and WBAT super-served its local listeners with no aspiration to dent the Cleveland market. About ten years prior to my arrival, WBAT-AM and FM were simulcast one hundred percent of the time. Remember, the AM station was a daytimer, so when WBAT-AM signed off at sundown, they urged their listeners to tune over to WBAT-FM to continue hearing the same programing.

To increase its listener base, the station advertised in major Black-owned newspapers pitching their Gospel music format. The WBAT ad contained a description of the BAT-BOX, a small AM/FM radio in a white plastic case adorned with a tiny black bat. The radio was sold at Henchman's Hardware for nine dollars and ninety-nine cents, and the ad promised listeners would "be able to hear Gospel music twenty-four hours a day, seven days a week." The BAT-BOX was sold for years, and if you visited the home of an African American family, it was highly likely you would see that little white radio somewhere in the kitchen.

At a recent NAACP meeting in Ashtabula, a woman was critical about WBAT-FM reducing their Gospel music programming in favor of rock songs. She was particularly miffed that there was no Gospel music at night, and a committee was formed to study the matter. In most cases, a problem assigned to a "committee" is a conflict about to die, but in that age of burgeoning equal and civil rights this committee was motivated by highly vocal and well-organized Baptist warriors.

Buddy was one of WBAT's jazz jocks who also held a managerial position at the station. One particular night, he came into the studios around 2:30 a.m. This wasn't a business or social call, however. Buddy was accompanied by a beautiful, young woman, and they went directly to the conference room, turned off the lights and closed the door. About twenty minutes later, a call came in on the engineering phone line. I answered, and a woman's shrill voice drilled into my ear,

"Is this the DJ? This is Mrs. Audrey Perkins. Is my husband there?"

"Ah, sorry, who is this again?"

"AUDREY PERKINS! Is Buddy Perkins there at the station?"

I replied I didn't know and politely asked if I could place her on hold while I checked. I did my break into the next song and started to walk toward the conference room. Just then it dawned on me. This was Buddy stepping out or, as they sometimes say, *picking up some strange*. I waited for about two minutes before lifting the phone again,

"No, sorry, I'm the only one here, but if Buddy comes in, I'll tell him you called."

She disconnected the call without saying another word. It would be months later when I learned the station had a simple rule, don't ask, don't tell. That being said, I never understood why some radio people used their station for sex and drugs. I thought it should be used strictly for rock 'n roll.

It wasn't unusual for me to be the last to know about things that happened around WBAT-FM. Being one of the few white guys at the station, and working the all-night shift to boot, meant I didn't have the comradery and interaction I so enjoyed with my colleagues in college radio. One day I found a plain, white envelope in my mail cubby. I opened it and out tumbled a small block of fragrant hashish. Inside was a brief note from WBAT's sales manager,

"Great job on the Anderson Chevrolet spot!"

While I was surprised and appreciated the compliment, I didn't produce that spot. It was recorded by Captain America, a known pothead. I passed the note and hash on to Jimmer and never spoke of it again, until now.

Captain America worked from 1 p.m. to 4 p.m. Monday through Friday and we saw each other only occasionally. One day I was at the station picking up my paycheck when Jimmer pulled me aside and said,

"Man, there were lots of Black people in the station today. They were mostly men but there were also a few women, and all of them were impeccably dressed and carrying expensive looking briefcases. They weren't here long before Hal ushered them into the conference room"

I flashed to the fact they were meeting with our general manager around that big conference room table which just a few days ago had been used as a love lounge. I snickered inside,

"Do you have any idea what the meeting was about?"

"I don't know but later in the day the receptionist made a snide remark about how it wouldn't be long before 'all you white bellbottom boys will be packin' your bags.'"

Well, Jimmer smoked too much, and I never put much credence in anything he had to say, but this time his words penetrated, and that small dark spot in my brain widened a bit more.

I remember that day like it was yesterday, or maybe the day before. I still didn't have a phone, so I had given Marilyn's number to Kenny and a few others at the station in case they ever needed to get ahold of me. It was a Thursday, and I was boiling water for my afternoon Kraft mac and cheese banquet when there was a knock at my door. It startled me because no one ever visited. I opened the door and there was Marilyn, wearing a flimsy T-shirt with no bra underneath,

"Hey Gemini, hey, my eyes are up here."

"Yeah, sorry Marilyn, what's up?"

"You need to call the station. They said it's important that you get in touch as soon as you can. You wanna use my phone?"

I turned off the stove, walked with Marilyn down to her place and called Kenny Reeves at WBAT. He sounded down and depressed, which was highly unusual for him. He was always chipper and upbeat, but on this call all the trappings of the hip beatnik dude had vanished. Kenny was coming off like a strait-laced businessman saying he needed to chat with me in person but not at the radio station. He asked me to meet with him in Conference Room 3 at the Holiday Inn as soon as I could get there. I hung up the phone and looked at Marilyn who asked,

"What's going on?"

"I'm not sure but I heard a rumor that some of us are going to be fired and I think this could be it. My boss wants me to meet him at the fucking Holiday Inn. This can't be good."

"I'm so sorry, Herbie. Please keep me posted."

I got dressed in my most conservative shirt and pants, jumped in my butt-ugly, yellow Beetle, headed down Bunker Hill and hit the main highway toward the Holiday Inn. I was holding some hope this might be a joke. I fantasized walking into the conference room to find it filled with all my buddies from WVUD, which was certainly possible. They could have hooked Kenny into a surprise party.

After arriving, I quickly found the small conference room off the lobby. I was greeted by Kenny Reeves, Hal Connors, the general manager of the station whom I had never met before, and Public Affairs Director Buddy Perkins. Yep, it turns out that the guy who was in charge of the station's public affairs was also an expert in private affairs. Mr. Connors started,

"Jim, ah… sorry."

He shuffled the papers in front of him and restarted,

"Herbert, beginning tonight WBAT-FM will be returning to all Gospel music. I'm sorry to say your services are no longer needed at the station but I want you to know that your exemplary work on the overnight shift has been very much appreciated."

A lump rose in my throat as my heart sank. I looked at Kenny Reeves, whose head was down as if praying to the dirty shag carpeting. Then Buddy spoke, and I had to stop myself from laughing at his screechy, high-pitched voice,

"You see, Gem, for many years we pledged that we would always play Gospel music on the FM after the AM had signed off. We have a ton of listeners who remember that commitment and they have asked us to keep our promise."

I looked up, and made a last-ditch attempt to save my job,

"I can do Gospel. I did Top 40 at college. I love the Edwin Hawkins singers."

Kenny finally looked up,

"Nah, kid, you wouldn't be able to do remote broadcasts, you're white."

And so it was, fired because of the color of my skin and not the quality of my work or character of my soul. Okay, you win God. I should have never stolen that fucking Twix bar.

The station gave me two-months' pay and made me sign a document saying I would never sue them and that they now owned everything I created while working at WBAT-FM. I was sure the Gospel jocks would be fighting over who would get to play my radio movies, ha! I shook all their hands and walked out the door. To this very day I hate Holiday Inn conference rooms.

But as ABC's great newscaster and provocateur Paul Harvey used to say, "And now for the rest of the story." It seems that the format change and my demise were, indeed, bigger than all of us.

Initially, WBAT-FM's ownership had politely stonewalled the NAACP complaint about the rock music. The pot was now boiling, however, and the station had seriously underestimated the group's cause and resolve. The lawyers from the NAACP had gently hinted at finding another broadcaster to challenge ownership of the station's license. This was a serious move, which should have clued in the executives that the gospel coalition was determined to win at any cost.

The Monday before I got my walking papers, four Black men strode into the station. They were dressed in black leather jackets and all of them were wearing the now infamous black berets with FREE HUEY buttons. Two men stood outside the front doors of the station, each holding a rifle. The sit-down meeting between the Black Panthers and Hal Connors was short.

The leader of the group asked him when the station would change back to a full-time Gospel format. Connors launched into a feeble explanation about the need to make money and blah, blah, blah…

The leader of the Black group, who shall remain nameless for my personal safety, then stood up, looked at the name plate on the GM's desk, and said,

"You don't seem to be getting it, Hal. If you don't change WBAT-FM back to gospel we will burn this whole place down, you dig? So, let me ask you one final time, when will your loyal WBAT-FM listeners get the gospel music they want?"

Connors, a short white guy wearing a four-hundred-dollar gray three-piece suit, calmly answered,

"Will Friday work for you?"

The Black Panthers didn't answer, they just marched out of the office through the lobby and into the street. Someone mentioned they saw the receptionist, with her astonishingly large afro, raise her left fist and wink at the leader as he passed her desk.

When I got back to the apartment, I climbed the steps slowly. My shoulders were bent in defeat, but someone brightened my day on the second-floor landing. Marilyn was there,

"How bad?"

"It's over. I am surprised you didn't see this in my horoscope."

She chuckled and walked over to give me a big hug. I could feel her breasts pressing against my chest,

"Come down for dinner tonight at six. I'll talk you off the ledge."

I looked at her and joked,

"Maybe you should just push me over the railing."

"No, not yet. I have plans for you."

I started the climb to the third floor and stopped halfway up,

"Can you believe I got fired because I'm white?"

She laughed and threw her hair back,

I resumed plodding up the stairs and shook my head when I reached the door, wondering how in the hell I was going to pay for this place. Shit, I'll probably have to move back home so I can hear my dad utter those terrible words, "I told you so." Marilyn looked up and said forcefully,

"It's just a damn job, Herbie, not the end of the world. Besides, I like white guys. See you at six."

12. Tail Between My Legs

Radio disc jockeys use the term "tease" for things they say to get the audience to listen through a commercial break or to create anticipation and excitement about something they will soon hear. Another radio expression is "stopset," which is a cluster of back-to-back commercials. Putting these two words together, you might hear a DJ lay out this tease right before a stopset, "A song that was written about a woman who had an affair with a president is coming up next." The goal is inspiring listener curiosity. If they're wondering which song or which president it is, they'll most likely stick around during the commercials to get the answer afterwards.

A tease can also come in handy when writing. Did you see what I did there at the end of the previous chapter? Our hero had climbed to the giant comfort blanket of his small apartment after our female heroine had hugged the poor, unemployed soul and invited him to dinner at her place using the sentence, "I have plans for you." Now, if I have done my job, you are certainly wondering what will happen next, and I would be a terrible author if I didn't deliver the goods after teasing you.

Marilyn's apartment was warmly inviting with the dim light of glowing candles scattered around the room. It had an almost Christmas look and feel. Incense wafted through the cozy apartment, a wonderfully calming sandalwood aroma. She put on the Van Morrison album *Moondance* and opened a bottle of Mateus, a Portuguese wine that, once consumed, became a candle holder for every respectable hippy's abode. The overt roundness of the bottle's bottom reminded me of a full-figured woman.

Marilyn was wearing a flimsy burnous, which is a hooded Arab cape, and hers was draped loosely over her shoulders. I was taken by her extremely white skin. The two of us quickly consumed the bottle of wine while chatting, but our girl was at the ready with another chilled bottle of the same. We headed to the dinner table as she popped the cork, and once seated we dove into her meal, ironically, a tuna casserole. It was exceptionally good, and we laughed about how life is one big crapshoot. Thankfully, she avoided any discussion about Gemini's recent career demise. Through the candlelight I could see that she was constantly gazing into my eyes and, of course, I kept looking at that beautiful garment loosely wrapped over her shoulders.

I don't know if you're familiar with a typical 1970s vinyl record changer, but if you loaded only one album it would play repeatedly. That was happening this evening as side one of the *Moondance* LP played again and again with Van Morrison singing, *"Well, it's a marvelous night for a moondance, With the stars up above in your eyes. A fantabulous night to make romance…"*

Through the smog of the Mateus, I saw the bedroom bathed in black light, and that garment I had focused on for the last hour had now been tossed on Marilyn's bedroom floor. She was undressing me and pulling me into her bed. Oh, sweet Marilyn, tall and round in all the right ways. I was young and inexperienced, and she was older and commanding.

Caravan was now playing. It's one of my all-time favorites because of the way it celebrates friends and radio. As I was feeling the sensations of a thousand firework finales on the Fourth of July, Van was singing, *"Turn up your radio, And let me hear the song. Switch on your electric light, Then we can get down to what is really wrong. I long to hold you tight, so I can feel you, Sweet lady of the night, I shall reveal you."*

The joy of the moment was interrupted by a sudden onrush of sharp pain at my bare feet dangling out of the bed covers. Curly, Moe and Joe had come out of their closet hiding space, and they ferociously attacked when they saw my feet moving and pushing. The three cats were biting and scratching, protecting their mother, or maybe I was their prey. My yelp of pain startled Marilyn. She switched on the light by the bed and began apologizing for her unruly felines.

It took a little while to patch and clean my wounds in the morning, but I managed to get down the long flight of stairs to the first floor where I met with the landlady. I explained my predicament of a job loss and she was understanding and gracious, cancelling my lease right then and there. In gratitude, I sat through a long story about how her husband was laid off from his job in 1937. I made a few trips up and down the stairs, emptying my apartment and packing the Beetle.

I said goodbye to Marilyn, who hugged me and told me I would be famous someday. She apologized again about the cats, but I just shrugged it off and told her that, somehow, I thought I might recover. She giggled and added,

"You know, it's me who usually screams during sex."

My eyes opened wide. I wasn't used to a woman being so bawdy and direct, but I was digging it. I have always been pro-feminism, yeah, burn those bras! On that final day in Ashtabula, Marilyn handed me a small, brightly wrapped box and asked me to open it in front of her. It was a woman's mannequin hand. I gazed at her quizzically,

"What's this for?"

"It will remind you of me. Keep my hand safe."

As I hit the road in my beat up, dirty, yellow VW, I had a heavy moment of doubt. What is radio all about? Is it something I genuinely want to do? It had only been four months at WBAT-FM, and now I was canned and having doubts about wanting a place in this crazy business.

I took I-217 to I-71, then picked up I-70 out of Columbus. As I listened to the radio stations in Cleveland, then Columbus and finally the disc jockeys in Cincinnati and Dayton, I kept thinking how good they all sounded. I also heard a few female DJs on that return trip, musing how they come in one of two boxes. Some women jocks try to imitate their male counterparts while others lean into a softer, sexier approach, which is the one I preferred. I didn't think a woman could ever possibly work a Top 40 format. The idea of a female DJ being a high energy "boss jock" was inconceivable to me. Well, I turned out to be absolutely wrong on that one.

Of course, my mother embarrassed me with an enormous banner draped across the front yard screaming "WELCOME HOME HERBIE!" They must have had radar to know the exact moment I turned onto our street because they were standing on the porch as I pulled into the driveway. My father was holding a newspaper in his left hand as he reached out with his right hand to warmly shake mine. My dad's firm grasp was deeply comforting, and I was grateful to have such positive, encouraging and understanding parents.

It was wonderful sitting down to a full course homecooked meal, and my parents were smart enough to avoid discussion of what had happened during my four months in "professional" radio. Dad was adept at working suggestions into conversations, and I was sure that when we talked later, he would gently share his thoughts in a natural and off-the-cuff manner rather than delivering a preplanned lecture. My father mentioned he ran into his Kiwanis buddy Frank at the hardware store who said he needed a shipping clerk at his bed factory. Frank explained his boy was getting back from Vietnam in December, so the job would be short term, only a few months at most.

Perfect timing! Desperate not to sit around the house and suffer any prosecution for not working and casting aside a college education, albeit one that lasted only a year, the opportunity was good. I took the job at the Restonic factory and worked for Mr. Siegel, packing eighteen-wheelers with mattresses to be delivered all over Ohio, Indiana and Kentucky. Little did the customers know that their new "handcrafted" bed was built by a gaggle of ex-cons and failed football players. Frank Siegel was a tough boss but a kind-hearted person who helped men down on their luck by hiring them. His five-foot-four frame was not physically imposing, but when he spoke his husky workers respectfully listened.

I learned a hard lesson the first time I packed a huge truck with dozens of mattresses. It was demanding work, and I was ready for a compliment when Frank came by to check on me,

"You totally fucked up the packing and now *you* have to fix it! I don't care how long it takes."

I stood there dumbfounded. Mr. Siegel walked out the door and one of the guys overhearing the exchange explained what was wrong. I loaded the truck exactly according to the manifest, but in the wrong order. I had packed the first stop on the truck first. It was behind thirty other orders, when it should have been in front. Dumb shit Herbie had loaded the truck backwards!

The news of my plight quickly made its way around the plant. Some of my co-workers laughed, but a it wasn't long before a couple of the biggest men I have ever seen walked over to my side. We unloaded the entire truck onto the shipping room floor and then restocked it in the correct order. I thanked them but they just grunted and walked away. I always wondered why they helped me. I guess even ex-cons can take pity on a young kid who made a mistake.

I stayed away from WVUD so I wouldn't have to tell my WBAT story over and over and suffer the shame of now being a mattress maven. Billy called when he heard I was back in town and invited me to lunch. Intuitively he understood my state of mind, so he suggested a Chinese restaurant off campus.

After his 10 a.m. class, Billy picked me up at my parent's house. Once at the restaurant it wasn't long before we were laughing and goofing around. He told me about things going on at the station, all good, and explained how thrilled he was to be finally graduating. He asked me if I would be coming back to school but quickly discerned my answer and jumped to another subject,

"Hey Herbie, I have an inside tip for you."

"What's that?"

"You've heard of WGAR in Cleveland, right?"

"Sure, they have that crazy morning guy, Uncle Don Remus, right?

"It's Imus, not Remus, and there's no Uncle. Anyway, I heard their FM station is going to flip to a rock format and they're looking for jocks. They started hiring a few weeks ago so it may be too late, but you should send in a tape and see if you can get a job there."

Billy mentioned a guy named LeBlanc was the program director and he gave me his full name and mailing address on a slip of paper. I scrunched the note into my pocket and asked,

"So, they are going to call it WGAR-FM?"

"Well, Sarah called the FCC, inspired newshound lady that one, and she found out that they applied for the call letters WNCR-FM."

"What? National Cash Register owns them?"

"Well, I didn't think of that, but no, they are owned by Nationwide Insurance Company, a huge enterprise out of Columbus. I assume the call letters stand for Nationwide Communications Radio."

We finished eating and back in the car switched on WVUD. What we were about to hear would be utterly shocking.

One of Dayton's commercial radio stations was an affiliate of the Mutual Broadcasting System radio network, and they had given us permission to broadcast Mutual news feeds on WVUD. The network programming came into our station over a specialized broadcast audio line which we leased from the local telephone company, which back then was known as TELCO in the radio biz. We broadcast the five-minute Mutual newscast at the beginning of every hour to practice "back-timing" into the network feed and to keep our university audience informed about happenings in the world.

On this day, May 4, 1970, we heard the Mutual news logo. Billy checked the clock in his car and said,

"Why are they running a newscast now? It's not the top of the hour?"

Billy turned up the radio. The Mutual newscaster proceeded to tell us that four Kent State students were shot and killed on their campus by members of the Ohio National Guard. The troops had been called to the school by Governor Rhodes, a huge supporter of President Nixon, who felt the demonstrations needed to be stopped.

This was a time in our country when many campuses had been protesting the Vietnam war and several of those demonstrations had turned violent. It was recently learned that the United States Army had gone into Cambodia to fight the Vietnam war, a clear violation of international law. The newscaster explained how students at Kent State University had burned down the Reserve Officers Training Corps building yesterday, and that protest concluded with those tragic deaths today. I couldn't hold back my question,

"Why? What for?"

Billy answered in anger,

"They were killed for protesting the goddamn war! We have to react to this. We must do something! Let's get to the radio station."

Billy parked his car and the two of us rushed into the WVUD studios. We didn't know exactly what, but knew we had to put something relevant and special on the air. We commandeered the air studio and worked together, intermixing our thoughts, songs of protest, phone comments from our audience and the dynamic reporting of the Mutual newscaster. The feedback from our college radio audience was heartfelt and gratifying.

You'll recall that in the summer of 1969, Neil Young had joined CS&N to form Crosby, Stills, Nash and Young. Immediately after the Kent State killings, Neil took his guitar into the woods and wrote a song titled *Ohio*. The band recorded it on May 21, 1970 and released a 45 RPM single the following week. The song's chorus repeats the lyrics, "*Four dead in Ohio.*" The semester was almost over when the *Ohio* 45 arrived at WVUD, and we played it every ninety minutes in honor of the lost souls. Those killings touched everyone our age because we realized the dead could have been us or people we knew and loved. It was a sobering time for us kids in America.

I was no longer a university student or a member of the WVUD staff, but it didn't matter at all in that moment. Billy and I were broadcasting timely, relevant content to our listeners in a show of solidarity with the Kent State students. The fools in DC and the Ohio governor's office didn't understand they had just united a force to be reckoned with, in time.

13. Taking the Next Step

A growing trend in the radio business around that time saw successful, non-broadcasting companies getting into radio and TV as great investments and places to park their profits. At the dawn of broadcasting, radio owners were electric companies and department stores, like Westinghouse, Sears, Roebuck and Company and General Electric, having a principal intent of selling radio receivers. In fact, Chicago's famous WLS call letters stood for "World's Largest Store." Things changed in the 1970s when insurance companies, labor unions and billionaire playboys began buying out small radio owners. Newspapers selling off some of their biggest AM and FM combos was also altering the face of radio. The good news was these radio newbies were hiring some of the best managers to run their million-dollar properties.

At dinner that night, I told mom and dad I would be sending my letter, resume and tape to a new station in Cleveland hiring radio announcers — using that somewhat outdated term in deference to my parents to make them think it was not just DJing and playing records, which is precisely what it was. My father showed some curiosity,

"Which station is that?"

I paused, took a sip of milk, then said confidently,

"WNCR-FM."

"Wait, my company owns a radio station?"

"No, dad, Nationwide Insurance."

"Well, that's our insurance company. Good move, Herbie!"

Later that night, as I put my head on the pillow and pulled the covers up to my neck, my thoughts drifted to Van Morrison and that second line of my new favorite song, *"I can hear the merry gypsies play…"*

Then I mentally felt those damn cats clawing and biting my toes. The idea of radio people being gypsies and continuously moving from place to place raised a question. Would I soon be moving again?

I have often wondered why some people referred to Cleveland, Ohio with such disdain. Perhaps the mocking could be attributed to the decay of the steel and shipping industries in the city. Later in its history the Cuyahoga River became so polluted it would sometimes catch on fire, but even with the city's 1970's declining population it continued holding onto a rich past.

Before the year 1900, the city's Euclid Avenue was known as Millionaires' Row. More than two hundred and fifty mansions were packed into a four-mile stretch with owners such as Standard Oil's John D. Rockefeller. In the late 1800s, Cleveland had at least twelve steel mills, giving Pittsburgh a run for its money. The city was also home to many foundries, which produced machine parts, then later, cars. Curiously, Cleveland also produced tons of clothing for America.

Cincinnati and Cleveland were polar opposites, not only geographically but also with respect to people and styles. Cincy was a clean, German-influenced city, whereas Cleveland was a mix of cultures from all over the world. Here in the 1970s, litter and dirt would often blow through the city streets. Cleveland radio, however, produced some of the industries' most colorful personalities and trendy formats.

About a week ago I had packaged my cover letter, resume and rock aircheck and sent it off to the name and address Billy had given me. Today my Beetle was in the shop to fix that overheating problem, and while waiting at home for the car to be ready the phone rang. The program director of WNCR-FM, a guy named Alan, was on the line and I was totally ecstatic hearing him ask if I could visit him tomorrow. That, coupled with my fixed-up car, gave me hope that positive energy could be swinging back in my direction. Before leaving for Cleveland the next morning, I reached out for some good luck by touching the mannequin hand Marilyn had given me.

The drive was only three hours, but I left early to make sure I would be on time for my 11:30 a.m. appointment should I hit traffic along the way. Travel went smoothly and I got to Cleveland early. I stopped at a Frisch's in the Parma Heights suburb because I didn't know if the meeting with Alan would include lunch. I bought a Big Boy for forty-five cents, but only ate half of it because my excitement was peaking. By the way, there was ongoing derision between teenagers from Parma and those from Cleveland proper, with the latter claiming that all the kids in Parma wore white socks. Somehow that was meant to be a derogatory taunt, but why that would be was a complete mystery to me.

I quickly spotted a parking space in the eleven-hundred block of Euclid Avenue near the station but discovered there was a two-hour limit. A little farther down the street I found a parking lot that charged two-fifty a day and I felt much better about that situation.

There was quite a hullabaloo when I walked through the front door of the station and entered the lobby. Holding court was a long-haired guy dressed like a cowboy. I recognized his voice as the morning man on WGAR, the AM station, and he was obviously huddled with members of his team. My first thought was how unprofessional this was. A radio station lobby is not an acceptable location for a meeting. Don Imus was sitting on a white leather couch with an open bottle of red wine between his legs while loudly reading letters from his fans. After finishing one letter, he raised the bottle to his mouth and took a substantial swig. His cowboy boot-clad feet were parked on a small coffee table across from the sofa. I later learned that his bad-boy attitude and presentation earned him a fifty-thousand-dollar annual salary.

The receptionist was aware I had just walked into chaos and waved me over,

"Hi, may I help you?"

"Yes, hello, I'm Herbie Klotenfelder. I have an appointment to see Mr. LeBlanc about an opening on your FM station."

I didn't think I was talking loudly, but Imus obviously heard me,

"Oh look, it's another calf headed to the slaughterhouse."

I turned and looked directly at him, sure that my face was turning crimson, but I had to retort,

"Where exactly is the ranch, Buffalo Bob?"

Those in the group sitting around him laughed, and Imus was pissed,

"Shut up, Clarabell!"

I was saved by the receptionist,

"You can go back now."

She pointed to a door next to a large window looking into the AM air studio, and once beyond it I felt safe from the crazy morning guy. The walls of the long hallway were covered with sound proofing material, but instead of being the typical gray or brown it was white. Large photos of WGAR's personalities and newscasters, all of them men, covered the area. The hallway ended in an open office area where a few women were sitting behind brand-new red and blue IBM Selectric typewriters. I stole a glimpse and watched one of the ladies typing an artist name on a five-by-seven index card, *The Beatles*, and then tabbing to the right to type, *Hey Jude*. I was thinking the card must be for a music library system. One of the women looked up,

"May I help you?"

"Yeah, I have an appointment with Mr. LeBlanc."

She pointed to an open doorway across the room on my left,

"That's his office over there."

I walked over and gently tapped on the doorjamb. The program director, about twenty-five years old, was completely decked out in denim including shirt, jeans and one of those Carnaby style hats. He had a full beard and a set of beads hung around his neck. He certainly looked the part of a rock radio guy. He was holding a phone to his ear and waved his other hand to a chair in front of his desk indicating I should sit down. He was finishing up a phone call,

"Look man, I don't have time for this shit. If you want to come onboard you will work six days a week, and that means a Saturday shift." There was a slight pause and then he continued.

"Well, Mitch, if you can't work weekends then this gig isn't for you. Yes, okay, go ahead and think about it but I need to know today. I have a lot of people in the lobby waiting to be interviewed."

He listened for a bit longer, said a goodbye and then hung up. Now, unless he was going to be hiring those Don Imus sidekicks, there were no applicants in the lobby. I took that to mean Alan will lie when backed into a corner and filed that away for future reference. He turned to me,

"Far-out man, thanks for coming all the way from, where is it again?"

"I live in Dayton but used to work at WBAT-FM in Ashtabula."

"Okay, listen, I liked your tape but I'm not looking for bits or routines. I just want you to play the songs, do the back sells, do the front sells and occasionally drop one of those many musical facts you have."

Picking up on the phone conflict, I offered,

"I don't mind working weekends."

"Well, that's good, because I want you to work weekend shifts."

"Okay, what are they?"

"There are three, 10 p.m. to 6 a.m. on Friday night, then 6 p.m. to 12 midnight on Saturday, then overnight Sunday starting at midnight and going until 6 Monday morning, but there's a lot of taped syndicated programming during that shift."

"Sure, I'm in. When do I start?"

He picked up the phone and quickly punched three buttons,

"Shirley, can I send a new hire down your way to get his paperwork settled?" He paused, then looked over at me and smiled, "Okay, ten minutes, got it."

He picked up a legal pad from his desk with a written list of maybe fifty things. He reached for a pen and drew a line through one of them, then turned to me,

"Okay, I don't want you to get bummed out, but I totally hate the name Gemini!"

"Me too! I hated it from the beginning! It was because my PD had a gimmick in mind... "

"We need to get you a new name. You've seen the movie *Five Easy Pieces*, right?"

"Yeah, sure, Jack Nicholson."

"How about calling yourself Bobby Dupea, or maybe Sonny something, like a street tough guy?"

"I prefer Sonny, but what about no last name? My real one would never work."

"Okay, I'm there, Sonny Bob?"

"How about Sonny Joe?"

"That's great! Perfect, just like that old Rocky Fellers song named *Killer Joe.*"

I didn't see any connection, but at least I had some input regarding my new air name. I would be Sonny Joe on the radio. That rhymed and was certainly a huge step up from Herbie da K. I had to inwardly chuckle thinking how quick and easy it was to manufacture an identity. It was like being inducted into the witness protection program. I followed Alan's directions to the personnel office and filled out the paperwork. Wow, I was going to live and work in Cleveland!

My WNCR shifts would require being in the city only from Friday afternoon to Monday morning, but I wanted to be available for extra shifts or other station work that may come along. I picked up a copy of Anger City Press, the local hippy newspaper, and wondered what in the hell they were so angry about. Flipping through the rag, I found an ad for an apartment to share. I called the number and made a 4 p.m. appointment to meet with the guy.

The place was on Coventry Road located in what was once a primarily Jewish neighborhood, but in the 1960s became the epicenter of a growing counterculture movement in Cleveland. Now here's where my story takes an interesting twist, but some background will help.

A musician named Thomas Gregory Jackson was born in Dayton and later moved to Niles, Michigan. You probably know him by his stage name, which was also part of the name of his band, Tommy James and the Shondells. Their first hit record was *Hanky Panky* in 1966, and by 1970 they had several others including *I Think We're Alone Now* and *Mony Mony*. Their sound was very pop, not the type to get airplay on an FM rock station. You'll soon see how this plays into my story.

The apartment rental was the entire second floor of an older home, which was most likely a mansion in the 1930s. I was amazed at the size and layout of the place. There were three bedrooms, a large kitchen and a spacious living room, which appeared smaller than its actual size because it was cluttered with guitar cases and large amplifiers. My first thought was this place might be all about loud music which could conflict with my work schedule.

The guy introduced himself as Carey Coverdale and he claimed to be the lead guitar player for the Shondells. I wasn't sure I believed him, but then I spied a bunch of hefty road cases stashed in the dining room. Stenciled in bold, silver letters across each of them was "Tommy James and the Shondells." I was impressed, but I had to set Carey straight,

"Okay, I need to explain something here. I'm going to be working three all night shifts at the new FM rock station and I will be sleeping during the day and…"

He stopped me,

"Far-out man! A rock DJ living here with me? That's perfect! We are about to head out on a four-month tour of America and Canada, so I'll be gone, and you'll be cool. I just need someone I can trust to keep the pad safe."

I nodded yes, and then he pointed to a large tropical fish tank in the corner glowing with a soft backlight,

"And you'll have to feed my fish."

"No problem, man. When can I move in?"

"Right now. Give me a hundred bucks and I'll get the rest at Christmas. Here's the master key for the front and back doors, and here's your room key. Let me show you."

The room was about twelve-by-twelve feet with an eighteen-foot ceiling. The bathroom across the hall had a shower and a large mirror, which when opened revealed several deep storage shelves. Carey seemed like a nice guy, but I couldn't help wondering if he was a batshit crazy rock star.

On my drive back to Dayton that night all the confidence that had drained away was now back at full steam. I listened to WMMS and realized competing with them would be tough. Nationwide Insurance wasn't in the radio business to lose money, so I figured we'd get all the marketing support we needed, but that little dark spot in my brain was still there to nag me.

I pledged to myself I would stay positive and move forward. I was just turning off I-71 onto I-70 when it dawned on me, Alan never mentioned money and I, like the young foolish college dropout I was, never asked. Shit! Where was my head? As soon as I got home, I called Alan at the station. After a considerable time on hold listening to WGAR programming coming down the phone line, he picked up,

"LeBlanc, who needs me?"

"Ah, it's Herbie Klotenfelder."

"Who?"

"I mean Sonny Joe…"

"Who?"

"You just hired me today. That did happen, right?"

He laughed and then apologized saying how nuts everything was and of course he remembered. I got right to the business part,

"You never told me how much I would be paid."

"Oh, fuck, I'm sorry man. It's a hundred and fifty dollars a week. Is that cool?"

"Yeah, just needed to know."

"You'll have to punch a timecard. Someone will show you how to do that before your first shift. Welcome aboard Donny Joe."

"You mean Sonny Joe?"

"I know, man. That was an Imus dig, you dig?"

"Yeah, I dig."

"Oh, one more thing, Jack Daniel the boss man doesn't like one name jocks, so he wants you to use his grandmother's last name which is McPherson. That's cool, right?"

"Yeah, sure. The name Sonny Joe McPherson will sound great on the radio."

I was so glad the money was more than I made in Ashtabula, but I had to be careful. Carey the rock star was not upfront about what I will owe him at Christmas. Who knew where all this was headed? Nonetheless, I was energized and back in radio, even though it was a part-time job. Cleveland was the ninth largest city in America in the 1970s, so I would be working in a top ten market and making six hundred dollars a month before taxes.

I hoped this would not turn into a mistake for me. Among so many other things in my young career, I had learned that radio could be a terribly cruel and dysfunctional mistress.

14. Major Market, Finally

Being settled into my new apartment felt wonderful. Carey had finished packing up the Shondells' musical gear and was about to head out the door and meet with his bandmates to begin their tour. He asked me for another hundred bucks and repeated the line about getting the rest after Christmas when he gets back to Cleveland. I handed him the cash but didn't think to ask how much more money he would want upon his return.

All of us new WNCR-FM disc jockeys were called to a meeting with General Manager Jack Daniel. Of course, Alan LeBlanc was there, constantly pulling his long, greasy hair. Mr. Daniel explained we were going to "transition" the station into full rock programming. See, back then the radio business had a notion of programming commitments. A potential owner seeking a radio license from the FCC was required to list the public interest programming they would broadcast. This content, which excluded playing music, was known as public affairs programming, and was typically scheduled during overnight and weekend hours when there were fewer listeners.

When AM broadcasters were forced to create nonduplicated content on their FMs, many rearranged their public affairs programming obligation by moving some portions from their AM station over to their FM. For example, if a station promised ten weekly hours of public affairs programming when their AM station license was renewed, they might fulfill that obligation on their FM station, even though it had a separate license. It was a sort of "silent deal" with the FCC, a bit of a game in the radio business.

The next part of my story involves the word "daypart," another radio term unknown to most listeners. As its name implies, a daypart is a part of a day or days. For example, the common radio daypart known as "Morning Drive" is typically defined as 6 a.m. to 9 a.m. Monday through Friday. Similarly, "Afternoon Drive" occurs from 3 p.m. to 7 p.m. Monday through Friday. Incidentally, The Morning and Afternoon

Drive dayparts on most stations are the most listened to hours of a week. Some dayparts overlap. The 6 a.m. to 12 midnight Monday through Sunday daypart includes both the Morning and Afternoon Drive dayparts. The radio ratings companies calculate listening levels for every station in each daypart. It's a huge slice-and-dice arrangement, which gives advertisers and radio stations many lenses for viewing and analyzing listenership. I'll share more about ratings later.

The Nationwide lawyers were busy working their magic in Washington D.C. to reduce the public affairs commitment of WNCR-FM, but for the launch of its new format the station had to live up to its promise of airing fifteen hours of local talk programming every week in a prime daypart. The GM and PD had already decided when the new rock format launched, a talk show would be on the schedule from 6 a.m. to 9 a.m. Monday through Friday to account for the weekly fifteen-hour public affairs commitment. Alan said contemporary and youthful subjects would be the focus of the program and a few relevant rock songs would be sprinkled in along the way. It was hoped the lawyers would eventually be successful in lifting that heavy obligation of so much talk content, allowing the station to run with one hundred percent rock music throughout the week.

Jack and Alan hired a woman to host the new morning talk show. She was highly intelligent with three doctorate degrees and an amazingly powerful voice coming out of her slightly less than five-foot frame. Her name was Kathleen Benson-Smith, and as a woman using a hyphenated name, she was totally unusual in the male dominated radio realm back then. Benson-Smith had no radio experience and only a glimmer of knowledge about the workings of the business, but her audition tape was compelling and got her the job.

Kathy B, her nickname among the station staff, was recently featured in a Cleveland Press article. It told the story about how she worked herself into what was then the mancave of radio, especially that of a rock station. Newsweek saw the coverage and, as we all later learned, they wanted to run a story, maybe even a front-page-cover feature, on Ms. Benson-Smith. The management was so busy with the launch of the new station they ignored the P.R. Kathy was getting. She would eventually be phased out, so her newfound fame wasn't even on their radar.

Now here is where things get crazy. I am about to tell you a story that may cause you to shake your head in disbelief, but I promise it's all true. I was both an eyewitness and an "ear-witness." I was just wrapping up my Sunday overnight into Monday morning show during my first week at WNCR-FM when Alan called me on the hotline. He asked if I could come in tomorrow, Tuesday, to work a production shift.

In the radio business, "production" is not as glamorous as it sounds. Back in those days, a big part of the job was getting commercials ready for air. Some were recorded at the station, while others arrived on five-inch reels of tape or on specialized sixteen-inch phonograph discs known as ETs, "electrical transcriptions." Regardless of their origin, all commercials had to be recorded onto tape cartridges. It's tedious work, and precise timing is critical when transferring audio from an ET or tape to cart. One must first start the cart recorder then, just an instant later, start playback of the commercial. If the commercial starts too late, the cart will have a bit of silence at the beginning of playback. Such a poorly recorded cart was said to be "loose." If the commercial starts too early, it's initial audio will be cut off and such a cart was said to be "upcut." After recording a cart, a conscientious producer will play it back, paying particular attention to how the audio "hits" when the start button is pushed. It should be nearly instantaneous.

As Alan had previously told all of us, executives from Nationwide, the station's owner, would be visiting on Tuesday. The company's President, Vice President and National Director of Programming would be touring their newly launched rock station and meeting with the full-time air staff. I guess I had impressed my new boss because he assigned me all the production orders for the day since the full timers would be in meetings. Alan offered some guidance during the hotline call,

"You should wear some decent rags tomorrow. I mean, not Sunday goin' to church clothes, but something cool. We want to give our owners a good impression. You'll be on the clock, and you should see Louise first thing to get the production assignments."

We said our goodbyes and ended the call.

I didn't think much about what would happen as I drove to work the next day. I just had to hold down the fort while the weekday on-air staff attended their meetings. I was in for a shock when I arrived and almost couldn't believe my eyes. The breakroom had been completely deep cleaned all the way down to a freshly mopped linoleum floor, which I had no idea was green!

I headed to Louise Sommers' office. She was WNCR's traffic director, and just about every radio station on the planet has one of those. In broadcasting, the word "traffic" applies to the process of gathering and readying commercials for broadcast and then scheduling them according to specifics in the sales agreement between the station and advertiser. It's a highly responsible position because it directly affects advertising, a radio station's revenue stream.

The sales department often provides "copy," lingo for a commercial script, which is read live on the air or recorded by one of the DJs. Many commercials, especially national spots, required a "tag" to be voiced at the end of the spot, telling listeners the local outlet that sold the product. Sometimes these were recorded, but many times disc jockeys read them from the "copy book," which contained all the commercial scripts scheduled to be read live that day. Preparing the daily copy book was one of many tasks Louise oversaw.

My first stop was Louise's office, where I picked up a container of tapes, a few ETs and the production orders she had prepared for my workday. In a small storage area next to the production studio, I rifled through a collection of previously used carts to find ones of the proper length for each commercial. I had to break into a box of brand-new Fidelipac seventy-second carts to complete my collection. Sometimes a sponsor provided multiple spots, and these would be recorded onto a "multi-punch" cart, meaning a different commercial would be heard each time the cart was played. One of my production orders for the day required recording five sixty-second Pepsi Cola spots onto one tape cartridge, so I grabbed a five-and-a-half-minute cart for that one. I could see it would be a busy day for me. I had more than forty spots to dub to carts.

"Dub" is interesting radio jargon in that the word can be used as both a verb and a noun. As a verb, dub is the process of making a copy of audio. "Please dub these Kraft Mac and Cheese commercials to a cart." As a noun, dub is a physical copy of audio. "Here's a dub of the Jenkins Jewelry spot."

On my way into the production studio, I saw a black stretch limousine pull up in front of the station. Jack Daniel quickly walked out the front door to greet the dignitaries. His body language screamed he was large, in charge, and ready to kiss the ass of each visitor. The entourage entered the station and Jack led the way to his office.

In keeping with the goal of youth-oriented topics, Kathy B. had invited one of the recently hired radical professors at Case Western Reserve University to appear on her show this day. He was an expert in language and linguistics and had published more than a dozen books on the subject. I could hear Kathy B's show over the house air monitors, which are loudspeakers spread throughout the station playing what was going out over the air, but I wasn't paying much attention. I stopped in the Master Control Room, which was a centralized control booth for both WGAR-AM and WNCR-FM, with a window looking into each station's air studio. I walked up to the engineer on duty,

"Hey man, I'm Sonny, and Alan asked me to do some production work today. Could I borrow a razor blade?"

My question was first answered with a chuckle,

"You want to kill yourself already? I've been here for twenty years, and still haven't gotten up the nerve."

I laughed and asked his name. He introduced himself as Domenic Conti, saying I should call him Dom. He carefully handed me a single-edge razor blade I would use to peel off the scotch tape covering the previous labels on the carts I would reuse today. The tape kept the labels from falling off the carts, but it created a sticky, hard-to-remove mess. I also grabbed some isopropyl alcohol, a small dab of which would help dilute and remove the gummy residue left behind once the labels were removed. WNCR-FM's audio was quietly playing in the background,

"So, Professor Dykeman, why are certain words considered verboten or even obscene?"

My attention snapped and I peered into the FM air studio window. I wondered where Kathy B. was going with this. I turned to Dom,

"What do you suppose this is about?"

"Hey man, same shit, different day."

We were both stunned when we heard what Kathy B. said next,

"So, when people use the word "fuck," what are they trying to communicate?"

The professor, looked over the top of his glasses and leaned into the microphone,

"That happens to be one of the most versatile words in our language — it's a verb, a noun, an adverb and adjective having both positive and negative connotations."

Kathy then asked the professor,

"Is the word derived from the German verb *ficken*, meaning to hit or strike?" The prof was quick to correct her,

"Well, that's a distortion, but clearly the word "fuck" can have a negative connotation, such as being 'fucked by someone' in a business deal."

I looked at Dom and quietly asked,

"Is this on the air?"

Conti walked over to the audio console in front of the WNCR air studio window and flipped a switch from the studio feed to the on-air audio and back again. Both sources were the same, although the broadcast audio lagged behind because of a seven second delay device. Should any speech need to be censored, the DJ had seven seconds to hit a "dump button," which stopped the offensive audio from being broadcast. In this case, however, the announcer was overseeing the cursing and not doing any dumping!

I dashed off to find Alan and saw him walking down the hall toward his office. Much to my surprise he was wearing a light brown tie over a dark-brown shirt. I thought to myself, "Oh my God, they made him wear a fucking tie." He was arriving late on this special day, and I couldn't help but imagine that tie as a noose. He opened his office door and turned on the lights,

"Hey Sonny Joe. How's the production going?"

"Alan, turn on the air monitor! Now! You've got to hear this."

He walked over to the house monitor control panel on his office wall, switched it from WGAR to WNCR and raised the audio level. The speaker in the ceiling came to life,

"…but "cuntalinguist," well, that is more slang than anything else, Kathleen, it's not a meaningful term. On the other hand, cunnilingus…"

The blood drained from Alan's face, and he began frantically tugging at his hair as his breathing became labored and panicked,

"Why is she doing this to me?"

Back in Master Control, Conti was racking up a large reel-to-reel tape to capture all the forbidden words being broadcast. He said,

"Man, we're gonna lose our fucking FCC licenses!"

The engineering union shop steward, ironically a guy named Nixon, rushed into the room rifling through the union contract trying to locate the language about who was responsible for what went out over the air,

"It says here that the station's ownership and management have the sole responsibility for broadcast content and an IBEW member cannot be terminated for any audio that goes out over the air."

There it was, in black and white. It was not an engineer's place to disrupt the broadcast, and that reel of tape was capturing it all. Kathy B. was now graphically discussing the association between bodily functions and obscenities. Sweet Jesus!

Meanwhile, Louise was back in the traffic office working on the next day's commercial log when the background of the air monitor quietly playing in her office suddenly became foreground. Her eyes widened as she heard what was being broadcast. She scribbled a terse note, got up, switched her air monitor from WNCR to WGAR and tore off down the hallway, quickly finding herself behind General Manager Jack Daniel leading a station tour for the visiting Nationwide execs. She briskly walked ahead of them and stopped at every air monitor panel she encountered, flipping the switch to WGAR if it wasn't already selected. If the panel was located in an office, she sternly instructed the workers,

"DO NOT switch this back to the FM station!"

Everyone at both stations knew you never fucked with Louise.

After making sure every air monitor on the floor was playing the AM station, Louise made her way to the conference room. Jack and the bigwigs were just settling in to enjoy breakfast goodies spread across the large, oak table. Louise walked right up to Daniel and handed him her note. Jack carefully unfolded the small piece of paper and saw the bright red letters,

THEY ARE SAYING FUCK ON YOUR STATION!!!

Daniel quickly excused himself from the meeting and ran over to Alan's office,

"LeBlanc, what the hell is going on?

Alan briefly explained the premise of Kathy B's show and Jack had only one blunt question,

Why haven't you stopped her?"

Jack marched into the air studio. A commercial was playing, and he pointed directly at the professor,

"You! Out!"

He turned to Kathleen and said,

"You're off the air until further notice."

Jack stormed out of the studio and grabbed me, fisting up my shirt, my one good shirt,

"Sonny Bob, get in there and play some music."

Feeling no need to correct him about my name, I didn't hesitate to "get in there." First things first, I grabbed the Van Morrison *Moondance* album. I was at least going to play songs I liked. The next shift would begin in thirty minutes, so it was going to be a short show for me. Alan popped into the studio and told me to host the three-hour morning show for the next five weekdays. I later learned that Ms. Benson-Smith was suspended for one week, with pay.

I felt sorry for Kathy B. She had ascended to an on-air radio position without the knowledge that would have come from working her way up the ladder and learning all aspects of the business. I liked her immensely and knew she believed her show that day was simply a highbrow discussion of language when she was actually putting the broadcasting licenses of her employer in serious jeopardy. I couldn't help remembering the goofy way Brewster Billy would sometimes answer his phone,

"Hello, you're on the air so whatever you do, don't say fuck. Oh shit, I just said fuck. Motherfucker I just said shit!"

That was funny because it had been drilled into us radio kids that saying dirty words on the radio was something one must never do. More on this later. For now, I had a morning show to host.

Unknown to me, the station's sales department threw a favor to Belkin Productions, the concert promoter in town, and arranged an hour-long interview with Three Dog Night. It was the final day of Kathy B's suspension and I learned of the band's scheduled arrival only minutes before they showed up. This was going to be my very first broadcast interview, with a famous rock group no less, and I was half energized, and half panicked. One is the loneliest number, and I was the "one" in the hot seat.

Alan led the group into the studio, but there was no Night, no Dog and two guys instead of Three. The band had sent their manager and lighting guy. Some artists and bands hate radio interviews, and this was clearly one of them. On the air I asked a few questions and the two of them did their best to give answers, but they were uninformed, lame and boring. I played more than a fair share of music to get my interviewees, the audience, but mostly me through that excruciating hour. Near the end of our time together, one of the two dogs opened a big plastic bag of white powder and poured a generous amount on the table between us. I was quick,

"Wait! You can't do that here. These guys will have you arrested."

Like children caught with their hands in the cookie jar, they pushed the bulk of it back into the bag, then the manager licked up the dust from the tabletop. Class act! I couldn't wait for this day to end.

We later learned that Jack Daniel wore a straight face to get through the rest of the day plus an evening dinner with the Nationwide muckety-mucks. They left Cleveland and went back to Columbus without an inkling about what all of us were now calling "The Fuck Show."

Jack Daniel anguished for several days, until hitting a mental wall with the realization he had to reveal the regretful event to his bosses. His greatest fear was a listener sending a complaint letter to the FCC, so he faced one super-big mega-conundrum. Jack confronted every engineer in the building and demanded they hand over any tape of The Fuck Show they might have recorded. He received several, but who knows? One or more might still be out there. Man, I'd just love to sit and listen!

The final motivation pushing Jack to come clean with the brass was a call from the Newsweek reporter who was authoring the story about Kathleen. She had told the reporter her side of The Fuck Show story, and now that reporter had Jack Daniel on the phone asking questions about censorship and which words cannot be spoken over the airwaves. Daniel did his best to brush away the questions, but he knew the fuck was out of the bag and word would sooner or later reach his superior, the President of the Nationwide Broadcasting Company. So, on the same morning the Three Dog Jerks were about to snort cocaine in our FM air studio, Daniel called his boss and told him about The Fuck Show, but probably not using that name.

After a long discussion with the attorneys, Nationwide told Jack that Alan LeBlanc would have to be fired or, as we used to say in the radio biz, "go bye-bye in the car-car." Kathleen Benson-Smith could return to the air, provided she sign a waiver detailing what she must NEVER EVER say on the radio. Daniel was told to hire a new program director as soon as possible. Jack, knowing how much Imus hated the "FM hippies," instructed Don not to make any on-air mention about what happened on WNCR-FM unless he wanted to lose that brand new car WGAR had leased for him.

Jack Daniel and I crossed paths in the hall Friday, and he asked me into his office. I was somewhat nervous wondering if he was going to blame me for what happened, but quickly decided that was crazy. He asked me to sit and then took his place behind an impressive maple desk. This would be the first of many times I would observe a strange habit of this man. He took a small length of Scotch tape from the dispenser on his desk and connected the two ends, making a sticky-side-out loop. He then stuck the loop between the thumb and index finger of his right hand and continuously opened and closed those fingers, disconnecting and then reconnecting the tape and his thumb. I was reminded of Captain Queeg and his ball bearings from *The Caine Mutiny*. Jack peered at me and asked,

"If you were the program director, and heard someone saying "fuck" over the air, what would you have done?"

"I would have walked over to the equipment rack, switched the station to the automation system and fired her."

The GM liked my answer and asked if I wanted to become the station's program director, I was honest,

"I'm not ready, Mr. Daniel, but I have a buddy who just graduated from the University of Dayton. He would be a great PD for you."

Taking a pen in hand while somehow still working the loop of tape, he paused and said,

"Tell me more."

"His name is Billy Kalpolski, but everyone calls him Brewster Billy."

15. Why Do We Sin?

Just like radio waves blasting through the ether, things move rapidly in the broadcasting business. One of the ways radio people kept informed about what was happening in those days was reading Billboard magazine, particularly a column titled "Vox Jox" written by a guy named Claude Hall.

Not only did the column disclose things like the latest new formats, changes in on-air personalities and job openings, it also revealed radio's behind-the-scenes intrigue and rumors. Claude had an amazing array of trusted industry insiders who were the source of his almost always factual material. Billboard was such a powerful music and radio publication that should you get a mention there you would cut out the article and mail it to your parents.

It was great seeing Brewster Billy's name in the latest edition of Billboard, and I became much more confident after he became the new program director of WNCR. Things moved quickly for me. I was given better weekend shifts and Billy moved me up to full-time status by appointing me to the production director position. I was able to take occasional Tuesdays off, but "working" was never a problem for me. This wasn't a job; it was an engaging and enjoyable hobby.

After the Nationwide lawyers got approval from the FCC to reduce WNCR's public affairs commitment Kathy B. took on a teaching position at McGill University in Montreal, Billy's first focus of his new job became hiring a new morning show. He had received an aircheck from an on-air team out of Des Moines, Iowa who went by the name W3 and Suzy. The duo was W.W. Walker and Suzy Cream Cheese, a Frank Zappa reference. Jack Daniel listened to their tape and was not overly impressed, but Billy was selling hard and convinced Jack the station should fly in the two so he could meet them face to face and maybe have them do an on-air audition. Jack agreed and the team winged their way to Cleveland.

At that time, the Cleveland Swingos Hotel was an infamous hostel on Euclid Avenue. All the touring rock bands called Swingos home when they played Cleveland. The name originated with the Greek family that once owned the place, but it also had a connection to the word "swinging," as in swinging from a chandelier or swinging with another couple. Its reputation for debauchery and parties motivated tourists to stand in front of the hotel's Keg & Quarter sign to snap a photo or two. The hotel was made famous back in the day by the King of Rock 'n Roll, Elvis Presley, when he booked four floors of the hotel and made it his Midwest headquarters. So, to impress W3 and Suzy, Billy put them up at Swingos. At the time they were a couple, so the station had to pay for only one room.

Now William the Wonderful, as some people called him because of his amazingly magnificent voice, had a strong weakness for alcohol. One of W3's lines was, "Hey, it's 10 a.m. somewhere!" On the ride from the airport to the hotel, W3 asked the cabby to stop at a rundown liquor store he spied outside the cab window in what he didn't know was the wrong side of town. Once inside, the clerk joked that W3 was smart to buy his own bottle because Swingos would charge him an arm and a leg. I hear you asking how the clerk knew where William was staying. Well, let's just say W3 was a typical DJ who never knew when to stop bragging or when to shut up. He also carried what was known as a "gangster roll," paying for the bottle of Smirnoff by peeling bills off his large wad of money. That move was carefully observed by two particular customers in the store.

Suzy and W3 checked into the hotel. William hit the ice machine, got back to the room and poured himself more than two fingers of vodka before starting to unpack. Suzy was looking at the room service menu when they heard a knock at the door. She looked up,

"Wow that was fast! I haven't even ordered."

Now I don't want to say Midwesterners are slow and naïve, but these two certainly grew up in a less crime ridden environment. W3 walked to the door,

"Yes, who is it?"

From the other side of the solid wood door came,

"Room Service."

Without looking through the peephole or even thinking, W3 opened the door and was confronted by two burly men wielding guns. One wore a bandana type mask and the other a black opera mask. A seasoned disc jockey like W3 has a fast response time and a quick wit,

"You have the wrong room."

The visitors pushed their way in and waved their guns to motion W3 and Suzy back. One of the guys turned on the TV and then demanded,

"Give me all your money."

Only then did it dawn on both Suzy and William this was real, and they should comply. W3 gave his clump of cash to one of the intruders while Suzy handed the other guy her handbag. He dumped the contents out on the bed, which included a baggie of pot and a checkbook. The robber stuffed everything into his jacket and then ordered,

"Get down on the floor, motherfuckers, faces down!"

Both did as they were told, then out of nowhere, two long pieces of rope appeared. While one man aimed his gun at their heads, the other guy hog tied both Suzy and William so tightly that some of the buttons on Suzy's close-fitting blouse popped right off. One of the muggers turned up the volume of the TV full blast, and William later said he believed the last thing he and Suzy would ever hear was drama from the latest episode of *The Guiding Light*.

The hearts of the two calves on the floor were pounding so hard their bodies were rocking back and forth. They were having difficulty breathing when suddenly the door slammed, the robbers were gone and both of them were still alive. That was the good news. The bad news came when, after much detangling, W3 and Suzy headed straight to the airport and jumped on the next flight back to Des Moines. Suddenly, the WNCR search for a morning show was back on.

There is a common situation that sooner or later affects most disc jockeys and it's all about the radio "groupie." The dictionary defines the word as a person, typically a young woman, who follows a celebrity in the hope of meeting and getting to know them. In the case of rock stars staying at Swingos, there was an understanding that when a groupie arrived, sexual favors followed.

I was green and never thought being a DJ brought that kind of celebrity status, but like any red-blooded male I loved attention. So, one night after searching for something to say, I came out of a Who track with this banal patter,

"Boy, I don't know why, but that song really made me hungry. I'd love to have a steaming bowl of spaghetti right now. I would suck up those noodles and lick up that sauce for days. Speaking of hot, here's Grace Slick and the Jefferson Airplane with *We Can Be Together* on NCR!"

The song was five minutes and forty-eight seconds long, so I decided to take some calls on the listener line. The very first started with,

"Hi there, Sonny Joe. You know, I made some truly tantalizing spaghetti, and my sauce is really exceptional."

Now there comes a moment when the best thing to do is politely end a conversation. That didn't happen. Two opposite entities, on each of my shoulders, the angel and the devil, began to argue. Her voice was so deep and sexy that the devil won the disagreement,

"Well, I'm a little busy right now, but that does sound good."

"What time do you get off? I mean, when would you like to get off?"

I took her meaning and fell into the trap,

"I'm working until ten."

"Why don't you come over after? You'll probably be starved by then."

I hesitated, then asked for her phone number. She complied and I called her when my shift ended. I was falling headfirst into a basic sin of the American DJ. You see, many radio personalities have been tempted into situations with young girls, you know, girls under the age of consent. Just recently I learned the term "jailbait," and I knew about a few DJs who got prison time.

My lady phone caller, who will remain nameless, lived only a few blocks from my apartment. I knocked on her door at about 10:30 p.m. and was relieved after seeing her face through the window in the door. She appeared to be in her mid-twenties and her eyes were the most fantastic shade of green I had ever seen. Her complexion was light brown, a Southern Italy look, and she had jet-black hair down to her shoulders.

She opened the door, and I took in a surprising spectacle. She was wearing multi-colored tights and a robe-type top tied around her large girth. I wondered if she was pregnant. She invited me into her first-floor apartment which was in one of the old homes gentrified by its owner for renters. We walked down a dark hallway and into a small kitchen. She broke the silence,

"My, you are a young one, dear. I don't have any pasta, but I'll throw on a porkchop for you."

"Yeah, sure, that's fine. So, do you live here alone?"

"I got divorced about a year ago and I have a baby. I just got her down for the night."

She bent over to get the porkchop and I could see her large derriere, which just about completely blocked out the light from the fridge. She plopped the meat into a black cast iron pan. Shortly it was sizzling.

I asked about her story, and she explained that she had moved to Cleveland after falling in love with a famous disc jockey I won't name. He got this lady pregnant, and when he found out she was with child he dumped her for a younger woman. I'm not saying the porkchop lady was a groupie, but having invited a DJ to her house she certainly was acting like one. The smell of the cooking chop had filled the room and I became a bit nauseous.

After I finished munching my meager meal, she turned on the radio and invited me into her bedroom to see pictures of her posing with famous musicians. So, I'm an idiot; I followed her. Ironically, the radio was playing a song by Sugarloaf, *"Green eyed lady passion's lady, Dressed in love, she lives for life to be, Green eyed lady feels like I never see, Setting suns and lonely lovers free"*

As she led me down the hall to the bedroom, I saw her untying the loose top from her enormous waist. After entering the room, she turned around, threw the top on the floor and there she was, full-frontal and showing off the large girls on top. She grabbed me and started kissing me while undoing my belt.

I wasn't at all aroused. I didn't find her attractive, and I just felt uncomfortable. I took off my shirt while she reached into my "tidy-whities" attempting to get my turntable arm ready to play. She pulled me down onto to the bed, took off her tights and jumped on top of me. I could feel not only the air going out of my chest, but whatever little blood was there leaving my manly part. Then, just as she was asking me to enter, with what I had no idea, her baby started to cry, and I mean bawl. She rolled off me, and I exhaled my *mea culpa*,

"Hey, I can't do this tonight. Maybe another time."

She laughed,

"Sure, it's no big deal! It happens to the best. I gotta feed the little one. Next time I'll cook spaghetti, promise."

I got dressed, kissed her goodbye and got the hell out of there. What an awkward, colossal mistake.

One aspect of WNCR's programming had been bothering me tremendously — the station's musical direction. Most of the jocks were heavily playing songs by early Genesis, Gentle Giant and King Crimson, leaning the station in a "trippy" direction. I favored a more accessible and commercial sound, and I felt a bit out of place. Our competitor, WMMS, brought in some DJs with serious album chops and moved the station onto a pure rock and roll path. They focused on David Bowie, Mott the Hoople, Lou Reed and other more approachable bands. I could almost see the writing on the wall.

The friendship Billy and I had developed was tight and we each knew anything said in confidence would never go beyond the two of us. He shared a troubling concern about the radio station, telling me that Nationwide was having serious doubts about their format choice because they had underestimated the strong foothold WMMS had with rock listeners. He revealed something else was brewing but made me promise to take it to my grave. Well, Billy and I are still alive, and our friendship remains, so I asked him to review what I am about to share with you and cancel that old promise. He did so, with an explanation,

"Well, it's not nearly as heavy now as it was back in those troubled days so go ahead and tell the story. After all, you're sharing true confessions."

The brass in Nationwide's broadcast division were extremely close with Ohio Governor James Rhodes, a conservative Republican. You might remember it was Rhodes who called up the National Guard to go to Kent State University where they shot and killed four students during a Vietnam anti-war protest. WNCR-FM was one of the more radical stations in the Nationwide chain, and our content didn't sit well with Rhodes who asked Nationwide to monitor and control our programming. The counterculture, as it was then known, had been annoying and angering national political figures. Vice President Spiro Agnew said on television that being anti-war was un-American and those radio stations taking the side of the protesters would have their licenses reviewed and perhaps revoked by the FCC. This was before Agnew was forced to resign and the Watergate scandal changed everything.

In fact, I was part of the problem. Remember when I played the Jefferson Airplane's *We Can Be Together* a few days ago? Well, it was the full length, uncensored version with the lyrics, *"We are forces of chaos and anarchy. Everything they say we are, we are. And we are very proud of ourselves — Up against the wall, Up against the wall, motherfucker!"*

All my sins were coming back to haunt me, to terrorize me and to screw with my career. I didn't put any thought into playing that song and that oversight would soon cause a seismic shift in my radio life.

Nationwide circulated a list to all its rock PDs containing songs they were not allowed to air. The one that really infuriated Billy was Crosby, Stills, Nash and Young's *Ohio*. One of our jocks named Mitchell B. Munchausen went on the air that night and played that song over and over for an entire hour. Jack Daniel drove into the station and personally ejected Mitch from the air studio, backed by half a dozen of Cleveland's finest. When Munchausen got to the end of the line of cops strung from studio to sidewalk, the last one looked at him and exclaimed,

"Boy, you must have done something really bad."

That was the very last time the verse *"Four Dead in Ohio"* played on WNCR. The jocks were fed up and started to search Billboard for openings at other rock stations.

And from that time forward, I held a hatred of political forces, radio censorship, and fucking pork chops.

16. Santa Fe Calling

It was almost Christmas, and I promised mom and dad I would be home for the holiday, which fell on a Friday that year. I planned to head back to Dayton right after my Wednesday shift and just thinking about being home and the amazing Yule feast my mother would set out made me incredibly happy.

Billy was waiting for me at the station when I arrived on Wednesday and pulled me into his office,

"Sonny Joe, we need to talk."

"What's up, Billy?"

My friend and boss explained that a listener had called to complain about the obscenity in the Airplane song I played on my show. That call was routed to Jack Daniel, and he had an engineer pull the logger tape to confirm. Jack called the Nationwide National Director of Programming who escalated the issue up the chain of command. Word soon got back to Jack that I had to be fired and he gave Billy his marching orders.

"I'm really sorry, man. I know you have deep passion about the political scene, but that song was one toke over the line."

"I know, Billy. I wasn't thinking straight. Actually, I wasn't thinking at all, and I have no one to blame other than myself."

"Go ahead and work your shift tonight, but it will be your last. And please, I am asking you as a friend to go out responsibly. I'm counting on you not to do anything stupid or radical."

"Don't worry, boss-man, I'll be good. I promise."

I thanked Billy for all the kind things he had done for me at WNCR and again assured him I, not he, was responsible for my demise there. So, chalk up another lesson for me. As all radio people eventually learn, station owners don't care about the DJs; they care only about ratings, money and maintaining their broadcast license. Playing the song was risky and I deserved my punishment, but I certainly knew Billy and I would remain friends and would surely run into each other again somewhere up radio road.

Billy later told me that he was heartbroken pulling the rug from under my feet, but he also knew more than he told me. Shortly after the first of the year, the whole WNCR airstaff would be fired and the station would launch a Top 40 format. He was glad I wouldn't be there for that explosion.

Meanwhile, the rest of the jocks went on strike over the increasing tension caused by management's programming manipulation, so Billy had a shitload to juggle until the upcoming format flip. Don Imus volunteered to help negotiate a peace treaty, but that would have been something like Ho Chi Minh negotiating peace with the White House. Deploying the bleak radio management style of the early 1970s Jack Daniel fired all the DJs, which sent a clear message to WMMS that the rock arena was all theirs.

Shortly after this insanity, Jack Daniel became the new GM of WNBC in New York and his first move was stealing Don Imus from WGAR. See, that's how radio works. Imus negotiated a yearly salary of a hundred thousand dollars, sending us newbies a message that being irreverent and breaking the rules earns a big raise. Of course, that's not always true.

Meanwhile, being dismissed allowed me to apply for unemployment, although I had already gotten interest from a new rock FM station in Pittsburgh and another in Santa Fe, New Mexico. I had no clear idea where that city was located, other than it was far from Cleveland.

I respected the playlist during my final show on WNCR-FM and was, as they say, "a good boy." I did break the format just a tad and ended the program by playing *Lay Lady Lay*, a song from the recent Bob Dylan album titled Nashville Skyline. I dedicated the song to my favorite librarian. No foul, no crime.

I filled out paperwork and punched my timecard for the very last time, took my headphones and other personal belongings from my cubby and slipped a note under Billy's door,

"Thanks for everything, dickhead. See you 'round the campus. Stay safe and rock 'n roll. Later, Herbie da K!"

It was after 12:30 a.m. when I got back to the apartment, and while pulling into the parking lot I was surprised to see the living room lights on. Once inside, I saw a collection of road cases and amps in the dining room, and I heard music and voices coming from Carey's bedroom, indicating he was back from the tour. It had been a draining day for me, so I quietly went to my room and slipped into bed. Then it hit me. Oh shit, I wonder how much I owed in rent? My checkbook was ready for whatever the number was, and I decided it could wait until morning. For now, I pulled the blanket up to my chin anticipating sleep. Then suddenly it started.

More than talk and music was now coming from Carey's bedroom. What I assumed was Carey's headboard started to bang forcefully against the wall, and I heard a woman exclaim, "Oh my God!" This was embarrassing and I wondered if I should get out of the house so Carey the rock star could have some privacy with his girl. I decided against that because I was so damn tired and just wanted to fall asleep. How long could this go on? I mean the guy just came off the road. Hadn't he already sown his wild oats across America? The pounding continued, and then she started to scream. First it was somewhat tolerable, but it got louder and louder. Her crescendo was a major outburst that surely rattled the heavens. Then silence.

I thought, "Oh good, now I can sleep." And just as the sandman was delivering his final dose of sleepy to me, it started again. I lost count of the climaxes, but they went on through most of the night. I have no idea what time I finally drifted off, but I know it was late.

I was first up in the morning and sitting on the couch for all of five minutes when Carey's door opened. He dashed to the bathroom and was yawning and scratching like a cat ready for a new day when he entered the living room. I looked up,

"Far-out, welcome home Carey."

"Hey, man. How's it hangin'?"

"I'm good, well not so good."

"That's a bummer, man. Why?"

"I got fired and I'm going to move today. So, how much do I owe you for rent?"

"Those assholes fired you? Well, fuck them! Money, okay, just give me three hundred dollars and we'll call it even. Where you headed?"

"Going back to Dayton for now."

"That sucks."

Now we don't make our own luck and we certainly don't control the way the world turns. There are life coincidences that become joyful events and there are other happenings that can tear the happy right out of your heart. I heard Carey's bedroom door slowly squeak open and I'll admit I was ready for the big reveal. Who was that screaming lady of the night?

There she was, wearing a man's large shirt and adjusting her long hair. It was Marilyn, the librarian. Time stopped for a few seconds. She looked at me,

"Herbie? What are you doing here?"

Carey jumped in,

"He's my roommate, dear."

The rest of the morning was one of those walking-on-eggshell occasions I would rather forget. Marilyn and I had no meaningful connection, but last night demonstrated how she reacts when being significantly satisfied, and that hurt my manly pride. But then again, I might be overreacting because I just got fired… again.

I packed up my meager belongings and made the journey back to Dayton. I couldn't bring myself to listen to the radio along the way; there was no joy in this boy's heart. It was time to close the Ashtabula – Cleveland chapter of my radio book, so I pulled into a rest stop on the interstate and threw the mannequin hand that Marilyn had given me into a trash barrel. I had been saving it for a rainy day, and now it was raining. I've often wondered if that hand gave the person emptying the trash can a stark chill thinking they had discovered a dead body.

Once back home, I was surprised when my father pulled me aside for a man-to-man. His approach was gentle, thoughtful and kind,

"Look, Herbie, I have no problem if you think this is the profession you want to pursue, but you need more experience, hopefully with a stable and compassionate radio station. I am frankly surprised that a solid insurance company like Nationwide would treat you like this."

Of course, my father didn't know the full story and I thought it best to leave it at that. The details were too complex, and I was merely glad he was on my side. He did point out that he and my mother preferred I take the Pittsburgh job so I would be closer to home. Dad said New Mexico seemed a universe away.

A few days after Christmas, I received a present of sorts in the form of a call from Rick Lynch, who was the GM of KSFR in Santa Fe. It was a twenty-five-hundred-watt Class A FM station with an antenna 312 feet above average terrain. I didn't fully understand the population in that part of the country. I knew only that it was sparse, and few people lived between the cities and Indian reservations. Should I land a job there it would be fun learning all about the city and the region.

Rick sounded young and enthusiastic as he explained,

"My father built the radio station in his garage as a hobby, never thinking FM would catch on. He passed away and now my sister Matilda and I run the place.

"I'm sorry for your loss."

"I love the air work I heard on your tape, but I will let my program director make the final call. I just wanted to touch base and see how you felt about moving across the country to play radio with us. Is this something you genuinely want? Say yes and I'll have my PD get the ball rolling."

"Yeah, for sure man. I gotta get out of here. Time for me to spread my wings and soar."

"See, that's what I mean. You use colorful language, like a writer."

"I don't know about that, but when do you think I could start?"

"I'll have our PD Dr. Bobby call you. Let's see how the two of you connect. If he agrees that you'll fit in here he'll lay out the particulars. I'm pumped."

Not too long after, KSFR PD Dr. Bobby called, and we had a great chat. After some back and forth, he offered me the 7 p.m. to midnight shift, and we discussed salary and a start date. During our conversation I learned Dr. Bobby was also the station's afternoon drive jock using the air name "Dr. Bobby, your rock 'n roll medic ." It reminded me of college radio, and I genuinely liked that.

My father took the news rather well, but my mother was depressed and kept hugging me knowing I would soon be too far away for an embrace. Dad offered a thousand dollars cash to help in my relocation, and we headed to the Salvation Army store where I bought a bed frame, mattresses, a dresser, two chairs, a small dining table and a comfy sofa.

I scheduled my departure, and as I've said many times, if radio DJs bought stock in U-Haul, they would be able to retire early. I sold my VW Beetle, which gave me a little more cash for the westward move. I figured I would buy a cheap used car when I got to Santa Fe.

On the day before my departure, which was to happen on January 2, 1971, my father and some neighbors helped me pack all my belongings into a U-Haul. Just as I was ready to close and lock the back of the truck, my mother ran out with my old acoustic guitar, a Guild D-40, which I never learned to play well. She had a notion I might finally master the instrument and write her a song. Tears ran from her eyes and fell onto the body of the guitar. She used her apron to wipe off a mother's sorrow then handed me the Guild.

On the night before leaving, Dad and I watched the Ohio State Buckeyes play the Stanford Indians. The boys from California, whose star quarterback was Jim Plunkett, won that New Year's Day game. Ironically, Plunkett is part Native American and a few years later, due to pressure from Native American groups and students, the team changed their name to Stanford Cardinal, becoming one of the first schools to make a choice of doing the right thing. My father got depressed when Stanford won the game. The loss meant Nebraska would take the national title instead of his beloved team the Buckeyes. Time to get out of town.

My father had taught me to always have a plan and traveling almost fourteen hundred miles on my own would be a challenge. I decided I would hit the road at 4 a.m. to beat the Indianapolis morning traffic. My first stop would be St. Louis, about a six-hour drive. When the need arose, I would sleep for a few hours at rest stops along the way, then get back to driving. I brought my warm sleeping bag and a major care-package of food mom had put together for me.

After St. Louis I would head to Oklahoma City, Oklahoma, repeating the drive-then-rest routine. I promised myself that whenever I got tired, I would pull off the road for a snooze. The ride from Oklahoma to Santa Fe would be roughly eight hours, and I figured that would probably be the last leg of my journey. The U-Haul truck was brand new and had an AM/FM receiver, and I listened to radio stations all along the way.

Closing in on St. Louis, I tuned into a station I had read about in Billboard, KSHE 95. They had launched their rock format by playing entire album sides without interruption or commercials, although that didn't sound like a money-making proposition to me. The Billboard story detailed how the FCC had fined KSHE for not broadcasting legal IDs, like never. That was one station I would keep on my radar for a potential future gig. I giggled at their pig mascot staring down at me from the station's billboards along the interstate.

KSHE was certainly quirky. They played Midwest bands that hadn't yet become successful in the eastern part of the country. Styx, Head East, REO Speedwagon and a Canadian hard rock band named Rush were prominently featured. It was all new and fresh to me, and even though the music was hard it was extremely melodic.

As we moved into the new year of 1971, lots of soft rock by artists like James Taylor, Carole King, John Denver and George Harrison were hitting the airwaves. Keepers of the FM rock format were struggling to decide if they would include these songs or stick strictly with rock. Even though George Harrison's *My Sweet Lord* was a major hit by a Beatle, many rock stations passed on it, feeling it was too mellifluous and folksy. We later learned that the melody line was a rip-off, intentional or not, of the Chiffons song *He's So Fine.*

The radio stations through Oklahoma and Texas were mostly Gospel and Country with a few Top 40s along the way. Sleeping at rest stops eliminated concern about my cargo and saved money that I would otherwise have spent on motel rooms.

It took three and half days to reach the outskirts of Santa Fe. I stopped at a gas station and called Mr. Lynch, who gave me driving instructions to the station. I was listening to Dr. Bobby on the radio, and I really enjoyed his style. He had a friendly, upbeat presentation, and his music knowledge was fantastic. One of his clever taglines was, "It's your desert doctor on KSFR 101.1, the rock of the Rio Grande Valley!"

Dr. Bobby played a new song from Led Zeppelin III called *The Gallows Pole*, which was a variation of an old English folk song by Huddie William Ledbetter, better known by his stage name Lead Belly. Robert Plant and Jimmy Page rearranged the timeworn tune, and its hypnotic chords and lyrics always drew me in, *"I couldn't get no silver, I couldn't get no gold, You know that we're too damn poor, To keep you from the gallows pole."* I certainly felt poor at this point in my life's journey. All my worldly possessions were in either the U-Haul or my pockets.

I drove into the parking lot of the station, which was situated in a small adobe building on the edge of town. The sun had gone down, twilight had settled in, and the blinking red lights on the broadcast tower in the station's backyard set against the purple sky was an electrifying and welcoming sight!

The receptionist escorted me to Rick Lynch's office, and I was wide-eyed, gazing at all the desert artifacts on the walls. There was a framed rattlesnake, a prehistoric tool of some sort and a painting of a native woman cooking tortillas on an open fire. Rick was a large man with a crimson face. His combed back hair was crazy-red, and after shaking my hand he handed me a shot glass. I looked down,

"Okay, what's this?"

"Mezcal son, drink up."

Rick and I chatted about radio and the infant album rock format. Meanwhile, Dr. Bobby's air shift had ended, and he stepped into the office. We introduced ourselves and Rick suggested the three of us go to dinner. Afterward they would drop me at an inexpensive hotel for my first night in the city. When we got to the parking lot, I asked Rick whether I should bring the U-Haul and he was quick to respond,

"Nah, I see you have a lock on it. It'll be safe here. This is a good neighborhood."

During dinner it became apparent these young guys were truly into what they were doing. Rick wanted the jocks to have freedom to play the music, Dr. Bobby was a talented leader, and the three of us were getting on perfectly. I felt this was a beautiful beginning in a new market, a new station and a new place for me to learn and grow. After too many tequilas to count, they dropped me at the hotel. I registered at the front desk then made my way to the room.

I woke up early the next day and took a cab to the station. My heart immediately sank when we turned into the driveway. The U-Haul was nowhere in sight. Did I give Rick the key so he could move it? I reached into my pocket and felt the truck key with its big plastic identification badge.

I walked into the station and quickly found Rick,

"Hey, Rick, where's the U-Haul?"

He looked at his secretary, then back to me,

"Oh shit, this isn't good."

17. The City Different

Santa Fe is an extremely old city. It was founded in 1610 by the Spanish, you know, the ones from Spain. Santa Fe is nestled in the foothills of the southern Rocky Mountains at seven thousand feet above sea level. It's the highest and oldest capital in the US and America's second oldest city. Its original name was Villa Real de la Santa Fé de San Francisco de Asis, or in English, the Royal City of the Holy Faith of St. Francis of Assisi. Yeah, a bit too long for a bumper sticker so the city fathers went with Santa Fe. Because of the presence of so many cultures, they adopted the nickname "The City Different." it was a way of glorifying and unifying the distinctive mix of Spanish speaking citizens, Anglo population and Native Americans.

New Mexico didn't achieve statehood until 1912, and in 1926 Route 66 was paved directly through Santa Fe. While I was enjoying the discovery of my new city different, I was also worried about the U-Haul and all my stuff. What had started out with so much hope and optimism was now turning into a flurry of phone calls with a detective at the Santa Fe Police Department. After two days, the police reported the truck was found in the desert. Rick Lynch and I climbed into his Jeep and trucked out to what the detective called "the crime scene." Ha, like most of my life so far!

We arrived at the site, and there were two cops sitting in their squad car not far from the U-Haul, which was encircled with yellow crime scene tape. I jumped out of the Jeep and walked toward them,

"Thank you so much."

The cop opened his window and barked,

"You can't go in there."

"Why? Those are my things."

Just then, an unmarked car sped up the dirt road and stopped at the parked cop car. Detective Edward Rodrigues got out and walked over,

"Hey there, are you Herbie?"

"Yeah, that's me."

"It's okay guys, I have been talking with this guy over the phone. We just ran the plate and the U-Haul dealer verified it's his rental. They're sending a tow truck over to pick it up."

Detective Rodrigues shook my hand and then gave Rick Lynch a high five, so I assumed they were friends. I tried to be cool by saying thank you in Spanish but Eddie, as I learned everyone called him, waved me off,

"I'm Portuguese and don't really speak Spanish, except when I'm in a knife fight."

The scene was hard on me. My belongings were scattered across the desert floor and the beautiful Guild guitar had been smashed against a large rock, quite symbolic in so many ways. Most of my clothes were ripped and ruined. I guess whoever did this wanted to joy ride until the truck ran out of gas, then concluded their game with some destructive fun. All my furniture was gone but a few things were left intact. Curiously, my briefcase containing paperwork and checkbook was left unopened. Rick helped me pile the salvageable items into the back of the Jeep, and just as we finished the local U-Haul guy arrived. I showed my ID, signed a bunch of forms, then they hauled the truck away.

When we arrived back at the radio station, Rick introduced me to his sister Matilda, and I was a little surprised. She was Native American and dressed in what I thought at first was a costume, but it was actually her style. She looked to be in her mid-thirties, with smooth, youthful and very dark mocha-gold skin. Her hair was black and straight, her cheek bones high and her eyes a piercing brown. I felt connection with an ancient spirit.

Rick explained he had a meeting with bankers and clients, and Matilda would transport me to a furnished apartment where I could stay rent-free for two-months until I found a place of my own. This was unexpected, but I figured Rick was feeling bad about my disastrous beginning there. Kevin Winslow was the station's chief engineer, and he helped move my surviving gear from Rick's Jeep to Matilda's large pickup truck. She gunned the vehicle out of the parking lot, stirring up a thick cloud of dust. As she drove, I said,

"I was so sorry hearing about your father passing away. Is your mother still alive?"

"Yes, we live together. And if your next question is whether she is native American, that answer is also yes. We are members of the Jicarilla Apache tribe. I like your hair, but I no longer do scalps."

She laughed seeing the stunned look on my face,

"Relax, I'm joking. This is probably a proper time to get one thing out of the way. Should you ever sense tension between Rick and me, it's related to our father being gone. He gave Rick all the advantages and treated me and our mother like squaws. There are some ill feelings between us."

I had to stop and wonder why so many people tell me all their secrets, good or bad, as soon as we meet. I diverted the conversation,

"So, shall I call you Ms. Lynch?"

She offered a little chuckle and pushed her long hair away from her face,

"You may call me Matilda, and if we get to know each other better I might give you permission to call me Kanti, the fox that sings."

"Sounds good. So, where are we headed?"

"Rick invested in an apartment complex years ago and it's a wonderful place up on the ridge. There's a magnificent view, but unfortunately your unit faces a hill so it's a tad dark. All the furnishings are brand new. Rick originally put it on the market as a condominium but abandoned that plan when there was a downturn in condo sales. How long did he say you could stay there?"

"Two months."

"Well, if you like the place, you might convince him to rent it to you. That would kill two birds with one stone, although killing a bird with anything is a sin."

"What's your role at the station?"

"I don't do much. I'm more or less the 'fixer' when Rick messes things up. Did he really tell you the station is in a safe neighborhood?"

"Yeah, he did."

"Well, there you go."

I was impressed with her candor and her physical strength. She helped me unload my belongings and steered me through a thorough tour of the apartment, opening every closet, cupboard and compartment. She handed me the key then asked,

"What are you going to do about transportation?"

"Well, I had planned to buy a car when I got settled"

"I can help you with that."

We jumped back in her truck and ended up on a strip of road populated with dozens of car dealerships. Matilda pulled into one with a weathered, cheap, wooden sign hanging out front, CHIEF POWAW'S

USED CARS. A large man dressed in native garb walked over, Matilda jumped out of the car and the two of them exchanged a big bear hug,

"Sister Kanti! What brings you here and how is your mother?"

I learned that Chief Powaw was a true American Indian chief who owned this car dealership. Matilda told him the story of my arrival in a way that made it seem like I was a distant traveler from another land, which wasn't all that far off base. I was feeling like my alien airship had crash landed on the edge of a demonic desert.

Now any American who has ever bought a car knows how long and convoluted the process can be. Well, this wasn't that. It was a miracle transaction. The Chief made a call to his bank, gave them my name and social security number, then asked me for two hundred dollars. I handed over the cash and he gave me a receipt, title and car keys. Minutes later I drove off the lot in a red 1962 Datsun station wagon.

When I got back to the station, Dr. Bobby called me into the air studio for a training session. He went over all the controls on the audio console, ran through the procedures to adjust the transmitter and take meter readings and demonstrated various other devices I would need to know before my first show. It was a totally casual approach, and I learned a lot just by watching and chatting with Dr. Bobby while he worked. My new PD was quite the DJ. His patter was up-tempo, but his style was far removed from a jive Top 40 presentation, it was a knowledgeable but also cheerful, casual and friendly on-air presence.

Several things jumped out while hanging with Dr. Bobby. First, he was wearing crisply pressed blue jeans with a white, woven belt. Also, I couldn't help noticing his shape was more like a woman's. I quickly blanked that out of my mind. Bad one, Herbie. When taking calls from listeners, Bobby tended to be short and business-like with women but more outgoing and warmer with the guys. Maybe nothing, maybe not.

Dr. Bobby sat with me during my first shift and things went well. While chatting as songs were playing, he mentioned frequent weekend trips to Los Angeles explaining he had "a really tight relationship" with the music industry. Record people who promoted new songs would do just about anything to get a record they were "working" on as many radio stations as they could. Most promoters were record company employees, but some became extraordinarily successful at getting airplay and went out on their own as "independent record promoters." These indies had no ethics policies or in-house lawyers, so record companies would hire them to have plausible deniability and isolation from any skullduggery. I'll share some details about that sort of malfeasance later.

Fresh back from one of his trips to LA, Bobby brought a reel of tape containing an album by a new group named Jethro Tull, which wouldn't be released until a few months later. He dubbed the title track named *Aqualung* to a cart and said I could debut it on my show. He insisted I use the term "KSFR exclusive" over the intro of the song. When I asked him if this guy Jethro was from the US or England, he chuckled and explained Jethro Tull wasn't a person but rather the name of the band, which was valuable information since there was no album cover for reference.

On the air I made repeated references to an upcoming exclusive play of a fantastic song by a new band. Yes, I was teasing. I loved the track and was struck by not only the hard, definitive guitars but also the angry articulation of the lyrics. The opening lines really stood out, *"Sitting on a park bench, Eying little girls with bad intent, Snot's running down his nose, Greasy fingers smearing shabby clothes, Hey, Aqualung!"* The poetry was fantastic, and the words painted an incredible picture. After a few spins it dawned on me this song was about homelessness, probably the first such song ever. The phones went crazy with listeners clamoring to hear it again. The same wild response would happen later in the year when I gave *Stairway to Heaven* by Led Zeppelin its initial spin.

An amazing feeling arises when playing a new song on the radio for the very first time. Most disc jockeys, especially those who work in FM rock radio, experience an intense rush when turning hundreds of thousands of listeners onto a new piece of musical art, perhaps a song that would very well withstand the test of time. That phrase may be brushed aside by historians, but it's impossible to know how many thousands of times, probably millions, *Stairway to Heaven* has been played on radio stations around the world after the time I pushed the Start button of Turntable #2 to roll the vinyl on the air for the very first time.

Back then, three basic kinds of DJs inhabited the rock radio world. There were the music freaks who wanted to explore fresh artists and songs and turn the world on to the best of them. Record companies loved these kinds of broadcasters because they could manipulate them with enthusiastic promotions of new product to get airplay. Then there were those addicted to the power and attention of being "famous." I once heard a guy say he got into radio to "pick up chicks." Yes, that's surely an out-of-date expression now, but he was voicing his true motivation. A third group of radio freaks didn't care much about the music and perhaps even less about the audience. They were taken with a love of broadcast equipment and the thrill of sending RF, radio frequency, signals into the air. These engineering types would be called nerds or tech-heads today. Most of them had a tolerable on-air presentation but not much more.

Rick Lynch and Dr. Bobby had boundless energy and I worked my ass off just to keep up with them. We held promotions at bars and car dealers. These live broadcasts are called "remotes," and they're designed to draw listeners into a sponsor's establishment to increase sales. Most remotes are simple affairs, with a DJ standing in front of a banner making live "call-ins" back to the studio and onto the air inviting listeners to the broadcast. In those days, the signal travelled from the business to the radio station on a rather low-quality, leased broadcast telephone line, but high-fidelity microwave transmission with dish antennas on trucks was under development and would soon be ubiquitous at these events.

Many DJs have a drive to get close to the audience. Yes, as I discovered in Cleveland, the radio groupies are always there, but sometimes a young lady was hired by a station to target a disc jockey at a competing station to gain inside information or perhaps create a scandal. Rivalry between broadcasters has always been fierce and ruthless and that sort of monkey business continues to this day.

The only intriguing and intellectually deep person at my new radio home was Matilda, but ours would remain an owner and worker relationship. Meanwhile, I got a call from Brewster Billy who was completely thrilled with the new Top 40 format he launched on WNCR. The station owners were much happier playing Tony Orlando and Dawn's *Knock Three Times* and the Bee Gees' *Lonely Days*. I told him I was equally happy in Santa Fe and expressed confidence my work here would eventually lead to another major market.

My downtime was consumed by reading books, watching TV and going to the movies but I hadn't connected with anyone, so I was delighted when Dr. Bobby invited me over to his apartment for dinner. He explained his roommate, Sly Epstein, was a famous chef who owned a local restaurant in the early sixties. They planned the party for Sunday night when I was off work. Dr. Bobby also mentioned a few locals would be there, as he said,

"Just to make things interesting."

I wondered what that meant, hoping the extra guests wouldn't muck things up. But, hey, it was a free dinner.

18. Too Much Desert Snow

I have always tried to avoid evil people, but it's sometimes difficult to discern between the damned and the delightful. In college, I avoided the YAF-ers, the frat boys and the sorority girls. I was more attuned to the kids who wanted to work in radio or in other artistic fields like journalism, photography, acting and playwrighting. These folks, more often than not, were free spirits or hippies. I also knew the radio and record industries had more than their fair shares of wackos, weirdos and wisenheimers, so I taught myself to tread lightly.

I was feeling great on this perfect "not a cloud in the sky" Santa Fe Sunday. The sun was nearing the horizon to the west, and that reminded me of the song lyric "*purple mountain majesty.*" What I was seeing was a perfect display of an American southwest sunset. I arrived at Dr. Bobby's place on Museum Hill, a one-story adobe structure on Sun Mountain Drive. Seeing all the cacti in the front yard rock garden made me think, wow, no need to ever mow this lawn. Stenciled on the mailbox were the names Epstein and Stapleford, and that made it obvious Dr. Bobby's legal name was Robert Stapleford.

I could hear exotic music coming from inside the house, acoustic guitar mixed with electronic music. I knocked on the door and it swung open a bit. I called out,

"Hey, Bobby, it's Sonny Joe, you here?"

The positive response was shouted from deep inside and I stepped through the doorway. I walked three steps down into a sunken space with a dirt floor and smooth, round rocks bordering a small spring-fed stream. Multi-colored lights were recessed into the crevasses of the stone wall, and it was apparent this elegant house was built over a large rock formation. I followed a walkway to another set of stairs leading up to a large living room. The eyes of everyone in the room turned to me as I entered, including Bobby's,

"Brother Sonny, welcome to the house of insanity featuring a menagerie of desert night creatures."

"Thanks, man, great to be here. Wow, that entryway would be tough for a drunk person to navigate!"

Everyone laughed and Dr. Bobby introduced me to three of his guests, two sitting on bean bag chairs and a third lounging on the sofa. Each of the three had a cartoon character name, Rasper, Chop and Steeple. I can't believe I still remember those oddball handles. Bobby grabbed a skinny guy sitting next to him who had a long beard like Rasputin, the Russian mystic and self-proclaimed holy man whom I learned about in my Political Science class at Dayton. Bobby managed to get him to his feet; both men appeared to be high as kites,

"And this guy is my absolute best friend in the whole universe. Meet the magic man, Sly Epstein."

The obvious affection and Bobby's body language made it clear they enjoyed something beyond friendship. I had encountered gay men at UD in the drama and dance programs, so I was not at all uncomfortable, but Dr. Bobby's lifestyle didn't align with the machismo rock 'n roll doctor image he projected on the radio. I guess we are all actors in a sense, casting off our real skins to appear as, and appeal to, whoever our audiences wanted us to be.

I asked Sly about his name. Was it short for Sylvester or was it like Sly and the Family Stone? His wispy, nasal voice answered in song,

"I am everyday people, yeah, yeah, There is a blue one who can't accept, The green one for living with, A fat one tryin' to be a skinny one, Different strokes for different folks."

Rasper came over and asked if I would like some pasta. What is it with pasta and parties? Two pots of tomato sauce were warming on the stove. Rasper explained that one was laced with L.S.D. and the other with just a little pot, so there was the menu. Now should you be from another planet, L.S.D. is short for lysergic acid diethylamide, a powerful psychedelic drug I was never tempted to try. I remember what it did to Woody, an exceptionally bright guy at college. After just one acid trip he was remarkably changed. He never smiled or laughed again, and I wanted none of that.

I had the "just a little" pot pasta and some red wine from France, but within ten minutes Rasper's lie was uncovered. I was having an out of body experience with my attention captured by the multitude of brightly colored lights dotting the house. It wasn't helping that I was consuming delicious pasta with pot-laced sauce, which only made me want to eat more.

As the night wore on, I learned Sly was once fired from the best restaurant in Santa Fe when his boss learned he was dealing drugs out of the kitchen. Mr. Epstein then opened a head shop named Sly and the Family Stoned. Yes, not at all subtle but he was somewhat of a folk hero in town.

Sly was dressed in cowboy denim and he wore tons of silver jewelry with green and blue turquoise. His hair was woven into small tails intertwined with Native American painted leather. I surmised that Epstein came from a wealthy family, which was more or less confirmed when Rasper mentioned Sly's cousin back in New York was a prominent investment banker who helped the chef with money management.

There was a moment when Sly left the room and Bobby explained Sly was somewhat uptight and not himself that night. It seems several local church groups were collaborating with the police to close his head shop. He was also being harassed by some nearby merchants, and his only saving graces were Rick Lynch and Eddie the detective who were volume customers at the head shop. Sly was also a major advertiser on KSFR. Just a few weeks ago I had cut a spot for his store.

Sly came back into the room carrying a beautifully carved wooden box and sat down on the large sofa. Like moths to the flame, everyone else in the room flitted over and gathered around the coffee table. Sly slid an eight by ten mirror from a shelf under the table and placed it on top. It didn't take me long to figure out that Sly Epstein was a major coke head, and I was already planning a way to get the hell out of this place.

Sly was meticulous with his green American Express card, laying out a dozen fat lines of the white powder. After finishing, he said,

"I go first motherfuckers, because I paid for this shit!"

And so, the rotation began, with each person taking their turn of an initial large snort with several inhalations following after to make sure all the stuff got to where it was meant to go, the brain. The breaths and sighs of each partier sent a clear message this was powerful cocaine. When the rolled-up, hundred-dollar bill was passed to me I had to qualify,

"I'm not really into this so I'll have just a bit and then go back to my apartment. I promised my parents I would call them tonight."

That wasn't true, of course, and the razzing I got from these freaks was more funny than hurtful. I was feeling no pain and I thanked Bobby and Sly for a great night. The coke relieved some of the woozy buzz from the pot-laced spaghetti sauce and I was praying that I didn't get pulled over by one of Santa Fe's finest while driving home in my not-so-subtle bright red Datsun wagon.

The cocaine felt good, but it's a terrible, nasty drug that makes you experience two things at once, a wonderful euphoric rush coupled with an almost immediate and maddening desire for more, more, more. The more you did the more you wanted, a stupid loop spinning over and over in your brain until, ten hours later, your body crashes into restless sleep.

I spent more than twenty minutes throwing up when I got back to the apartment. It dawned on me that the cocaine may have been cut with baby laxative, a common way to stretch one's stash back then. I was experiencing the double dilemma of a sleepless high and a wakeful restlessness brought on by that wicked white powder.

I didn't know it at the time, but my fellow partiers were also high on quaaludes. Methaqualone was first made in India in 1951 and patented in the United States in 1962. It was manufactured by Rorer, a drug company based in Fort Washington, Pennsylvania, under the brand name Quaalude, a clever combination of the words "quiet and interlude." The drug was a small, round, white tablet stamped with "Rorer 714." It was classified a hypnotic drug and prescribed legally to people who had trouble sleeping due to anxiety, but it had some harsh risks. An overdose could lead to nervous system shutdown, coma and even death. It also lessened inhibitions and was probably an early date-rape drug, but that wasn't talked about. The US government eventually declared quaaludes an illicit drug and manufacturing ended.

My view of Dr. Bobby changed following that night at his and Sly's place. It dawned on me his endless energy was the result of constant drug use. Yes, he was a gifted disc jockey with vast musical knowledge, but he was not a caring or giving person. I now viewed him as somewhat of a lost soul in an unhealthy relationship with Sly. I believed Bobby allowed Sly to control him and it was just another case of "love is blind."

Meanwhile, the summer of 1971 was fantastic for music. We had the new *Who's Next* album and it's wonderful songs like *Baba O'Reily* and *Won't Get Fooled Again*, with that fabulous line, *"Meet the new boss, Same as the old boss."* Those words stood out because I was beginning to think that every radio boss was somewhat tilted, but let's stay with the music. The Rolling Stones released *Sticky Fingers* with *Brown Sugar* and the driving *Can't You Hear Me Knocking*. The LP cover was ultra-cool with an actual zipper on what one assumed to be Mick Jagger's jeans. That cover was eventually changed after people complained. Who were those folks?

I was making extra money during the day hosting remote broadcasts at car dealers and Dairy Queens, and my nightly radio show was a hit. A local TV station ran a feature named *Sonny Joe on the Go*. A film crew followed me around from breakfast to late night chilling in my apartment. The show included a lengthy segment of me doing my show in the KSFR air studio.

The job paved my way to meeting some dynamic people and having a couple of great dates with strong, smart women. One was a producer at the public TV station and the other was an art teacher at the Santa Fe University of Art and Design. I didn't want to get into a "serious" relationship because I never knew when I might find an opportunity to bolt to a bigger market. I will mention that any new date who didn't like Led Zep was immediately taken out of rotation.

I also developed a once-a-month lunch liaison with Matilda. It was a symbiotic association with her getting information about what was happening at the radio station and me acquiring some KSFR background that helped flesh out the psychological profiles of a few of my co-workers. I learned that the entire family of Kevin Winslow, our chief engineer, who called himself the "cheap engineer," was killed in a plane crash ten years ago. That's why he was so immersed in his work.

It was September now and at one of my lunches with Matilda she revealed her Native America alignment and sense of mysticism were giving off a "very bad odor," meaning something grave was afoot. Quick swerve, how can a grave be a foot?

Now I'm not at all religious but have always adhered to a set of values based on morals and spirituality rather than an organized dogma. As Matilda and I parted ways in the parking lot she looked at me, touched my arm, and stared at me with those piercing brown eyes,

"No matter what happens, Sonny Joe, it's best you stay silent. Walk with light feet through the desert of deceit."

Yeah, that was a bit creepy. Her words echoed in my mind and made me want to smoke some pot, but an event that followed showed Matilda was perhaps a soothsayer from ages past.

It was September 9, 1971, and the morning was crisp and unseasonably chilly, but the sky was a deep, pure blue, the kind eagles use in their photo shoots. I got into my red Datsun and headed down to the station for a production assignment with a finicky client whom I was to meet at 11 a.m. Instead of listening to KSFR, I punched up 770 KOB, the big AM station out of Albuquerque. I thought their newscasts at the top and bottom of each hour were in-depth and well produced. This is what I heard,

"This just in to KOB radio news, Dr. Bobby Stapleford, one of the top FM DJs in Santa Fe, has been found dead in an apartment near his radio station. That's all we have on this story for now; more details when they become available. And in other news..."

I pulled off to the side of the road. My face turned white as I put the car in park and switched off the radio, hoping that would make the sad news go away. Wanting to deny what I just heard, I flashed back to that dinner party at Dr. Bobby's months ago and had a sickening feeling. Shaking off my thoughts, I put my station wagon back in gear and hightailed it to the radio station, hoping to find answers there.

When I arrived, the KSFR parking lot was full of cars, including two police vehicles. I rushed in and the receptionist was crying through phone calls to relay terrible answers. I made my way to Rick's office and saw he was meeting with two uniformed cops and Eddie the detective, who looked up,

"Hey, Sonny, can you please give us a minute, but don't go too far. I would like to talk with you."

I had no reason to fear any questions from Eddie, but there was a tight knot in my stomach and a cacophony of questions in my mind. What happened? Was it a drug overdose?

The police moved on to others in the station and Rick asked me to cover Dr. Bobby's afternoon drive shift, saying he would get a part-timer to host my nighttime show. The client I was to meet heard the terrible news and canceled his recording session. I was walking around like a zombie and turned to Rick for some advice about how to present the news about Bobby on the air. This wouldn't be the last time I had a need to speak directly and personally to my listeners about the death of a DJ, rock star, or major celebrity, but this first one was unquestionably tough.

After the funeral a week later, Rick Lynch pulled me into his office and offered me the PD job. I broke down in tears and told him that as much as I loved the station and the city, Dr. Bobby's death was just too much to take. I told Rick I wanted to move on soon. He was totally cool and understanding which made me feel much better.

As once-famous newscaster Paul Harvey would say, "And now the rest of the story." It seems that after a night of hard partying, Dr. Bobby got into an argument with Sly Epstein. Bobby was pissed that Sly "let him" do too much coke. That's rich. Sly suggested Bobby try one of the Rorer 714 pills he got from a friend. Sly, not remembering if Bobby took one, three or a dozen, later found Bobby's lifeless body on the bathroom floor. He called Rasper to come and see if they could revive Bobby. Rasper needed only one look,

"Shit, Sly, he's dead as a doornail."

Now I don't know exactly how dead a doornail can be, but Sly worried he would lose his business if he called the cops. So, with a total absence of logic and thought, he and Rasper moved Bobby's body to an apartment across town and then asked one of Sly's workers to send police to that address. As typically happens, the story unraveled and Sly and Rasper went to jail for hindering the investigation by moving the body, not for the drug overdose. One can kill a lover in America, but once you move a body, oops!

The coroner released his report stating that said Dr. Bobby died not only of an overdose of cocaine but also from heart failure caused by the substantial amount of methaqualone in his blood stream. The quiet interlude between life and death was way too short for Bobby. The good news is he felt no pain on the way out.

19. Rising From the Ashes

There are times when inspiration arrives in an unexpected way. Two young men in their twenties were driving back from the historic Woodstock rock concert that took place in 1969 between August 15th and 18th in Max Yasgur's Bethel, New York cow pasture. Eric Hauenstein and Dwight Tindle were making the drive from the upstate New York concert to the Tindle family home in Philadelphia. There they talked about buying a radio station.

The pair were chatting about the first commercially licensed radio station in America, KDKA in Pittsburgh, and they wondered why the station's call letters began with the letter K like those in the west. Dwight asked a quirky question,

"Okay, there's a KDKA but is there a KDKB?"

They liked the sound of the those call letters, found they were available and decided they would use them for their station, not knowing at the time it would take two more years to realize their vision.

The two fantasized about how their radio station would play the music they loved. Dwight, who was from Philadelphia and listened to WMMR in its early days, and Eric, who worked as a sales rep at WEBN in his hometown of Cincinnati, realized that a progressive rock format in the right city could be extremely successful. You see, radio has always inspired more radio and there were times an entrepreneur would duplicate the format of his or her favorite radio station in another market. Some purists chastise such behavior, but hey, all's fair when chasing a radio dream.

Dwight cashed out a trust fund from his father to the tune of three hundred and fifty thousand dollars and moved to Eric's Cincinnati stomping ground so they could begin working in earnest on their plan to acquire a radio station. The two decided they wanted a property in the western US, and they drove cross-country searching for a station to purchase. They eventually decided on KMND at 93.3 FM, a station licensed to Mesa, Arizona, a city just east of Phoenix. The "Woodstock boys" closed the deal and applied to the FCC for a call letter change, which was granted, and thus, KMND became KDKB.

Eric and Dwight took out a long-term lease on a building that was formerly a Safeway grocery store on Country Club Drive near First Avenue. The street name didn't project a particularly good image for a rock 'n roll station, but the structure had tons of space they would use to expand the minds of radio listeners in Mesa, Chandler and Phoenix.

On August 23, 1971, our heroes launched a Progressive rock format on KDKB. Meanwhile I was still in Santa Fe mourning the untimely death (um, is a death ever timely?) of my station's program director and reading a story in Billboard about the launch of KDKB. I wanted to find out if they were hiring disc jockeys, so I called. Al Murdoch, the station's program director, picked up the wrong line and that wonderful mishap allowed me to speak with him directly. I spit out a laugh when he answered the phone because it sounded like he said, "Elmer Duck," but then quickly realized I hit paydirt. Al listened politely while I rapidly ran down my resume, then he rattled off a Mesa post office box address and asked me to send my tape and resume.

I had always been a hard worker at the Santa Fe station and that was especially true after Bobby's demise. Rick was nothing but helpful and gave me a wonderful letter of recommendation, which was a rare commodity in radio. It turned out that Al in Phoenix was more impressed with the production samples on my tape than my DJ work, so he offered me three hundred dollars a week to come to Mesa and become KDKB's full-time production director, along with one or two weekend air shifts. No U-Haul this time. My Datsun wagon could easily hold my belongings with plenty of room left for a comfortable seven-hour trip to Mesa. So, once again, I was packing for a move.

Before leaving Santa Fe, I had a final lunch with Matilda at a Mexican restaurant near her home. The place was poorly lit, and everyone was speaking Spanish, except us. Matilda turned to me,

"I'm so glad you are getting out of here, Sonny."

"Why? Which way do you mean that?"

"You're better than this tiny town, plus I know something you don't."

"What's that, Matilda?"

"Those meetings with bankers were not client meetings. Rick has been spending far too much money and the station is not profitable, so something has to give."

"What exactly do you mean?"

"In a few months, we are going to sell KSFR to the local college and they will be changing the format. We will dissolve the business, and everyone will be fired, but you must not say anything to anyone. You've already dodged a bullet here by escaping what will soon become a messy situation, so please, just quietly move on."

I felt she was talking to me like the son she never had. I liked Matilda, but her mystic perceptions did freak me out somewhat. After Ashtabula, I had a dim view of astrology and other paranormal pursuits; it was all a pile of poop to me.

Death was always lurking for one of radio's own and, like any profession, ours had its fair share of mishaps and mistakes. When microwave remote setups became the rage for broadcasting promotional appearances, more than one engineer was electrocuted by carelessly raising the dish antenna and hitting high tension electric lines. He would be fine while inside the remote truck, but should he step out onto terra firma while holding onto the vehicle chassis, the bodily connection between high voltage electricity and earthen ground would send him to his maker in a cloud of smoke.

Speaking of death, if you enjoy a great murder mystery, you'll find a ton of them in the radio business. A legendary one occurred that year centered on famous Los Angeles DJ "Humble Harv" Miller, who allegedly shot and killed his wife. Several tales surfaced because he initially pled not guilty and later changed his plea.

One account was his wife, who was said to have been a more than difficult partner, used to call Harv while he was on the air to brag about her infidelities and Harv had his fill and took action. There was also a rumor that Harv's wife Mary was having an affair with a woman, and their daughter caught her mother in a compromising situation and killed her with Harv's gun. One theory was Harv took the rap for his daughter, and that gained credibility when he changed his plea to guilty. The version the judge believed was that Harv and Mary got into an argument, she held the gun, and as Harv was attempting to disarm her the weapon discharged and killed Mary.

Harv's problem was he went missing after the shooting. Some say famous record producer Phil Spector helped Harv avoid capture, but then what would Spector know about killing a woman? Harv served a little more than three years in prison, and upon release he returned to an on-air radio gig at KIQQ-FM in Los Angeles, which was branded as K100. The station was operated by famous radio programmer Bill Drake, who in 1965 debuted the extraordinarily successful Boss Radio format on LA's KHJ. It was a streamlined Top 40 format that reduced disc jockey chatter, eliminated long jingles and clustered commercials into stopsets, all designed to throw focus on the music. The success of KHJ prompted Top 40 stations around the US to adopt its elements which became known as "The Drake Format."

As for Harv Miller, I'll conclude with this dark, gallows humor statement. If a baseball pitcher can throw a good curve ball, he can get away with murder, and several have. As for radio, if a DJ can get big ratings he can also get away with murder.

Like the Phoenix rising from the ashes, I departed Santa Fe and aimed my car at Arizona. I took I-25 to I-40, through the Petrified Forest National Park, which always made me feel young. I mean, the wood is so hard and ancient; it's two hundred and twenty-five million years old. I used state roads for the remainder of the roughly five-hundred-mile trip to Mesa.

Immediately upon arrival I checked into the Pioneer Hotel and started making calls to find a furnished apartment. I soon located a place not too far from the station in what looked like a typical 1970s neighborhood, which was perfect for me.

Just like Cleveland, Phoenix was a major market, meaning the station ratings are the gods determining the future and the fate of our team. If the ratings went down, a big discussion by management, sales and programming would follow. Declining ratings raised an immediate need to determine what needed to be "fixed," and employees had to live through the incredible stress and tension caused by "bad numbers."

Archibald Crossley, Elmo Roper and George Gallup have been described as the fathers of election polling, and grading politicians came along well before rating radio stations. It was Mr. Crossley who originated the term "rating." In 1934, Claude E. Hooper brought us "Hooperatings," which measured the popularity of radio shows using concepts of available audience and average minute ratings. Later, Arthur Nielsen, Sr. designed the first probability sample, which would become a fundamental aspect of radio ratings. Most of these early polling companies battled to the death or were consumed by each other with buyouts and mergers.

A research company cannot measure radio listenership by interviewing every single listener, so they work with a "sample," which is a carefully selected smaller portion of the audience. The measure media usage within the sample and project that as being representative of the entire audience. So, you see, radio ratings are actually listening *estimates* having margins of error. If a large enough sample is surveyed, and its composition reflects percentages of the actual population with respect to gender, race, ethnicity and age, the listening patterns of that small group will most likely reflect the behavior of the population at large. It's far from a perfect and infallible system, but it's the best we have, and broadcasters and advertisers need those estimates.

In 1949, a guy named Jim Seiler started a company named the American Research Bureau, later referred to as ARB, and that company's radio ratings product carried the name Arbitron. You may know the name if at some point in the past you participated in an Arbitron survey of radio listening.

I was a duck out of water in Phoenix, which is dumb imagery for a desert setting. I am not a math expert and numbers have value to me only if I can picture their meaning. Some radio people fueled conspiracy theories about rating companies and their methodologies, especially when their numbers were terrible, but even though estimating listenership wasn't a precise science most in the radio and advertising businesses treated the results as firm reality.

I don't want to pull you down into a black hole with an abundance of complex details about how radio ratings work but having a superficial view will help you understand some facets of my story. Back then, Phoenix had a population of close to a million people, but Arbitron surveyed only fifteen hundred listeners in the market. The fate and fortunes of those of us working in Phoenix radio were in the hands of that small sample.

In the early days of radio ratings, companies would go door to door or make telephone calls asking people which stations they listened to. Arbitron devised an approach they believed would lead to more accurate results. Their idea was a "secret ballot" of sorts, a listening diary with a separate page for each day of a one-week period. Those taking the survey would fill in a date page with the names of each station they listened to, along with the times they started and stopped. As an incentive, Arbitron paid one dollar to each diary keeper for their involvement. Participating households received a separate diary for every family member, and Arbitron asked them to honestly record their daily radio listening in the little booklet. Now, here is where controversy erupts.

You see, the diary wasn't capturing *actual* listening but rather *recollections* of listening. Sure, some pedantic types filled out the diary at the radio each of the seven days, logging the exact times they listened to each station, but most people treated the diary-based survey the same way their kids managed school assignments. They waited until the last minute and then completed the entire one-week diary in a single sitting, doing the best they could to remember their radio usage across seven days. One theory was some people wrote in stations they felt made them "look good" by sprinkling in entries for the public radio station here and the all-news station there, even though they had never listened to them.

Radio owners and programmers could travel to the Arbitron office in Laurel, Maryland to look through all the diaries for a rating period, and that was often eye opening. The ten diaries of a large family might all be in the same handwriting and pen, evidence of one individual taking charge of the survey in the household. Each person was paid to complete the survey, so a big family would make sure they earned the money, even if that meant dad filled out all the diaries on deadline day. Such diaries were most likely inaccurate, of course, but their impact was lessened by all the others in the sample.

There were cases of radio station employees getting a dozen diaries by lying to the ratings company during the initial recruitment phone call. Manipulating just a handful of diaries could affect rating results profoundly. There's a legendary story about a certain San Diego radio station programmed by a mystical madman who scored thirteen diaries for a rating period. We'll hear more of his story soon.

Most station plots to cheat the ratings system were uncovered, and a station caught in a grand scheme to defraud the system would be "delisted." That meant their rating results weren't published, which could have a damaging economic impact. Advertising agencies use ratings to determine the stations on which they will buy commercials, and radio stations use ratings to decide how much they charge the advertisers. In other words, ratings are central to the business of radio, and when a station is delisted and doesn't have rating results a negative fiscal impact follows.

Disc jockeys often don't know or care about the details of ratings, but a good program director will study survey methodology to fully understand the process. After all, their success or failure is directly tied to the results. More than a few programmers tried to play into Arbitron's methodology by adding on-air slogans such as, "You're listening to WXXX, *write it down!*" A typical radio listener might have wondered why they should "write it down," but an Arbitron diary keeper could have been inspired to do exactly that. Radio guys and ladies were open to any nuanced twist or trick that could massage the system because heads rolled if the numbers weren't favorable.

Phoenix radio was fiercely competitive, and it wasn't just rock being heard on FM stations. Country music had always been popular in Arizona and there were also stations catering to the Hispanic community. This raises another gripe broadcasters once had with the diary ratings method. Minorities were less inclined to participate because of language barriers and basic mistrust. Over the years, ratings firms adjusted to these realities with non-English diaries and bigger cash incentives for minority group members to increase their involvement.

Arbitron recruited survey participants via phone calls, so if one didn't have a telephone they would never participate in a ratings study. More than a few radio programmers wondered if the listening patterns of non-telephone households varied significantly from those with phones. Such musing might seem silly, but ratings results are fundamental to the success of a radio station and much attention was paid to every aspect of the measurement system. The Arbitron story is fascinating, and I'll share more later.

Strange as it may seem, serious competition for KDKB came in the form of Top 40 radio. One was an FM station at 97.9 called "Cupid," a nickname derived from their call letters KUPD. The other was KRIZ at 1230 AM. Both stations were vastly different than ours, but they were well programmed, exciting to hear and really gave us a run for our money.

So, there I was in a major market and the college guys who owned and operated the station were extremely smart and thoroughly understood the radio business including ratings, budgets, ad sales, programming and engineering. I read as much as I could about the business so I wouldn't come off as a hick from Ohio with a straw hanging out of his mouth. I was a long way from Dayton, but radio was in my blood, and I was having a blast working and growing in the business.

The KDKB jocks resembled the station's audience, sporting long hair and a deep appreciation and love of the music. They were desert dogs to the max, just like their audience, and the station exploded in popularity. It was a Class C FM with a hundred thousand watts of power and an antenna located over sixteen hundred feet above average terrain. The station covered a radius of a hundred-plus miles, and its signal was so strong that occasional reception on false teeth or hearing aids occurred.

Because KDKB was the hip station playing all the newest rock album tracks, many folks who worked at other radio stations listened to us. It could be uncomfortable meeting someone from a competing radio station, especially if they asked a question like,

"So, what is Dennis McBroom really like?"

Rising From the Ashes

I would toss a flippant reply like, "Oh, he's cool" and walk away. Some broadcasters are more like "radio-groupies," and I avoided those characters as much as I could.

As one would expect, progressive music, well, progressed. From that one genre, a term originally coined by musical snobs, many tributaries became etched into the sands of creativity. Styles would evolve, split and divide into new forms, much like a single cell organism. The Beatles showed musicians how varying their approach and pushing the envelope further with each new release could bring immense success. It was a magical time for music and radio. Top 40 stations had the challenge of designing appealing programming with dissimilar musical styles like R&B, English rock, US rock, Motown and softer artists like James Taylor and the Carpenters, but rock stations had a more focused allure by their concentration on a single musical type, albeit one with depth and diversity.

The music I was playing on KDKB in early 1972 was certainly varied. Southern rock, exemplified by a major hit album from the Allman Brothers, emerged as an appealing sound. Hard rock was alive as well, with Black Sabbath releasing their fourth album. The Grateful Dead had been around since 1967, blending country, folk and rock into long concert jams leading many into mystical experiences.

Then there was a style some called "art rock" or "orchestral rock," represented by the fantastic music of groups like the Moody Blues, Yes and Emerson, Lake & Palmer, often shortened to ELP. The song *Lucky Man* is an ELP rock classic, and KDKB played it frequently. It starts with a folksy twelve-string guitar pattern, which Jimmy Page of Led Zeppelin sometimes employed, but on this song it's Greg Lake strumming and singing. As the song progresses, the powerful Moog synthesizer playing by Keith Emerson embellished the lyrics and, along with the military tattoo drumming of Carl Palmer, provided an immense bottom end giving the song power and enormity. The lyrics tell the tale of a man who goes off to war, *"He went to fight wars, For his country and his king. Of his honor and his glory, The people would sing."*

The irony of the song's title is revealed when the soldier was brought down by a bullet, and he died. That's why he was lucky, you see.

The Vietnam War would not end until April 30, 1975, and more than fifty-eight thousand American soldiers would die, but was that for honor or glory? The music we played questioned the authority of those in charge of the military-industrial complex. We deeply believed we were making a difference with every song we cued up on our trusty turntables.

20. The Clout of Money and Music

If you meticulously examine how a given thing actually works, you just might be disappointed by what you learn. Curiosity about how Congress works, how the Catholic church works or how your favorite radio station works can uncover complex answers. Most radio listeners turn on their favorite station and listen until it plays a song they don't like, or begins a stopset, then they dial around or punch into another station. These are not fans; they're consumers.

I'm sure you've had the experience of tuning into your favorite radio station one day to find it's gone and something completely different is in its place. Maybe your rock station is suddenly playing Spanish music. You may want to burst with anger or sink into disappointment, but always remember this. While the airwaves exist in the "public domain," citizens don't get to vote on where Bearman and LeRoy host their morning show. You might also want to know that getting a request played on demand is mostly fantasy. If you hear the song you requested soon after your call to the DJ, most likely it was already scheduled to play.

We didn't keep music logs in the 1960s. We had only a commercial log for business and billing purposes. Many music radio stations eventually required their DJs to write a list of songs and the times they played. When someone called the station to ask, "What was that great song you played last night around 7:15 where the lady asks the Lord to buy her a Mercedes Benz?" the music log provided a quick answer.

There are organizations that pay money to music publishers when their songs are played on the air. Two of the most familiar of these are ASCAP, the American Society of Composers, Authors and Publishers and BMI, Broadcast Music, Incorporated. SESAC, the Society of European Stage Authors and Composers is lesser known and once focused on publishers of more traditional song catalogs. In recent

171

years, however, more and more pop music artists have become affiliated with SESAC.

Once a year, BMI requires radio stations to list every song played over a one-week period. These official logs show the date, time of day, artist and title of every song broadcast. BMI collects and analyzes the logs to determine how much money each publisher will get for the airplay of their songs. A decades-long war broke out between the US Copyright Office, licensing agencies and record companies, which eventually led to artists receiving radio broadcast royalties along with the record sale percentages stated in their contracts. When an artist didn't own the publishing rights of their songs, millions of dollars were taken by ravenous record companies, greedy publishers, plotting producers and con-artist managers. The rights to song publishing started decades earlier with sheet music and piano rolls and the music industry adjusted over time.

A radio station may own vinyl records and CDs, but they don't own the music contained on them. Each station pays an annual fee for the music they play on the air. The fees were small in the beginning, but when those "non-profit" associations and groups learned about the massive profits of radio stations, they raised the fees. The associations calculate payments based on market size, and any station that refuses to pay the fees will receive a cease-and-desist court order listing the artists they may not play. Imagine being told one day you couldn't spin any Rolling Stones or Beatles records! So, to remain successful stations paid the piper, or in this case, the piper's agency.

The progressive music of the early 1970s played right into the hands of the new FM rock stations, but our potential popularity was diminished due to the lack of FM radios in cars. Some novel ideas emerged, like an FM tuner in the shape of a tape cartridge that you slid into your car's eight-track player. With the success of FM rock, many young people took their cars into small shops that installed powerful, customized AM/FM sound systems. It wasn't long before I would be stopped at a red-light hearing KDKB blasting out of the car right next to me through powerful speakers coupled to a two-hundred-watt amplifier. One guy had the bright idea of placing sensitive microphones at stoplights as a way to quantify radio listenership. That scheme was no more viable than estimating viewership of *I Love Lucy* by measuring water consumption caused by toilets flushing during the show's commercial breaks.

Corruption often creeps into businesses. Consider the grocery store that gets free product if they rack a vendor's bread at eye-level, or the restaurant owner who takes a bribe from a record company to fudge the jukebox counters that determine music licensing payments, or the scurrilous used car dealer who winds back odometers so he can charge more. Just as in these examples, the radio business was not immune to the wicked ways of powerful but corrupt people in high places.

Us KDKB disc jockeys were music freak hippies, and we looked the part. My hair was down to my shoulders and a well-trimmed black beard covered my face. It got more than a few kind comments from women. Lucinda Waterman was our music director, and with respect to lifestyle she was just like the rest of us. Of course, she took phone calls and visits from record promoters, whom we derisively called "record ducks," but she was an independent thinker and discovered new songs on her own. She shared her findings with the rest of us and, providing PD Al Murdoch had no objections, we were free to play those songs we liked. Record promotion people have a goal of getting their songs played on the radio while radio programmers have a goal of getting and maintaining high ratings. You're on the right track if you can sense conflict between the two. Music directors, or MDs, became a thing when program directors wanted to avoid "wasting time" with record promoters, both label guys and independents. The MD would listen to the new releases brought in by the promoters and recommend only those they felt would help station ratings.

Which brings us to the laws of the land. In the beginning, no one thought regulation would be needed for radio or television, but that changed over time. The producer of the TV quiz program *The $64,000 Question* passed answers onto contestants to make for a more exciting show as the potential cash prize grew and grew. Radio program directors were easy targets for ruthless promoters. One particular PD was offered a brand-new color TV to play a certain record. Confused and cautious, he called his famous boss and asked,

"I had already planned to add the song, so is it okay if I take the TV?"

Without skipping a beat the boss answered,

"Get two; I need a new television."

In the Top 40 world, a record company's goal was getting newly released songs on the Billboard Hot 100 chart as fast as possible, then having those songs rise higher and higher every week with a hope of it peaking at number one or at least in the top ten. It was a kind of self-feeding loop. Airplay of a record made it move up the chart and that movement caused other stations to play the song. More airplay and upward chart movement produced more record sales. The biggest gainers on the weekly charts were indicated by graphical markers known as "bullets." A promo man visiting a station might open his pitch by exclaiming, "Hey man, this week Cher is number five with a bullet! How could you not be playing her record?"

Rock programmers were never keen on judging a song by its Billboard chart position. Later in the life of industry newspapers and magazines there would be rock charts, and record label pressure would increase on that genre's programmers, but in the early 1970s we didn't care when or if Top 40 stations played rock songs because we had been airing those song for months before they did, sometimes even years.

I was shocked when Murdoch asked me to take his place on a panel at a radio conference in San Francisco. MD Lucinda would be going as well so, as they say, I would have someone to show me the ropes. My panel was titled, "Will FM Radio Kill AM Radio?" That was not exactly a subject I felt qualified to speak about, but hey, I had been winging my radio career from the git go.

After checking into the San Francisco Fairmont and getting settled in our rooms, Lucinda and I met in the lobby bar for drinks. The old hotel was incredibly impressive and once used in the TV show *Have Gun Will Travel* featuring the character Paladin as a bounty hunter. It was also used as a shooting location for the movie *Vertigo* and TV shows like *Hotel* and *Streets of San Francisco*. I was awestruck by the number of well-known radio folks who stopped by our table to tell Lucinda the fantastic things they were hearing about KDKB. She was always humble and polite and introduced me as the "Creative Production Director," which wasn't exactly my title, but in this business a little hyperbole goes a long way.

Suddenly there was loud reaction to a toast being made at the end of the bar. Standing there was a tall, handsome man with a perfect haircut and dressed to the nines in a tailored suit, crisp white shirt, red silk power tie and expensive, shiny shoes. Clustered around him was a throng of some of the hottest ladies I had ever seen, and just like him they were clothed to kill. The man spoke with a raspy voice and a thick southern accent. Lucinda looked at me,

"Sonny Joe, that's him."

"Who him?"

"That's Charlie Minor, the new head of promotion at A&M Records"

"Oh really, I was thinking he's a movie star."

A&M Records was the brainchild of Herb Alpert, the trumpet player with a funny first name, and his partner Jerry Moss. Their first hit record was released on a label they had named Carnival Records. *The*

Lonely Bull by Herb Alpert & The Tijuana Brass sold more than seven hundred thousand copies. When Moss and Alpert learned that another record company owned the Carnival name, they changed theirs to A&M, the first letters of the last names of the two principals. They moved into Charlie Chaplin's former Hollywood studio, and they added another Charlie in the form of Minor.

We sipped our beers and abruptly Lucinda looked shocked,

"Get ready, he's coming over."

I didn't even have a chance to react as Charlie and his "angels" descended on our sofa. The man dipped down to give Lucinda a substantial kiss on her right cheek,

"Well don't you look fabulous darling."

Lucinda introduced me, but once Minor realized I had nothing to do with selecting the music played on KDKB he refocused on her,

"I have been trying to get Murdoch to listen to this new band we signed named Supertramp. Baby, can you do me a big favor and make sure he listens to this when he's in his car?"

He handed her a brand-new shrink-wrapped tape cassette of the band's album and continued a rapid-fire delivery, which was an odd tempo for a southerner,

"What you're holding is going to be a smash and I already have a commitment from Buzzy Bennett at KCBQ to add the single. Y'all are going to be making the biggest mistake of the century if you don't jump on this right now, darlin'! Hey, Sonny Joe, good to meet you man."

First, I was floored Charlie remembered my name and next I was shocked watching his hand move down the small of the back of one of his women companions. They strolled across the barroom as Charlie cupped an angel butt while shucking and jiving at just about every table and sofa in the place. I turned to Lucinda,

"What the hell was that?"

"Well, he's a funny guy."

That is certainly not the word I would have used, but there will be more Minor later.

I picked Lucinda's brain about how to tackle my upcoming seminar panel. She suggested I mention our station call letters as much as possible, but not reveal any programming tactics or upcoming promotions. She warned that other Phoenix radio people would be there, and leaked information could do damage. I listened intently, but had to ask,

"So, what is the answer?"

"The answer to what?"

"Will FM radio kill AM radio?"

Without any hesitation, Lucinda answered,

"Absolutely."

It was late the last night of the convention, and I was ready for sleep. I arrived at the elevator and three guys were standing there waiting. They appeared a little spaced out, but I probably looked the same after a long, tiring day. The elevator arrived, the four of us walked in, then I gulped reading the industry-famous names on the tags of my fellow riders. It was the San Diego Top 40 radio mafia, starring programmer Buzz Bennett and Chuck Browning of KCBQ along with Bobby Ocean, the morning drive DJ on KGB. I was mightily impressed and tried to be cool,

"Hey, guys, how was the convention?"

Bennett looked at me, then down at my name tag,

"Oh, Sonny Joe on the radio. Nice FM beard, man. Righteous!"

The most embarrassing aspect of this encounter with radio royalty was the elevator doors had just opened and closed at my floor, and I was in such a daze I remained frozen in place until they opened again at the top floor. As the guys walked out, Buzzy looked back at me,

"This is the bar, Sonny Joe. You comin'?"

"Yeah, I mean no, sorry. I just missed my floor."

Watching them walk away I heard Browning say,

"Those FM guys always have the best drugs."

Both KGB and KCBQ were well-programmed, extremely exciting Top 40 radio stations in San Diego. Buzzy had been a dancer on a local TV music show in New Orleans and over time he advanced to an immensely successful on-air program director position at that city's Top 40 radio station, WTIX. Later, he became the PD of KGB, which was running Bill Drake's Boss Radio format. Soon, a legendary radio battle between Bennett and Drake would take place.

Buzz had applied for the PD opening at the flagship station of Drake's Boss Radio format, KHJ in Los Angeles. The opportunity became available when Paul Drew, the former program director, was elevated to VP of Programming at RKO Radio, KHJ's owner. Buzzy was crushed when he didn't get the KHJ job, and in revenge he quit KGB and took his act across the street to KCBQ. Radio legend Charlie Van Dyke says, "When Buzz was programming KGB, he told the staff their station was unique because it had only three call letters. When he rolled over to KCBQ, he made THAT station unique with only one call letter — Q!"

Mr. Bennett was a mysterious, almost unknowable person. He dressed in old-time Western garb, which at times included a cowboy hat, boots, and even chaps. Maybe this reflected a personality trait some psychologists refer to as "Cowboy Syndrome," a deep-rooted belief that a man should never show emotions because doing so would make him appear to be weak.

One major aspect of Buzzy's programming style was an alignment with psychology. Hear what legendary San Diego radio personality Shotgun Tom Kelly has to say, "When I got hired by Buzzy, he told me to prepare for my new on-air job by first reading a book." Dr. Joseph Murphy had penned the 1963 best-seller *The Power of Your Subconscious Mind*. In that tome, Murphy presented a metaphor of the subconscious mind being a magnet, "A magnetized piece of steel will lift about twelve times its own weight, and if you demagnetize this same piece of steel, it will not even lift a feather." Murphy claimed the subjective, subconscious mind controls the objective, conscious mind of every individual. Bennett latched onto that and produced promos planting seeds in the subconscious minds of his listeners, enticing and urging them to be loyal to his station.

Slick marketing, on-air contests with huge cash giveaways and great, sometimes unexpected, songs in proper rotations were more practical aspects of Bennett's masterful radio programming. I should also mention that dirty tricks were a part of his arsenal. The audio lines to the KGB transmitter were cut on the very day Buzzy launched his new format on KCBQ, giving the "Q" a serious advantage until repairs were made at KGB. Yes, sometimes radio people go to an extreme just to get a leg up, even if it's totally against the law.

KCBQ killed KGB in the ratings under Buzzy's leadership, so it's fair to say he "out-Draked" Bill Drake. I cannot overstate what a huge event this was in the radio industry. Bennett had dethroned the king of Top 40 radio programming, and his stature in the radio industry grew instantly and tremendously.

As for me, I was called into the PD's office after returning from the Gavin convention in San Francisco The general manager was also there, and both men had stern, serious looks on their faces. Al Murdoch motioned to the chair in front of his desk, and I took a seat while the

GM settled himself on a small filing cabinet. I flashed on that meeting with Rev Ray back in college and wondered what in the hell was going on. These guys looked like they meant business and I was internally freaking out. Al threw down the latest copy of Billboard, open to the page covering the conference,

"Do you know about this?"

I moved closer and read the headline: PHOENIX FM PD PREDICTS THE DEATH OF AM RADIO. The article contained a picture of the panel which stunned me because Al Murdoch's name was printed on the plaque in front of me. The article and captioned picture indicated Al had made the statement, not me, probably the result of my last-minute placement on the panel. I took a breath,

"I'm so sorry. Ah I didn't...."

Suddenly, the two guys burst into laughter. I was just about to have a heart attack and my bosses were cracking up,

"We're just messing with you, man. This is fabulous press! We are reprinting it and sending it out to the buyers at all the advertising agencies."

The GM was now grinning ear to ear,

"Sonny Joe, we want to grab as many AM bucks as we can, and this will ring the bell on our cash register. Fantastic job!"

He shook my hand and walked out of the room, leaving me to unravel a lesson in all of it. I concluded that bravado, braggadocio and bluster were key elements that made radio tick. That aside, I would never want a quote of someone else being attributed to me.

After our trip, Lucinda was enthusiastic about the song *It's a Long Road* from Supertramp's debut album released in the summer of 1971 and a few of the jocks began playing it. I thought it was a rambling piece of self-indulgent musical masturbation and couldn't understand why

Lucinda suggested the song. I had the utmost respect for her, but I wondered if that Minor guy used more than the power of persuasion. There was no way Buzzy Bennett would ever add that song to KCBQ.

Eight years later, Supertramp would release their musical masterpiece with a similar name. *Take the Long Way Home* which became a smash in 1979 and, yes, they did indeed take the long way. We must give credit to Misters Alpert and Moss because they stuck with the band far longer than any other company would have. That's called loyalty.

Phoenix was growing on me. I even bought a pair of cowboy boots, but I refused to wear one of those heavy hats. I was a baseball cap kind of guy.

The station had gone through some minor changes those first couple of years. Our crazy night DJ caused an uproar by bringing a loaded gun into the studio, but he was excused after claiming to have seen a rattlesnake in the parking lot one night. Frank was a paranoid guy who was exactly the person you didn't want to be carrying a loaded weapon. The management scolded him, and he promised not to do it again, but guns and radio stations have a long history of strange coexistence. We'll get to that shortly. See, another tease.

21. People Die, Eventually

I called my mother shortly before Christmas 1972 to chat about coming home for the holidays. She seemed somewhat off, so I probed,

"You don't sound like yourself. What's up, Mom?"

"Oh, Herbie, your father is sick and I'm so worried. The doctors don't know what it is."

Well, I was on the next plane to Cincinnati, which was the fastest route to Dayton. I was given five days off work, but even this early into the trip my strength and positivity were completely zapped. Dad was sick and it had something to do with his lungs. He once mentioned to me a few of the guys who fabricated parts at the cash register factory had lung problems. We would later learn the cause wasn't the nature of their work but rather the building where they worked. The factory was insulated with asbestos and the men were suffering from mesothelioma, the asbestos-related cancer discovered in the 1960s. Dad's prognosis wasn't good.

I asked my mother if I should take a leave of absence from the station and stay with her and the old man, but she was adamant,

"Herbert, you go back to work. You'll be home soon enough, and you'll need more time off for …."

She started crying and I hugged her. Talking with dad was troubling. He had lost a lot of weight and his words were forced through short breaths and much coughing. I had to sneak off to my old bedroom for a good cry.

The long flight back to Phoenix gave me time to process the situation, and there was nothing easy about knowing the person who brought me into this world would shortly be leaving it. I was saddened by the events in Dayton, and I kept thinking about a phrase I heard a Santa Fe asshole say after Dr. Bobby's death, "Well, people die, eventually." It was true, but so blunt a statement no grieving human would get the meaning, instead they would resent the words.

In February 1973, I got the call from my Uncle Carl telling me my father passed away on the last day of the month. I headed back to Dayton with a heavy heart.

My father was a conservative, God-fearing man, but he had an unquenchable thirst for knowledge about how things worked. He taught me so much, and I inherited his sense of humor and electromechanical mind. I truly am my father's son, his only son. My deep sadness worsened when I realized he would never meet his grandkids, take a walk with them or show them how a clock worked. If only he could have lived a little longer. If only he could have slowed down the damn clock.

The funeral was quite a proper event, just as my dad would have wanted. All the relatives from seven states came and the food, oh God the food. Our home was full of currywurst, schnitzel, German potato salad and deep-fried everything. The menu didn't blunt my sorrow but did produce ample amounts of gas.

KDKB had given me a two-week leave, which was a truly kind and generous allowance. One of my high school chums invited me to Wright Brothers Beef and Brew for drinks, and I was absolutely floored when I walked in. I spied my friend immediately but sitting with him at a large round table were Brewster Billy, Skip, Brady and even Sarah Lee along with, wait for it, a cake for me! That gathering was the absolute best thing that could have possibly happened at such an otherwise sad time. The beer did flow, and the stories were told, properly embellished of course. Brady was spinning one of the yarns and I just had to stop him,

"Hey, you know Brady, I was actually there and that's not what happened. Rev Ray did not paddle me!"

The night wore on, the bar was about to close and what started as a bar gathering among four amigos ended up as two radio buddies chatting. Completely out of the blue, Billy started to lay out plans for a road trip to Pittsburgh, but I was having trouble following his cryptic and disconnected words. It didn't help that he probably had one more beer than he should have. Then Billy posed a question,

"You ever hear of a guy named Buzz Bennett?"

That directness and clarity snapped me to immediate attention,

"Yeah, for sure, he's that batshit crazy PD from KCBQ in San Diego and KRIZ in Phoenix. I briefly met him at a convention."

"Well, he's no longer out west. He's in Pittsburgh."

"What?"

"An influential Hawaiian broadcaster who I think is also a US Senator bought NBC's oldline radio stations WJAS AM and FM in Pittsburgh. They are going to flip the stodgy AM programming to Top 40 in a couple of weeks."

"Billy, how can you possibly know all this?"

"Bennett called me to interview for the station's production voice, but I didn't get the job. He hired a guy named Mark Driscoll, a real radio pro."

We learned the esteemed US Senator from Hawaii was Cecil Heftel, who owned KGMB-AM-FM-TV in Honolulu. Cec, as he was known, was a powerful, non-native in Hawaii and a well-respected businessman. His company was Heftel Broadcasting, and the FCC had already approved its acquisition of the two WJAS properties.

Our hasty plan was to jump in Billy's Plymouth and head for the Steel City to hear the launch of a new radio station. Soon, the entire broadcasting industry would buzz, pun intended, with the radio news coming from the Steel City. Fate and timing handed Billy and me the perfect opportunity for a radio travel adventure.

The trip was a wonderful antidote for my father's passing, and my mother so loved Billy she endorsed us leaving her alone to settle dad's affairs. Billy, organized as ever, had booked a room with double beds at the Greentree Marriott. It was only a short drive through the Fort Pitt Tunnel to reach downtown Pittsburgh. The room rate was great, but what we found waiting for us at the hotel was something far better than we could have ever imagined.

You know that old expression, "I would love to have been a fly on the wall when…" right? Well, Billy and I hit the jackpot. Because of its proximity to the airport and the city, our hotel was also being used as the headquarters for all the newly hired Heftel broadcasters who were gathering in the city to prepare the launch of their new radio station.

I was concerned that, should we bump into one another, Buzzy Bennett would recognize me from our elevator encounter and splat one of the flies on the wall, namely me. Billy had no connection to that San Francisco encounter, so he was safe. My best attempt at a disguise was shaving off the beard I had been wearing for more than three years. Billy laughed hard when I came out of the bathroom, sans face covering,

"Well lookie here, it's little Herbie Klotenfelder from Dayton!"

We found out that the owner of this new station had a loose, casual style, and the best-in-the-radio-business team Cec had assembled was taking advantage of that by partying hard at the hotel twenty-four hours a day. They were encamped in a wide-open hospitality suite they called radio central, feeding on an endless buffet of chilled shrimp, lobster, cold cuts, breadsticks, beer and hard liquor. The large table was constantly restocked by the hotel staff. After checking in, Billy and I casually strolled into the suite to check things out, and soon encountered a voluptuous lady named Peggy, holding her cigarette in a very sensual way. She looked a bit like Elizabeth Taylor and just assumed we were part of the new station's staff,

"Hey, if you guys want something special just call fucking room service but watch the pot smoking. Do that on the balcony."

Do you remember that fast talking DJ we heard on the way home from the CSN&Y concert in Cleveland years ago? Well, that guy, Jack Armstrong, was about to become the prime nighttime jock on Pittsburgh's new radio station, and the woman we just met was his wife Peggy. Seven months later she would be awakened by the station's morning DJ to do a sketch with Jack. Not realizing she was on the air, Peggy said, "Fuck you!" to a guy asking if Jack was going to run for the recently vacated office of US Vice President Spiro Agnew. That prompted the FCC to enact a rule declaring a phone call could not be aired unless the person on the other end of the line knew they were being broadcast. All DJs were now required to ask permission off the air, before putting someone on the air.

Billy and I ate a yummy free lunch, then spied a poster board leaning against a wall. It was a stylized graphic of the famous Keep on Truckin' cartoon image of R. Crumb, the famous "underground" artist who created Zap Comix. Central to the image was the number 13 and the letter Q — 13Q. The bright orange lettering had a strange yellow shadow; I mean, shadows are supposed to be dark. The Q was a cartoon record, with its little tail shaped like a turntable tonearm, or a limp male organ, depending on your point of view.

The station had an average signal at 1320 AM, but it would soon become clear that wouldn't hurt them in the least. The new Pittsburgh station would launch running what was now known throughout the industry as the Q Format, which originated with Buzz Bennett's programming of KCBQ in San Diego. Trends pop up quickly in the radio biz, and Buzzy's masterful skewering of Bill Drake's KGB in "America's Finest City" was now legendary. Across the country radio stations were changing call letters to add a Q and adopting Bennett's programming techniques.

Some background information might help here. NBC was one of the oldest radio broadcasting companies in the United States. David Sarnoff started the radio group back in 1926, and those stations became the most popular in the nation. Before the 7-7-7 rule was enacted, NBC owned radio stations in all the major markets, such as WNBC and WJZ in New York. To keep the FCC at bay, NBC divided their empire into a "Red network" and a "Blue network." By 1941, however, the radio sheriffs in Washington decided that NBC had way too much influence with so many owned stations and a large network that provided programming to a multitude of listeners. They forced NBC to sell the Blue Network, which eventually became ABC Radio.

When TV developed into the major bread earner of the network, NBC decided to sell off its less profitable radio stations. Because NBC was a large national company, their owned local stations were strapped with huge union contracts for the engineering and announcing staffs. Also, the stations were being run like they were operating in the 1950s, with massive production teams, commercial writers and creative directors. I'm surprised they didn't have makeup and hair stylists. Whatever NBC stiffness still existed at what would soon become 13Q, was about to be blown up with the new owners.

In our capacity as official flies on the wall, Billy and I observed the 13Q crew partying into the wee hours of the morning with everyone drifting away by sunrise. We realized that if we got to the suite early each morning, we would be unobserved while grabbing some goodies and carrying them to our room for a feast.

In addition to Jack Armstrong, we learned that Heftel was bringing other major radio talent onboard, including Batt Johnson from KCBQ, Dennis Waters from WPGC in D.C., Sam Holman from too many stations to mention and Mark Driscoll, who was also working in D.C. While the team was preparing for their Monday, March 12, 1973 sign-on, Buzzy Bennett was plotting some devious magic he would perform when the station was officially handed off from NBC to Heftel.

I crossed paths with Buzz late one night and he didn't recognize me. I don't think it was my beardless face; he seemed to be completely wasted. People said he had three apothecary jars in his room, one filled with quaaludes, one with cocaine and one with amazing weed. Bennett looked the part of a druggie with long, gangly hair and a devil beard. He wore dark rimmed glasses and was always smoking… something. His costume was eclectic, somewhere between street hippy and desert rat, with an inside-out denim jacket far ahead of its time. However, when Buzz talked the whole roomful of his disciples fell silent so as not to miss a single word of this radio-wise, mythical creature from some distant land. He worked incredibly long hours because he could, then he would crash for a day or more.

The day the FCC officially transferred the WJAS licenses from the National Broadcasting Company to Heftel Broadcasting, Buzz Bennett was fully prepared and ready to go. The man was intimidating even to crazy radio people, so just imagine how he came off to folks totally removed from the rock and hippy lifestyles. Bennett was like a Cheech and Chong character, only with an almost terroristic presence.

Mark Driscoll describes the scene that day in the WJAS offices and studios located in downtown Pittsburgh's Kossman Building, "Mr. Bennett confidently strode into the station's lobby, preceded by two immense Dobermans and followed by all the ragtag members of the new on-air team." As if that grand entrance wasn't enough, much more would soon unfold.

The receptionist greeted Buzzy with a turned-up nose, as if she was confronting a homeless derelict,

"May I help you sir?"

"Hey man, I'm the new owner. What's your name?"

"I'm Dorothy Miller, sir. How may I help you?"

"Well, man, big changes are coming."

At that time, every NBC-owned station had a large corporate logo on the wall of their lobby, which I always thought was bizarre because the station's call letters were dwarfed by those huge NBC letters. Buzzy walked over to the wooden NBC/WJAS logo, reached up, and ripped it right off the wall. Then, in what has come to be known as the "walk-through from hell," Buzz approached each desk in every office, and in his slurring hip lingo asked its occupant their name and role at the station. No matter the reply, Bennett said only,

"Well, man, big changes are coming."

The WJAS staff freaked out, and many just dropped whatever they were doing and left. A station that had about fifty employees at 9 a.m. was reduced to maybe twenty by noon, mostly union engineers and newscasters. Buzzy summoned the subconscious mind of each of his targets and triggered their fight or flight mechanism to the latter option. Their conscious minds urged one thing, "Get the hell out of here."

The Pittsburgh radio community didn't know what to make of the 13Q newcomers. Most felt they were "radio carpetbaggers," entering the city with deep disrespect and an unruly attitude. As for the radio audience, well we'll soon see their story was much different.

13Q was most likely the only Top 40 station in the country not using call letter jingles. I'll explain why in just a bit, but this is an opportune time to talk about radio jingles and their storied history in broadcasting.

Back in the late 1940s, roughly ten years before the Top 40 format was born, many radio stations featured live orchestras and vocalists as entertainment. Often the bands would perform "little songs" to sell the benefits of their sponsors. These were known as jingles, and they sang the virtues of almost every product imaginable from soap to soup to cereal to cigars. A few radio stations had their own in-house orchestras and vocalists create jingles to promote themselves, which helped them stand out and "cement" their call letters in listeners' minds.

Bill Meeks was a Dallas, Texas native and bandleader who led two orchestras at his hometown radio station KLIF. Meeks wrote jingles for both the station's sponsors and KLIF itself. In 1951 he formed an advertising agency named PAMS, which stood for **P**roduction **A**dvertising **M**erchandising **S**ervice. The company's main focus was music for advertising, but Meeks produced a collection of ten radio station jingles he named "Series 1" and sent a demo tape to radio stations.

Bill recorded the music first so it could be used for multiple stations, meaning only vocalists would need to be hired when a jingle package was cut for a particular station. Meeks wrote the music in a way that the call letters could contain various numbers of syllables and be sung with different melody lines. So diverse station names like "Seventy-Seven W-A-B-C," "Big D in Hartford" and "Wonderful Radio London" could each have a unique musical signature. Thus, syndicated jingles were born.

Over time, jingles found a place within just about every radio format such as Country, AC and even News. Other jingle companies came and went, but PAMS had the lion's share of radio clients during the heyday of Top 40 on AM radio. Jon Wolfert, a producer and audio engineer at PAMS, struck out on his own in 1974 to open JAM Creative Productions, also located in Dallas. That prosperous company still exists today, producing jingles for commercials as well as radio and television stations around the world.

Now, let's get back to Pittsburgh and 13Q. Previously, radio station giveaways were mostly concert tickets, 45 RPM records and small prizes provided by sponsors, but Buzzy's 13Q was about to reach into its own pockets in a legendary way. The lack of jingles gave the station a unique and remarkable sound. In their place was a magnificent promo, voiced in a breathless, hypnotic cadence by Mark Driscoll, suggesting listeners were about to become rich because of this new radio station.

"When your phone rings, don't say hello, say 'I listen to the new sound of 13Q' and win thirteen thousand dollars instantly!"

That promo ran repeatedly, and the bombardment of listeners' subconscious minds triggered conscious and immediate loyalty to this new radio station. Bennett was masterfully applying the concepts covered in Dr. Joseph Murphy's book *The Power of Your Subconscious Mind*, and that juju worked. Years later, radio historian Jeff Roteman would write, "In 1973, 13Q came on with a bang!" Boy, he was spot on.

Soon, just about everyone in Pittsburgh was answering their phone with that phrase, which helped further spread the word about this fresh, electrifying, high-energy Top 40 radio station. And while Buzz Bennett had the demeanor of a far-out hippy, he was also a deep-thinking, research-driven radio marketing genius. 13Q established an in-house call center that surveyed Pittsburgh radio listeners to determine the biggest hits and best songs to play. The kids making those calls were mockingly referred to as "phone turkeys," but many of those teenagers went on to have great careers in radio, research and music.

When I later met Mark Driscoll, he shared some advice Buzzy once gave him, and I'll do my best to paraphrase it here. "Our goal is to make the listener love us as we speak through a cold hard piece of metal." Could the strength of that magnetized metal be enough to lift an entire radio station into stellar ratings?

It wasn't long before drugs and hubris pushed things in a somewhat out-of-hand direction at the new station. One particular day, the DJ staff was welcomed into the station conference room and, incredibly, a substantial amount of cocaine had been artistically formed into a giant 13Q logo at the center of the table. Meanwhile, some of the jocks were not renting apartments in favor of staying on at the Marriott hotel, placing extravagant room service orders and, you know, sucking on the Heftel corporate teat. Cecil was livid when hearing about this and soon flew into Pittsburgh to close the hotel account. Some said the final tab amounted to hundreds of thousands of dollars in food and amenities.

On top of that, there were room damages. Cec previously had a good relationship with the Marriott family, but the 13Q shenanigans at their Greentree hotel tremendously stressed the friendship.

Mischief aside, 13Q was discharging a strategic assault on Pittsburgh's radio listenership that would have a ruinous result for one station in particular. A little background of the city's radio ratings history will help paint the perfect picture of 13Q's impact.

KDKA ran a Full-Service format, featuring a heavy emphasis on local news, civic events, traffic and weather, with music being a second-class entity. KDKA had always been the number one radio station in the Pittsburgh ratings.

KQV launched their Top 40 format in 1958, and for fifteen years practically always landed in the number two ratings spot with occasional burps and ratings aberrations. They were far and away the favorite station of teens and young adults. When industry rumors hinted at 13Q's programming intentions, KQV made a programming change which in hindsight would be seen as a tactical misstep. They softened their sound by removing all rock songs and placing an emphasis on slow ballads. They purposely abandoned their young listeners, thinking that catering to an older audience would keep their ratings strong in the face of 13Q. They essentially rolled over and played dead, handing off an important audience segment to 13Q before they even hit the air.

The first measurement of 13Q's audience came in Arbitron's ratings for the fall of 1973. KDKA remained far and away the market's top radio station with a 25.4 share, the same sort of number they had always earned. 13Q roared into the number two position with a 14.8 share of the audience. KQV, which had scored a 6.2 share in the previous ratings book, tumbled to 3.9 and became the sixth-ranked station in the market, a devastating defeat. Now, despite 13Q's imposing ratings debut there was a strategic miscalculation hidden in their numbers, which I'll share in a bit.

The revolutionary tactics of 13Q taught radio programmers a valuable lesson. Giving away money was not only fun but doing so earned a large audience quickly. Not all stations could afford ongoing cash calls, but those who copied the idea raised the bar by increasing the amount of the monetary prizes. The radio industry learned that compelling, well-produced promos, voiced with drama and authority, were better than jingles because they told a story. The 13Q cash call promos were emotional triggers. The station created even more excitement and energy when Driscoll produced dynamic promos featuring the voices of excited listeners screaming they had just won thirteen thousand dollars, giving Pittsburghers the vicarious and visceral thrill of getting rich.

13Q also applied some technical trickery to the music they played. Cecil Heftel was a partner in Nashville's Ken-Tel recording studio. Working with the station, the studio applied audio compression and frequency equalization to their music, making the songs louder, punchier and more sparkly on the air. The station also increased the playback speed of their songs, making other stations playing the same records sound slow and sleepy. Even though it was an AM station, 13Q had an incredible aural presence.

At the time, some stations called their on-air giveaways "rip offs," as in, "Be the tenth caller and rip us off," but Buzzy came up with the term "zip off." Walking around Pittsburgh's Point State Park one night, probably high, he glanced toward one of the inclines traveling up and down the side of Mount Washington. The incline tracks were outlined with red and white lights, and Buzz imagined the sight as a giant zipper. He fantasized pulling that zipper to open the mountain as prizes and money exploded all over the city below. Now it could be a myth, but there you have one account of how the 13Q zip off was born.

13Q's debut ratings were so hot that Cecil dispatched Buzzy to the other Heftel-owned stations to work his magic. Eventually, programmers like Bill Tanner, Robert W. Walker and others would caretake and refine what Bennett had created. Heftel also had a mature adult in the room to oversee all the programming, a guy named Dick Casper. He and Bennett argued constantly, and this undoubtedly constrained some of Buzzy's more outrageous plans. Genius is not always understood, especially when the bill arrives at the table.

Despite all the careful planning, an invisible wrench in the works would eventually trigger the failure of 13Q. When the station first hit the air, the programming was simulcast on the AM and FM signals Heftel had purchased. They were under time pressure, knowing the FCC would not allow them to simulcast forever. Their plan was to change the FM call letters to WSHH, brand the station as WISH-FM, and broadcast a syndicated package of beautiful music. That format was sold by a guy named Jim Schulke, an ex-Paramount TV executive and Harvard MBA, and the station spent some time negotiating the deal with him. The programming would be supplied on large reels of tape to run on an automation system, and it took considerable time to purchase and install the necessary hardware. Months had passed before WISH-FM debuted on the air.

Now here's where the flaw comes in. WWSW AM and FM were two of the oldest stations in the 'burgh. Seeing 13Q's ratings success and knowing part of it flowed from their FM signal, WWSW's owners flipped their FM to a Top 40 format and named the new station WPEZ. The PD was Bob Pittman, yes, the same guy who would go on to invent MTV and even later head up the large iHeartMedia radio conglomerate.

Consider this bit of statistical analysis. The ratings book after 13Q stopped simulcasting, their 14.8 share dropped to 7.2. That was quite good for an AM station at 1320, but less than half of what they had for their debut. Once WPEZ steadied, they earned a 4.5 share, remarkably close to 13Q's FM share when they were simulcast. This illustrates the concept of audience fragmentation, which we'll further investigate later.

Gamesmanship was taking place on both sides of the 13Q/WPEZ battle. The WPEZ general manager interviewed two guys for the PD position at what would soon become Pittsburgh's newest Top 40 radio station, Bob Pittman and a guy named Ron Brindle. After the two met, Brindle believed Pitman was better qualified for the job. In a rare radio moment, Brindle told the GM that Bob Pittman should be the PD. The GM handed the program director job to Bob and Brindle became the station's assistant PD. Now, here's where it gets rich. Pittman wanted Brindle to use the air name Buzzy Bennett to play a major head game with 13Q's architect. Brindle pushed back, and the two compromised on the name Buzz B. Brindle. Ron continued using that moniker throughout the rest of his radio career.

WPEZ wasn't as flashy and outrageous as 13Q, but many listeners were attracted to that powerful signal playing their favorite pop songs in full-fidelity FM stereo. WPEZ dented 13Q's ratings, and the two stations ended up splitting smaller pieces of the ratings pie. As for all the historical AM Top 40 radio stations in the United States, the FM writing was on the wall.

There was one stop between San Diego and Pittsburgh for Mr. Buzz Bennett, whose legal name was Russell Bennett. Let's jump back to San Diego for this part of our story. Bartell Media Corporation, the family-run owner of KCBQ, went through some corporate stress when Downe Communications bought a considerable number of Bartell stock shares. This probably spooked Bennett, who convinced his assistant Chuck Browning and four other DJs to quit their jobs and move to Phoenix to work at KRIZ-AM. It was an abrupt and foolish act, but something else was driving radio gypsy Buzz. The two forces of his conscious and subconscious minds were at war. Certain addictions were taking their toll.

According to Shotgun Tom Kelly, Bennett took a rare day off at KRIZ, his new AM Top 40 station, and told Chuck "The Chucker" Browning he would be large and in charge. Buzzy was livid when he returned the next day and discovered Browning had added one song to the KRIZ playlist, a song Buzz did not like. Bennett ordered The Chucker to remove the song, but he belligerently refused to do so. Buzz then bounced his buddy Browning, who promptly pulled a Buzzy by running across the street to program KUPD, the Phoenix Top 40 FM station. A potent powder was fueling Mr. Bennett's judgement.

Buzz needed to be the absolute and final arbiter of which songs would air on his radio station and this was often demonstrated in the way Bennett dealt with record promoters. A guy from Mercury Records came by to play Buzzy the new Rod Stewart release *Reason to Believe*. Bennett wasn't impressed, and he flipped over the 45 to hear the B side. He loved that song rather than the one the label was pushing. The promo guy insisted he not play it on the radio because it wasn't Mercury's "priority." Buzzy recoiled like a rattlesnake and added the song to the playlist.

To show his power over the label guy, who claimed he would get fired if KRIZ played the wrong side, Buzzy put a contest on the air. It urged listeners to count the number of times KRIZ played the new Rod Stewart release during an entire week, the length of one Arbitron survey period, and the listener with the correct answer would win ten thousand dollars. The song was *Maggie May* and Buzzy broke that record, radio lingo for being the first to play a song that goes on to become a huge nationwide hit. So, another legend was added to the Buzz Bennett folklore.

According to Shotgun Tom, "Buzzy wrote an ongoing collection of promos claiming KRIZ played the fewest commercials, when in fact the AM outlet played a ton of spots per hour. Browning, knowing how Bennett would fabricate any claim to reach the inner mind of each listener, decided to do something about his habit of lying." Soon, billboards went up all around Phoenix that read, "KUPD – Cars, Cash & the Truth." Not long after, Buzzy Bennett packed his bags and headed for Pittsburgh to make radio history yet again.

People Die, Eventually

It was exactly as predicted in the misattributed quote of a famous Phoenix PD. FM eventually did kill the AM star — and a few legendary radio programmers along the way.

22. It's a Damn Business

I was looking forward to my return to Phoenix and KDKB, but most of all to sleeping on my waterbed that first night back. Five years earlier, a guy named Charles Hall handed in his thesis project to his prof at San Francisco State University. It detailed filling a thick, plastic membrane with gel and using it as a bed mattress. The idea was the gelatinous mattress would conform to the shape of the body lying atop it to provide ultimate comfort. Before coming to market, Hall replaced the gel with water and yes, you guessed it, the waterbed was born. Hall later added a heater to address complaints from initial purchasers about the mattress being too cold.

As I sloshed my way into bed that first night back, I was uncomfortable with something I heard was happening at my radio station. Suddenly it was feeling less like my good old college radio days and more like a business. It had to do with the relationship between the programming and sales departments at KDKB.

Imagine a Venn diagram showing the logical connections of three typical departments in a radio station, programming, promotions and sales. When those teams are fine-tuned and working in unison, they produce great radio, productive interaction with the audience and revenue for the sales team. As for the latter, salespeople are paid slightly lower salaries, but are awarded commissions on the advertising they sell. Some get fifteen percent while top dogs might net twenty percent of each sales contract. The station never pays salespeople upfront. Commissions are paid quarterly, or at another interval stated in the salesperson's contract. The essential point is salespeople don't see the green until the station has cleared the commercials, aired them and placed the sponsor's dough in the bank.

Radio stations have always done promotions, and the best PDs work with their sales and promotion managers to get desirable prizes, either through trade deals in which the station exchanges commercials for goods from the advertiser, or the client gives the station free samples of products they want to push. Ideally, the program director will have the final say in any station promotion because he or she is responsible for the station's image and ratings. A poorly designed promotion can adversely affect either or both.

There are times when a station's general manager is sold a bill of goods by the sales department, and the unlucky PD is forced to run the promotion despite its unfavorable effects on listenership. An example would be having your morning crew broadcast from an outdoor billboard twenty-four hours a day until they raise a million dollars for a local hospital. The hospital promises the station an advertising purchase when the goal is reached. What could go wrong? Well, if the morning team doesn't reach the goal, the station's image suffers and the team becomes disheartened. Maybe the morning team hates the idea of working outside in cold weather and offers lackluster on-air support of the promotion. Perhaps the worst-case scenario is the promotion successfully ends, and the hospital spends their hundred-thousand-dollar ad campaign on another station. A great PD always speculates about the terrible things that could possibly happen, and that's why they should be the final checkpoint before a promotion hits the air.

When I returned to Phoenix, a standoff between management, sales and programming was underway. An account executive brought in a proposal from his biggest client, Waterbed City, who wanted to sponsor hourly weathercasts. These were certainly commonplace in the business, but the audience of a hip, Progressive FM station didn't care about weather. KDKB did have a sharp focus on news, far greater than the average rock station in those days, and perhaps that motivated the sales guy, but there was a subtle distinction between meaningful newscasts targeted to the station's audience and a mundane weather report.

The proposition was a weather forecast that would run twice an hour bracketed with ten-second commercials for Waterbed City. For my non-radio readers, bracketed means before and after. The PD said no, but the salesguy was waving a five-thousand-dollar monthly check in the face of the general manager.

There are times I believe I have a tattoo on my forehead stating, "Ask me, I know what to do," so I wasn't surprised about what he wanted when the GM pulled me aside,

"Hey, Sonny Joe, you got a minute?"

He asked me to come into his office and closed the door behind us. He opened with,

"First our deepest condolences on the passing of your father. You, okay?"

"Yeah, and thanks for the flowers. My mother was deeply touched by them, and she wanted me to thank you for the time off. It meant a lot."

"No problem, man. You may be wondering why I called you in. Have you heard about the Waterbed City situation?"

I was a little hesitant to say anything that could get me in trouble with PD Al Murdoch, but I felt compelled to respond,

"Sure, that's going to be a challenge."

He leaned in and listened for the why,

"Our audience doesn't care about the weather, besides it's Phoenix. All they care about is how hot it's going to be."

"But the temperature would be in the weather."

I sensed he was pitching the idea to get my buy-in, but I had to defend KDKB's programming,

"Sir, go to happy hour at the Rusty Spur this afternoon and ask our listeners if they care about the weather. That might give you an answer. Besides, we should never slow down the flow of the music. Why doesn't Waterbed City just buy commercials? I'll produce some killer spots for them."

He thanked me and the next day he smiled and gave me a big pat on the back,

"Sonny Joe, you were right. A hundred percent of the listeners I talked to don't give a shit about the weather. Thanks for your input. I get it now!"

About a year later my GM, the same guy, handed me a newspaper article from his hometown paper, the Cincinnati Inquirer. I was blown away that a Cincinnati paper would run a story about a radio station in Pittsburgh, but it seemed 13Q was making news everywhere. When he handed me the article, he winked and said,

"I think you'll enjoy reading this. It's a story about conflict between programming and sales."

First, some background. In the late 1800s, Pittsburgh was an industrial juggernaut with steel mills operating twenty-four hours a day, even before automobiles were invented. The steel industry was cranking out metal for buses and streetcars, which provided the majority of public transportation.

The Monongahela Street Railway Company followed the lead of its counterparts in many other forward-moving cities with a brilliant plan. They built a park at the suburban end of one of their new trolley lines to induce weekend travel to a relaxing destination. These were called "trolley parks," and on May 30, 1898, Pittsburgh's Kennywood Park opened. Originally it was a destination for picnics and ball games, but soon the rail company added amusement rides and food to boost revenue. Early on, Kennywood became one of America's major amusement parks and its success continues to this day.

Kennywood had several wooden roller coasters, including one named the Pippin which first opened in 1924. Many years later, in 1968, that coaster was restyled and renamed Thunderbolt. It developed a reputation as having some of the most thrilling drops, curves and bends of any rollercoaster in the world.

Kennywood and 13Q entered into a Labor Day promotional agreement. The idea was to have the station's midday disc jockey, Dennis "The Menace" Waters, continuously ride the Thunderbolt leading up to a world record for the most consecutive rotations on a roller coaster. Dennis, not wanting to look anything less than a team player, didn't reveal his lifelong challenge with gastrointestinal bleeding and it wasn't more than two hours of round and round on Thunderbolt before Dennis started coughing up blood, which earned him a trip to the emergency room. So, 13Q turned to their superhero nighttime jock, Jack Armstrong, to get over to Kennywood Park.

The promotion was cooked up by 13Q's GM, the station's sales department and Kennywood and the station heavily promoted this big event weeks before the holiday. The fall is typically a slow time at amusement parks, and it was hoped the promotion would attract a lot of visitors to the park on the Labor Day weekend. Kennywood, stating concerns about safety and insurance, insisted one of its employees, a guy named Bernie Kusibab, ride with the 13Q jock the entire time.

Jack, armed with a case of Pepto-Bismol and a great attitude, climbed aboard the roller coaster. Folks from the Guinness Book of World Records were in attendance, and they would not consider the rotations of Waters, so the count had to restart at the beginning. Sadly, there is no official record of exactly how many rides would capture the crown, but some sources claim it was seven hundred and fifty rotations.

Jack persisted through Friday night, all day Saturday and into Sunday. He was obviously spaced out and grumpy while closing in on the world's record, but nothing was going to stop him. Once Jack broke the record, the public would be allowed to board the famous coaster, which was one of the most popular attractions at Kennywood. The place was packed with families and station listeners waiting for Jack Armstrong to cop the award so they could take their turns on the Thunderbolt.

Jack was just about to make the final rotation on the Thunderbolt for the record when park management asked him to get off the coaster. Jack, believing he was either tripping on acid or had died and gone to hell asked,

"Wait, I need only one more ride. What do you mean get off?" The Guinness representative agreed,

"He's right, the contestant must have one more ride to achieve the world record."

At this point in reading the article, I began to understand the meaning of the words my GM spoke in Phoenix when he handed me the clipping. Armstrong, a tall, imposing man, stood in silence. 13Q's GM walked over to the motionless Thunderbolt to explain to Jack why he had to get off the ride. You see, the sales department's deal was intended only to promote the park and the ride. There was never any mention of who would officially set the record and Kennywood Park figured it would only be right for their employee to achieve that distinction. So, the Thunderbolt left the loading station for a final rotation with only Bernie Kusibab onboard. Jack was livid, and in front of all the 13Q fans and park attendees waiting in line he exploded in his loud, resonant voice,

"Well fuck you, FUCK YOU! I cannot believe you motherfuckers would con me into this promotion. I will never, ever, do any promotion for this fuckin' radio station ever again — you assholes!"

According to eyewitnesses, mothers stood in shock, placing their hands over their kids' ears, and with that, the promotion ended. 13Q had their money, Kennywood had a vast crowd, but Jack's days at the station were numbered. That legendary radio gypsy would soon pull up stakes and move his newborn daughter, his wife and himself to Indianapolis to work at, coincidentally, a station named WIFE.

There was one line in that article I will never, ever forget. As Jack was walking away, 13Q's general manager said,

"Jack, it's a damn business!"

Radio people must learn to balance the goal of a promotion with rules and total transparency about how the game or event will proceed, or inevitable disasters will occur. We'll get into some other promotions that went more than sideways later, but for now let's deal with the symbiotic relationship.

For decades in the radio business, a career promotion to the position of general manager was awarded only to a person who had moved up through the sales ranks. It would take decades before the industry would realize this top station position could be filled by a smart and accomplished programmer. There was a clear divide in the business back then. First and foremost, radio sales guys and women drove expensive cars and dressed well, indicating they were making more money than the DJs and the program director. This became a point of envy with those in the programming ranks. Also, salespeople partied with the clients to get their money, which didn't seem much like work to a DJ who spent hours in the production studio creating the commercials. More often than not, the client would give the salesperson credit for the creative work.

As Progressive Rock and Top 40 stations got wiser about how things worked, many began hiring hot looking saleswomen to pitch the station to advertisers and close deals. Car dealerships were the bread and butter of the radio business, and their owners would melt in the hands of these ladies. Some stations with mediocre ratings would get more than their fair share of advertising dollars due to this strategy.

As an example of this ingrained misogynistic attitude, one GM said he hired a saleswoman who looked like Sophia Loren, and after her first week on the street she became "Salesperson of the Month" for bringing in the most advertising dollars. When asked how she did the second month, he answered, "Well, she obviously fucked her way across New York and signed a bunch of contracts, but she must not have been very good at sex because hers were mostly one-time deals." He fired her soon after that. It was all too true that being the "head" salesperson became a full-time job for some young women in radio sales.

Back then, you see, radio held an "end justifies the means" attitude. New hires to the sales department weren't given courses in selling, and their communication skills were often less than perfect, but radio needed them. Without a solid income, a station would try a format change, and when that didn't work, the owners often took their losses and sold the facility.

FM radio was playing eight to ten minutes of commercials per hour, giving us a programming advantage over those AM stations that were airing eighteen to twenty minutes of spots. Clearly, some bright minds in this "damn business" were figuring out the money side of things. Many station owners who were more radio geeks and less businesspeople were starting to get offers to sell their underachieving properties. Perhaps they invested twenty-five thousand dollars to build their station in the fifties, and now in the seventies they were getting offers to sell for nine hundred thousand dollars. A substantial number of them cashed out. With the asking price of a station based on cash flow, a seller would increase the spot load to reap a financial reward at the closing, but the new owners often kept the higher spot counts.

As for me, I was facing the reality I would not be displacing any of the full-time DJs at legendary KDKB. I enjoyed the production work and compliments from my bosses and co-workers, hell, I even won a couple of awards, but my creative soul was dissatisfied. The low point came when I was asked to take one for the team. Lots of radio stations had mascots. KGB's San Diego Chicken was a national treasure and WMMS in Cleveland had their famous Buzzard appear at promotions.

Well, KDKB's mascot was, wait for it, a Carrot! At one of our hot-air balloon festivals, the kid we hired to wear the carrot costume got deathly sick, so the GM asked me to dress in that foul-smelling, germ-infested outfit for three days. I don't want to sound like a prima donna, but that was just too much for me. To top things off, I came down with some strain of the Malaysian flu after that weekend.

It was time to do some digging to see what other job opportunities might be out there, and something happened in the fall of 1973 that not only helped me but changed the way radio people got their information.

Bob Wilson was a radio kid from Los Angeles who founded a trade newspaper he named Radio & Records. Two of his financial partners were Bob and Tom Kardashian, yes, *those* Kardashians. Finally, the radio and record industries had a printed, weekly publication that featured news, job openings and tasty gossip as well as an up-to-the-minute Top 40 chart.

That music chart was key to the publication's success. It was an extremely current and accurate listing based on all the song adds and chart moves across the most successful Top 40 stations in the nation. Most local stations published a weekly chart for their listeners, and Bob collected and tabulated that data to produce a national chart. Most radio programmers believed the Radio & Records chart was far superior to Billboard's because the latter publication was more aligned with the record industry. Some suspected money could buy the number one position on Billboard's Hot 100.

Radio & Records became the gold standard in the radio and record industries, and soon my path would intersect its.

23. Fear of Flying

On December 1, 1974, a well-known Washington D.C. radio newscaster named Ross Simpson was enjoying a quiet Sunday morning at his home in Northern Virginia. This Simpson guy had a long and storied career, as well as a knack for being at the scenes of many news-breaking events. Later, he would figure out a way to implant himself in the hospital where President Ronald Reagan was being treated after an assassination attempt. He would also be in the lobby of the D.C. City Hall when a radical Hanafi Muslim group tried to overtake the government. One of the people killed during that thirty-nine-hour siege was Maurice Williams, a WHUR-FM reporter. Simpson also went back to work after retiring to be an embedded reporter during the second Iraq war, which motivated his incredible book entitled *Backseat to Baghdad.*

Simpson's quiet Sunday morning was interrupted when he got a call from a radio station asking about the news bulletin of a plane crash near Mount Weather, Virginia. TWA Flight 514 had slammed into that mountain and the crash of the Boeing 727 killed all ninety-two people on board. As Ross told me the story later, "I saw my next-door neighbor, an NTSB crash investigator running to his car. When I yelled, 'Where are you going?' he said, 'Mount Weather, follow me.' I grabbed my tape recorder and trailed him through police lines to the crash site, where bodies covered with tarps were being carried to the road."

Ross painted an extremely thorough picture, for sure. Being of not-so-sound mind, I became paranoid about flying after this TWA incident, mostly due to Simpson's detailed coverage of the crash. When a person talks about a fear of flying, I totally understand their dread. Panic isn't logical because most planes don't crash, but this incident prompted me to learn the details of other crashes and I mentally locked up. This was clearly a case of my subconscious overruling my conscious mind by obsessing on the least probable outcome. Hey, it happens.

While I was in Phoenix and perfectly happy to be working at a great radio station, I was also trying to figure out a way to get more radio industry exposure. I've always been a decent writer, so I started to pen some articles and send them out to magazines. I submitted one to Record World never expecting it would get published but, low and behold, they ran my piece covering the history of FM rock radio.

My article featured Tom "Big Daddy" Donahue, a large man with a bushy beard, who launched his concept of Free Form radio on many California FM stations. Tom's wife was Rachel Donahue, and she went on to become a successful rock programmer at KSAN in San Francisco. I detailed their NO FORMAT format, under which disc jockeys played anything they wanted on radio stations many folks didn't even know existed. Tom is credited as the father of FM rock, and while there is some truth to that honor, a lack of ratings didn't sit well with the people who had to pay PG&E to keep the transmitter running. That being said, Tom was instrumental in getting people, especially the trade mags and advertising agencies, to understand the power of FM.

Donahue wrote a 1967 Rolling Stone article titled, "AM Radio Is Dead and Its Rotting Corpse Is Stinking Up the Airwaves," which lambasted Top 40. That piece made Tom a menace to mainstream broadcasters and the maestro of the FM movement. In the early days, FM stations were getting eighteen dollars for a sixty-second spot, while our AM brothers and sisters were cashing in with two to three hundred dollars per spot. No one wanted to kill the golden goose, but feathers did fly and most of those AM broadcasters wanted us FM radio weirdos to get the flock out of their domain.

I was working in the production studio at KDKB when the phone lit up. Totally out of the blue I heard this,

"Hey, Sonny Joe, this is Bob Wilson, editor of Radio & Records magazine. Have you heard of us?"

I sensed someone was pranking me,

"Yeah, but who is this really?"

A hearty chuckle came across the phone line and then he added,

"It's me, Bob, and I wanted to talk with you about that great article you wrote for Record World. Your insights were totally brilliant. How about you fly over to LA and let's pick each other's brains?"

I stopped breathing, not because the editor of the most popular industry trade magazine wanted to talk to me, but the idea of flying was petrifying,

"Yeah, sure, um when? I'll drive over."

"No, no, we'll pay for your flight. How about next Tuesday for lunch?"

"Yeah, sure, that's cool, but I'll drive. You know, my station might be a little wary about someone related to the record biz paying my way."

"That's a great point and makes me want to talk to you even more. Okay, see you next week in our Hollywood office."

He gave me the address and I immediately headed to my boss' office to disclose the meeting and arrange the day off. I didn't think my article was a big deal, but I guess Wilson saw something in it. Okay, a road trip to LA. Here I go again.

There wasn't a lot of traffic on Sunset Boulevard, and I got to the office sooner than I expected. I passed A&M records along the way and thought about that Charlie guy I had met in San Francisco. Back in those days it was easier to drive in Hollywood, but just as hard to park. I finally located a spot and headed to Radio & Records.

I was a bit thrown once ushered into Bob Wilson's office. There was a phone with a long cord in the middle of the room with two large pillows on either side, but no furniture. Bob was sitting on one of the pillows while scribbling on a notepad, probably drafting an article. I didn't know if the décor was some sort of hippy-spiritual thing or if furniture hadn't been delivered yet. Bob asked me to sit on the other pillow and I just had to mess with him,

"Shall I take my shoes off?"

He snickered and as I settled in, then he immediately launched into a story about how Radio & Records came to be. Bob got exposed to the radio business as a young man, parking cars in a lot near KFWB, and becoming friendly with the DJs at that major Top 40 station in LA. He later landed a disc jockey gig at KROY in Sacramento, and then advanced to KDAY in Los Angeles where he became program director. He applied for the PD job at KLOS-FM, an ABC owned station, but that job went to Tom Yates, who for some reason gets credit for creating the Album Oriented Rock format while there are so many others worthy of that trophy.

Bob shared his workflow in compiling the centerpiece of his publication, the weekly music chart. I was impressed with the methodology and care applied to that process.

The intercom buzzed while we were chatting, and the receptionist announced visitors. Seconds later, two gentlemen dressed in suits and ties entered the bare office. One of them was named Robert and he had a dashing gray streak in his hair. He told Wilson the office furniture would be delivered tomorrow and asked if the staff could work from home that day. I will always remember how those two guys seemed so out of place in a radio and records company. The Kardashians apologized for the interruption and quickly left the room.

A woman dressed in white go-go boots and a tight dayglo green dress brought us lunch on trays. It was a dish I never had before, but Chinese chicken salad was truly a Californian culinary delight. Bob said that if he ever opened a restaurant, he would place this delicious concoction on his menu.

Wilson next talked about using that new/old technology known as the fax machine to send out midweek news reports to his subscribers and asked what I thought about the name HotFax. I loved the term and told him so, but now I became even more curious about the intent of our meeting and why he was asking my opinion. Bob said there was a magazine published in Washington D.C. that had a definite edge on industry news flashes. He went on to explain the sale of a radio station, or filings to increase a station's power or move its transmitter site, often hinted at a future format change. He also wanted a leg up on major FCC rulings, and Broadcasting Magazine was covering all of that better than anyone else. Because it was based in the nation's capital, that publication had a serious advantage and Bob wanted a piece,

"So, I want to open a Washington D.C. office and I'm looking for someone like you to write articles, keep an eye on all industry and FCC activity and work with a small staff of radio freaks just like us."

I was thinking a job had just been offered but sitting on a floppy hippy pillow made me feel uncomfortable, both mentally and physically. I told Bob I would think about his proposal and promised to get back within twenty-four hours. He said that was fine and then I thought to ask,

"So, how much would this job pay?"

"Well, it's a new position and I'm thinking we could start you at twenty-one-five annually."

I was making thirteen thousand in Phoenix, so the offer was definitely attractive, but I had one more question,

"So, Bob, if I were to take the job would it be okay if I did some part-time radio work on the side provided it didn't conflict or interfere with my work for Radio & Records?"

"Sure, that would be great. Just don't work for a record company."

211

The salary and possibility of radio work in D.C. convinced me to give Bob a yes right then and there. He called his secretary for a contract I could carry back to Phoenix to share with the attorney I didn't have. I guess I came across as a skilled professional and he just assumed I had legal counsel.

Now I needed to figure out how to respectfully end my position at KDKB without hurting the station and then transfer my body from Arizona to Washington without using an airplane that I knew would certainly crash and kill me. As the song goes, *"Paranoia strikes deep, into your life it will creep. It starts when you're always afraid."*

I spent the next couple of weeks preparing for my twenty-three-hundred-mile drive with my growing collection of personal possessions stuffed into a U-Haul trailer my trusted station wagon would tow across America. When not working those final days in Phoenix, I hit the public library to bone up on the FCC and the radio and record businesses. I hired a lawyer to go over my employment contract before I signed it, and he got me into the local law library to research and understand some of the engineering aspects of my new assignment at Radio & Records, which now had the industry-wide nickname of R&R. Quirky but true, the Rs in the magazine's logo were designed by Dean Torrence, one-half of the surfer-song duo Jan and Dean.

KDKB threw a fantastic party the Friday before my departure. You know, there is something in common between a bachelor at a wedding and a single guy at a rock radio station going away party. I don't remember much, except the sloshing of my waterbed rocking back and forth pretty much all night long. Anita, one of the sales ladies, wanted to thank me for helping her so much over the years, and she certainly was grateful. That made me feel a little guilty though. I mean, not to brag, but there were two other soon-to-be former co-workers who wanted to show gratitude in that same personal way. Hooray for women's liberation! I didn't mean to be rude not accepting thanks from traffic and billing, but I decided to save any further sex, drugs and rock 'n roll for my new job and city. I distracted myself by thinking about applying for a part-time job at a D.C. radio station once I got settled there.

I was floored by the cost of living in Washington. I didn't expect to live in the Watergate, but it took time to find a reasonably priced apartment in the Cleveland Park section of town. With nearby public transportation to the office, my new, one-room place was perfect. R&R had rented a small office on Connecticut Avenue. The names of the D.C. streets were numbers, letters or state names, perfectly laid out by a Frenchman named Pierre Charles L'Enfant. Of course, one of the plazas carried his name. What an amazing coincidence.

Getting around the city was easy, but I wasn't used to the high volume of traffic and pedestrians. The government employed piles of people, some reimbursed for their loyalty and others who were honest, civil servants working hard at making America's gears properly turn. It was a totally different class of citizenry than the hippies and desert dogs in Arizona. I immediately realized a serious need for new clothes so I wouldn't look like a faraway alien. I went shopping and bought several decent trousers and button-down business shirts and those would do the trick for now.

I had no time to doubt myself, get paranoid or think I didn't belong, but I knew that somewhere along the road I would need to jettison my silly fear of flying. Travel was going to be an essential part of my new job.

I walked into a bar named Jason's on M Street in Georgetown one night and sat next to a round-faced man wearing circular specs. We got to talking and he asked where I was from. When I told him I just moved to D.C. from Phoenix, he pressed me, almost like he was conducting an interview. When I told him I worked in radio, he introduced himself,

"Wow, pleased to meet you! I'm Ross Simpson, Mutual Radio News."

Only then did I recognize the voice and almost fell off my chair. I ordered him a drink and when I told him I drove from Phoenix, he asked,

"Why did you drive? Why not fly?"

I explained to him I had been fine with flying until that TWA flight ploughed into the mountain. He took a long sip of his beer and put the glass down, then centered it perfectly on the coaster,

"I was one of the first reporters on the scene after that plane hit the mountain. When I got there, they were loading up black body bags."

He paused slightly, then proceeded to share every detail of that day, all the way down to the smells, the sounds and the reality of death. His words kicked my flying fear into overdrive.

That first barroom conversation eventually evolved into a friendship, and on days off we would drive to a small parking lot at the end of National Airport's main runway to watch airplanes take off and land. Ross would do a play-by-play of each plane's movement as we listened to the fascinating chatter between the tower, pilots and flight controllers on his aviation radio. Over hundreds of landings and departures Ross became my healing doctor. Every single time a plane took off and disappeared into the sky, Ross would turn to me and say,

"There's another one. Didn't crash. You see that?"

We both laughed.

I was cured.

24. Power of the Personal Touch

One of the best things Bob Wilson taught me was the power of the personal touch. When I asked how he got the major Top 40 radio stations to reveal their playlists to his new and unproven publication, he replied,

"I personally called each program director."

Radio programming consultant E. Alvin Davis would later say,

"That's powerful voodoo."

When I began making calls, I would speak only to the PD, and that technique opened some incredible doors for me. Wilson's personal touch launched a magazine, and I followed his lead while on the job by compiling a little black book containing names, numbers and notes.

I should mention here that R&R's music chart did not include data from all US Top 40 stations. Bob analyzed Arbitron numbers and recruited only the highest rated stations. Being an R&R reporting station was a privilege, and playlists of unproven stations could not dilute the accuracy of the publication's chart. One of the worst possible days in a PD's office would take place with a phone call alerting the station they have been dropped as an R&R reporter, the ultimate confirmation of a string of bad rating books.

The writers at R&R coined the term Contemporary Hit Radio, and that moniker became the title for their Top 40 chart. It's a tribute to the power of R&R that Contemporary Hit Radio was soon shortened to CHR, and that mnemonic quickly replaced Top 40 as a music radio format name. Mike Harrison, a PD who had worked at many FM rock stations became the rock editor of R&R and he originated the term Album Oriented Rock, AOR in shortened form.

The R&R CHR chart rapidly became the industry standard for radio. Record companies all over the world coveted placement and upward movement of their songs on that chart. The Billboard Hot 100 remained important, but it included record sales and jukebox plays along with radio airplay. Joel Whitburn was a chart guy from Milwaukee who published books of record chart statistics, but his sole source was Billboard. Because of its exclusive focus on radio, that industry propelled R&R to immense success. Radio programmers eagerly anticipated the publication every week, and record companies placed full-page ads there to announce new releases. That advertising helped the newspaper grow and prosper.

One of the most popular features of R&R was a column named "Street Talk." It was a fabulous collection of hires, fires, format flips, new stations, sold stations, DJ tales and radio rumors written in a tongue-in-cheek style. Many readers would immediately flip to Street Talk when their copy of R&R arrived. Part of my job was tracking down bits of information for that column and advising the LA office about the details of the intelligence I uncovered.

One of my early R&R projects was researching and writing a feature story about the first radio station in the United States to play the Beatles, WWDC-AM right here in Washington, D.C. I believed a DJ there named Fred Fiske received a 45 RPM record from a friend in Great Britain, and I wanted to confirm the accuracy of my sketchy information before digging further. I called the station and got through to Fred's producer, a lady named Nance.

When I told Nancy Underwood I was with R&R, she probably thought I worked for a government agency and became confused about why I was asking about the Beatles. I explained a bit about the trade newspaper and my position there and she confirmed my basic fact was correct. She also gave me more background on that happening and I took notes for the article. Suddenly she asked what I was doing Saturday night, believing I would fit in at a party she was hosting. I feigned checking a bulky appointment book by furiously rifling through a pile of papers on my desk,

"Oh, okay, Saturday night. Uh, let me see, oh, okay, here it is. Well, look at that. I am wide open."

Her hearty laugh revealed a wonderful sense of humor and she rattled off a Georgetown address. Nance ran down the guest list and it included some of the movers and shakers in the political press corps along with some GS-3s and GS-4s. The federal government's "General Schedule" indicates work responsibilities and pay scales. GS-3s and GS-4s were internships or student jobs handed out to kids whose daddies gave a bunch of money to a politician, and that's how our government works, or in many ways, doesn't work. Those government goons were college friends of Ms. Underwood with no power.

At that time, AM stations were still the dominant force in radio broadcasting. Two of the top D.C. stations were WMAL-AM, the number one station in the market owned by the Evening Star newspaper, and WTOP-AM, Arthur Godfrey's local radio home for years. It was now running an All-News format and owned by the Washington Post. Are you seeing this picture? While FM stations in most cities were moving forward and separating themselves from their AM counterparts and newspaper ownerships, Washington D.C. was slower making this transition. Of course, why would radio move faster than everything else in our nation's capital?

I was wearing my brand-new shirt and slacks and felt like I was attending a major social event when I arrived at the party on Saturday. Nancy was a slender, tall, pale woman with chestnut brown hair, just like my mother. At first, I thought hers was a New England accent, but on further listening it sounded more like that intellectual New York snobby patois that William F. Buckley and William Safire deployed. I would later learn Nance knew both of them. I spied an ancient Underwood typewriter sitting on a small desk in the foyer and thought that was an interesting touch.

Nancy was totally wired into the D.C. scene, and later would work in communications for the Reagan administration. She knew I was there to make contacts, and her first order of business was a motherly touch. She spoke kindly and softly,

"Hey, Sonny boy, the price tags are still on your shirt and slacks."

I was utterly embarrassed, but she deftly glided me into a bathroom and used a pair of scissors to fix me up. As Nancy repaired my unintentional fashion statement, I couldn't help noticing a poster of an Underwood typewriter on the wall in the powder room. Strange. I thanked her and as we walked out Nance stepped over to a beautiful woman who had just arrived,

"Hello, MC, how are you? Let me introduce you to the new writer for Radio & Records magazine here in Washington, Sonny Joe McPherson."

I shook her hand and was captivated by her screamy blue eyes and orange-freckled face. She was Mary Catherine McGillicuddy, as Irish as a lass could be. Of course, I used the line that she probably got from every guy who met her, "Say, that was Lucille Ball's maiden name." I got what I believed to be her standard answer, in a southern accent so slow and thick I could almost taste mint juleps and honey,

"Well, we are the Charleston McGillicuddy's, Lucy's from Jamestown, New York. She's a Yankee!"

As she spoke, I focused on her pouty little mouth which was oh-so-perfectly painted with the reddest of red lipstick. Her southern accent was very appealing to this "Yankee" from Dayton. She explained that she wanted to be an actress, but after graduating with a pre-law degree from the University of South Carolina her new dream was attending Georgetown for a law degree, but instead she became a paralegal at the FCC. When she said FCC, it was as if she was asking me to rip off that shiny-blue, silk Chinese dress right there. Her auburn hair twisted into a tight bun with bright green chopsticks holding the wad up on her head was a fabulous touch.

Referring to the name McPherson, she questioned my Scottish heritage. I had to break the news that I was not really a McPherson, and when she heard my real name she smiled,

"Well darling, do stick with the radio moniker. It suits you better. With those high cheek bones and that well-manicured beard, you do look a little Gaelic."

Here she was, a single woman, a beautiful young lady who worked at the FCC. Yes, contact with an insider! She had the body of a dancer, well-shaped legs and sensuous curves that drew eyes to her dancer's derriere. She was fit but certainly not a busty woman, which prompted her to adopt a no-bra policy when socializing.

When I called her Mary Catherine, she quickly asked that I use the name MC, just like all her friends did. She pulled a business card and pen from her purse and jotted down her home phone number, saying I could call her any time. She departed early with the excuse she had to work that night. I wondered what an FCC employee would be doing on a Saturday night, but it was too early in our relationship to dig into the details of her job. That could come later.

It was around this time in the radio business when some of the best programmers in the nation were seeing a limited path beyond being the PD of a single radio station. There were only so many dollars available for that position and some wanted a higher income and more industry recognition than they had. As was true in many other industries, the most accomplished radio programmers often broke away from day-to-day employment and started small companies to consult radio stations. By charging a station a retainer fee for their services, like a lawyer, these major programming guys could pocket five hundred to two thousand dollars a month per station. Of course, they were on call night and day, and using the power of the personal touch they made each station feel as if they were the small firm's only client.

Bill Drake, the former head of RKO Radio and father of KHJ's phenomenally successful Boss Radio format, struck out on his own, guiding CHR stations to more successful programming. Drake partnered with radio businessman Gene Chenault to form Drake-Chenault, a syndication company that sold distinctive radio features like the History of Rock and Roll.

Then there was George Burns, no not that one, and Kent Burkhart, who had worked for Todd Storz, one of the Top 40 format fathers. Both of them hung out their consultant shingles after working for major broadcasting companies in programming and management. Burkhart was the President of Pacific and Southern Broadcasting Company before he went out on the road as a consultant. Paul Drew, one of Burkhart's programmers, also began a consultancy.

That old saying about consultants knowing six ways to make love but not knowing any women definitely did not apply to these guys. And the old yarn that if you knew how to do it you did it, but if you didn't know how you become a consultant, also didn't apply. These guys were at the top of their game and devised every detail at the successful radio stations they advised.

A programmer can become a radio consultant and charge stations for their advice only if they can help a station improve in the ratings. If the ratings are stagnant or dropping, the consultant might hire a new PD, rearrange the DJ staff or even change the format, but should those ideas not work the consultant will be gone in a New York minute.

One afternoon while having drinks at Gallagher's in Georgetown with my newfound friend Nancy, we overheard two FCC guys and a few Congressional aides from the Hill,

"Zeke, those asshole radio consultants are becoming too powerful. It might be time to introduce some legislation to license the bastards so we can examine their books. You know, they are probably taking payola to play records."

We finished our drinks and Nance went to work with this fresh fodder she may be able to work into the nightly talk show she produces. As for me, I have always been skeptical of government agents and that overheard conversation was proving me right. Now here's a good place in my story to bring the word "payola" into sharper focus.

Payola is money paid by a record promoter to a broadcaster in return for playing of one or more songs on the air. It dates back to the days of shellac and vinyl records and jukebox play counters that could be changed to give certain record companies bigger royalty checks. The earliest records were played on a Victrola, which was the brand name of a gramophone. It reproduced music when a needle in the tonearm pulsated according to etchings along the groove of a rotating record, and those vibrations were then amplified acoustically. So, if you combine the word "pay," as in money, with the last three letters of the word "Victrola," the result is "payola" which is a perfect word to describe pay for play.

The US Congress will not hesitate to butt into any business it believes is doing something wrong. Payola had been around since the 1880s when music publishers paid popular singers to perform their songs. The word itself first appeared in a 1938 Variety magazine editorial. In the 1950s, there was little prosecution for the use of payola, but by 1960 Congress amended the Communications Act of 1934 with Sections 317 and 507, which specifically outlawed under-the-table payments for song airplay. If a broadcaster didn't disclose over the air that airplay of a song was bought, they could be jailed for one year and fined ten thousand dollars. Smaller record companies had everything to lose, so they complained to the people in power about the payola activities of the bigger companies, and this resulted in hearings. That's when the real fun began.

The powerful Subcommittee on Legislative Oversight, the body that recommends laws to deal with discovered wrongs, conducted the initial inquiries. The 1959 headlines concerning that first of many hearings centered on a New York City DJ named Alan Freed, whose silence basically was his raised middle finger to the committee. Some people assumed he didn't talk because he was guilty of taking record company bribes for airplay, and Alan later confirmed that to be true. Freed paid a small fine, but his radio career waned after his hearing. Famous baby-faced radio and TV star Dick Clark also testified before the committee, but that was after the ABC Television Network directed him to divest ownership in many of his music-industry holdings. Laws making payola a federal offense eventually followed.

As mentioned earlier, record labels could circumvent payola allegations by utilizing independent record promoters then hauling out that old, "I know nothing" excuse. Still, people were caught and hurt. In 1976, DJ Frankie Crocker was indicted in a payola scandal which forced him off New York City radio, but after those charges were later dropped he landed a gig hosting MTV's video jukebox. Later in the payola timeline, previous New York District Attorney Eliot Spitzer, of all people, focused on record business corruption and uncovered evidence that executives of the Sony/BMG record labels had made pay for play deals with several large commercial radio chains. A clear violation of payola laws was proven, and those guilty broadcasters paid twelve point five million dollars in fines, then tougher restrictions were put in place. Like much of what happens in Washington and the good old US-of-A, however, they paid the fine and moved on. But let's return now to my story in D.C.

Like any healthy red-blooded American twenty-something, I wanted to learn more about how the strength of the personal touch worked in the most powerful city in the world. I found the business card I had tucked away and called MC to see if she wanted to go hammer down some drinks. MC was thrilled to hear from me, well, as thrilled as a prim and proper southern girl would allow herself to be.

She had an efficiency apartment on Dupont Circle in one of those old mansions that William Taft and Teddy Roosevelt lived in a hundred years before. It was exactly fifty steps up to her place on the top floor, but she modestly asked that we meet at an uptown bar named The Royal Warrant. Let me tell you that was the craziest drinking establishment I have ever patronized, and that's saying a lot. Don't forget, I'm a radio guy.

The bar was one-hundred feet long and worked by a staff of fit females with gigantic arms. These ladies looked like Russian weightlifters! Could cocktail shaking do that to a woman? MC and I arrived in cabs at exactly the same time and that spoke of immense potential, at least in my tiny, horny mind.

When asked for our drink order, MC straight away said, "My usual please Marge." The tough looking lesbian barkeep reached back and grabbed a gallon jug of Chivas Regal, poured more than twelve ounces into a large, ice-filled glass, then slapped a lemon twist into it. She filled another glass with ice water and set both down in front of my date. I slyly said,

"I'll have the same."

Now I know what they say about Irish people, but it's quite unfair. Sure, many of Irish descent drink a fair amount of alcohol but most of my German relatives drank beer until they fell over, which at my family events would mean barrels of beer. It was clear this lady could drink anyone under the table, but it didn't take long before we were slurring our sentences, and most of our attempted remarks were paired with a touch to the arm or hand of the other. It was good neither of us had to deal with driving that night, because our three monster drinks each threw us three sheets to the wind. I paid the tab, then we stumbled out onto Connecticut Avenue and hailed a cab. Since we would pass my apartment on the way to hers, I said,

"I'll pay for the cab ride when I get off in Cleveland Park."

She briefly looked at me then grabbed me by the ear, pulled me close and planted a wet, sloppy kiss on my face, which also plastered a smudgy streak of hot red lipstick on my mug and beard,

"Y'all not going to your place Sonny boy. You need to see my gargantuan apartment on Dupont Circle."

That was the very first time I ever heard "y'all" used to address one person, but she was now the boss. I came to discover that "large" apartment, had a small sofa and a room-divider curtain hanging from hooks in the ceiling, which concealed a small mattress on the floor. When I woke in the morning, half of my body was on the mattress and the other half was on the hard, cold, Parquet flooring. MC had all the blankets and was naked underneath, so I guess we did the number. I spotted a large, unopened bottle of Chivas Regal sitting on top of the fridge when making my way to the bathroom and just had to smile.

25. Rotations and Connections

The Earth is moving at about a thousand miles an hour, but we don't feel it. A full rotation takes twenty-four hours and causes planetary day and night as well as light and dark times for humans. It takes about three hundred and sixty-five days for the Earth to move around the Sun and return to where it began. We count the days by many methods, one of which is the shape of the moon. Of course, the moon doesn't change its shape at all, it's an illusion caused by sunlight reflecting off its surface with the moving Earth casting a shadow which gradually alters the silhouette through a monthly cycle.

Early on, radio programmers figured out that when listeners like a song their favorite station plays, they will want to hear it again. That might seem obvious, but Lucille Ball and her husband-co-star Desi Arnaz opened eyes when they negotiated financial benefits to what we now call television reruns. One CBS executive asked, "If a viewer already watched a show, why would they want to see it again?" Media management did have some C-students at the top, but once Desi and Lucy owned their shows, they sold them for millions. CBS ended up buying back the first one hundred and eighty episodes of *I Love Lucy* for five million dollars. Who's the dumb, silly redhead, now?

One of the rating measurements radio folks paid attention to during the late 1960s was "cume," which is the cumulative audience or total number of listeners. The cume of a CHR station was typically fantastic, frequently number one in the market, while its quarter-hour ratings were often smaller than traditional AM stations that held people through long foreground programing like Don McNeill's Breakfast Club or a baseball game between the Brooklyn Dodgers and New York Yankees. So, without getting too "mathy" here, the ratings companies provided numerical breakouts that allowed stations and advertisers to evaluate the listening audience in numerous ways. A good salesperson could find something to sell in every rating book, even if the station's overall listenership was sparse.

Another ratings measurement was the percentage of the total population listening to any given station. That figure was called a "rating" or "rating points." Radio people especially liked another calculation, which was the percentage of total radio listeners who consumed their station.

I used the term "popular vote" to describe a station's cumulative audience during the 6 a.m. to midnight Monday through Sunday daypart. It's the number of people who tuned into the station for at least five minutes at any time during the week. Each listener is counted one time only, so the cume consists of unduplicated listeners. Ratings companies later added a deeper dive into listenership some called psychographics, in which groups and spectrums were defined and measured.

All the above are good data, but far too limiting to get a true picture of listenership, especially for advertisers, so along came reach and frequency. Reach is the total number of listeners who will hear a given commercial (or song, or DJ, or promo), while frequency is the number of times they will hear it. These metrics weren't directly available from the ratings companies, they had to be mathematically extrapolated from the published numbers. An accomplished stats person could show an advertiser that, say, for a particular advertising campaign thirty thousand listeners would hear their commercial an average of fifteen times each.

Back then we were using station cumulative listener figures to help get advertising money which otherwise would have been spent on newspapers. In a sense, a newspaper or magazine's circulation numbers were similar to a radio station's cume ratings. Radio salespeople sold the "sound" of their radio stations and got advertisers to buy lots of spots, which would be scheduled through different dayparts to maximize reach and frequency.

It didn't take humans long to start relying on the daily cycle of light and darkness. I can imagine the first time an ancient saw an eclipse. To them, it may have been like your favorite radio station suddenly changing format. Music radio programmers eventually learned that people genuinely cared about music and were willing to wait through annoying, shouty, fast-talking ads for used cars and racetracks to hear another favorite tune. Should the listener hate the next song, they often would switch to another station. Not good. Some CHR stations were playing the biggest songs every hour and forty-five minutes, while FM AOR stations might rotate their biggest songs from the top albums every three hours and fifteen minutes.

It was always clear to me that when two stations were directly competing in the same format, the station that played fewer "stiffs," a radio term for a song with limited appeal, and the one with the fewest commercial interruptions, would win ninety-nine percent of the time. New stations often aired fewer commercials and were extremely appealing right out of the box.

Airplay of bad songs happened for several reasons. One was a program or music director with a godawful ear, but more often than not a record company was the driving force. Some record promoters became adept at developing "friendships" with their radio contacts. It was phony bullshit, but if a PD or MD fell for it, they sometimes added songs the promoter pitched because they were psychologically manipulated, not because those songs would help their station's ratings. Another common record label trick was giving a radio station an exclusive right to promote the local concert of one of their major acts, with the condition the station add one or more of the label's marginal songs not getting the kind of airplay the record company wanted. Of course, the classic staples of payola — money, drugs and sex — have been used many times to garner airplay of limited appeal music.

When I was in Cleveland, a local RCA Records guy offered me a marijuana joint to play a song by the band named Forever More. I declined the proposition by asking,

"Why would I want your joint? I like their music and will play them anyway."

That band, then a minor blip on the radar, eventually became the Average White Band and enjoyed success, but the meager bribe of one joint for my airplay of a record was eclipsed by direct deposits in bank accounts, bags of cocaine, luxury cars and/or hookers that others in the biz received. I knew my reputation would rise by following my brain and gut on music and ignoring any illegitimate incentive to play a song I didn't think would help my station's ratings.

MC's schedule and mine finally found another date night and we met at Rive Gauche, a haughty Georgetown restaurant where I had seen Barbara Streisand a few weeks before. Now we all know a gentleman should never ask, but I just had to know,

"So, MC, that night I stayed over after the Royal Warrant, did we, um, you know…"

"Darling, you are a such a fresh breath of air, like dew on the morning grass, but I can see right through you."

I smiled and didn't say another word, which is a technique I learned from some of the top-notch reporters on Capitol Hill. Allow room for your subject to continue talking and often there will be a slip up, divulgence or leak. MC continued,

"Well, Sonny boy, if you are asking if you hit a homerun, I do believe that neither Mrs. McGillicuddy's precious daughter nor the simulated Scot from Ohio did the big number. The only integer we got to that night was those fifty steps up to the spacious home of yours truly."

I didn't want to seem needy, so I just dropped the topic right there. Instead, I decided to dig for a scoop,

"So, what's new at the Federal Candy Commission?"

She laughed at my nickname, took a sip of her expensive French red wine, and leaned forward,

"Big things at WWDC. A construction company is going to buy both the AM and FM stations."

I acted like this intel wasn't at all important,

"Really, why would a construction company want to get into the radio business?"

"Well, they built the new headquarters for the FBI, the J. Edgar Hoover Building. By the way, the Director loaned me this dress for the night."

We both chuckled and I got the feeling she wanted to talk about other things. Suddenly there was a yelp from across the restaurant and we turned toward a woman moving quickly to our table,

"Oh my God, MC, I haven't seen you in weeks."

When she arrived, this loud, overly-made-up woman glanced down at me as if checking out a batch of cookies in a bake shop,

"Oh, now I see why you haven't called, sweetie."

MC's facial expression changed into what I learned was her phony southern charm smile,

"Teresa, this is Sonny Joe McPherson, and before you open your large and ungovernable mouth, he's a reporter."

"Well, howdy there Sonny, I am Teresa Cushman and which paper do you work for, the Post or the Star?"

MC explained a bit about me and R&R, which was good because I was really enjoying the escargot dish she had ordered for me. Those little guys were succulent but after dipping the bread in the butter, wow that was a savory slice of heaven. The effect diminished, however, after she told me they were snails. Being the polite person she was, MC invited Teresa to join us, but she quickly retorted,

"Love to dear, but I've got to work tonight."

Teresa punctuated that sentence with a knowing wink and left the restaurant. I couldn't help noticing her beautiful butt gently moving and swaying as she walked. My inner voice asked, "How do women learn to do that, or is it just a natural thing?" MC brought me back,

"Hey, I saw that!"

"Oh, just looking, but why does she have to work?"

"I'll tell you later."

The following week, the R&R LA office was abuzz about a big format change in Washington. At that time, WPGC-FM was an R&R reporting station playing CHR, while WASH-FM had significant older demographic ratings with an Adult Contemporary format which some old timers called "chicken rock." The format consisted of pop songs but all on the lighter side, no rock or fowl involved. It was becoming a mainstay radio format, often abbreviated AC by those in the business.

WMAL-FM was doing a format they called "soft explosion," which was neither. I always believed the jocks at WMAL-FM were overinfluenced by WHFS, a Class A FM licensed to Bethesda Maryland. WMAL-FM was trying to out-hip those lower power guys who had a loyal cult following with a format that would best be described as Free Form.

WHFS was the Little Feat station, while WMAL-FM was the *White Bird* station. That was an obscure song by the San Francisco band named It's a Beautiful Day. That folksy, six-minute track from 1969 had limited appeal, whereas the LA band Little Feat would sell out six nights at George Washington University's Lisner Auditorium. The biggest jock at WHFS was Cerphe, a constantly tanned guy with straw-like yellow hair. So, the guessing game was whether WWDC-FM would challenge WPGC in the CHR format or become another FM rock outlet when there were already two "successful" rockers in the market.

I was sitting with my news-guy friend Ross at the Third Edition on Wisconsin Avenue in Georgetown enjoying their scrumptious Eggs Benedict. Ross was talking about giving up network news reporting and jumping to a local station because he missed the beat. Yes, it's cop terminology, but a local radio reporter also has a beat. They roam the streets observing their surroundings, asking questions, conducting interviews and digging up facts.

I liked Ross, and like many of us in radio he had an Achilles' heel. Offer a compliment then immediately ask a question, and you'll get far more than might have otherwise been shared. Radio folk tend to talk too much, and the narrative Ross revealed was well worth the money I spent on our meal,

"So, Ross, I heard you were honored at the Broadcaster's Association dinner. You should be really proud."

"Yes, I was extremely grateful. After I received the trophy, I smiled at all those people sitting in the front row who never hired me."

"Yeah, they missed out."

"McPherson, you need to keep this between us but I'm about to become WWDC's News Director."

"Wow, are you going to be working at the AM, the FM or both?"

"Both, but tremendous changes are coming. I was there yesterday and saw that famous consultant, the one who constantly puffs a pipe and has a massive, curly-gray hairdo, like a white-guy Afro.

"Oh really, Kent Burkhart?"

I knew from talking with radio people that one of Kent's nicknames was "The Pipe." He was also called other names, particularly by those DJs he replaced during format changes.

The brunch was delightfully delicious, but the information Ross just fed me was equally digestible. I was now near certain that WWDC-FM would rebrand and become a CHR station, but I had forgotten about Burkhart's secret weapon until I chatted with Bob Wilson later. He reminded me that the firm was Burkhart/Abrams, not just Burkhart.

Lee Abrams was a Chicago boy who dreamed of running radio stations. As a precocious teenager, he operated a travel agency out of his suburban bedroom. While vacationing with his parents in Florida, Lee fast talked his way into a radio station with an unbelievable but true pitch that has become legendary in the radio industry. Lee told the crew at the station he had been hitching rides with strangers and observing their radio listening habits. He would ask questions like, "Why did you just change that station?" or "Do you think that disc jockey talks too much?" This primitive research gave Lee insight into radio listeners that few others had.

It wasn't long before this loquacious, brace-faced, "Jew-fro'd kid" would talk his way into WRIF, the ABC-owned FM station in Detroit, which had recently changed to a Progressive Rock format. This happened at the same time the New York ABC big wigs, and some of them did wear wigs, decided the inmates would no longer run their FM asylums.

The President of ABC Radio was a guy named Hal Neal, whose claim to fame was being the booth announcer for the 1930s radio show *The Lone Ranger*, which coincidently, was produced in Detroit at ABC's WXYZ, WRIF's AM sister station. Neal and his VP of their owned FM stations, Allen Shaw, believed their FM stations would perform much better with some discipline and tighter control. When Neal asked Mike McCormick, his PD at Top 40 WLS in Chicago, what he thought of the ABC FM stations, McCormick barked,

"They all suck canal water."

Abrams impressed WRIF's GM, who soon fired his hippy programmer and gave Abrams the job. Lee immediately installed a tight playlist featuring only the best songs by the Who, Led Zeppelin, Rolling Stones, Yes and others. He eliminated both unfamiliar album "deep cuts" and marginal bands, instead rotating familiar rock songs by major artists around the clock, like celestial bodies moving across the sky. The ratings were fantastic, but Abrams, the youngest programmer ever hired by ABC, was a free-spirited teenager who didn't play the corporate radio game. He regularly skipped out of the FM program directors' conference calls, didn't return messages and was mostly aloof from the corporate powers that be. He focused his energy on lining up stations to use what he would later name the Superstars format. Lee didn't copyright the name and ABC TV later used that tag for a sports feature.

Abrams convinced WQDR in Raleigh, a large college town, to plug in Superstars, and it achieved astronomical ratings straight out of the gate. Abrams was quickly developing an industry-wide reputation as the new wunderkind and a trade magazine favorite. Kent Burkhart took notice and believed Lee could bring rock format expertise to his existing radio consulting stable of CHR, Country and Adult Contemporary clients. Burkhart brought Lee to Atlanta for an interview and, as they say, the rest is history.

Both the R&R format editors and I figured WWDC-FM was either going CHR, which wasn't a terrible idea given WPGC's less than stellar signal in the market, or they would flip to Lee Abrams' new AOR format. Being the ever-aggressive reporter, I called Burkhart/Abrams and got straight through to Lee himself, who wasn't at all secretive or guarded. It was like he didn't care what he shared with me. You see, Lee had a style. He would make a contact believe they were getting super-secret, exclusive information, almost a leak of sorts. It helped grow his reputation and mystique.

What I didn't know was Lee had just concluded calls with Billboard, Record World, Broadcasting and the Wall Street Journal and he gave them the same details he just shared with me. He swore me to secrecy but admitted he was already lining up the best people to execute a rock format. He said the station would be named DC101, a combination of the call letters WWDC and their 101.1 frequency. Abrams didn't disclose when the new format would launch, saying only I should keep listening. I asked if I could interview him about the new format the next time he was in the area,

"Hey, man, I'll be there at the International Inn next week. Call me."

I was so pumped! I had just made a contact in a sky-high place, and would soon interview him, but I was curious why he would stay at that particular hotel. It was on Thomas Circle, the infamous roundabout where hookers and pimps hocked their wares every night. The mystery was quickly solved when I discovered that Blake Construction Company, the new owners of DC101 also owned the hotel.

My life in radio has been one of learning lessons, and D.C. brought an important one I will never forget; connections tie everything, and everything means something.

26. Capitol Hill Capers

Dayton's own little Herbie Klotenfelder was making his way in D.C. without anyone to guide him and getting to know hundreds of people along the way. Every page of my black phone and address book was filled, well, not the Q-page... yet. R&R had published a good handful of my editorial assignments and feature articles under a byline, and when I called radio people, they picked up.

My relationship with MC was blossoming slowly. At times, it seemed she was working twenty-four hours a day, but I was also traveling to research a story here and there so we spent time together when we could.

Since R&R was a young company in what could be an extravagant business, the LA partners and accounting office kept a close eye on budgets and expense accounts. Recently I had obtained some pertinent information from the Radio-TV Editor of the Washington Star during a lunch at an overpriced Capitol Hill eatery. It was clear he opened up because he wanted to be my friend, yes that kind of friend, but the details he shared were going to fill an immense chunk of a story I was writing so I picked up the tab. My expense report was later returned from LA and denied with a terse note, "We don't feed our competitors." Okay, a hand slap and another lesson learned, the kind not taught in colleges.

I had confirmed that DC101 would flip to a rock format and was even able to track down the DJ lineup: 6 a.m. to 10 a.m. would be hosted by Johnny Holliday, a Washington mainstay but not a rock jock. He was an AC guy who for years had been doing mornings on WWDC-AM. A guy from WKTK in Baltimore, Gary Chase, would be the midday jock from 10 a.m. to 3 p.m. Denise Oliver from WDVE in Pittsburgh would be on the air 3 p.m. to 8 p.m. and Dave Brown, a local guy who graduated from the University of Maryland, would cover 8 p.m. to 1 a.m. There were two questions I wanted to ask Abrams. Why the nonstandard air shift times and why have a morning guy with no rock format experience?

I called Lee as he had asked me to do, and we agreed to meet at his hotel. I packed up my small tape recorder, because good reporters always document their interviews to get the details straight and protect themselves later if need be. I knocked on the hotel room door and was greeted by an extremely enthusiastic guy. He was wearing a purple striped dress shirt, casual slacks and high-top black leather shoes like the Beatles and other British rock stars wore. We sat at a small table in the room, and I asked permission to record our interview. Lee cupped his hands around his mouth and replied loudly,

"Sure, here, I'll give you a level. DELTA 375 HEAVY, CLEARED WASHINGTON DULLES VIA THE CHATTANOOGA FIVE DEPARTURE, NORCROSS TRANSITION, J86 RICHMOND, SENATE FIVE ARRIVAL. MAINTAIN FOUR THOUSAND, EXPECT FLIGHT LEVEL THREE THIRTY IN TEN MINUTES DEPARTURE, 128.5 AND SQUAWK 5254!"

I was floored to hear Lee's perfect imitation of an airplane pilot during takeoff, but that made total sense later when I learned he had a pilot's license.

Just before starting the interview, Lee pulled out an unusual pack of cigarettes, Dunhill Reds, produced by an English manufacturer who promoted the brand as "hygienic." Yeah, right! The smokes had a "royal warrant" from 1927 until 1995, meaning Kings and Queens endorsed the Dunhill brand. They were also preferred by Hunter S. Thompson, the famous Rolling Stone writer. Lee explained that Chris Squire, the bass player of his favorite band Yes, had turned him onto Reds.

I declined when he offered me one of his costly ciggies, and suddenly we were off to the races. Lee launched into a speech he had obviously pitched to hundreds before me. He stood up and began pacing the room, moving his body as if he was conducting a symphony, his hands constantly in motion while he swayed back and forth. He paused to take a large drag of his cigarette and then continued,

"You see, it's really a blend of science and emotion. Radio should be a cinematic experience for the listeners and the jocks ought to be their buddies, not some high and mighty aloof DJ." I finally found space to pose a question, and Lee responded,

"That is a fantastic question!"

I soon realized that was his constant reaction to any query and followed by an immediate return to his speech, which never properly answered the question. He explained that DC101 would have a soft launch because of advertising commitments and the air shift times would become normal once they got off the ground.

I asked about the common characteristics of great radio stations and Lee went into overdrive,

"Well, Sonny, first you have to have great production to create a theater of the mind that delivers sonic magic. You must also turn to what I call the 'Bible of Music,' which includes printed playlists and countdowns of the most popular songs in the city as determined by the station."

I pressed him, "Is that a Top 40 thing or an AOR thing?"

"It's a radio thing, essential for any music format."

Abrams was on a roll,

"Live personalities twenty-four by seven are a must, and they are not shifts but shows. Never forget that every daypart matters, even overnight. New Yorkers still talk about Charlie Greer's 3 a.m. commercials for Denison Men's Clothiers on WABC."

For years, Greer was the all-night disc jockey on WABC and his outrageous live spots for the all-night clothing store either rhymed or told a funny story. The men's shop was next to a strip joint, and it was the candle to draw customers into both. Of course, only the clothing shop could legally advertise. Each Denison ad contained the line "money talks and nobody walks," which became a commonplace expression. Lee continued,

"Eccentricity is a vital ingredient to successful radio, from crazed DJs to whacked out promotions. Appall the parents and their kids will swarm to the station."

I asked Abrams if he thought his new AOR rock format would ever be "mainstream?"

"Of course, it's already happening. Unlike the generic, pablum radio of today these new stations ooze the vibe of their cities; they are true soundtracks of their communities."

I asked some direct questions about DC101, but he talked around them without providing any useful information other than he would be bringing in a top PD to steer the ship. He then resumed his script,

"A good station constantly raises anticipation. The listener must believe there's always something major coming up and if they tune away, they will be missing out. The station must also have *swagger*, a confident vibe that everything it does, on the air and off, is special, meaningful and perfect."

I was either being sold the biggest thing since sliced bread, or this guy was the radio version of P.T. Barnum. By the way, why is sliced bread the biggest thing? I would have gone with fire or the wheel, but I digress. Lee continued,

"Every station has to be a well-oiled machine and hold the basics in high regard."

In a moment of high drama Lee raised his voice significantly,

"The station must have respect for the audience — and I mean, RESPECT! No bullshit. A radio station must never resort to tricks and it's imperative that they always keep their promises."

I thought back to Ashtabula and BAT-FM's disrespect of their Gospel audience and what it wrought. Watching Lee Abrams perform was already tiring me out, and I was just the guy asking questions. He was into his third cigarette as he wound down his well-prepared, well-rehearsed, incisive presentation,

"Look man, there has to be a completeness in a radio station, so the audience has no reason to listen elsewhere. And there's another essential ingredient, smartness. A station must be a hub of local information and the DJs must be plugged into everything going on in the city."

I challenged him,

"But aren't those things that every radio station strives for?"

"Yes, but to be the clear winner you have to be on the cutting edge and do things before your competitor even thinks about them. Oh, and here's another thing, graphics. The visual identity of a radio station has to mirror its on-air presence and convey a really cool vibe."

I asked him what bothered him about today's radio, and he answered,

"The lack of fresh ideas. Every few years, "new ways" come into play. From Storz to Drake to Bennett, things evolved, but not much beyond. It's sad that these days radio is still executing an old playbook."

Of course, Lee was talking about Top 40 pioneers Todd Storz, Bill Drake and Buzzy Bennett and I moved to wrap up the session. I felt if the guy went any longer, he would die of lung cancer.

My interview with Lee was published in R&R the same week DC101 went on the air. Sadly, the station's sales department had sold commercials into the future for the Johnny Holliday show with the understanding they would air on both the AM and FM signals, so rock music didn't start until Gary Chase hit the airwaves at 10 a.m. The goal was keeping Johnny's AC listeners tuned in, but one didn't need a job with the CIA in Langley to know this was not a terrific way to launch a new rock station. Despite that, DC101 would soon become a major factor in DC radio and would be at the center of an incredible radio explosion just a few years later.

I was living a good life in Washington, but I was what we all referred to as "rent poor." Most young people in the nation's capital were surviving right on the edge, and some would have to sell blood or their old guitar for rent money. On the other hand, I was having fun and dating a woman who wasn't afraid or ashamed to pick up a few checks along the way.

MC and I were having a wonderful lunch on a government holiday afternoon at Clyde's of Georgetown. That hip hangout had a happy hour menu named the "Afternoon Delight," which was the inspiration for what became a hit record for a musical group named the Starland Vocal Band. I once interviewed the two main members of the group, Bill Danoff and Taffy Nivert, to get background for an R&R feature story about John Denver. Bill had written *Take Me Home, Country Roads*, a smash hit single for Denver in 1971. The song is a tribute to the mountains of West Virginia and was later adopted as that state's official song. Being from Ohio and knowing the true beauty of West Virginia, I asked Bill,

"Wow, that song is so serene and iconic. Have you ever visited West Virginia?"

Bill smiled,

"No, I wrote that song in my Georgetown basement apartment. I just needed four syllables."

So, sitting there in Clyde's, MC decided since we were both off, we should both get off. She picked up the Afternoon Delight menu and we started sampling some of their more famous cocktails. We were somewhat "randy" as folks from "down under" say, and it wasn't long before we were counting those fifty steps up to the top of the building MC called home.

The apartment was sweltering with summer, and other, heat, and I remember her taking off her clothes and asking me to do the same. MC was standing by that little mattress, her body wet with sweat. She held out her long arms. I couldn't resist and I began by kissing her lips, then her neck. Hungry and hot she pulled me onto the bed. I tasted the flavor of the last drink she had at Clyde's, and it wasn't long before she pushed me from her small breasts with large nipples to another area that tasted much different.

Later in the afternoon, the sun had started its slow descent and MC was sitting on the bed, a shadow covering half her naked body. She was smoking a cigarette and asked me to pour two tumblers of Chivas. When I returned with the drinks, she turned to me and said,

"Sonny, love, this will be a nightcap for us."

I handed MC her drink. She looked up at me and carefully said,

"Sit down, we need to talk."

Now I didn't know what this was all about, but women have a weird timing mechanism I have never understood. Suddenly I was feeling as if we just had breakup sex and I was about to be the last one to find out. She started,

"It's time you know that I have a part-time job which is the reason we can't go to Rehoboth Beach this weekend."

"Man, the government must not pay much. What kind of job is it?"

She took a long drag of her cigarette, like a guy with a noose around his neck, and then finished off the few ounces of scotch before continuing,

"You remember Teresa, right? Well, she has this little side business and it's not something I'm proud of... but, um, it helps pay my rent and..."

I pulled my underwear on and sat down next to her and touched her shoulder,

"MC, what are you talking about?"

"Teresa runs an escort service on the side. We get paid five hundred dollars to go out with Congressmen and other rich guys."

My heart took a beat, and then another hard one,

"What the fuck, you're a prostitute?"

"No, no, the money is just to hang with a man and be seen. You know, just to be there. Some of the girls get a grand or more to do other things, but that isn't me."

"So, Teresa is a madame?"

"No, Teresa is just a contact person. She's in a long-term relationship with a Congressman from Buffalo."

I stopped for a second and went through my rolodex of big-name capitol Hill people,

"Is it Jack Kemp, the former football player?"

"I can't say, because a lot of these guys are married and if the word got out... well, you know."

I cradled her shoulders and took some time for thought before responding,

"MC, why would you put yourself in a position that could lead to scandal? This could kill your chances of getting into Georgetown Law."

She started to cry, the tears landing on her beautiful stomach and then dripping down to that special place, which was the source of her deep excitement and pleasure just a short while ago. She added this,

"The guy who I am going out with tomorrow night said he would help me get into the school and pay my tuition."

"In exchange for what?"

"I'm sorry Sonny, I should have been honest. I should have told you about this from the beginning."

Now she was outright bawling her eyes out as she stood up and poured herself another drink. I was stunned, and from my shoulders I heard those devil and angel voices, but for once they both were saying the same thing, "Get the hell out of here."

I slowly finished dressing while MC sat on the single chair at her card table substitute for a dining table. I turned to her before I left,

"You know, you need to figure out what you really want in life. You can't get everything on your back in this town; there has got to be a better way."

I closed the door and walked out into the smoggy, sweltering night air and tried to find a cab. D.C. is the only city where each cab company has different colors. I finally spotted and hailed one, and as I sat down in the smelly vehicle an old phrase buzzed through my mind, "You just dodged a bullet, Herbie." It was fun while it lasted, but I had to chalk it up as another learned lesson; things aren't always as they appear to be.

27. Stayin' Alive

Over the years I have met many people in the male-dominated record business, but beyond a single dinner few developed into a worthwhile friendship. There isn't anything particularly wrong with these folks, it's just they are so laser-focused on "working" their latest "project" and pushing their label's current "priority" that it was next to impossible to get to know most of them on a personal level.

It was 1977 and I was in Atlanta for a convention of the radio and records industries. I saw him almost immediately outside of a banquet room. Charlie Minor, the VP of promotion at A&M Records, was holding court under the intensely bright lighting. Instead of a bevy of blonde bombshell babes, this time Minor was surrounded by a group of men, all wearing dark, well-tailored suits with padded shoulders, which was the current rage. Charlie stood out because he was wearing a white, raw-silk dinner jacket and tuxedo pants. He looked like Jesus visiting the city on Palm Sunday. As the group began walking about, Charlie was back slapping, glad handing and vigorously working every radio guy along his path.

I spied a DJ in the group surrounding Charlie whom I really wanted to meet. His name was Scott Shannon, and until just recently he worked at Top 40 WMAK in Nashville. I'd heard a number of his airchecks and was always impressed with his effective presentation, a perfect radio communicator. Scott was an Army brat who had not one accent but a mix of many, which made him universally appealing. I followed his career and believed he was destined for greatness in radio. What I couldn't understand was why this talented radio personality would leave a major radio gig to go into record promotion. It felt like a sellout to me.

Shannon had recently started a job at a new record company named Ariola which was owned by a large German media company named Bertelsmann. At first, I believed the label's name was a wordplay on areola, an anatomical term, but I was told it was the combination of "ar," as in airplay and "ola," as in Victrola — once known as the Victor Talking Machine Company and famous for its hand-cranked record players back in the day. I was astonished when Charlie Minor grabbed my shoulder and pulled me into his group,

"Sonny Joe, do you know Scott Shannon?"

First, it was almost incomprehensible that Minor remembered me, but somewhere beyond coincidental he thought I should meet Shannon. Some say I lead a charmed life. Scott and I stopped walking and stood to talk for a bit,

"So, Scott, I really liked what you were doing in Nashville. Why the move to records?"

He smiled under his swept back hair, his gentle eyes and sharp, chiseled, cartoony chin painting a friendly countenance. He responded in a southernized patter,

"Hey brother, just wanted to see what it was like to live on the other side for a while, plus they're paying me a shitload of money."

"Do you miss radio?"

"You should be asking yourself the same question, Sonny Joe. Weren't you a baby disc jockey back in Cleveland, Santa Fe or was it Phoenix?"

That blew me away. He knew all the markets where I worked, and I suspected that if pressed he could rattle off the call letters too. See, that's why this new record company wanted him; he had vast radio knowledge and knew the players. Ariola would have a few chart busters straight out of the gate, including Mary MacGregor's *Torn Between Two Lovers*, but it wouldn't be long before Scott Shannon was back in radio and making himself a household name in major markets.

Rosemary Winter was the Programming Assistant at DC101. Her claim to fame was researching the Patent and Copyright office and uncovering documents which proved the Canadian rock band Klaatu was not the Beatles, ruining a promotion/scam/myth that was selling tons of records. I never believed that story. Klaatu sounded only slightly like the Beatles; a trick most Holiday Inn bands could have easily pulled off. Rosemary was hosting a gathering of Washington radio, music and record people in a small conference room.

As I stepped into the party, I quickly noticed a young, dark, Jamaican woman in the crowd I wanted to meet. Never being shy, I walked right over and introduced myself. After our name exchange, Simone Marley declared she was in no way related to international superstar Bob Marley. I didn't press her on that, simply taking her at her word.

Simone was truly exotic, far beyond her model-like appearance. Maybe it was her accent, or perhaps the way she moved, almost like she was dancing, not walking. Then again, could it have been her large, perfectly shaped breasts? Sorry, but maybe my amygdala was trying to control a primal need, or was I just missing my mother?

Simone lived in D.C. and worked freelance promoting music to reggae clubs. As we talked, I discerned her deep passion for rhythmic songs. It was almost as if she was on a mission to hype me on that musical genre. I thought back to my boyhood record collection with all those Black "race records," as well as those vastly different, more polished songs from Motown, Stax and Philadelphia International. I recalled those days when I was home from school and sick in bed, flipping over to the R&B station when I got bored with WING playing the same pop songs over and over. I have always loved all styles of Black music and, you surely know, "some of my best friends are Black."

When I told Simone what I did for a living, she became somewhat forceful, pressing me about why Radio & Records didn't do more to cover rhythmic formats. The term "Urban Radio," was coined by New York radio DJ Frankie Crocker in the 1970s as an umbrella term for Black musical styles including rhythm & blues, hip hop, disco and rap. It stuck.

Simone was tall, about five-foot-ten, so we were on the same physical level. Her deep brown eyes competed with her skin tone for attention, and I did all I could to focus on them. Her complexion contrasted sharply with her large, white teeth which almost seemed to glow in the dark.

I was saying my goodbyes while getting ready to leave the gathering when Rosemary, a gregarious, talkative woman from Pittsburgh, walked up to me and said,

"You looked like you were interested in Simone, or were you just entranced by her cleavage?"

She laughed as if she was the one to talk. Rosemary also has a balcony you could do Shakespeare from, thank you Firesign Theatre. I asked Rosemary for Simone's phone number, you know, just in case.

My office telephone rang early the next morning. Bob Wilson was on the line asking me to interview Bob Henabery, a guy who used to work at ABC Radio in New York. For the past two years, and very much under the radio business radar, Bob had been programming a new format on Washington's WKYS, the FM sister station to NBC's old-line WRC. Henabery was an older New England gentleman who had vast connections from his many radio jobs over the years. Bob was instrumental in transitioning ABC's owned FM stations from Free Form to Progressive rock and then onto AOR, bringing discipline and contemporary formatics to rock music programming which vastly increased ratings. I called Henabery at WKYS and he invited me to visit him at the station.

Bob was a tall guy, about six-three, and at the time we met had a gray, scraggly beard he constantly massaged, scratched and pulled. His voice was an amazingly deep baritone, and he used it effectively. Although Bob was a no bullshit, straight ahead kind of guy, he pontificated in a theatrical way, tossing in smiles at times, making his underlings feel he was more a caring father than strict authoritarian.

Although Henabery was a "format guy," he was equally a trend explorer. He wanted his clients and associates to not only understand the "what" of his programming policies but also the "why," the reason a given strategy made sense and would likely succeed. Bob sprinkled the term "disco" in our conversation and, silently, I was trying to grasp meaning. I knew the French word *discothèque* was a play on the word *bibliothèque,* which means "library," so I was imagining a collection of vinyl records. I didn't know then the word had been shortened and repurposed to define clubs in Europe where vinyl records, rather than a live band, provided the music, nor did I understand the style of the songs those clubs played was now called disco music.

This bearded consultant was completely open to R&R authoring a story about the groundbreaking format he was airing on WKYS-FM. The music was rhythmic in nature, and Bob claimed the song mix, sprinkled with a few jazzy songs by artists like Herbie Mann, had mass appeal to a wide range of listeners. He claimed his disco format would reach way beyond inner city kids, attaining massive audience success in the suburbs as well. Call me a doubting Thomas, but I had to probe,

"But Mr. Henabery, your playlist primarily consists of music by Black artists. Doesn't that make it just another Urban format?"

My question today might seem somewhat racist, but at that time it struck a nerve. Bob suddenly became a wiggling fish, impossible to hold in my hands. The veneer of a calm professor using logic, stats and reason suddenly evaporated, and he erupted,

"You don't know what you're talking about! If you did just a speck of research, you would understand I am totally right and soon there will be hundreds of stations running this format."

Driving back from the station, I was grappling with mixed feelings. One was Henabery's intense commitment to his disco format, and his past successes in radio surely required that I look more closely. I was turning one question over and over in my mind. What came from England or Europe that worked in America? Well, it didn't take me long to realize that *All in the Family*, an American television smash, was once a British TV show. My cab passed by a McDonald's, and I thought about French fries and their Belgium roots. Then there was that marginally successful Liverpool music group known as the Beatles. Maybe I was being closed minded.

I needed to set all that cerebral churning aside for another time. My mind was suddenly on Simone, and I decided to call and invite her to a weekend dinner. She was incredibly spirited on the phone,

"Hey, Sonny, what took you so long? I've been working my dreadlocks for days."

I snickered and we chatted, deciding on Saturday evening at the Thai Room, a restaurant near Nebraska Avenue, which, ironically, is where WKYS-FM was located. I probably didn't need to, but I asked anyway,

"Do you like spicy food? Their Thai fish dish will melt your face."

"Jo, Jo, I am a Jamaican woman; my body is one large piece of hot spice."

I loved her Jo Jo nickname. It made me think of Jo Jo Gunne, a rock band formed from the remnants of the late sixties group Spirit. They took their name from an obscure Chuck Berry song named Jo Jo Gunne, which barely cracked the Billboard Hot 100 in 1958. The members of Jo Jo Gunne would later sue Led Zeppelin for allegedly ripping off one of their riffs and using it in *Stairway to Heaven*. There are times when even I marvel at some of the obscure connections between rock music and my personal life.

After eating scorching hot Thai fish and walking out into a frigid night, Simone asked,

"Jo Jo boy, you know how to dance?"

"Well, I'm a white guy, but I have been known to 'bust some moves.' What do you have in mind?"

"You ever been to Tramps?"

"I've heard a lot about it. Let's grab a cab and go. It'll be a fine way to work off those four beers each of us just had."

You probably have seen a poster, once widely printed and sold in stores but now available on the internet, picturing a man dressed in an English horse-riding outfit and leaning on a Rolls Royce. He's holding a riding crop in one hand and a glass of champagne in the other. A bucket of ice with the remaining bubbly sits on the bumper of the car, illegally parked near what looks like a government building. Splashed prominently across the top of the poster are the words POVERTY SUCKS in a roaring twenties show font. That man is Mike O'Harro, the owner of the discothèque Tramps in Georgetown, whose name was most likely stolen from, I mean inspired by, Tramp, a private London club.

When he opened his restaurant and club in Washington DC in 1975, Michael had no idea he would be smack dab in the middle of a cultural phenomenon, but who writes history before it happens? Because of her connections to R&B and reggae bands, Simone was a regular at the club and the doorman whisked us straight inside. I later learned that Tramps was the first and most successful discothèque in America. In the club I saw a mix of upscale African Americans, gay men and young, white, suburban adults with white powder on their noses. The music sounded like it was recorded directly off WKYS, the dancefloor was packed, and it was obvious all the patrons were having a blast. I flashed back to my interview with Bob Henabery thinking, "Shit, maybe he's right."

Mike the owner was always in his disco club surrounded by an entourage of beautiful, well-dressed women, just like that record guy Charlie Minor. It was precisely the image he wanted to project. The club's décor was straight out of an old western movie; the only thing missing was an upstairs brothel. Oh, the cocaine did flow, but O'Harro stayed away. He was a businessman who later created Champion's Sport Bars and knew making money and doing drugs was an ill-advised mix.

I was amazed at how movie stars, politicians, and music people claimed Tramps as their own. I ran into some people I knew, including a funny guy named Izzy and an enthusiastic New York lady named Roxy who worked for Atlantic, a record label that had signed many disco acts like Chic, the Average White Band, Sister Sledge and later, The Trammps, whose *Disco Inferno* was perhaps the best damn disco song ever. I figured at least some of those clubgoers were researching the kind of songs that pulled people to the dance floor. I was captivated by the flow of music and the upbeat energy enveloping the place.

Some women say they can tell how a man will be in bed by how he dances. I was trying my best to keep it going with Simone, whose style was less disco and more reggae. Her moves were channeling Bob Marley's motions, a kind of swaying trance with accents on the upbeat. We left the club at 1:30 a.m., and Simone wanted to head back to her flat near Chevy Chase. I said it was time for me to call it a night as well. I waited while she hailed a cab,

"I hope my dancing didn't embarrass you."

A taxi pulled to the curb, and I opened the back door for her. She started to step in, but quickly turned back,

"Where are my manners, Jo Jo?"

She gave me a big hug, her breasts pressed tightly against my sweaty shirt as she planted those thick lips on my mouth, devouring my lips and tongue. That took my breath away and she said,

"Hey, call me. There's more where that came from."

The maroon and pale-yellow cab made a U-turn, and as it moved up Wisconsin Avenue, lyrics from the dancefloor were booming in my brain, *Voulez-vous coucher avec moi, ce soir? Voulez-vous coucher avec moi?* I was thinking about all that happened to me in my short radio career, and I whispered to myself, "You know, Bob Henabery just might be onto something with his new format." Equally insightful was this self-realization, "Hey, I really like disco!"

28. One Special Night

On September 15, 1977, I got a call from my friend Rosemary Winter over at DC101. It seems Warner Brothers Records representative Doc Dembrak had visited her station to promote a new Steve Martin album, and he brought along Martin's road manager, a guy named Bill, who, like Rosemary, was from Pittsburgh. The two mentioned Steve would be hosting an upcoming Saturday Night Live. While Rosemary liked Steve, she became energized hearing Jackson Browne would be the show's musical guest. Now I don't know why so many women think Jackson is the "cat's meow," but Rosemary was far beyond meow for this guy. She WANTED HIM, lock, stock and Stratocaster. Rosemary went behind her boss's back and boldly asked the record promoter for tickets to SNL. Her plan was meeting Jackson Browne backstage after the show, knocking him off his feet, marrying him, then having his babies. [violins up, roll ending credits, couple walks off into the sunset]

Rosemary told me she scored two SNL tickets and I replied,

"Hey, that's wonderful. Have a fantastic time. You deserve it."

Then she popped the question,

"Would you drive me to New York and attend the show with me?"

She began "pitching" the idea, saying we could use her car and she would treat the gas and food. Trying to remain cool and not expose my enthusiasm, I questioned,

"Rosemary, why not take a date or girl friend?"

She expressed her desire to keep the trip top secret and was concerned if she brought a girlfriend, well,

"She might get in the way."

I got it and reluctantly agreed to drive and attend the show, and she countered with an offer to drive back to D.C. afterwards. The deal was done, and we made plans to leave at noon on Saturday, September 24, 1977.

On the drive to New York, she revealed the tickets were in my name at NBC and I was not at all happy about that. I wanted to see the show, but I was worried my boss in LA might find out and I would be called on the carpet for accepting a record company favor. Other than this, the drive to the city was uneventful.

Unbelievably, we found a free parking space in New York's Greenwich Village. We ate at Ray's Original Pizza on St Mark's Place, and then hightailed it uptown in a taxicab, leaving Rosemary's parked car behind. The excitement was mounting as we got out of the cab in front of the NBC Studios. When I asked for our tickets at the will-call desk, I was told there was nothing there under my name.

Quickly, Rosemary moved front and center to an NBC page and started to spout the names, ranks and serial numbers of her contacts. We waited in silence until the page called to verify her story with the record company, and just a few moments later he reappeared and handed us our two tickets to paradise.

We got on the elevator, and when the doors opened Rosemary and I stepped into a long hallway painted in industrial shades of gray and green. As we waited in line, costumed characters from the show darted in and out of doorways on both sides of the hallway, just like the scene in *Yellow Submarine*. The big double doors to Studio 8H finally swung open. We made it! Our SATURDAY NIGHT LIVE tickets were in the fucking FRONT ROW! We were in heaven, and the program hadn't even started.

Steve Martin came out shortly before the show went live to warm up the crowd. He launched into some of his non-airable material, which included blowing up a condom and releasing it into the crowd. Steve certainly set the stage for a night of uproarious excellence. We were already in stitches when the live TV program began.

The show was one of the all-time classics and the comedy exploded continuously before our eyes. The routines were excellent, and we laughed until it hurt. I had to restrain Rosemary when Jackson Browne and his band of renowned LA studio musicians played their two numbers. I looked at Jane Curtin, Laraine Newman and Gilda Radner standing on a side stage watching Jackson singing and thought they were three of the skinniest ladies I had ever seen. Those women looked normal from the front, but when they turned sideways, they almost disappeared. Dan Ackroyd did his fantastic Jimmy Carter routine, and Steve and Danny were hysterical as a pair of Czechoslovakian brothers Jorge and Yortuk Festrunk, those two "wild and crazy guys." It seemed like only ten minutes had passed when the cast and guests were all standing on stage wishing America a good night.

The show had ended, but everyone just stood around like they were at a high school dance no one wanted to leave. The band kept jamming for a while, then they abruptly stopped, stood, gathered their instruments and sauntered off the stage. Show's over.

We moved into the hallway outside the studio. Nearby, Jackson Browne and Bill the road manager were having a conversation. Rosemary walked over and said hello to Bill, and he introduced her to Jackson. She froze, so I gently steered her into position. Bill turned to say hello to another and got pulled into a different conversation. I looked at the musical guest saying, "Great show Jackson," and Rosemary shook his hand. She looked down at the floor, clueless about what to say or do next. She will forever remember his shoes and I will remember his large, 'luded-out pupils.

I was totally satisfied, gratified and ready to hit the road. Rosemary returned to Doc and Bill and their circle of friends to give thanks for the tickets. I leaned against the wall, feeling the evening gaining on me. Rosemary returned with a "please, pretty please" look on her face, saying we had been invited to a post-show dinner at One Fifth Avenue. I shook my head and reminded her of the plan to get back to D.C. before sunrise, but Rosemary was adept at getting her way.

We were the first to arrive at the restaurant, which had a small bar in the front. Between the bar and the seating area stood the maître d' station, a "social-barricade" separating the common drinking folk from the famous. Rosemary leaned over and handed me two of her diet pills, and whispered,

"Here, you'll need these."

Five minutes later I was ready to party all night long, especially when I realized we were sitting at the star table. Perfectly dressed in a slightly less formal suit than he wore at the evening's performance, Steve Martin sat down at the table. A waiter asked me what I wanted, and I just pointed at something with a strange name on the menu, steak tartare. I later learned that's a fancy name for raw meat and, depending on how it's prepared, consumption can be challenging. Bill's date, a beautiful Hungarian model, was sitting next to me but soon got up and headed toward the restroom.

I felt a sharp pain in my thigh right above my knee cap. It was Rosemary's fingernails digging deeply into my leg. Her eyes motioned to what I thought would be the empty chair next to me, vacated by the Hungarian on a mission to powder her nose. I turned to look and there, sitting right next to me, was Mick Jagger! He glanced in my direction, and I said,

"Hi."

"Eh mate."

And thus ended my moment with stardom, as Mick resumed chatting with Bill, who apparently knew everybody in the music business.

Looking around the room I saw Gilda, Jane, Laraine, John Belushi and Paul Simon, along with a who's who of New York music and showbiz celebrities. Wow! Could it get any better than this? Shortly after dinner, Steve Martin politely departed but Bill insisted we all meet at a club named TRAX for some music. I figured what the hell. We left the restaurant and headed to the nightclub located in the basement of an office building.

Just as we entered the club, the house lights dimmed, the stage lights came up and, to my total surprise, and Rosemary's delight, Jackson Browne's band began playing. How the hell did they get here and set up so quickly?

Rosemary found a chair and ordered a drink while I walked around the room. As I neared the edge of the stage, I noticed John Belushi and Lorne Michaels in the front row sipping champagne and rocking out. Then, as if it was planned, Belushi jumped on stage and started to sing with the band. This was before John's Blues Brothers act with Dan Aykroyd, and he belted out a perfect Elvis parody. I was impressed at how well he sang, and I nudged the guy standing next to me,

"This is great. This is fantastic!"

Just then I noticed "that guy" grinning ear to ear was Bill Murray, he said,

"Hey, you know what they say? Yellow is mellow!"

Then we both said in unison,

"But brown goes down."

After that, he just walked away. There was a major water shortage in California at the time which was the origin of the slogan. I don't know whether Bill was referring to Jackson Browne or if Bill was just being Bill.

Now it was time for Browne to get down. When the band began playing the intro to *Redneck Friend,* the stage lighting washed into the audience revealing a sea of humanity, and as my eyes adjusted, I could clearly see the first five or six rows. Like perusing the *Sgt. Pepper's* album jacket, I started to recognize some folks in the crowd. There was Carly Simon and James Taylor, Hall and Oates, Andy Warhol, along with a boulder of a bodyguard, and a multitude of other famous faces.

At around 5 a.m., a rousing rendition of *Running on Empty* concluded with a long, sustained chord. The house lights faded up and the stars started scurrying away before the daylight could destroy the magic of the evening. I walked the littered floor of the club and found Rosemary for the drive home.

Outside it had started to rain and we were desperately trying to hail a cab. Belushi and Michaels came out with the champagne bottle and glasses along with two hot ladies on their arms. The entourage popped into a big, black, stretch limo then, bang, they were gone. The rain kicked up and it was clear a nor'easter had blown in. The deluge was slicing east to west, and we were getting pelted. I felt like a seal. All I could think about was getting back home, having had enough stimulation to last a lifetime.

Miraculously, a cab stopped and picked us up. Once back in the Village we rushed to the car, only to see one of its tires was flat as a pancake. I had to change it in the pouring rain when all I wanted was safe haven in my warm, firm bed back in D.C. The waterbed did not make the trip from Arizona.

After wrestling with the tire change, I took off all my clothes and tossed them into the back seat. I found an old beach towel and covered my essentials, climbed into the driver's seat, started the engine and put the heater on full blast. I didn't want to get pulled over and have to explain why I was under-dressed, so I drove the speed limit. While Rosemary dozed off next to me, I asked myself if I had only imagined her saying she would drive us home.

One Special Night

I dropped Rosemary off at her house, retrieved my car and finally made it back to my apartment, twenty-two hours after this crazy night started. I began thinking about Simone and my need to tell her this adventure was a friend thing and not a romantic escape. Truth leads to trust.

29. Push, Push, in the Bush

On December 9, 1977, I had a date with Simone which would come to be a combination of toxins, timing and a time bomb, none of which I could prevent or stop. Was it the blue wire, the red wire, or just all the colors of the rainbow that would explode over my special pot of gold? You might say I was very quickly falling in lust with the young Jamaican entrepreneur, but we both would soon see the light, the bright beam of a trend or maybe just a fleeting fad whose beginning held so much promise.

I invited Simone to the Washington premier of *Saturday Night Fever*, a new John Travolta movie. Her first reaction was,

"You mean that guy who played Vinnie Barbarino on the TV show, *Welcome Back Kotter*? Okay, I guess, Jo Jo, but only because I'll be with you."

The temperature on our date-day stayed just below thirty-two degrees. I felt a little tingle in my throat while working in the office and thought, "Oh, no, don't get sick now, Herbie." I have always liked Drambuie, the Scottish after dinner drink. For those non-alcoholics in the audience, that liqueur is a blend of aged Scotch whisky, spices, herbs and heather honey. They say it was a secret recipe created for Bonnie Prince Charlie by his Royal Apothecary in the Eighteenth Century. Having adopted the name McPherson obligated me to know all things Scottish.

I picked up a bottle during my lunch break, and to ward off the throat tickle I added a shot to my afternoon coffee. Well, one shot led to a few more and soon not only was the tickle gone but I was also starting to slur my words. Herman Kauffman, our accountant, came into my office to ask a question about one of my expense reports. He looked down at the open bottle on my desk,

"You know, dat it's against da policies of da company to consume dat in the vork place?"

"Oh, my doctor prescribed it. I have a sore throat."

He quickly left the room. At the end of my workday, I took the bottle with me and put it in the backseat of my brand-new car. I had a friend who worked in sales at the Bethesda AMC dealership, and several weeks ago he came to me in a panic saying his boss would fire him if he didn't sell a car that week. I bought an unusual, weirdly shaped car that was more spaceship than "chick magnet," a bright blue Pacer, which I lived with and laughed at for the next three years. My sales friend was fired three days later, and I was stuck with a bizarre ride.

Simone met me outside the theater, and she looked fantastic in her long fur coat with mock puff-sleeves. She briefly flashed open her coat to show me the fantastic red mini dress she was wearing underneath. Yes, it was freezing out and that short dress certainly wouldn't keep her warm, but she was the hottest lady on the planet and those gorgeous long legs beautifully balanced her dancer butt.

We entered the theater, watched the movie and afterwards sang *"Stayin' Alive, Stayin; Alive"* all the way back to her apartment. To say we were blown away by the film was an understatement. Simone had already figured out how this "disco movie" would add a huge push to her business, and I took it as more unmistakable evidence that Bob Henabery was correct; disco was here to stay. I was in her kitchen pouring two glasses of Drambuie when Simone asked for hers on the rocks. She had these tiny, square ice cubes, which for some unknown reason made the drinks taste better. We were sitting on the carpet in the middle of the living room, having crackers and cheese with our drinks, when I excused myself to take a call from Mother Nature.

While in the bathroom, I smelled that distinctive scent of the herb from Simone's native land. I quickly finished my business, washed my hands and looked in the mirror to make sure I wouldn't see someone on an all-day bender looking back at me. When I returned to the living room, Simone was still wearing her fur coat and smoking what can best be described as a mega-Marley spliff — six inches. She reached out to hand me the joint and her coat opened, revealing she was wearing nothing other than her knee-high boots under that furry wrap. I took a hit and then, magically, I was in her bed totally naked.

Simone was still wearing her boots as we thumped to the beat of reggae music coming from two large speakers on either side of the bed. Bob Marley's song *Exodus* was playing, and I saw a tear fall from one of her eyes. She let out a muted scream and grabbed my ass hard. She then reached down and pulled her right breast up to her lips, and while staring into my eyes she showed me what she wanted. She dabbed Drambuie on each of her areolas and pushed her breasts toward me. Man, they were full-sized, delicious and eighty proof!

A momentous radio event took place on July 24, 1978, when Disco 92 WKTU hit the New York City airwaves. Kent Burkhart had convinced the partners of San Juan Racing Association, whose broadcasting company was named SJR Communications, to flip the station to a disco format. By this time, many people were aware of the consistent growth of Bob Henabery's success at WKYS in D.C., and perhaps it was the "purity" of WKTU's disco format that so quickly attracted a huge audience. Remember, WKYS sprinkled in some danceable jazz songs which 'KTU didn't.

Meanwhile, everyone in the Big Apple was talking about Studio 54. Steve Rubell and Ian Schrager, once college roommates at Syracuse University, got into the nightclub business after the failure of their first venture, a chain of steak restaurants. Studio 54 was openly snobby and shamelessly turning away all but the most chic, famous or beautiful patrons. The exclusivity and hype brought the moths to the flame.

Of course, the movie *Saturday Night Fever* and the colossal sales figures of the RSO soundtrack album meant that people from Des

Moines, Decatur, Duluth and everywhere else across the land were stayin' alive, stayin' alive and dancing their hearts out.

WKTU shot to the number one position in its first rating book, a seismic explosion in the radio business that not only made the station worth ten times more than it was previously valued, but also made Paco Navarro a huge star. He was a Puerto Rican DJ with a highly sultry, accented voice who crossed all ethnic demographics and became the linchpin of this fresh broadcasting phenomenon. Subway conductors in New York City imitated Paco when making their stop announcements.

Disco also propelled women into positions they hadn't held before, like Wanda Ramos as music director and then PD in New York, who then went on to become a consultant at Burkhart/Abrams. Female music directors propelled the disco format and helped other women climb the ladder to become programmers and managers. Women had an intuitive feel for dance music. They knew which songs worked and they were incredibly valuable to the format and the radio business.

I flew to LA for a major strategy session with all the R&R reporters and format page editors. How shall we cover this new format and how far should we go? It was important not to overstate the success of two stations and we also realized our CHR reporting stations didn't want to be thrown aside because of a new musical style. Besides, those mainstream stations had already embraced disco by playing the crème de la crème. They edited out any inappropriate words and shortened the disco hits to make them blend into their format. When a Disco station attracted a wide audience in a major market, the sales department of the competing CHR station would counter-pitch by saying only African Americans were consuming the disco station. However, such false talk certainly didn't affect the ratings or stop the multitude of fad chasers in radio looking for instant success. Within a few months, Burkhart/Abrams would deploy disco on fifty stations from Boston to Honolulu and from Denver to Des Moines.

I was surprised when I heard Kent Burkhart on the phone offering me a job to launch his new disco station in Indianapolis. I had to ask,

"That's really a compliment Kent, but where did you hear about me?"

"Well, I was having a conversation with Scott Shannon, and he went on and on about your great radio sensibilities. I'm looking for someone to guide us to prominence in this new format and I think you're my guy. Indy is a fabulous town, and don't be fooled by that lie that a large Black population is needed to get numbers."

I hadn't even thought about that. I was focused solely on the idea of a move to Indianapolis. My mother would love me being only a hundred miles from her, but what about R&R? What about Simone? I told Kent I would think about it, which seemed perfectly fine to him as long as he had my answer no later than 5 p.m. tomorrow.

First, out of deep respect and a growing love for Simone, I called her and asked if she would like to meet for drinks at Jason's on M Street. When she walked in, every head in the place turned. Several onlookers were dazzled when she sat down next to me and slapped a giant open-mouth smooch on my kisser.

"Hey Jo Jo baby."

She seemed somewhat stressed and not at all herself,

"You look uptight, gorgeous. Difficult day?"

"No, actually it was a good day, but I'm facing a strange situation I never thought would happen, but now, well, it's on the table and I need a drink."

I was already nursing a Johnny Walker and she ordered a Vodka gimlet. Her cocktail arrived quickly and as she sipped, I turned to her,

"So, what's happening?"

"Well, there's this guy who has been talking with me for about the last six months. He's from Chicago."

I suddenly feared a breakup meeting was about to unfold,

"What does he want?"

She quickly replied,

"He's offered me a job to manage his club Faces, which is the Studio 54 of Chicago.

I started to laugh. She looked at me in disbelief which quickly became a scowl,

"Oh, is that funny to you, Jo Jo?"

"No, no, I was just offered a job in Indianapolis to run a new radio station there."

I had already investigated the map in my head. Chicago was maybe two hundred miles from Indy. Her disdain turned into a beaming smile, her white teeth lighting up the room,

"Oh my God, Oh my God, that's fantastic!"

Yes, once again I saw my life being programmed with only a bit of talent but a ton of luck. Bob Wilson was nothing less than kind and understanding on the phone call when I told him I would be leaving R&R. He said he was more than happy for me and knew I would do well. It occurred to me that he was a genuinely good man.

I arrived in Indy and met with the GM of the station. We mapped out some early moves and my new boss asked me if I would be okay hosting a weekend air shift. That was no problem for me at all. I loved the music and felt that nurturing my on-air chops would be a good thing.

So, we launched Disco 99 in the city that gives us the Indianapolis 500, which became my opening gambit. We flipped the format at 3 p.m. on a Friday with a tight playlist of the most popular disco songs and constantly rotating promos promoting the Disco 99 Indy 500, five-hundred songs in row without talk or commercial interruption. During our first weekend on the air, the station would play nothing but music then, starting at 6 a.m. Monday, we would bring in DJs and, of course, spots. I was hearing my station everywhere across Indy that weekend, and it felt as if we were primed for success.

Simone had already arrived in Chicago, and she was doing well with the club. We had a call and she eagerly spoke of her venue and how its music was not only a disc jockey spinning records but also cutting edge and headliner bands playing live.

Simone often brought in major reggae artists like Peter Tosh and Lucky Dube, and I would drive up to Chicago for those extravagant events. It reminded me of the night we saw Bob Marley at Georgetown University in D.C. That was one of our best nights together and an almost mystical music experience for each of us, without drink or drugs.

Things were going well at Disco 99. Sure, there were negative comments from the Rock and CHR stations in town, but that flew in the face of our respectable ratings and increasing sales. I suggested to the sales manager he hire some African American salespeople to give us an edge when pitching Black-owned businesses. He hired only one.

It was now the Summer of 1979, and I was planning a big event for Disco 99 at the Indiana State Fair. It was hard to believe that little Herbie Klotenfelder was the program director of a successful, major market radio station. I was living large and happy as a clam, but why are clams so damn happy? Could it be the security of a shell? I spent many of my weekends with my baby in Chicago. She was making tons more money than me and her apartment overlooking the lake was like a movie set. Life was good, and I was outside of my shell in so many ways.

Push, Push, in the Bush

July 12, 1979 is a date that will "live in infamy." I was having a drink with some of my jocks in a little tavern near the station. The Chicago White Sox were big in Indy, and the owner of this establishment had Sox banners and pennants lining the walls and the large black TVs dotting the place were always tuned to the games. Today the Sox were playing the Detroit Tigers in a doubleheader at Comiskey Park. The first game had concluded, and a between-games event was about to begin. Here's where the story takes a turn.

Because of the success of *Saturday Night Fever*, the White Sox held a "Disco Night" at Comiskey Park in 1977, the same year Chicago's WLUP, The Loop, launched a Rock format. Now, two years later, The Loop was at the top of the ratings, and they put together a promotion with the Sox. The event, named Disco Demolition, was concocted by Sox' owner Mike Veeck, WLUP's Sales Manager Jeff Schwartz and the station's promotional whiz-kid Dave Logan.

When the moment arrived, The Loop's top DJ Steve Dahl, and his sidekick Gary Meier, appeared in a Jeep circling the field. The duo warmed up the crowd by leading the entire stadium in a chant of "disco sucks." Dahl was dressed in an army outfit and ready to wage war by blowing up a pile of disco records that had been stacked on the pitcher's mound. Yes, blowing them up!

I couldn't help wondering why this promotion was so openly aggressive, then it hit me like a ton of bricks. The words Lee Abrams spoke during our interview came back to me like a bullhorn blaring in my brain, "Eccentricity is a vital ingredient to successful radio, from crazed DJs to whacked out promotions. Appall the parents and their kids will swarm to the station."

White Sox officials had hoped for a crowd of twenty thousand that fateful night, about five thousand more than usual. Instead, some fifty thousand packed the stadium, many of them WLUP fans. Dahl set off the explosives, destroying the records and tearing a large hole in the field. After the blast, accompanied with bits of vinyl flying all about, a mass of kids stormed the turf and the White Sox had to forfeit the second game. I'm sure they "appalled" their parents, but more importantly, the event was the lead story on every TV network in the world.

There I stood, watching it all unfold on TV, daft but not drunk enough to ward off the disbelief and angst. Lee Abrams and Kent Burkhart were partners in the same firm. One was launching disco radio stations around the country while the other was declaring war against the format. What were those guys thinking?

The State Fair people called the next week and canceled my radio station's big event. Articles popped up everywhere with titles like "Is Disco Dead?" and "Is the Last Dance Near?" Disco 99's owner got spooked and brought in a new consultant to steer the ship out of "troubled waters." I became a casualty of the negative press. Yes, I got canned!

Across America disco stations were unloading the format. Some modified or morphed from disco to pop-oriented Rhythmic formats. One of those was stunningly successful KISS-FM in Boston. The PD of that station was Sonny Joe White, and he developed an impressive national reputation, but why wouldn't he with such a fabulous name? May he rest in peace.

Perhaps disco's final blow came in a 1979 op-ed piece published by my buddies back at R&R, "Around most of the world, disco was a frolicking music trend that pervaded, peaked then quietly receded," like my hairline in later years. The disco "trend" erupted so quickly the "fad" was an easy target to take down. Almost overnight, the word "disco" took on a heavily negative vibe. It was so bad that people who still liked disco songs would say in research focus groups, "Oh, I don't like disco at all." They couldn't explain exactly why, but I believed a certain overweight Chicago DJ dressed like a soldier had ruined the party. The lesson learned? Never chase a fad, focus on steady trends and stable ideas.

Push, Push, in the Bush

For the rest of 1979, I lived with Simone in Chicago and looked for work. At least I was with my love in a city with friendly people and amazing food. Chicagoland had everything I needed.

30. Rockin' Rockford

I was up early that morning, the Ides of March 1980, the day in history when sixty conspirators, led by Marcus Junius Brutus, stabbed Julius Caesar to death in the Roman Senate. I was watching a documentary on the Chicago PBS TV station about Congo leader Patrice Lumumba. Having a Black girl friend, I thought it wise to bone up on some African history.

Lumumba was the first Prime Minister of the Republic of the Congo after he and others broke away from Belgium and became independent. Seven months into his term, on January 17, 1961, he was assassinated. Anyone who has studied American intervention and the Dulles brothers' efforts in US politics know we have been far less than honorable in changing governments around the world. We usually took the easy route by having the CIA assassinate whichever leader we didn't like. Many of our moves were based on a fear of communism, and any possible spread was met with lethal, and I will add, unlawful force.

The phone rang and I almost tumbled off the couch as the call unfolded. An old buddy who was now the PD of WROK in Rockford, Illinois was on the line saying that his 7 p.m. to midnight jock suddenly left town and he immediately needed someone to fill in. Rockford is only ninety miles from our apartment in Chicago, so I agreed to come over and help him out. He explained he would try to find a replacement right away and the station would put me up in a small apartment near their studios.

The only thing I knew about Rockford was some rare baseball trivia about a women's baseball league formed during World War II and the Rockford Peaches were one of the teams. The movie named *A League of Their Own* honored the Peaches. As always, Simone had worked late the night before so I let her sleep, dashing off a brief note explaining my new gig along with a promise to call her from Rockford.

The station at the time was an up-tempo, tightly formatted CHR and it sure was fun being "Sonny Joe on the Ray-Dee-O!" I called Simone before going on the air that first night and she was thrilled for me. She apologized for being asleep when the call came, and I said,

"Don't be silly, it's all good. This won't be much money but it's going to help me mentally."

I told her I would be back early Saturday morning and wished her a wonderful week. It was fun being with DJs again after a few months of isolation in Simone's apartment. The way radio people who are total strangers can strike up a conversation, and within minutes discover they are connected by stations, formats, people and cities is always fascinating. I've often said broadcasting is a small, incestuous business where a new associate often already knows key elements of their newfound connection's radio history.

I was having lunch with three of the station's jocks who had been around the horn, as we say, and I'm not talking about the horn of Africa. These guys had worked major markets, but in their advancing ages had decided Rockford presented an opportunity to stay in radio with little pressure. One of the guys there, who in his younger days looked just like Robert Redford, called himself "The Original Charlie Browne." He began telling a story about working as program director at CKGM in Montreal, which soon captured the attention of everyone around the table,

"So, I'm at the desk in my oppressive, windowless office at the station and the receptionist buzzes me and says there's a guy in the lobby who wants to talk to me. I tell her I'm busy working on tomorrow's music log and hang up."

One of wisecracking morning guys, Jay Baker, jumps in,

"That's your story, Charlie? What the fuck?"

The storyteller continued,

"She calls me again from the front desk, only this time she says, 'Charlie, he's coming to your office.' I look up and this man in an old army coat is standing there. He's maybe in his late fifties, has a scraggly beard and is holding a gun on me."

Baker now gets it,

"Whoa!"

"I ask him what he wants and in bad French and even worse English he says he wants to talk on the radio. I suggest he come back later when the boss is here so we can arrange a proper time for him to talk on our music station."

Early in my radio career I learned about people coming into radio stations for various random, sometimes scary, reasons, and there are many tales of DJs carrying guns into a station, but I never had to deal with a pure lunatic wielding a weapon. Charlie went on,

"I use my most calming voice and say, 'It can't happen right now.' With that, the walls echo with a sharp crack, and I feel a bullet whiz through my hair."

Now, I know you are wondering if this really happened. Well, it did, and back then Browne had an extremely thick crop of blonde hair which was always styled perfectly, but let's get back to the story,

"The room smells like sulfur, so I figure I am dead or in hell, but no, the wild guy is still in front of me waving the gun and instructing me to stand up. He says, 'Take me to where they talk on the radio.'"

Steve Hartman, the PM Drive jock, chimed in,

"I can't begin to imagine what I would have done."

"Well, we walk past the air studio window and the jock and news lady spot the guy with a gun trained on my back. They hit the deck and crawl under the console. At the end of the hall, I fake some absent mindedness and tell the guy he should talk from the newsroom. I turn and ask him to follow me, and we walk back up the long hallway."

Baker shook his head,

"I would have been pissing my pants."

"So, we're walking up the stark white hallway and there are two guys walking toward us. They look out of place and suspicious. One is wearing a Montreal Expos T-shirt and the other looks like a dock worker with a tuque and three-day old beard. I pass the first guy and he winks at me, then the madman looks through the window into the air studio with all the blinking lights and says, 'No, no, I want to talk in there.'"

Steve says,

"How'd they keep the music on the air?"

"My jock would reach up from his position on the floor to run the board and keep the format going, but now it gets rich. The newsroom door is on the left and the air studio door is on the right, and I leap into action. I push the guy into the newsroom and then take off running down the hall, almost knocking over the two undercover guys from the Montreal police. I get to the end of the hall and enter the station lobby where the receptionist has packed up her purse and is now heading to the elevators. She turns her head to tell me she called the cops as soon as the guy walked toward my office. The undercover cops were working a drug case nearby, so they quickly took the call."

We all sat there wondering if that was it, then Charlie smiled,

"I suddenly hear dozens of rounds exchanged along with breaking glass but figure with two on one it all might turn out okay. I hear shouting, obscenities and more gunfire, then the place gets incredibly quiet. Just minutes later the two cops walk out of the studio area with the lunatic in handcuffs. Then, five uniform guys arrive to haul the gunman away."

Baker asked,

"Wait, they fire off dozens of rounds and not one shot landed on any of them?"

"Amazingly true, but the destruction was intense, shattered glass across the floor, plasterboard blown off the walls and bullet holes in the ceiling. It took weeks to get the station back to normal."

Meanwhile, it was a good week and a bad week for me in Rockford. Good because I was having a blast being back on the radio. The audience response was all positive and one caller asked if I was the same Sonny Joe from Phoenix; that meant a lot. The bad piece? I was totally missing Simone.

Being away from Chicago and working in Rockford radio made me think about the future of my career. Perhaps it's time to expand my job search, and that might mean a fateful decision about Simone. Many radio couples had the dilemma of two different jobs pulling in opposite directions, and some dealt with it by having every other job move be a sacrifice for the other partner. He would get the big job; she would quit and move with him. Then she would land the cherry position, and he would rearrange life to move with her. Such a bargain was far from guaranteed, and in some cases a breakup still occurred. Sometimes it's just impossible to give up a fantastic job.

I got to thinking about Charlie Browne and how close he came to death that day, but also wondering why he called himself the "Original" when there were more than ten guys who had used that name before him. His memory was terrific, however, and he explained the case of the whack-job at CKGM, was highly political. The gun-wielding man was part of the separatist movement that believed in Québécois people and wanted a Quebec nation separate and independent from Canada. We had that same fervor here in the States with our revolution against England, and later, that tear in democracy known as the Civil War. As for the death of Patrice Lumumba, it was more than racism. Those fighting for independence angered many foreign and local interests in the Belgian colonial state who were making tons of money extracting Congo's mineral resources. It's always something vast that drives the fortunes, fates and fabrications of powerful people.

I got up early that Saturday morning and drove to Chicago from Rockford, my temporary home away from home. Being the early hours of a weekend day, the traffic wasn't bad at all. The sun was coming up in the east, which is a stupid thing to say because that's where the sun always comes up. I had to lower my visor to escape the blinding light.

Once in the city, I didn't waste any time getting into the parking garage of our high-rise building. I figured I would check the mailbox in the lobby before going upstairs and quietly entering the apartment. I knew Simone would still be sleeping, such is the life of a nightclub manager. After grabbing some bills and circulars I was making my way to the elevators when I passed Kerry, our doorman. He looked dejected and upset as if he had just lost his best friend.

"Hey, Kerry, how you doin'?"

"I am so sorry Mr. McPherson."

I stopped in my tracks. The sun had just hit my eyes, so I moved a few steps closer to him. He was slightly trembling, and his watery eyes appeared ready for a major cry,

"What do you mean? What are you talking about?"

He took a deep breath and then uttered words that instantly made no sense, had no meaning,

"Oh my, you haven't heard. I'm so sorry, Mr. McPherson, but you'd best brace yourself. There was some sort of a gun battle outside her club last night and Miss Simone and several others were killed. It's so terrible."

This happened to me only one other time in my life, but I suddenly lost control. While my brain was processing the words, my knees first weakened then failed. I dropped the mail and keys, then the design of the carpeting immediately rushed up to meet my face. I was probably out for a few minutes. When I drifted back to consciousness, three people were standing over me, one of their hands holding a smelling salts inhalant under my nose. I looked at Kerry and asked,

"Is what you said true?"

He was now crying and confirmed,

"Yes, Mr. McPherson, it's true. Here, let me help you to your apartment."

I remember looking down at Kerry's hands as I was leaning against the back wall of the elevator. He had my keys and mail, and I was trying to fend off guilt, sadness and despair. Was it possible to get into the fetal position while standing?

It would be years before I would step into a nightclub again. I sorted through the facts I'd been given, but I just could not fully comprehend what had happened. Why would the owner of a competing nightclub do this to someone I cared so much about, and what was up with Chicago and fucking guns? Have we not moved beyond Al Capone?

Once again, dark, evil forces of the world were knocking at my door. For weeks I didn't go anywhere, and many days I didn't even attempt getting out of bed. This was the lowest of lows, the very bottommost and worst part of my life. All I wanted was to see the sun come up again. It would be a while.

31. Living to Learn

Within days, every Marley from Nine Mile Road to Kingston, Jamaica was in Chicago. I was amazed Simone had so many relatives and, as expected, famous singer Bob Marley wasn't one of them. Identifying Simone's body at the city morgue was perhaps the most disturbing, depressing and debilitating event of my life. I will carry that dreadful experience with me forever and would never wish such a task on anyone, even my worst enemy.

I believe death brings out the best in some people but the worst in kinsfolk. In just months, "Tuff Gong" would leave us, and major arguments over royalties and ownership of Bob Marley's songs would begin. Simone's relatives from Jamaica were claiming rights to her property left and right, but I was just "the boyfriend." I packed up my stuff and grabbed a few treasures, mostly personal memorabilia and a handful of photos.

Feeling lost I drove home to Dayton to stay with mom for a while. She was incredibly wonderful and had some great salt of the earth advice about life and death. One afternoon, we were having her famous grilled cheese sandwiches with Cincinnati chili on the side when she said,

"Herbie, your father used to always say when you hit a bump in the road go read a book or get some more education."

I don't remember my dad ever saying that, but surely this was a teaching moment,

"He put away money for your college education and we never withdrew it from the savings and loan. You should take it. Why don't you go back to school?"

My mother touched a nerve. I greatly regretted never receiving a college diploma. Maybe resuming my education would be a productive way to fill the void created by Simone's death. I wasn't that old, and if I went after an associate degree, I could wrap it up in under two years.

I found a well-respected Journalism program at the University of Michigan. The school was located in Detroit's Dearborn section, which wasn't the main campus. That was fine by me because I wouldn't have the distraction of all those cheerleaders. I could soak up some Detroit radio while hitting the books and learning. I discovered all of my credits from Dayton would transfer, giving me a great leg up on my degree.

Soon after arriving in town, I found an interesting music project right under my nose. The University was soliciting students to collaborate with an unusual guy in Ann Arbor who was building a large music database. I never met the man, but I learned he was a compulsive archivist, noted astrologer, Buddhist scholar and a musician. Well, that astrology bit made me nervous, but there's much more to his story. In the mid-1970s, Michael Erlewine began using computers for his astrological work, and in 1977 he founded a software company named Matrix — clever name. He later teamed up with a Russian software developer at the university's main campus and began digitizing his music database to CD-ROM, which had begun life in 1992 as a twelve-hundred-page reference book. He named the database AllMusic.

I found out the project involved writing short, accurate descriptions of artists, record albums and songs. The recruiter was impressed with my Radio & Records credentials, but she warned about being a critic or overly opinionated. I was impressed the credibility of the project hinged on unbiased content.

One of my classes at the university was taught by an old, disgruntled radio broadcaster named Floyd Peccorino. Now, this may seem farfetched, but Professor Peccorino, The Pecker as we called him, looked just like "Floyd the Barber" from *The Andy Griffith Show*, bow tie and all. While teaching a class in Government and Communication, Peccorino warned that deregulation would be the end of radio as we know it. This was early 1980 and I couldn't fathom how or why such a change would unfold, but I took notes.

Professor Floyd described the three kinds of broadcast regulation, horizontal, vertical and technical. Horizontal regulation specified the total number of TV and radio stations one company may own in America. Vertical regulation set limits on the number of facilities an owner may have in one market or city. Technical embodied regulations concerning transmitting power, signal direction and radio frequency spectrum utilization put in place to protect stations from interfering with each other. The FCC classified these as Part 15 Rules, which also governed other communication devices like walkie-talkies, hand-held phones, radio receivers and low-power transmitters just like my old Knight Kit Broadcaster. Over time, the layers of governmental misadventures and missteps surrounding deregulation would be revealed.

I was immersed in my university classes and sucking in knowledge. Late afternoons I would walk over to the small research office to create entries in the AllMusic database using a classic computer terminal. By my estimation, the work would never finish, but what began life as twelve hundred pages eventually became more than three million album entries with thirty million tracks listed. By the way, AllMusic continues as an online music database to this very day.

I was wrapping up one night when a short, bespeckled young woman with a stunning stack of red hair asked me if I wanted to get a cup of coffee. She worked at a desk just a few feet from mine and we regularly greeted each other. I suppose that casual connection led to the invitation. Her wide smile and sharp blue eyes reminded me of someone from the past. She tossed her stuff into a large, black, leather suitcase and we were soon on our way to a local coffee shop.

Her name was Vanessa Smithgaard, and with a name like that she obviously had family roots in Denmark, so I ordered a strawberry Danish and coffee, and she did too. After some chit chat about the music database project, Vanessa told me that she wanted to get into radio, but her teacher-parents made her go to college. I couldn't help but laugh,

"I worked in radio, and may have some ideas for you, but there is nothing wrong with getting an education."

"You sound like my fucking fuddy duddy father. How old are you?"

I explained that I was closing in on thirty and would soon be someone she shouldn't at all trust. She let out a giggle and pressed me,

"So, why here? Why now?"

I asked her the same question. We talked for two hours, and I revealed my year-by-year story, like a dog-eared resume on the coffee-stained desk of a struggling PD not knowing whom to hire. She listened and smiled often. Vanessa gave me a pass on my age, and when she learned I was still in the grieving zone, she became exceptionally warm and caring. She asked me to describe Simone in detail, and I assumed she was coaxing a cathartic release from me. I sensed she was a good, kind person.

Vanessa was from South Pasadena, California and grew up in the sunshine of that LA suburb listening to the music played on KROQ, one of the most successful and unique rock stations in America. Competing against both KLOS and KMET for the rock audience, KROQ's brilliant programmer named Rick Carroll found a niche with a mix of new wave, punk and hip rock music wrapped around a stylish CHR presentation. One of their signature bands back then was Depeche Mode. The station had tight music rotations, with new songs turning over frequently. KROQ was very well programmed, and it was sad when Rick eventually died of an HIV/AIDS related disease.

Vanessa's voice was a bit like Bernadette Peters, who was dating Steve Martin at that time. This redhead's mouth was small and pouty, reminding me of that old cartoon character Betty Boop. Of course, she wanted to immediately springboard into the chair behind the console at KROQ, spouting her musical knowledge and playing only music she liked, but Vanessa was a long way from home and had much to learn about broadcasting.

If you're wondering how I was doing, well, I was getting better but there were moments when something on TV would trigger my tears. Sometimes I saw a Black girl walking in front of me and picked up my pace to catch a glimpse, but she was never Simone. I imagined the ladies on campus thought I was suffering from a "jungle fever" thing, but I was truly mending mentally.

I vowed to all the cart machines in the sky that I would not take advantage of my relationship with Vanessa. I would become her radio teacher and ease her out of her naïve state by nurturing and mentoring. She was a perky, pretty girl with the same radio dreams we all had back in the day, but her youthful enthusiasm made me feel old.

My data entry co-workers were in their diapers when the music they were annotating was first released. I thought of that old maxim "the blind leading the blind" but these kids were focused and hard working. Besides, all our entries were reviewed by editors who were experts in music, footnotes and all that jazz.

Meanwhile, there were others thinking about all the world's data and wondering what in the hell to do with it. Before the IBM Personal Computer rolled out to the world, large companies and universities had mainframe computers to assist with business operations. The NBC, CBS and ABC networks used their mainframes to administer payroll, analyze ratings, manage accounts payable and receivable and track and predict national election results.

Dr. Andrew Economos was in charge of the National Broadcasting Company's mainframe system. One day in 1979, he was chatting with an NBC cohort from the company's radio division who expressed a need for radio stations to automate their primitive music scheduling process. When Andrew left NBC, he took his co-worker's advice and opened a company he named Radio Computing Services, later shortened to RCS. His first software venture was a computerized music scheduling program called *Selector.* More on that soon.

We spoke about song rotations earlier, and before computers came along some stations would have their DJs refile a song cart upside down to signify that it had been played. Such an inverted song could not be replayed until all the others had been aired and turned over. Other stations used a more sophisticated "card system" to control music rotations. Information for each song on the station's playlist was typed on an index card and stacked in individual containers according to category. Disc jockeys were instructed to play the song listed on the card at the very front of the stack, jot down the date and time of airplay on the card, then place it in back of the stack, providing a notion of rotation as the song in the back eventually made its way back to the front. A hand drawn "format clock" on the studio wall was a pie chart, indicating which category to play at the various clock positions.

Radio DJs were given numerous "rules" about music flow, such as preventing the play of songs by the same artist within an hour, not playing two slow songs in a row or separating Motown songs by twenty minutes. Some jocks were better than others executing this, but these simple structures gave radio stations some sense of musical consistency throughout the day.

As a first step in his new company, Dr. Economos enlisted the help of radio programmers and consultants to learn their thinking about how music should be scheduled. He met with these folks often, took notes, and coded *Selector* accordingly. His first sale was to the NBC owned radio stations, which gave him additional contacts for feedback and ideas about music scheduling. RCS was first in the space of computerized music scheduling, and today *Selector* is used by more than ten thousand radio stations worldwide.

At first there was pushback from some programmers who claimed music scheduling was an art and could not be done by a machine having no feelings or emotions. That idea faded quickly when station ratings soared after implementing *Selector*. Radio consultants were early adopters of the technology because they loved the control it gave them, and their support helped spread the innovation throughout the industry.

The time I first heard a record promoter say to a PD, "Hey, can you add this into *Selector*?" I knew that radio song database management and computerized scheduling had truly arrived. This was a profound change in the business because the need to learn and grasp cutting edge technology had now become a job requirement.

I enjoyed helping Vanessa and felt she appreciated my guidance. She always brought her papers to me for review before handing them in. This wasn't cheating because her writing was well-thought out and provocative, and other than a small comment here or a grammar tweak there I was hands-off. One day she tossed me a paper her professor had graded B-minus, and I was as pissed off as she was. We drowned our anger that night in dark beer, a brew I never would have believed a young, sophisticated California woman would consume. I thought they were all wine people.

Another thing I liked about Vanessa was her love of sports. She knew every Los Angeles Dodger who had ever played, and she constantly wore LA Rams jerseys along with her USC baseball cap.

We had a comfortable older-brother/younger-sister relationship and came the day I invited her over to my small apartment to watch Monday Night Football on ABC. She was genuinely enthusiastic and pledged to bring a six-pack of Guinness stout. My contribution would be the Sonny Joe Mega Nachos plate, with the hottest peppers to be found in Michigan, which is to say they would surely be mild. I reminded myself of my hands-off personal vow and made sure I had enough Mexican cheese.

It was a frosty night in Dearborn, but the football players would be warm. The New England Patriots were in Miami to play the Dolphins and the game-time temperature at the Orange Bowl was seventy-five degrees. It was a back-and-forth affair with the Patriots' points coming in the second quarter with two field goals. In the third quarter, Miami kicked two field goals in this defensive struggle, tying the score six to six. We had already finished the first batch of nachos, but my crazy red-headed guest wanted more. As I was cooking up the next bunch of chips, I thought, "Six to six... now all we need is one more six to make six-six-six, the mark of the Devil!"

Vanessa and I were polishing off the last of the beer when the game wound down to the final three seconds with a score of thirteen to thirteen. I thought, man, that's bad luck. John Smith, the kicker for the New England Patriots and, yes, that was truly his name, was readying to kick the winning field goal.

Suddenly Howard Cosell announced that John Lennon had been shot in the back outside of his New York City apartment building. He was rushed to Roosevelt Hospital and pronounced dead on arrival. It was December 8, 1980. The kick was blocked, and the game went into overtime.

Vanessa and I looked at each other then she silently gazed into her large glass of beer as if trying to decipher meaning in the foam. My attention was on the TV, watching Frank Gifford and Howard Cosell repeating the Lennon story and adding additional facts once confirmed by ABC News. We hardly realized the Dolphins win with a twenty-three-yard field goal by Uwe Detlef Walter von Schamann because, as Howard and Frank kept reminding us, "It was only a game."

Vanessa and I embraced each other and cried. This wasn't happening; this must be a lie. We turned off the TV and I put on the Beatles' *Abbey Road* album. Later, I walked Vanessa to her car and we both sobbed again. She drove away and I sauntered back into my apartment, crying harder than I did when my father died. What is happening to me? It was as if an evil force had swept into my life to steal my childhood dreams. It was too late to call my mother, so I pulled out the emergency whisky bottle and took a substantial shot to help me sleep.

After waking the next morning, I tuned the radio to one of the four Detroit rock stations. WWWW-FM had hired a guy named Howard Stern from a station in Hartford, and I found it odd that I went to bed with one Howard and now I was waking up with another. I also thought about those call letters and how much I hated them. The station called itself W4, which sounded good but didn't line up with their 106.7 dial position.

As I was sipping my coffee, I was stunned by what I was hearing on the radio. Howard was just a normal guy sitting in my kitchen and talking only to me, sharing my anger along with some insights about the life and death of John Lennon. I could tell he really cared, and hearing such excellent communication was making me ache to get back into radio. The voice in my head chimed out, "This guy is going to be big someday, really fucking big."

Lennon's death shocked me and brought truth to the surface. I was thinking I have only one life, it's unfolding now, and it just might be short. Was I living to learn, or learning to live? Walking toward my first class of the day I saw Vanessa hugging a surfer-looking woman with long blonde hair and a rusty-orange suntan. Vanessa slowly pushed her against a wall, gave her a caring hug and then a deep, enthusiastic kiss on the mouth. That was certainly an unexpected sight.

Vanessa had come out and I was proud of her. Okay, a little jealous because of my single status, but she would be my friend for life. And life and living were never more paramount than right now.

32. Graduation, Then What?

The intense, biting cold coupled with the brisk wind made me wonder why I was still in Michigan. I would have my degree in just a few months and was scouring R&R and all the other radio trade rags for a suitable job opening. I had gone home for Christmas and realized my mother was going to outlast everyone, and that was good.

I was now a major fan of W4 radio, mostly because of morning man Howard Stern. He was outrageous, funny, topical and original. Then one morning in early 1981 I turned on my radio and W4 was playing country and western music. I figured Stern must be doing some comedy routine, even calling himself "Hopalong Howie." I checked my calendar, nope, it wasn't April Fool's Day. Then I looked at my radio, yep, it was tuned to 106.7. So, what's going on? Why wasn't W4 playing rock music?

A sudden format flip may surprise a station's competition, but it angers their audience. I have always believed each time this happened the average radio listener lost a little more faith in broadcasting. The radio station they loved and thought of as a friend had abandoned them. This abuse takes place in every market in every month of every year. So, let's explore this, put it in context, understand why it happens and why it occurred long before radio's major deregulation.

As radio markets grew in both population and number of radio stations, people typically listened to one or two favorite stations and perhaps a few others for specific programming like Friday night high school football games, a weekend music countdown show or a great personality on an otherwise poor station. Radio formats grew out of experiments. Top 40 was a gamble in the 1950s, but that highly repetitive rotation of songs drew in listeners.

I learned in one of my classes that every marketplace has a certain amount of durability based on what is offered. Yes, the well-known notion of supply and demand plays into that, but radio listening doesn't cost anything. Of course, you will hear commercials, but radio was "commercial" from the very first broadcasts in the 1920s and the listening public has been programmed to accept them.

When a Top 40 station becomes dominant in a market and garners a large chunk of cash from ad sales, another station might be thinking if they had just half of that big station's revenue, they would be doing much better. So, they take a chance, flip to Top 40 and begin selling commercials. If the number one CHR station had a twenty share, the second one in might acquire a nine share, but should a third station come along in the format they would be lucky to get a three share and probably wouldn't make money.

The term in play here is fragmentation, and business schools teach "…emergence of new segments in a previously homogeneous market which have their own distinct needs, requirements, and preferences may fragment, which reduces the effectiveness of mass marketing techniques and erodes brand loyalty." There are only so many ways you can cut the pie, and Howard Stern's show on one of the four rock FM stations in Detroit was a big deal; he was unique and gave the station an edge. Had W4 continued with their rock format, they would have had a compelling marketing proposition with Stern carrying the station to lofty success. After a few weeks acting like a country cowboy disc jockey, Howard wisely left W4 for greener pastures at DC101 in Washington, D.C. Remember them?

Stern left the Motor City for the madness of the nation's capital and a tough, three-way battle among rock stations. DC101's program director, Denise Oliver, wanted to have a newscaster/sidekick join Howard. She knew it would take a special person to feel comfortable with the shock jock, an absolute necessity for smooth and appealing interaction. Denise found the perfect candidate in Robin Quivers, who was a former registered nurse turned radio personality in Maryland. Robin had previously worked at Baltimore's WFBR with Johnny Walker, a shock jock in his own right, and she rolled with the punches and punchlines. Robin's robust and infectious laughter made Stern sound even funnier, and DC101 doubled in quarter-hour share and bolted to number two in cume behind WMAL-AM. Many advertisers bought spots on Stern's show but, yes, some clients did not want their commercials on the sometimes-shocking broadcasts. That aside, it was clear Howard Stern had arrived, and his presence outshined the radio station.

Meanwhile, I had been sending airchecks to many radio stations and the reaction was dead air. Program directors are busy, and it's risky to call after you've applied for a job because they may see you as irritating or needy, the latter of which could easily translate into "hard to manage." Besides, PDs have their calls screened, so getting through to them is difficult. It's frustrating to wait in stillness but it's similar to the movie business. A movie studio will not consider a script that hasn't been cleared by the gatekeepers. At this point, radio's gatekeepers were the consultants who had powerful connections with stations and record labels. It was far easier to wine and dine a single programming consultant and get your song added to fifty stations compared to pitching fifty individuals at the station level. As for DJs, program directors were now relying on their consultants to find the best candidates. It was dicey for a consultant to move a prize talent to a larger market with higher pay because the management of the station losing the jock could become alienated, but everyone deserves a chance to grow, right?

My phone eventually rang, and I was surprised to hear Bob Wilson, my former boss at R&R, on the other end of the line asking if I might be interested in getting back into radio. He was once a disc jockey at KROY in Sacramento and had a contact there who told him about an opening for the 10 p.m. to 2 a.m. air shift. Bob kindly mentioned my name. I thanked him for the lead, and he suggested I stop by for a visit should I get to LA. Yes, confirmed good guy.

I dashed off a tape off to KROY, a Rock station in Sacramento, California, a state often misunderstood by folks in the East and Midwest.

Some conservatives viewed California as Sodom and Gomorrah; the two biblical cities destroyed by God for their wickedness. California has many diverse citizens. There are the Hollywood crazies, the liberals of northern California with its large gay community and the many Republicans populating the state's sprawling, agricultural areas. John Steinbeck's masterpiece book *Grapes of Wrath* followed the journey of a poor family forced by drought and hardship from their home in Oklahoma. They, like thousands of other Midwesterners, came to California's Central Valley to farm.

About a week after dropping my tape in the mailbox, I received a call from the PD of KROY. He praised my air work, had checked my references and hired me right then and there over the phone. So, here I was again, packing up another U-Haul, with much appreciated help from Vanessa and her girlfriend, Trixy. Sounds like a stripper's name, doesn't it? As much as I "loved" my AMC Pacer, and not to flip the bird on Detroit, but I used some of the savings from my dad to buy a brand-new BMW 320i to pull the U-Haul trailer. I bought the biggest combination lock I could find to secure my belongings and started the long drive to Northern California. There was a sense of renewal and rebirth as I traveled from Dearborn to "Sac-KROY-mento," as the station cleverly called their city. I got a map from the AAA Travel people, who had marked my route in orange, meaning there was more than a fair chance I wouldn't end up in Alaska.

I listened to all the major radio stations as I traveled. Driving through Chicago, I got a healthy dose of Steve Dahl, that rotund Disco Demolition guy. He talked more than I liked, but his morning show was entertaining. I listened to Steve do a twenty-minute bit about keeping his son's circumcision foreskin in the freezer. That ruined any idea of stopping for breakfast.

It was a rite of passage for an AOR station to move away from music in the morning to focus on interactive DJ bits, routines, listener phone calls and conversations with guests or sidekicks. Humor became the primary means of propelling a station in the ratings. This tactic in the CHR format was formalized by the term "Morning Zoo," which Scott Shannon birthed in Tampa, Florida. FM Rock station humor was more mature, heady, highly suggestive or even lewd. Sitting on his high perch in Washington, Howard Stern proudly wore the shock jock crown, broadcasting from his studio only one block away from the FCC!

I heard a radio sameness as I passed through Iowa, Nebraska and Wyoming with little fragmentation of formats. Each town had one Rock station, one CHR and one Country. Of course, there were also a few Christian stations along my trail. I will suggest to anyone who is bored in their little shell they spent time in Wyoming to see how beautiful America is. Equally as impressive and awe inspiring are the mountains of Utah.

After gazing at shallow, mucky Salt Lake I wondered what force of nature created it. I supposed I could also ask the same about the Church of the Latter-Day Saints. It was the first rewriting of history that made America great back then and would ultimately become the plot of a hilariously profane Broadway play titled *The Book of Mormon*. The "sinless" city of Mormon power is right next the state of Nevada, and its gem, "Sin City" — Las Vegas. The difference between the states of mind of each geographic location's citizenry was stunning.

I made my way down to Sacramento and found the station, which was located in a stand-alone, office-park building. The general manager was Mark Milner from Columbus, Ohio. M&M, as the staff called him, was a driven guy who began his workday at 5:30 a.m. and finished by 2 p.m. Then he would play golf with the major powerbrokers of the town and advertising community. M&M did bring in the money and the station prospered.

I don't want to divert too much, but in hundreds of corporate office parks in northern California, innovative software development was taking place. Those algorithms would change the world and make billionaires out of geeks from Stanford, Berkeley and other institutes of technology. The IBM Personal Computer, or PC, was launched in 1981 and became a groundbreaking presence in techno-world, as I called it. Apple was five years ahead of IBM in the marketplace and it was to be a battle to the death of the two systems, but neither company perished. The competition between technologies drove innovation and better ideas came out of the battles. Bill Gates and Steve Jobs became legends and, do I even need to mention it, billionaires. Technology's effect on the radio industry was significant.

The groundbreaking work of Andrew Economos developing software to classify songs, schedule music and keep track of which songs played when, allowed radio programmers to better control their formats. It wouldn't be long before all the turntables in radio stations across the land were ripped out and replaced by CD players. The compact disc was made available to the public in 1982 and it quickly became the radio industry standard for delivering music. The final transition took place later when audio files replaced tape and compact discs. That's when the cart machines were scrapped, and all pre-recorded station audio originated in a computer system. This earthquake eventually killed vinyl, magnetic tape and CDs being the source of radio audio. The industry was going digital, and nothing could stop that evolution.

As for me, getting back to an FM rock radio station in one of the most important cities in America was thrilling. Some aspects of living in a capital city reminded me of Washington, D.C., but this town had cowboy sensibilities with a neat historical district, a train museum and acres and acres of rice fields.

After two terms of Ronald Reagan, the governor of California was now Jerry Brown, a guy who was dating Linda Ronstadt. His Lieutenant Governor was Mike Curb, a record company executive. I wondered if they all listened to KROY. The state had just lived through the ultra-conservative policies of its previous governor, but Jerry Brown would dramatically transform that. Meanwhile, Ronald Reagan was out to change more than a single state.

In Washington D.C., the legal powers were making moves with respect to media. Their acts would eventually eliminate the possibility of radio ownership by a single owner or family. There was an ongoing debate about whether deregulation would be good for radio or not. After thirty years preserving the 7-7-7 rule of ownership, some in the industry wanted a baby step to allow companies to own 12-12-12. I was pretty much disconnected from all of that, doing my late-night radio show, going to Sacramento concerts and making the occasional hundred-mile drive to San Francisco.

Since San Francisco had one of the largest gay communities in America, a heterosexual guy could benefit greatly because of the ratio of straight men to heterosexual women. A straight guy in radio had his choice of many magnificent women. Little Herbie was in heaven!

I always found it funny when a new female acquaintance would subtly probe about my sexual proclivities in a conversation. Some more open women would just pop the question directly,

"You're so nice. You're not gay, are you?"

I would just laugh and order two more drinks.

33. Radio Warfare

Some who inhabit various facets of American culture have a curious need to ascribe military terminology to their endeavors. Hearing a participant in a radio station strategy meeting saying, "We must protect our flank" or spout a line from Sun Tzu's *The Art of War* has always seemed ridiculous to me. For a while, the semantics of the radio business were awash with military terms and phrases, often initiated by a Dartmouth kind of guy who would bring an attorney to a gun fight.

Broadcasting isn't a military conflict, it's supposed to be entertaining, fun and collegiate, like a radio goofball who lets the air out of the tires of a competitor's van at a remote broadcast. Now there's an example of pure frat boy amusement without requiring camouflage overalls, helmets or automatic weapons.

A researcher or consultant might ask a radio programmer, "Do you want to die on that hill?" This typically happens when the counselor is trying to get a PD to make a strategic change. They're using the fear of military defeat and death to invoke action.

The year was 1982, and one of the most famous CHR stations in the country, 77 WABC in New York, the one where Cousin Brucie and Dan Ingram cracked jokes through a thick wash of reverberation and music, was about to make a MOMENTOUS change. ABC, the station's owner had made the decision not to die on the music hill and the gods of radio cried when WABC launched an All-Talk format. Was keeping music on AM radio like staying in the Vietnam war too long?

I remember when an old-line, Full-Service AM station in Fargo, North Dakota wanted to make a change. The Fargo station's researchers and consultants advised that a new Country format would keep them healthy for years to come. So, the station flipped their format, which in many ways is like flipping a house. The change happened on a Monday, and by Thursday most advertisers had canceled their contracts and more than a hundred people staked out the front lawn of the radio station protesting with shotguns, rakes, and a few axes. The general manager ran a contrite on-air announcement saying the station had made a mistake and would immediately change back. The stodgy format returned, and over the next two years the ratings continued to slide until the owners were forced to sell the station. They died on that Full-Service hill. More than one radio station has been killed in battle because the principals never learned one important radio lesson, a change requires time to bring success.

The Sacramento radio market of the 1970s looked more like a small market setup. KROY, which started out as a Top 40 station on AM at 1240, soon acquired an FM sister station with the call letters KROI, a phonetic twin of their heritage AM calls. By 1980, they went with the KROY call letters on both properties. KROY-FM was airing an AOR format, and I was thrilled to be going to a station to play and talk about the music from my favorite artists and albums.

I got to Sacramento in 1981, and by then KROY had a fierce competitor with a great identity fused into their call letters, KZAP. The battle between KROY and KZAP would eventually explode into all-out war, with KROY being the loser and switching to an Adult Contemporary format in 1984. For now, however, Sonny Joe McPherson was on the radio and having a blast.

In the late seventies, AC/DC, Pink Floyd, Led Zeppelin, Judas Priest, Scorpions and Van Halen were the mainstays of FM rock radio. After the disco era retreated into the clubs, rock radio reacted by embracing a "modal format" focused on harder music. *Raiders of the Lost Ark* was the big smash movie hit, and the DeLorean car was introduced, later to star in a trilogy of movies titled *Back to the Future*.

In the early 1980s, many of the legendary rock bands were having serious meetings with their accountants. They were running fast through their money and now faced the additional burden of heavy tax bills. So, the big bands of the 1970s went back out on the road in the 1980s to get solvent. Keeping in tune with the dawning age of branding, they gave their tours flashy names like *The Rolling Stones American Tour 1981* and the *Ghost in the Machine Tour* with the Police and its lead singer Sting.

Curiously, Black Sabbath fired vocalist and founder Ozzy Osbourne, and launched their *Heaven & Hell Tour* with Ronnie James Dio as lead singer. I was mystified they would even try to tour without Ozzy, but I guess the Prince of Darkness was too expensive and the band needed money. It was one of the worst ideas of the year, and it led to a major riot in Milwaukee when the band refused to play after someone threw a bottle onto the stage, sending Geezer Butler to the hospital for stitches. After the band left the stage, the crowd rioted and caused ten thousand dollars' worth of damages. It took the cops an hour to clear the venue of all the angry Black Sabbath fans. Yes, rock 'n roll was still appalling to the parents.

I loved hosting my radio show, talking about the antics of the rockers and playing their songs. Listeners wanted a minimum of talk, but they valued stories that put the music into context. When a radio listener hears a music tale told in a concise, relatable way, they eat it up. Many of the DJs I listened to on my trip across America sounded self-centered and disconnected from radio's essential entertainment, the songs. To hear some lame-ass disc jockey go on and on about how happy he was the temperature dropped to freezing last night because he left his Chinese food takeaway bag in the car reminded me of one succinct disc jockey critique I'll never forget. Speaking was the late, great CHR radio programmer, Bill Tanner, properly aiming his southern fried accent at a chatty DJ,

"Stop talking so much, that's just wretched excess."

The first day of August 1981 brought an eruption many feared would bring down radio. MTV, Music Television, was a cable channel launched as a partnership between American Express and Warner Communications. Eventually, radio-owner Viacom/CBS bought MTV.

It was no accident that the very first video aired on MTV was the Buggles' *Video Killed the Radio Star*. Bob Pittman headed MTV's programming, but he was a radio guy through and through. It didn't take MTV long to get cleared on most of the cable outlets in the nation, and by the end the 1980s they reached more than eighty million households. However, they slowly moved away from twenty-four by seven music and added what we now call "reality TV shows" — youth-targeted dramas about real people caught in the act of being stupid. At their launch, MTV believed they would indeed kill radio, but they waged war against radio by copying it with a staff of VJs, video jockeys, of course. They also featured well-written pieces presented by music newscasters.

MTV's marketing was cutting edge, modern and graphically sensational, reminding me of that conversation I had with Lee Abrams years ago. The channel's iconic "I want my MTV!" advertising campaign was launched a year into their life and was based on the 1950s advertising slogan "I Want My Maypo!" which featured a spoiled kid demanding his favorite brand of cereal. When Sting happened by a recording session of the Dire Straits' song *Money for Nothing,* with its wonderful poetry about the greed of rock stars, he adlibbed a short "I want my MTV" vocal over the song's intro, and that phrase became etched into the brains of rock music fans around the world. Greed, demand and a "feed me, feed me" youth culture, which had been given everything, got their participation trophy. It was their way of vicariously experiencing the excesses of fame and fortune.

I'm sure the MTV executives and programmers used the long-standing marketing strategy of asking themselves the question, "What is the single worst thing that could possibly hurt our brand?" The purpose of such an exercise is advance planning to offset any potential future attack. MTV studied how The Gap created Old Navy before someone else did, and felt they were onto something when they launched additional channels like VH1, which was aimed at the Top 40 audience. At the height of their popularity, MTV had more than twenty-five channels of different formats in every country around the world. If a government wouldn't let them in, they licensed the brand's name and concept to a local provider.

MTV was a powerful force in music, fashion and movies, but they had a dark side as well. They would toy with local video music channels and shows by signing exclusive deals with the record companies. If an over-the-air music TV channel like V66 in Boston wanted to air the new Dire Straits video, they might have to wait for a few weeks while MTV played it first, in power rotation. This practice hampered competition. Cable titan TBS, Ted Turner's superstation out of Atlanta, had trouble clearing the rights to videos for their Saturday Night Tracks show. Turner hated the idea of music videos and called them the work of the devil, but he knew they kept an audience tuned in after the live Braves baseball broadcasts.

Well, the devil is always in the details and those exclusive music deals the MTV lawyers dished out eventually annihilated most of MTV's competitors on their music television hills. As one TV station manager put it, "It wasn't worth the time and energy fighting to play a video that brought in no revenue."

I always felt a bit uncomfortable watching my radio brothers and sisters on MTV. I couldn't understand why they were needed but, truth is, had Bob Pittman called me to fill a VJ slot I would have crawled on my hands and knees to New York to suit up for the future.

Being a disc jockey is not a particularly lucrative job, unless you are a highly paid morning talent, but radio was in my blood, a common expression among those in the biz. It had all the great parts of college life; you didn't have to study much as long as you were readily available and always flexible with changes. One PD would leave, and another arrive with a slew of different ideas and ways of doing things. You had to adapt instantly, or you wouldn't be there much longer.

About this time "liners" came along, which were short scripts typed on five-by-seven-inch index cards "positioning" the station. "It's rock around the clock on Sacramento's K-R-O-Y." These were read live on the air by the DJs who had to sell the words and ideas of their bosses as if they were their own. I was a bad boy and skipped the ones that were awkward or poorly written because I didn't want to sound like a doofus.

Stations were increasing in value because their sales departments were doing more training and working with networks and syndicators in new ways. Creative bartering came along, with advertisers trading their products or services with stations in return for commercials or sponsorships. There was also a short-lived scheme in which a radio station would trade shelf space in a store and then resell the area to another station advertiser. That idea fizzled once the storeowners figured out radio was squeezing a big rock for extra blood.

There was also renewed interest in an old radio concept known as P.I., which means "per inquiry." The station would run a thirty or sixty second P.I. spot for free or at a reduced cost. It contained a phrase or keyword specific to that station. When a listener called the advertiser and spoke the keyword, the station received a fee for the inquiry. Ted Turner's superstation made a fortune with P.I. spots. Compared to TV and cable, radio advertising was a bargain, and sales teams would sell, sell, sell those P.I. spots. PDs hated them because they were stuffed full of blah, blah, blah!

The radio business has its share of nefarious characters in both sales and programming. One major market morning guy believed his ratings would be much better if there were fewer commercials. Stations often paid DJs large performance bonuses based on rating improvements, and such a disc jockey has great incentive to succeed. In this case, the station was going through a sale from one large company to another radio powerhouse. During the last rating period under the former owner something bad was going on.

After the new owner took over, a whistleblower traffic assistant leaked a story to the town's newspaper, a printed flamethrower with no love for radio. The paper ran the story about this station's morning guy not running commercials worth over two hundred and fifty thousand dollars during the rating period. Not only was this embarrassing, but the station sale agreement indemnified the former owner. BOOM! The morning guy was fired and turned to a life of drugs and wandering around America letting the air out of radio station van tires.

A station had to "clear" their spots by signing legal affidavits declaring the commercials had aired. If a station cheated and didn't run spots, that fraudulent practice was a perfect way to lose their license. The radio industry was generally good with self-governing, and a station that wasn't on the up-and-up usually got reported. Broadcasters know who the cheaters are in their market. I'll repeat what I said earlier. Radio is a small, incestuous business, and behind-the-scenes happenings at stations eventually become known to all radio folk in the community, and sometimes they gain nationwide notoriety in the industry.

Nuisance lawsuits were another way to get your station's butt kicked. KWOD in Sacramento was infamous for suing anyone and any company for activities that bothered their spoiled-brat owner. It was one of the reasons the state government passed a nuisance lawsuit bill, which said that the originator of the suit would have to pay all legal costs should they be defeated in court.

I attended a Van Halen concert in San Francisco at the Cow Palace where one of the radio stations was giving away a free trip to Hawaii for the best costume that night. It was September 15, 1982, and I was sitting next to a lady dressed as a sixties flower child, complete with a loose-fitting, flower-patterned dress, colorful makeup and a plastic daisy in her long and braided blonde hair. She was carrying a macramé purse and asked if she could perch upon me to better see the band.

Now I am not at all a big guy, so it's good she was a petite lady with strong, fit legs, as I would soon discover. I agreed to let her climb on me piggyback so she could have a better vantage point. During the song *Dance the Night Away*, she held on tightly around my neck and started to sway the rest of her body to the beat of the music. As the song progressed, she tightened up her legs around my waist. I could hear her breathing in my ear, then moaning as the song played on. I had to stabilize myself by placing my hands on the chair in front of me. Now she was moving up and down to the rhythm of the music and she screamed loudly in my ear during the Eddie Van Halen guitar solo.

I helped her get down gently and safely after the song ended, then gave her a quick hug. She returned the contact much more aggressively and then whispered in my ear,

"Thank you so much. I came."

34. Once There Was a Way

Whenever I went to a concert in San Francisco, I would habitually book a cheap motel near the venue so if I drank too much beer at the show, I wouldn't kill myself on the drive home. With Van Halen's music still ringing in my ears, I found myself walking around the auditorium's parking lot trying to find my car. I had lost my little humping friend when the show ended, and I was glad to have escaped. She was a tad too crazy for me. I finally found my BMW but a major panic, an electrical shock of sorts, jolted my body as I reached for my car keys. They weren't in my pocket. Just as I was trying to imagine where I lost them, I heard,

"Are you looking for these?"

And there, leaning against a flashy red Thunderbird, was the hippy flower dress lady, playfully twirling my keys in the air. I was pissed,

"Who are you? What are you doing with my keys?"

"Oh, so now you want to know my name. Well, I am Brenda Shaw and what should I call you."

"Give me my keys."

"Come and get them."

Well, you might think the story ended there, but that would be placing too much faith in my big head being more in control than the other. She had lifted my keys during that big hug after her fancy back dance on me. It was clear she was the owner of that 1977, Lee Iacocca redesigned, long, sleek, red Thunderbird she was leaning on. I had placed my motel door-card on my key chain, so now she knew I had a room there and, yes, she followed me to the motel. Little Miss Brenda was a total trip, and I must say despite spending most of her days designing user interfaces for computer programs, she was more than funny; she was also extremely intelligent, well-read and stimulating.

Around this time the news was filled with stories about a deadly disease killing gay men. Even though Ronald Reagan would never acknowledge the HIV/AIDS curse, it was real and becoming something straight men and women had to deal with as well. It was spread not only through sexual contact but also from blood transfusions, meaning the disease was not at all limited by one's gender or sexual orientation. I was becoming a bit more careful of my romantic partners, especially those from the San Francisco Bay area. By 1982 there had already been more than eight hundred deaths.

I was delightfully encouraged when Brenda whipped out a long string of condoms from her macramé purse, and over the evening we went through a few. She was fun, open, free and honest. She shared everything that snapped, crackled or popped into her mind and she was not at all impressed that I was a disc jockey, which suited me perfectly fine. Turns out she was working on the design of a computer system that could eventually make me unnecessary.

After our motel romp, she went her way and I headed back to Sacramento, but we stayed in touch, like almost every night. She was a late worker, knew when I got off my shift and how long it would take me to get home and settled in for a phone call. She wasn't at all an obsessive, oppressive or insecure type. We would talk for maybe five or ten minutes, then she would say,

"Okay, you're home. I'm going to sleep now; thanks for the hug."

It took a long time coupled with a growing understanding of her background before I could deduce Brenda's meaning of the telephone hug. She was a child of technology and grew up in the home of an artist and a brainiac. Her mother was a Stanford graduate with a PhD in mathematics and her father was an artist, a painter, whose works were a cross between R. Crumb, Dali and Picasso. Brenda Shaw was the product of her environment and she thought of words less as speech and more as human contact. I realized she interpreted my voice as far more than sound and words. Call me crazy, but I found her amazingly refreshing. Her total disinterest in my life as a radio personality intrigued me. Her attraction was not based on what I did but who I was.

Our relationship continued for years. Brenda became a good friend, a confidant, and on my occasional visits to San Francisco or San Jose for concerts we would have our fun. We grew closer by being geographically distant. On those rare weekend occasions when she wasn't working, she would drive her hot T-Bird to the Sac, and we would slip into the sack. It was a healthy and dynamic relationship.

After more than two years in Sacramento, I was still a late-night DJ and things unknown to me were churning. Motivated by a bunch of factors, my station was facing reality and about to admit that KZAP had beaten them. When KROY-FM ended its rock format on July 26, 1984, it was my time for a greener pasture. Even though the management knew I had major experience as a CHR jock, they were about to launch an Adult Contemporary format and wanted disc jockeys with direct experience in that format. They "broomed" the place, as we say in radio, and all us jocks were now on the beach. KROY would get its just revenge against KZAP much later.

I got cracking and sent out resumes and aircheck tapes to every station in San Jose. My motivation, of course, was a job closer to someone I wanted to see more often, but also San Jose was a steppingstone to San Francisco, you know, that city Grace Slick told us all was built on rock 'n roll.

I was ecstatic when I got a call from KOME, a San Jose rocker with an amazing history as a Free Form and Progressive FM. The station had always leaned in a radical and suggestive direction. They pronounced their call letters KOME as "Cum." Sweepers and liners embellished the enunciation with, "Don't touch that dial, it's got KOME on it!" or, "KOME all over your radio dial," or, "Wake up with KOME in your ear," and "The KOME spot on your radio dial." Even Playboy magazine cheered on KOME's aggressive sexual innuendos. I knew I would have a blast working at that place, no matter which shift. The PD had invited me to come to the station, no pun there, for an interview, but during our discussion it became clear they would not pay my moving expenses. I wasn't being a prima-donna, but a move from Sacramento to San Jose didn't exactly KOME with a million-dollar pay hike, and I told him I would think on it.

Just as so many other enchanted incidents have framed my career, a few hours later I got a call from KSJO, another AOR station in San Jose. Guess which job offer I accepted. Yep, I went to work for the guys with the U-Haul purchase order.

All the KSJO jocks were young and eager. I was most impressed with the fact they loved San Francisco but had no specific desire to be working at a radio station up there. They considered themselves part of both markets and enjoyed the better cost of living in San Jose. The music was good, but remarkably similar to KOME, and most listeners just punched between the two stations. KOME had a well-received morning team while KSJO was in search of an image and a solid morning show. I was hired to work the 10 p.m. to 2 a.m. slot, which was perfect for this guy who also wanted to have a real life. It was an added plus that Brenda worked basically the same hours.

When I told her about my new job, Brenda was excited and begged me to move in with her. She even remarked her lease renewal was coming up soon and she was thinking about finding a larger place. Her recent patent work, based on a decade old device called the cell phone, led to a huge bonus so she could afford an upgrade. I wanted to be with her and agreed to the move-in. I was beyond smitten; I think I was in love.

About a month after starting at KSJO, I was asked to train a new station hire. This threw me off because I was also a new guy, but the PD and GM said I was a good instructor. I didn't learn until later that they didn't want to "bother" any of their prime-time jocks with training. Strange.

The new guy was Ronald Mahoney, a Black man from New York and a Communications graduate of Syracuse University. He would joke, "Rockin' Ron, the orange man who's really Black!" Of course, the quip was an homage to the athletic teams of his university, the Orange Men of Syracuse. He was bright and "articulate," which at the time was still used to describe Black radio guys. Another common radio trope back then was, "Man, that guy is good. He doesn't even sound Black."

Here's some historical background to help this part of the story make better sense. President Lyndon B. Johnson signed the Civil Rights Act of 1964 into law, and its Title VII prohibited employment discrimination based on race, sex, color, religion and national origin. The Act applied to private employers, labor unions and employment agencies. Later, the feds created the Equal Employment Opportunity Commission (EEOC) to enforce the law. Meanwhile, behind the curtain, the FCC was holding hearings and voting on whether a television or radio station would get a license renewal if they violated Title VII. They formulated a rule requiring broadcast stations to keep a record of its hires, fires and minority recruitment procedures.

The FCC instituted a mandate requiring television and radio stations to maintain a Public Inspection File. Most listeners and viewers don't even know such a thing exists, but during business hours anyone has the right to visit a broadcasting station and go through its Public File. It contains documentation about how the station is operating in the public interest, details of a charity drive for example, and it also includes positive and negative letters from the public, citations the station received and all legal activities such as FCC filings, proposed ownership changes and any court actions. The Public File would be "soiled" if the EEOC sent a letter about discriminatory hiring practices.

The lawyers of many broadcasting companies put policies in place stipulating the percentages of minority employees must match the percentages in the station's community, but most stations simply employed at least one minority person in each department. The hurtful term "token" became woven into the structure of many industries, but the need to interview and hire minorities was mandated in broadcasting. The Black kid in the TV cartoon show *South Park* was originally named Token, but the show's writers cleverly revised history by revealing his actual name is "Tolkien," in honor of the author J. R. R. Tolkien. If only we could make life's regrettable things disappear just by writing them out of the script.

So, back there in 1980's San Jose, Rockin' Ron was my student, learning the station specifics so he could host the all-night show, where many minority hires began their radio careers. Interesting things can happen in radio because listeners cannot see the presenter. I remember meeting Howard Page, a tall, Black DJ from D.C., who was six-feet-five tall. Sometimes when meeting a listener at a remote broadcast he would get caught by a slip of the tongue,

"Gee, Howard, I didn't know you were…"

Before they could continue, Page would jump in,

"So tall?"

What a beautiful and clever retort!

The struggle for equality in real life, however, was a hard-fought battle. There was a guy who walked into my college station back in the day who had two mountains to climb, he was a Black man with an acute stutter. Tony wanted to do a jazz show, and some of the student management put him on the air for laughs, not out of compassion. Well, they were totally fooled. Once Tony slapped on those headphones and clicked the mic open, his stutter completely vanished! I think two things circumvented his disorder. His audience was invisible and therefore no "threat," and the powerful feedback of his own voice reproduced faithfully and loudly in his ears gave him overpowering confidence. Tony had a wonderfully deep voice and a tremendously knowledgeable presentation, perfect for radio.

I sat with Ron through his first three hours on the air at KSJO. After voicing the 3 a.m. legal ID, he turned to me with a huge smile,

"I got this brother. I'm a radio guy. Why don't you go home?"

A warm feeling flooded my body as I walked through the parking lot to my car. It wasn't because I helped Rockin' Ron get settled into his new gig, but rather that he called me "brother." I know this may sound strange but having a brother of any race felt good to this only child. Ron and I were brothers, truly, and I will always remember his unique style, friendship and sense of humor. He called me J-Man.

Ron went on to major market success both in Rock and Urban radio, and eventually ended up in Dallas hosting a nationally syndicated radio show. More than forty years later, Rockin' Ron's life would be cut down by a global fucking virus.

The battle between KOME and KSJO was intense and never ending, but none of us were blind or deaf about what was happening in San Francisco. In 1982, KFOG started to play rock and was consulted by the now more-than-famous Lee Abrams. The station's program director was Dave Logan. You may remember him as an architect of the Disco Demolition in Chicago. In 1984, KMEL dropped its rock format to become "the people's station" playing pop hits, but three years later morphed into a Rhythmic format. Disco never died in hip African American and gay communities, it just changed its name and kept on dancing.

Brenda and I were taking a late walk in San Francisco's Chinatown on the eighth anniversary of the Golden Dragon Massacre. That was the culmination of a decades long dispute between two Chinese gangs, the Joe Boys and Wah Ching, which erupted into a gun battle on September 4, 1977, in the "always open" Golden Dragon Chinese restaurant. Five people were killed and eleven injured in that combat.

Now I have no idea if they are connected, but the Doobie Brothers wrote and recorded a song named *Chinatown* that year, and they first performed it a month later, on November 4, 1977, at a concert in Florida. Brenda and I were looking at the Golden Dragon menu taped to the emerald tiles of the building, and as fate would have it, we heard that Doobie Brothers' song piped in from who knows where, "*Painted lanterns hang from balconies, People running everywhere, Chinatown, with all your dark mystery, Chinatown, Chinatown, Your spell is capturing me.*"

I was experiencing something but didn't know what. Maybe it was the power of music or feelings about a love I never thought I deserved, but certainly it was bigger than radio. I was under a spell of sorts, and after a very rough patch in my life I once again felt living was magical.

35. The Long Arm

American life ebbs and flows. Like the pendulum at the planetarium demonstrating the Earth's spinning, our country gradually swings over to the left and then back to the right, and neither political party ever admits or even believes they are wrong.

It was 1987, and the FCC was getting grumbles about DJs, mostly morning shows, doing routines that bothered listeners. Members of our audiences were so perturbed they were sending complaint letters to the FCC, and those good servants in charge of the electronic public domain were investigating.

The Communications Act of 1934 states the FCC is an independent government agency that regulates nonfederal government use of the radio and television spectrum as well as interstate telecommunications — telephones. The FCC has always walked a thin line between protecting our First Amendment rights and being cops, stopping the theft of our children's purity caused by hearing a lewd joke or naughty word on the radio or TV.

George Carlin clearly pointed out the FCC's challenge in his 1972 comedy routine titled *Seven Words You Can Never Say on Television*. According to Biography.com, "The bit was meant to highlight the absurdity of singling a few words out of the roughly four hundred thousand in the English language that would somehow corrupt our souls by repeating them for public consumption, and Carlin effectively made his point with silly voices and simple logic." Those seven infamous words are: shit, piss, fuck, cunt, cocksucker, motherfucker and tits. Now I'm quite sure there was never an official memorandum from the FCC stating this verboten verbiage verbatim, but Carlin drew the line in the sand for broadcasters.

I thought back to The Fuck Show in Cleveland and wondered if the FCC had any record of its occurrence, but now we were entering fresh territory and there were people in Washington incredibly uptight about those dirty FM DJs and their foul, nasty language on the radio.

At 2 p.m. on October 30, 1973, WBAI, a not-for-profit, publicly funded radio station licensed to New York City, played the recording of Carlin's routine, and that led to one of the biggest court cases in the history of radio, Federal Communications Commission versus Pacifica Foundation. It all began when a fifteen-year-old boy heard the broadcast, and his father decided the station had gone too far. Incidentally, the father was John Douglas, an active member of Morality in Media, which decided to take down WBAI's owner. Pacifica claimed all speech was protected by the Constitution and argued that radio should have the same freedom as United States newspapers.

After five years and what amounted to a football field full of files, the Supreme Court weighed in with an incredibly watered down and non-declarative five-to-four decision. The Court determined the routine was "indecent not obscene," but they also declared the broadcast was enough to justify special treatment as indecent programming. Huh?

In short, the FCC was allowed to fine a station or hold up its license renewal based on the broadcasting of what they called "bad speech," but the owner would be allowed to challenge said fine or action against them. One good outcome was the Supreme Court forced the FCC to refine their definition of indecency, which they did.

The long arm of the law became codified into rules when the FCC explained how they would decide what was obscene, indecent or profane, each with accompanying legalese to back up their words. Let's look at the FCC's definitions.

Obscene content is not protected by the First Amendment. The Supreme Court established a three-prong test to determine if content can be declared obscene: It must appeal to an average person's prurient interest; depict or describe sexual conduct in a "patently offensive" way, and taken as a whole lack serious literary, artistic, political or scientific value.

Indecent content portrays sexual or excretory organs or activities in a way that is patently offensive but does not meet the three-prong test for obscenity.

Profane content includes "grossly offensive" language that is considered a public nuisance.

Okay, let's start with obscene content. Now I don't know about you, but I think George Carlin was a linguistic artist and his routines were Shakespearean in nature. They had political and scientific value and, judging by how he stirred things up, they also had major influence on our culture. At worst, his bit was a two-prong offense, but I say it was probably a powerfully stiff one-pronger.

Out of the trio of FCC definitions, indecent content is the most straightforward. Imagine you are listening to me on the air, "Hey it's KSJO and you've got Sonny Joe with you and now here's the long version of *Suite: Judy Blue Eyes* which I know you'll enjoy while I go take a long shit." Yeah, that would be indecent content.

Then there's that little white sin, profane content, which the FCC defines in an extremely vague way. How can language possibly be "a public nuisance?" If one were to ask the FCC if that includes people who talk loudly in a restaurant, they would likely snark back, "You know what we mean!"

At least the FCC gave broadcasters a tad of leeway with the following language, "Broadcasting obscene content is prohibited by law at all times of the day. Indecent and profane content is also prohibited on broadcast TV and radio between 6 a.m. and 10 p.m., when there is a reasonable risk that children may be in the audience." I became saddened to learn that there weren't any kids listening to my nightly show on KSJO, but I was also quite aware that after the WBAI/Pacifica case, no

DJ in their right mind would ever again be naughty on the air, except Howard Stern.

After three extraordinarily successful years at DC101 in Washington, Howard moved to WNBC in his New York City hometown. He was hired in August of 1982 to host the 4 p.m. to 8 p.m. shift. Radio insiders wondered if he would be as successful outside of morning drive, and whether the absence of sidekick Robin Quivers would dent the quality of his act. Eventually the late, great PD Kevin Metheny, whom Stern derisively nicknamed "Pig Vomit," came to recognize the vast balance and contribution Quivers brought to the show, and he hired her to reunite with Howard on WNBC. Stern had gotten suspended several times at WNBC, and the dirty infighting between Howard, the station, Don Imus and the programming staff was public and legendary. It was almost as if the revolving door was already spinning when Stern first arrived.

After not being renewed by NBC in 1985, Howard and Robin moved to New York's WXRK, which was owned by Infinity Broadcasting Corporation, a far more liberal company. To satisfy his desire for a larger stage, Infinity allowed Stern to form a syndication company. By 1986, he was being heard in sixty markets across America. With his twenty million listeners nationwide, and some TV work on the side, his boast of being the "king of all media" could not be denied. Stern also became the poster boy of "shock jock" radio personalities, and more than a few folks believed he was obscene, profane and decidedly indecent.

To make it seem like they weren't singling out Howard Stern, the FCC cited many other disc jockeys they felt were "causing trouble." The Commission fined Bob & Tom, the top morning show at WFBQ in Indianapolis, for a line in a skit with characters posing as Richard Nixon and Elvis Presley staying at the local Holiday Inn. Knowing how much Elvis loved to eat, the hotel drained the swimming pool and filled it with stuffed potato skins. The argument between Elvis and Nixon about who could eat the most ended with the Nixon character saying, "Hell, I could eat Elvis under the table."

Now, if you are at all keen with words, you know the expression "drinking someone under the table" means to consume as much alcohol as one's drinking companion without becoming as drunk. I'm not sure the phrase in the skit was meant to be double entendre, but the folks at the FCC thought the comedic line was a much too direct reference to oral sex. One of the people involved in the skit said off-mic, "Fuck them if they don't get the joke!"

The FCC guardians were out to purge the airwaves of this "sinful" language, and some Congressional Senators had private meetings with broadcast companies and told them straight-up if they brought Howard Stern's program into southern stations, they would block license renewals and transfers. This all-out war raged on, and between 1987 and 1997 more than two and a half million-dollar indecency fines were imposed on radio stations. Some owners just paid the penalty and moved on, but others became cautious and put the Stern show on a seven second delay, with the local PD's index finger poised above the dump button to drop the transmission of anything he or she believed didn't meet their "community standards." It was an extreme price to pay to keep a highly rated radio show on the air.

It didn't stop with the fines and threats. WNEW-FM in New York City had a pair of goofballs named Opie & Anthony who hosted the afternoon drive show, which was syndicated on seventeen radio stations across the US. The duo ran a contest that awarded points to callers who allegedly engaged in sexual activity in public places, one of which was St. Patrick's Cathedral in New York. They were fined three hundred and seventy-five thousand dollars for that trick and eventually fired. They also pissed off the Pope.

Most Americans remember the 2004 Super Bowl half-time incident when Justin Timberlake ripped open Janet Jackson's bustier and exposed her right breast to the millions of viewers watching the CBS broadcast. Once again, an election-year political frenzy was triggered to "clean up the airwaves."

Howard Stern not only changed radio, but community standards as well. The man's talent could not be contained by over-the-air radio or the FCC. Our government drove Stern to satellite radio where a paid subscription model gave him total freedom to say whatever the fuck he wanted.

Brenda and I were talking one night about the whole censorship mess, and she had some insightful thoughts,

"The thing about government control of radio and TV is they go after disc jockeys and entertainers but let the politicians lie all the time. That's obscene to me, and totally indecent."

"Yeah, that's a great point."

Oh, she had more,

"They allow commercials pitching remedies for aches and pains, but if you listen closely, you'll hear, 'This product has not been tested and provides no clinical benefit.' Why do they allow tripe like that on television and radio?"

Brenda was a sharp cookie, and I realized how much she made me think. Her statements often opened my eyes to a perspective I hadn't considered before. I chimed in,

"The thing that gets me is some of the fines were based on innuendos, figures of speech or euphemisms, which fall far below obscene or profane words. Why can't a talent use creative language to circle around profanity? Shouldn't they get credit for their ingenuity and knowledge of linguistics? Instead of a fine, they should get complimented for colorful metaphors or similes that expand our imaginations, which is something radio does so well."

"Right! What would keep the FCC from one day declaring the word "bongo" to be vulgar?"

We both laughed at that. I could always count on Brenda to make any heady stuff go away. She used the word bongo as an example, but it was my go-to term for large breasts, as in, "Boy, she certainly has some bodacious bongos."

As she sat on the sofa, sucking passionately on the straw in her large root beer float, Brenda turned to me and spoke in her little girl voice,

"Mister Joey, would you want your sex tonight to be obscene, profane or just indecent?"

I chuckled and scratched my head, like I was pondering, and pronounced my verdict,

"Well, let's start with a little indecent exposure, then we can move to profane small talk that eventually lands right on some damn obscene positions. Of course, I will want to maintain my due process, if you catch my drift."

"Nice innuendo or is that 'in my end-oh?' You wish!"

We laughed, she put down the soda and I picked her up and carried her into the bedroom like a caveman. We made beautiful computer programmer – radio DJ love, whatever the hell that is. All I remember is I had to reboot several times.

36. Happy in Hawaii

My first two and half decades of radio experience taught me that the workplace could be playful, but at times explode into an unhealthy, sexually charged atmosphere fueled by alcohol and drugs. What started out as a neck rub, might escalate into ass slapping and grabbing that turned off the person on the receiving end. Sadly, some naïve boys and girls thought that was how radio worked, and they lived in blissful ignorance of how much they hurt others while behaving badly at their cool job.

Some in the radio business had a strange obsession with the Xerox machine, or whatever brand their station had. It wasn't unheard of to find a sheet of someone's photocopied boobs inside the folder of paperwork for a production order. Just as bad, a guy would Xerox his penis and send that back to traffic nestled within the completed production orders. Drug crazed lunatics would snort cocaine off the glass of the copy machine while it was running to boldly provide evidence of their usage. One night a screwball jock had a woman mount the machine and he ploughed her field while producing a legal-size sheet of proof. I believed most other fields and businesses were different, more serious and proper, but I never worked in any other industry so I didn't know for sure.

It was the spring of 1987 when I first heard the name Harris Stephano. Brenda's company hired him to head up her user interface development team, and she did not like her new boss… at all. Standing six foot seven Stephano was physically intimidating, but his creepy, nerdy posture made him repulsive in other ways. To make things worse, his body was completely covered with tattoos. While that's not so very unusual today, each of Stephano's tattoos was a fragment of computer code he had written. Yes, he was a strange unit.

A few days after the arrival of her new boss, Brenda complained to me about his behavior. She said it started when he stood behind her to see what she was working on at her computer. The first few times he would casually touch her shoulder and say, "Nice job" and then walk away. That quickly escalated to an attempted neck rub, which Brenda immediately rebuked. She was able to keep him at bay after that but had to be on constant guard, making her workplace much less pleasant than before.

It had been six months since Brenda's new boss came onboard when her company scheduled a retreat in Maui for a four-day brainstorming session. She asked if I would accompany her, thinking my presence would deter any monkey business her boss might try pulling. Plus, we could stay over for three days after the retreat to enjoy some personal rest and relaxation. I scheduled time off, and on Sunday September 27, 1987, we flew from San Francisco to Honolulu and then on to Maui.

I was surprised to find Brenda's software developer co-workers to be normal humans with two hands, two legs and all the rest, except for Stephano. He was a damn freak with his thick glasses and balding head. I couldn't help wondering when he would plant ink atop his cranium. During the day while they were thinking, I was on the beach drinking. I enjoyed the beautiful skies while getting a great tan and watching the amazingly talented surfers!

On the last night of the conference, Brenda came to me and pleaded I come with her to dinner with her boss Harris and his wife. I laughed and said,

"Sure, no problem at all. Hey, it'll be a free meal."

Harris Stephano's spouse was a tall, beautiful artist from San Francisco with jet-black hair, large red lips and a sculpted body, the kind a gymnast would have. I asked Mona why I hadn't seen her earlier in the week and she explained her flight had arrived just a few hours ago. Next week, she and her husband would be staying on Molokai, the infamous leper colony island. In the late 1800s, Americans with Hansen's disease were sent to Kalaupapa, a leprosarium located in a remote part of the wind-swept Hawaiian island. Remember Hawaii didn't become a state until 1959, making the Molokai "treatment center" an offshore dumping ground. Patients were still there in 1987, which made me think that unusual people must like peculiar places.

Brenda dropped her knife several times during dinner and each time our attentive waiter quickly replaced it. I looked quizzically at her, and she gave me an irritated expression. I filed that away and kept the conversation going with Mona. I learned she was born in Molokai where she was raised by her doctor and nurse parents who still lived there, thus her connection with the island.

Just as dessert arrived, Brenda dropped her fork and, once again, I looked over and tilted my head with the unspoken question, "What's going on?" She took the new fork from the waiter and cut vigorously into the chocolate dessert cake.

Once we all finished, I thanked Harris for dinner and told Mona how much I enjoyed meeting her and looked forward to seeing her paintings back on the mainland. After leaving the restaurant, Brenda, and I took a walk down Front Street to the Lahaina Banyan Court and sat under the largest Banyan tree in the USA. Brenda turned to me,

"Okay, we have a problem."

"Yeah, lady, what was up with all the silverware dropping?"

"I was purposely tossing them. That motherfucker kept trying to put his hands up my dress under the table."

I froze, wondering if this could possibly be a joke or comedic bit. I put my arm around Brenda,

"What? Seriously?"

She was noticeably perturbed by my question,

"I'm not being funny, Sonny. I was dropping knives and forks when I should have been stabbing him with them."

"What an asshole. Let's go back to the hotel and I'll confront him. I'll kick his ass."

"Really? That wouldn't be wise. He's my boss, and if I complain to that bimbo in H.R., he will just deny everything. Besides, there is something else I want to tell you. I got a tremendous job proposal from a company in Seattle, Washington that is developing an operating system for IBM. They are offering me a major pay increase along with stock options."

A thick lump congealed in my throat, and I was unable to speak for a few seconds, then I said,

"Well, that sounds great. When? How soon?"

She threw both her arms around me and kissed me passionately,

"I don't want to leave you, Herbie. I have become dependent on seeing your sorry ass every day. You got that?"

"But wait, you should definitely take the job. I can help you move, and I'll start looking for a job in Seattle. It's a great radio market and I could wait a whole lifetime before landing something in San Francisco."

"You know that asshole Stephano made this a much easier decision for me. I will explain the exact reason I'm leaving during my exit interview at work."

I was proud of her and hoped to never see that perv Harris again.

The rest of the week was fantastic, except when a farmer burned the sugarcane prior to harvest and all the hotel smoke alarms went off. We toured the island and snorkeled near Molokini, a sunken volcano from a hundred and fifty thousand years ago. Now both of us were getting great tans while looking forward to change and a new adventure.

As I said earlier, radio couples often do this. An amazing job opportunity comes up for one mate and the other must pull up and relocate. I was sure I could find work in Seattle, and I applied to all the radio stations there. I explained to my PD in San Jose why I was leaving, and he was completely respectful and supportive of my decision.

While walking on the beach with Brenda, I was thinking about how much we were alike and, where we were different, how well we complimented one another. She fancied my sense of humor, I adored her logic and intelligence, and the bedroom was the perfect place for both of us. There was no question I would relocate with her. She was the one, the yin to my yang. I also had deep thoughts about that incident at dinner, like how dare any man put his hands on my woman. Maybe that triggered a primal urge because when Brenda and I bedded down on Wednesday night, September 30, we made love like bunnies.

I woke up at 5:00 a.m. on October 1, and that ongoing primal desire was steaming up the mirrors in the room. After hitting the bathroom, Brenda tag teamed me for the facility, and I returned to bed. I was just about to fall back to sleep when a naked woman was on top of me and sucking my mouth before moving down for a look at the little guy, who was standing and demanding attention. I was more than turned on and she began repeating her lovemaking mantra,

"Let me please you, please let me love you."

Without thinking about it I looked over at the clock as she mounted me. It was 5:40 a.m. Maui time, and within a couple of minutes we both climaxed in mutual eruptions of sheer delight. Brenda let out an animalistic moan followed by an earthshattering scream I will never forget. She was shaking and I rolled over on her and said,

"Marry me."

Breathing deeply, she swallowed, and managed,

"What did you just say?"

"Let's get married."

There was this pause, and then she said,

"Okay, sure, but right now I need some more buddy. You got any gas left in the tank?"

We continued our lovemaking and then returned to sleep. When I woke up, Brenda was fresh from a shower wearing a hotel robe and sitting on the chair combing her wet hair,

"Sonny, was that a dream?"

"No dream baby; let's do it."

"Well, okay, but where's my fucking ring?"

"Oh, shit, I forgot that."

After a good laugh we talked and decided to slow down the process for now. We'll get the move, new jobs and new life settled before falling down a rabbit hole of wedding plans. Little did we know that something momentous was happening at that exact moment but in another place.

We were so happy as we flew back from Maui. Dionne Warwick was singing over the airport's P.A. system, *"Do you know the way to San Jose?"* We were uplifted as we plucked our luggage from the carousel in the SJC baggage claim area. We are here, we know the way, but we were also wondering where our lives will lead in the future.

As we passed a newspaper stand, a glaring headline caught my attention: MAJOR EARTHQUAKE HITS LA. I walked over to read the subhead, Whitter Narrows Earthquake Hit at 7:42 a.m.

"Wow, Brenda, remember what were we doing at 5:42 a.m.?"

She shook her head,

"An earthquake? Oh, okay, now I remember. Sonny, let's not make a big deal about this; people may have been hurt."

In fact, eight people died and more than two hundred were injured in that five-point-nine earthquake as it rumbled through Los Angeles. I couldn't help thinking it was time to move farther north.

37. Regional Radio Families

Sometimes a sort of invisible magic dust permeates all the stations owned by a single broadcaster. It's a synergy and sharing of mission among its workers that makes having a job at the owned radio station of such a company a totally feel-good situation. Walk into one of those stations and you'll instantly sense a positive and uplifting energy.

There's also a phenomenon of one or several disc jockeys staying within a single market for years by moving about from station to station. I remember asking one DJ why he was leaving a market after so many years there and he quipped, "I ran out of stations to work for!"

Let's take a look at two northwest powerhouse CHR stations, KJR in Seattle and KJRB in Spokane. At this point in our story, both were owned by Kaye-Smith Enterprises. That company opened their doors in 1958 as a joint venture between Seattle salesman and radio station owner Lester Smith and actor Danny Kaye. The firm owned and operated radio stations in Washington, Oregon, Kansas and Ohio. Kaye-Smith Enterprises launched Concerts West, which brought many famous performers such as Elvis Presley, Jimi Hendrix, and Led Zeppelin to the northwest. In addition, the group helped bring the Sounders and the Mariners professional sports teams to Seattle. Then there was the Kaye-Smith recording studio, which in the 1970s produced major hit records by Bachman-Turner Overdrive, the Steve Miller Band and Heart.

In a sense, Spokane's KJRB was the minor league training facility for KJR, the bigger station in Seattle. Talented radio personalities like Ichabod Caine and Scallops, Larry "Superjock" Lujack, Charlie Brown, Ric Hansen, Jim Kampmann, Danny Holiday, Jack "Commander Dunk" Gordon, Ross Woodward, Norm Gregory, Brian Gregory, Ricky Shannon, Suds Coleman, Rick Rydell, Marie McCallister, Steven West, Ralphie Koal and Frank Hanel with sidekick "Sunshine" Shelly Monahan made the Smith-Kaye group *the* place to work. Lujack went on to enormous success at WLS in Chicago, thus becoming the "superjock" he always claimed to be.

Because of Kaye-Smith's large roster of well-run radio stations, I applied to KJR, KISW, the rock station in Seattle, and KJRB, a CHR in Spokane. I heard back from PD John Sherman at KJRB. He was a gentlemanly, insightful and kind man who asked me to come visit him, see the station and talk about radio. John explained he had heard me on KSJO in San Jose and wanted to get together to see if I might fit into the family. Now there's a line I had never heard before. It was a cordial, comfortable call, and I was sincerely looking forward to meeting John.

A delightful surprise greeted me upon my Spokane arrival. The city hosted a World Expo in 1974, and they had restored their downtown area for that event. Old and lifeless industrial buildings and rusty railroad tracks were torn out and replaced by beautiful, sprawling parks, and the town adopted the nickname "All-American City." The remains of the tent structure used for the Expo still stood and looked like a giant king's adornment with lights from the top of the crown down to the ground. Unique! I didn't see any of the gray ash Mount Saint Helens had airmailed to his city years ago, but John did tell me his story about being caught on the golf course the day the cloud of volcanic dust surged forth.

John was a great ambassador for his city and company. He shared his love of Spokane, saying he felt vital and alive there, but also explained many disc jockeys had gone from Spokane to Seattle and then on to other major markets all across America.

I mentioned to John I had received a call from the PD at KZOK in Seattle, a competitor to his group, and asked him what he thought of that station and its management. He smiled and his answer was direct and honest. John said the current owners were okay, but he intuitively knew I would want to know about the station's history. Also, it's a given that most radio guys will pounce on an opportunity to bad mouth a competitor.

John explained that years ago KZOK AM and FM aired paid religious programming. The properties were owned by a couple from California, and husband Norwood J. Patterson was found guilty and sentenced to two years in prison for failing to pay taxes on employee withholdings. After the stations were forced into a court-ordered receivership, Patterson went ballistic when he realized he would lose the facilities. He drove to the transmitter site and pulled what are known as the "final tubes" from the transmitters, taking both stations off the air. Fortunately, there were spare tubes in the engineering locker so the damage was temporary, but Patterson's actions guaranteed he would never own a station again. Don't ever judge a station by its name, only by its licensee.

Basically, John was telling me to be careful, and I sincerely appreciated his candor. He also said he would let the guys at KISW know I was looking for a job, and he urged me to investigate possibilities at Kaye-Smith before any other stations in the market. It was a good trip and I left with immense respect for John and his radio company. I felt like I had made a new friend in the business.

Brenda was getting settled in at her new job and I was fascinated by her company's work with IBM and Microsoft designing an operating system named OS/2. She was putting in long hours and making a ton of money but never pressured me to get a job. We were setting up our new apartment with two large bedrooms and a small office where Brenda worked rather than going into Redmond or Seattle every day. She may have been part of the first wave of technology professionals who mostly worked from home, or wherever.

I spent time listening to the radio and discovered that disc jockeys in Seattle and surrounding areas truly talked a lot. Scott Shannon called radio newbies "baby DJs," and I'm sure Larry Lujack taught those youngsters the importance of being a personality. Problem was, the baby DJs misinterpreted his guidance by thinking they had to talk and talk and talk, neglecting the beauty and audience appeal of concise patter.

Surely by now you have realized that one common thread among radio people is their fantastic, often outrageous, stories. I met a jock from the Country music station who had just moved to Seattle from Orlando, Florida and he shared a tale about a famous DJ who cold-called at the home of a fellow broadcaster while he was hosting a garden dinner party outside by the pool. The visitor, let's call him Roddy, was drunk as a skunk and loudly complaining,

"Why the fucking fuck would anyone have an outdoor party in fucking August?"

The host told Roddy in plain language he was so dirty he reeked and said, "Go take a shower." Spying a garden hose near the pool's restroom door, Roddy proceeded to strip naked and spray himself off in front of all the guests, who could clearly see the miniscule microphone dangling from his porcelain white body.

Perhaps it was a Florida thing, but how could Roddy keep his job? Shouldn't he have been in a mental hospital? Truth is, gifted radio performers are often given a free pass for just about anything; call it a perk of the business. The more talented a radio disc jockey the greater the latitude extended to them for social misbehavior.

After just a short while I built bonds with the new Seattle radio friends I had met while job searching, and we would talk openly about the people and goings-on at the stations in the market. I met a jock from KZOK who spoke about his station's new general manager, a recent graduate of a progressive business school. On his first day, the boss announced he was a firm believer in an open-door policy. To prove it, he ordered the engineers to remove every door in the facility, except for the studios of course. It wasn't more than a week before employees adopted a habit of whispering in their open offices, and this infused a sense of paranoia rather than comfort. It's a given that unrest within a radio station can be "felt" by listeners, and when KZOK's ratings declined a new GM was brought in and the doors went back on their hinges. That old joke "don't let the door hit you where the good Lord split you" was summoned when discussing the dearly departed GM.

The management change at KZOK, the station with a logo of a hand doing the "OK sign," brought me opportunity. I was hired for the 10 p.m. to 2 a.m. shift and couldn't wait to get behind the mic.

One lesson I had learned was getting the money up front, and for this hiring I negotiated a great deal. The sad reality of the radio business is that on top of gas shortages, economic downturns and other such negative financial situations, you might end up at a cheaply run station and never get a raise. Some radio owners encouraged their disc jockeys to make personal appearances at advertisers for extra money, but they also kept their big-booted feet on their employees' necks. A ready excuse was giving a raise "right now" was a bad idea, but I was thrilled with my pay and didn't need to worry about that.

To best understand the next part of my tale, I should tell you a little something about me. I smoked cigarettes for a short while in college, but I gave that unhealthy habit a boot all those years ago. As a young adult, I began to get grossed out by that nasty nicotine and tar smell. Back in the old days, radio stations were cluttered with ashtrays and many broadcasters were addicted smokers. Sometimes the stale smell of tobacco on a studio microphone was intense.

There are extremely thin bands of metal inside a microphone that minutely vibrate according to nearby sounds, and those pulsations are then converted to an electrical signal. If one talks too closely to a mic, some of the more percussive vocal sounds will produce distortion. One of the most notorious examples of this is caused by words containing the letter P, which is known as a "plosive consonant." That's a great term because if you pronounce a P-word too close to a microphone, the force of wind against the delicate pickup mechanism inside comes across like an aural explosion. The radio slang for this is "popping your Ps," and it's just not cool.

Amateurs show their inexperience by not properly "working" a microphone, which means positioning it at a suitable direction and distance from their mouth to reduce the likelihood of popped Ps. That terrible sound drives veteran radio people crazy, and I'll bet you've heard it more than once. Seattle car seller Zeke Padgento voiced the radio spots for his dealership, and they were full of popped Ps. Perhaps your city has a local lunatic car dealer voicing their own radio commercials with popped Ps aplenty. Sorry for another digression.

When I sat down at the KZOK control board and adjusted the mic for my very first break, the acrid smell of cigarettes hit me like a rock. Between opening night jitters and that revolting odor, I almost threw up. I hadn't been that ill since college, so I grabbed the studio trashcan and kept her close. Which brings me to a question. How did I know my trashcan was female? Okay, back to my foul microphone.

I asked the chief engineer if he could replace the mic's foam pop screen. He seemed more than happy to help but sarcastically added, "I'll have to see if it's in the budget." He told me a short while ago he noticed the air studio mic was sounding almost as if it was wrapped in a dish towel. He opened it up and couldn't believe how much sticky cigarette gunk was coating the windscreen inside the mic. He asked the management if they would ban smoking in the studio but that went over like a lead balloon, or in this case, a led zeppelin.

I got through my first show and went on to do another twelve hundred shifts in that very chair, wearing my trusty headphones during each one of them.

I'm sure you've seen pictures or videos of a radio DJ wearing headphones, but do you know why? Well, if the studio loudspeakers were active when the mic was open, feedback would result. You know, that excruciating screech you hear from an event's poorly adjusted P.A. system. The loudspeakers in a radio studio immediately mute when the mic switch is opened, so headphones are necessary for the jock to hear the audio they're controlling.

One of the most popular headphones in the radio business was and continues to be the Koss Pro 4-AA, featuring soft, rubber cushions that completely encircle the wearer's ears to form a tight fit. The sound from cheaper headphones would occasionally seep into the mic causing a feedback squeal, but you could run the Koss headphones loudly and its rubber pads provided a perfect acoustic barrier. The design secret was those flexible earpads were filled with oil, which formed a snug seal around the wearer's ears. The Koss headphones had a downside, however. Many a disc jockey experienced "the leak," when the aged rubber became hard, eventually cracked, and gooey oil was now free to flow down. I know one poor jock who let out a yelp in the midst of reading a live spot when that goo started to trickle down his neck.

Brenda's company was coding the operating system that was supposed to rival Windows, which had become ubiquitous. Her stock options were growing every year and so was her compensation. We were too busy to get married, but I figured if the day came when we wanted to have kids we would tie the knot then. For now, though, we were living the dream in what I assumed was mutual happiness, but then, does one ever truly know what another's contentment entails?

My PD got sick a few days before he was to travel to Dallas for the R&R convention, and the GM asked me if I would go in his stead. Yes, please! I knew my college buddy Billy would be there, and it would be great seeing him and catching up. The manager made me promise that I wouldn't be looking for a new job while at the convention and I assured him I was extremely happy in Seattle and had no desire to leave the city or the station. Yes, radio was in my blood, and I didn't need to be looking for something better when I had all I really wanted in Seattle with Brenda and a great gig at KZOK.

38. When Did You Get In?

There is a funny circumstance about business conventions, and I'm sure it's true regardless of the industry. There's usually a cocktail mixer to open the event. When two cohorts meet, inevitably one of them pops the question, "When did you get in?" Even glib radio people cannot come up with something creative or witty to say in response. What's most strange is an answer to the question couldn't possibly change anything; it's just an icebreaker.

The R&R convention was being held in Dallas at the Anatole Hotel, which us radio ducks nicknamed the Ayatollah hotel. Ronald Reagan was in office. He had gotten the hostages back from Iran and soon he would blow up a fundamental, major rule of broadcasting. We'll get back to that shortly, but right now it's convention time.

The hotel is a massive structure on Stemmons Freeway, only two miles from Parkland Memorial Hospital where President John F. Kennedy was pronounced dead after being assassinated in 1963. More and more radio and records people filtered into the mixer, and I was proud to be working in an industry with so many talented yet outrageous people. My longtime pal Billy had moved on to the number three market in the country, Chicago, and was the program director of the leading CHR station there. He was no longer Brewster Billy from the University of Dayton. Now his radio name was Billy K. Polman, a mashup of his legal surname Kalpolski.

After cruising the gathering I finally ran into Billy. He was surrounded by record people schmoozing him in hopes of getting an "add," a shortened form of the word addition, meaning the placement of a song they were promoting on his station's playlist. An add in a major market like Chicago was invaluable to an artist's record label, producers and managers. I told Billy I would find him later, but he insisted I join them and sealed the deal by buying me a drink. I sat down with the group while Billy made the introductions, but I immediately knew there was no way I could possibly remember all the names and faces. Since I worked in what was then the fringe AOR format, there was little pressure on me to play a new single release. Plus, I wasn't a PD, just a jock on a Seattle FM radio station.

R&R conventions always attracted recording artists, sometimes major stars, to either perform or just mingle with the industry folk. Here in the mid-eighties, the hangover from the disco era was still intact with abundant amounts of cocaine finding its way to Dallas. For some it became a four-day, non-stop party.

I knew Billy wasn't into drugs, but during the convention there were times he seemed distracted and disconnected. It was also impossible to have a one-on-one with him. We would start a conversation and then a record or radio guy would suddenly appear and interrupt. I needed to be patient with this situation. My dear friend was in the stratosphere while my feet were on terra firma.

A few radio acquaintances grabbed me and took me to a hotel suite and the happenings there were remarkable. Seven people were present, and I knew a few of the radio guys from seeing their pictures in R&R. There was also a record promoter from Island Records pitching the latest Robert Palmer single *Addicted to Love* from his new album *Riptide*. Island was a label started by Chris Blackwell using his family's money. That's right, financing courtesy of Crosse & Blackwell. Several substantial lines of cocaine were in the middle of the coffee table and music was floating in from a radio in an adjoining bedroom.

I have always loved Robert Palmer's music and I played *Every Kinda People* over the years more times than I could count. I fancied the lyric, *"To make what life's about, yeah, It takes every kinda people, To make the world go 'round."* The song's point was not judging others no matter how different they were.

In the center of the room a famous New York City program director was lounging in an oversized armchair facing the couch. I looked over to the sofa and my eyes just about popped out of their sockets. Sitting there was Robert Palmer!

Now if ever there was a proper and impeccably dressed Brit, that would be Robert. He had a remarkably successful career as a singer-songwriter, but he eschewed the rock 'n roll lifestyle. Sadly, he was addicted to cigarettes, and some said he often smoked more than sixty in a day. He was a polite, sincere fellow, and the following events underscored my belief that not all radio people are well-behaved.

The New York programmer, who will remain nameless, was deep into his lines, his scotch and himself. The Island Records guy was plying his charm and white magical powder to get the PDs gathered there to commit to adding Palmer's new song when they returned to their radio stations. The bigshot program director took a great gulp of grit from his glass, put it down on the table rather sloppily and said,

"Robert, this song *A Dickhead to Love* really isn't your best work."

At exactly that moment, one of the guys went into the bedroom with a woman, closed the door and turned off the radio. Instant stillness followed, caused by the absence of music and the harsh words of a rude broadcaster. It was an uncomfortable situation, and instead of using the razorblade to cut the cocaine perhaps it should have been used to cut the tension. The Island guy spoke,

"Have you heard the hook in that song?"

When playing a new song for a PD or DJ, some record promoters have an extremely annoying routine. Instead of allowing their captive audience to appreciate a new song they're hearing for the very first time, the promoter insists on singing the hook in their ear. They're trying to convince the radio person the song is so enchanting that no human could possibly resist singing along. Besides the assault of their bad breath, they can't sing worth a shit. If they could, they would be making records instead of pushing them. So, the Island guy actually started to sing the hook of the song, the chorus, and looked at Robert as if to suggest he should belt out the tune himself to counter the massive turd the New York PD had just dropped into the punch bowl.

Robert lit a cigarette, leaned forward and tried to smile,

"Well, tell me mate, what don't you like about the song?"

The arrogant programmer picked up a straw from the table, took a large inhalation of the finest record company cocaine, snorted, coughed then spoke,

"It's just formula pablum. It's a contrived piece of shit designed for Top 40, and it certainly isn't any 'takin' sally through the alley.'"

Robert's face flushed with anger, the same kind of ire I was feeling about the behavior of this PD. I spoke up,

"I love the song. One of your best, Mr. Palmer."

Everyone in the room got a chuckle from my "Mr. Palmer," which gave the Island guy an opportunity to grab Robert's arm and extract him from the paddling of an overblown program director. I truly felt sorry for Robert, and I still vividly recall that night in 2003 when hearing the news of his death from a heart attack at only fifty-four years of age.

Sometimes karma is a part of this life. The PD's New York station had several negative ratings books in a row, and he was soon fired. He found work as a helicopter pilot broadcasting traffic reports in Jacksonville, Florida. Apparently, the guy's lack of judgement misguided him one final time. He was attempting to land in the backyard of the home owned by his paramour and misjudged the location of high-tension wires over her property. His career and life went up in smoke. I guess one could say he was addicted to love.

The convention wasn't all party with no substance. There were seminars designed to educate visitors from both the record and radio fields. I attended a few government and engineering panels and was astounded by the prediction that one day all of the audio we play over the air would come from a computer system. Little did we all know forty years ago that audio for today's radio stations would be stored in the "cloud," without the need for earthly hardware. Back then, a cloud was a white-fluffy thing in the sky.

I saw an incredible demonstration from the *Selector* people showing off one of their new products they called a "paperless studio." I also learned that Ronald Reagan was about to get rid of the Fairness Doctrine. Please allow me to give you some background on that one.

In 1949, the FCC created a policy that required holders of broadcast licenses to present controversial issues of public importance in a way, as they described it, to fairly reflect differing viewpoints. The doctrine was applied mostly to political campaigns. So, if a Grand Wizard in Alabama was running for office, and my station aired a twenty-minute speech by his opponent during afternoon drive, then the KKK guy was entitled to the same amount of time in an equivalent daypart. The Fairness Doctrine was cumbersome because some markets had more than ten people running for a given office. Reagan wanted to end the rule mainly because it would eliminate lessor known political candidates from the airwaves, but it would also give radio stations the right to refuse political speeches or advertising. The white supremacists would have to find other means of disseminating their poison.

I caught up with Billy on the last day of the convention and we had lunch at a Mexican restaurant on Ross Street in downtown Dallas. I was surprised, a bit shocked actually, at how much he drank during our time together. He summarized his success path from Cleveland to Miami to Pittsburgh to Chicago. He admitted that his financial situation was somewhat desperate because of two divorces, and now as a free man in Chicago he was paying alimony and living paycheck-to-paycheck. He asked about my career, and I gave him the fifty-cent tour of my life after college, which raised a chortle,

"You always land on your feet Herbie."

I smiled, realizing in my own mind I was no longer Herbert. I had fully assimilated my Sonny Joe moniker, and hearing Billy say my "old" name threw me a bit. Billy also warned me about the record industry and how often cash, drugs and/or women were used to get songs played on the air. I used that old Paul Newman quote about going out for hamburger when he had steak at home. Billy snickered and told me I was lucky.

Here I was, doing a 10 p.m. to 2 a.m. shift on the second rated AOR station in Seattle while Billy was the PD of the biggest CHR in Chicago, and he was telling me *I* was lucky. Maybe he was thinking about my great relationship with Brenda and the way I was happy and content with just about everything in my life.

We got back to the hotel and ran into, of all people, Charlie Minor, the flamboyant VP of Promotion at A&M Records. Two lieutenants were by his side when he walked up to Billy and spoke in a soft-southern whisper,

"Hey, I'm having a small dinner gathering for a few top PDs tonight and I'd like you to be there, Billy. Very intimate."

He turned and looked at me,

"Y'all can come too, Sonny Joe. It's Seattle for you these days, right?"

There, it happened again! Charlie not only remembered me but also knew where I was now working, but I supposed that was a requirement of his business. I agreed to go with Billy to Charlie's cozy event, figuring it would be good to see how the major market PDs who reported their charts to R&R were treated.

Our cab arrived at the five-star restaurant where the valet crew was busy parking gold Mercedes and black Maserati's. I paid our driver and turned to Billy,

"Are we dressed up enough for this place?"

Billy looked down at his satin radio station jacket and my denim jeans and said,

"Herbie, I'm pretty sure no one at this private party will care about how other guests are dressed."

We walked in the door and stepped up to the hostess stand, which was under the control of an exceptionally busty blonde in a tight red dress. The place was packed, and I was looking for the door that would lead us to a private dining room. Billy spoke,

"Hi, we're here for the Minor private party, Charlie Minor."

"Well, you are certainly at the right place. Have fun!"

With that, she swept her arms at the crowded restaurant, and we were now experiencing the Charlie factor full-on. We thought we would be attending a private dinner with a few radio people and hosted by one of the most well-known and loved record promoters in America, but we had been sucked into a mega-event where about a hundred radio folk would wine and dine on snow crab flown in from Miami and top-cut steaks from Omaha while surrounded by a bevy of the Metroplex's finest looking women.

I had the best time, and as the night wound down I found myself thoroughly drunk, stuffed like a tick and hoarse from loudly telling stories and jokes to be heard over the thumping music and cacophony of all those strident radio voices. I felt like it was time to leave, but Billy was nowhere to be found. I did see Charlie Minor, so I thanked him for the great party and then asked,

"Hey, Charlie, have you seen Billy, you know, Polman?"

In his raspy voice,

"Man, he left a while ago with some chick, but we'll get you back to the hotel. Meet us outside."

I appreciated the ride and when we got to the car Charlie sat in back with two amazingly attractive ladies, a blonde bombshell and a dark Italian looking woman who kept pulling up the front of her dress, while complaining how it was either too small or her breasts were too big. I was crowded together in the front seat with two other guys.

We were almost at the hotel when I heard Charlie whispering in my ear,

"Which one do you want?"

"Sorry, what Charlie?

"Take one of them, I can't manage two."

I smiled and said loud enough for everyone to hear,

"No, no, I'm okay."

We got out of the car, and I took a long look at Charlie's angels and how their butts wiggled and swayed when they walked. I suddenly realized this was some people's daily existence. The job of promoting records could be one long party, and some playing that game snorted so much blow and drank so much alcohol they became unable to perform. Many radio people are drawn to the fame flame, but at a base level everyone is the same — all human, flawed and sometimes self-destructive with those little blue meanies buried in their souls.

I called Brenda who was busy working on a tight deadline project, and I could read her voice, so I kept the call short. Besides, I had a plane to catch in the morning. I entered my hotel room, set the clock radio alarm to 5 a.m. and adjusted the volume to make sure it was loud enough to wake me up. Then I heard this,

"Well, Larry, this whole 'new Coke' idea was one of the worst. I mean, here they have a perfect product and now they've gone and messed with it."

"You might be right about that, caller. Okay, we have Jim on the line from Ypsilanti, Michigan!"

"Hi Larry, am I on the air?"

"Yes, you're on Jim. What's on your mind?"

"So, Larry, why do superheroes wear their underwear outside of their clothes? You assho…"

Calling into a talk radio show trying to beat the seven-second delay was a stunt some listeners liked to pull. I laughed realizing Larry hit the dump button with perfect timing. The word was long enough to know what the caller said but short enough to avoid any legal challenge. Then I looked down at my underwear. Gee, that was actually a damn good question. To this day I have no idea why Superman dresses that way. Larry King should have tried to answer the guy.

Another radio convention was under my belt, and I escaped without drinking too much, doing drugs or engaging in any "lay for play." I was worried a little bit about Billy, but I had a hunch he would overcome his poverty, which I had learned in D.C. truly sucks.

39. Birthday Cake Caper

Media people, and that certainly includes radio broadcasters, often get pulled into the hype of the moment. Because most of us read George Orwell's book *1984* either in high school or college, we believed that year would bring a brazen bang. It didn't.

Before the end of the decade, however, lots of innovation, inspiration and ingeniousness boiled to the surface of the radio industry. In the mid-1980s, Detroit radio guy Fred Jacobs was selling his Classic Rock format which, as its name implied, featured rock songs from the sixties and seventies. This new format had huge audience numbers in the right demographic, Men 25 to 54.

They said it could never happen, but in 1987 KMET in Los Angeles dropped its rock format and rebranded as The Wave, airing Frank Cody's over-produced, syndicated Smooth Jazz format. In that same year, WNBC in New York City changed its call letters to WFAN and became a full-time All-Sports radio station, a format which to this day wins audiences and revenues in large markets across the country.

The Talk format had found its home on many AM stations, and one conservative pundit and pontificator of massive girth took his act into syndication to change America for the worse, forever. Rush Limbaugh was attracting more than the toothless, the jobless and old ladies. Young men were being brainwashed by his vitriol and hate speech. Mr. Limbaugh was especially misogynistic and forced his "return to traditional values" on millions of listeners. Broadcasters who aired his show got rich and radio stations carrying his show revamped their overall programming to align with his right-wing rhetoric.

Sometimes a radio host suddenly swerves to a new direction, leaving the audience in the dust. One funny morning guy in a large market lost a major sexual harassment suit brought by his on-the-air newswoman, and this pushed him into an anti-government conspiracy zone. Once a staunch supporter of women's rights, the loss of the court case made him anti-feminist. His talk show was no longer amusing, instead he became even more hateful than Rush and the ideology he pushed on the airwaves was pure vindictive dung. That guy and Limbaugh may have shown the power of radio, but I just wanted to play rock 'n roll records and have fun.

The melting of a massive snowfall isn't a significant problem until water leaks into your home and causes thousands of dollars in damage. Over the late eighties and into the nineties, radio regulations were transforming in a way that shook and pressurized the industry's structure. One area of change affected non-entertainment program regulation. The FCC eliminated radio licensing rules governing the amount of talk and informational programming required on stations and replaced them with a vague obligation to "offer programming responsive to public issues." They also threw out the need to formally ascertain community needs, which once required radio executives to regularly interview community leaders for guidance with understanding and covering public concerns. In addition, the FCC abolished guidelines concerning the maximum number of commercials allowed, meaning a station could play nothing but commercials and still keep its license.

The mega-tsunami was the elimination of ownership maximums. Limitations regarding the number of radio stations a single entity could own became based on a sliding scale that varied by market size. In a radio market with forty-five or more stations, a single company could own up to eight radio stations, no more than five of which were in the same AM or FM service. In a location with thirty to forty-four stations, a single holder could own a maximum of seven radio stations, no more than four of which were in the same service. In an area with fifteen to twenty-nine radio stations one firm was permitted to own up to six radio stations, no more than four of which were in the same service, and so forth.

This deregulation sparked a buying frenzy which made many owners of only one or two stations rich when they sold their properties for top prices. Larger groups with seven to twelve stations faced a decision, either significantly increase their holdings or get out of radio entirely. FM stations with good signals were selling for ten to fifteen times cash flow. So, a facility that was paid off years ago with a current annual net revenue of two and a half million dollars could sell for as much as thirty-two million dollars. This fifteen-times cash flow metric was based on how the industry believed radio would perform financially in three to five years, but interest and principal payments came along with borrowed money. The pressure on local radio sales departments to bring in three to four times their previous billing was tough enough but could be even more brutal during an economic downturn.

Some shrewd radio owners bought twenty or more stations, hoping that one or two of their major markets properties would pay the bills for the entire group. When that didn't happen, those owners sold their smaller market stations at a loss, but that's not the worst of it. When the banks called in large payments, station owners often increased their spot loads, the maximum number of commercial minutes aired per hour. Station audiences who were comfortable with eight to ten minutes of hourly spots were now bombarded with fifteen to eighteen commercial minutes. When ratings went down, some station owners fired highly paid DJs to right the budget, and the loss of those talented on-air personalities caused even further ratings erosion.

Syndicated programming helped some owners with their financial obligations. Broadcasting Rush Limbaugh and others, for example, would fill a considerable number of daily hours without much of a cash outlay. Most syndication companies used "barter" as their business model. The station ran spots sold by the syndicator in exchange for a reduced cost of the programming. Of course, the station also squeezed in their own commercials to maximize profit.

As more and more old-time station owners cashed out, radio companies consolidated and were firing disc jockeys, newscasters, engineers and programming assistants, but never salespeople. Instead, the new conglomerates increased their sales ranks and turned them loose on the clients. If a salesperson survived, great, if not, they were replaced in a few months. The business of radio developed a revolving door reputation from which it has never recovered.

With pressure to generate revenue and keep up with huge loan obligations, fewer owners were willing to stick by a heritage format when directly attacked by a new competitor. One famous consultant spoke truth to power by advising a client, "Always go after a big company, they have pockets deep enough to leave a format behind, whereas a one-station owner has an emotional bond to their programming."

The game was clear; if you couldn't beat them, just buy them out and change their format. It was a game of cannibalization. A mega-owner could eliminate a competitor and pick up their highest rated DJs. Once a cannibal ate its competitor, they increased their advertising rates based on the lack of competition.

New kinds of companies were birthed to sell cable television ads using a technique named "interconnects," which streamlined and simplified advertising buys in local markets. With a single purchase, an advertiser could spread a commercial across many cable outlets to reach a sizeable number of households. The ads were automatically inserted into the programming of multiple cable television channels. The spots sold for less than radio was charging, and more than a few sponsors dropped radio in favor of cable TV commercials, which had both sound and video. With the arrival of the internet, newspapers were beginning to lose their clout but still taking a lion's share of advertising money. When the economic woes of 1986 to 1989 forced the Federal Reserve to raise interest rates, many radio operators felt the pinch.

Around this same time, automation became a trend in the radio industry leading to a quick and almost universal adoption of a dreadful technique known as "voice tracking." A single disc jockey working for an owner of multiple stations recorded breaks for maybe eight or ten stations every day. So, one voice would play in the automation systems of radio stations across the country, eliminating loads of local DJ jobs.

Radio station groups saved enormous amounts in their programming budgets, which was great for the owners but terrible for the listeners.

These automated stations had hardly any local content. If a major news story broke, the station's prerecorded automaton continued with no mention of whatever was occurring in the town or city. It's unlikely you would ever hear, "Take shelter, a twister is coming!" on a twenty-four by seven voice tracked station. Live disc jockeys weren't on duty and more often than not the disembodied radio voices conveyed no love or understanding of the cities where they were heard. Local happenings weren't covered.

Seeing the writing on the wall, I decided that some consulting work on the side would be an excellent way to protect myself from a capricious station owner or format change. Adams, a successful outdoor advertising company, now owned my station and said I may consult with two stipulations. I couldn't hire away any jocks working for an Adams station, and I couldn't compete with them in any market. That made perfect sense to me, and our agreement was put in place.

You'll never guess who became my very first client early in 1989. It was KSJO and I was amazed at how the morning team, Perry Stone and Trish Bell, had stirred up the market. On one of his first days in San Jose, Stone learned that KOME's Blazy & Bob morning show, hosted by Jeff Blazy and Bob Lilley, would be remote broadcasting from the lobby of the very hotel KSJO had booked for Perry during his first week at the station. He bought a cake with frosting forming the logo of KOME, KSJO's archrival, and the plot was set.

Stone, not known visually to the KOME team, walked in during their final hour of the morning show remote broadcast and took a seat in the front row. One of the producers noticed this guy in the crowd holding a box and urged Blazy to interview him. This is what was heard on KOME,

"Hey, we have an interesting guy here. Where are you from?

Stone, acting like a nervous listener, replied,

"Well, I am new to San Jose. Just got in yesterday and I wanted to see what your show was all about."

"Well, you got Blazy and Bob with KOME on your radio."

Perry stared at Blazy and asked,

"Aren't you going to ask me what's in this box I'm holding?

Caught off guard, the KOME morning man laughed and then said,

"Okay, the listener is telling me how to conduct an interview! That's rich. Sure, I'll bite. What's in the box?"

Perry Stone opened the box, and Blazy was quite impressed with the cake emblazoned with his station's logo,

"So, listeners, here inside the box is a beautiful cake with the KOME logo made of black and yellow frosting. Man, that looks and smells great! Did you bake it yourself?"

"No, my wife did."

"Dude, what is your name? What do you do?"

"I'm Perry Stone, your new morning show competitor at KSJO. Be sure to tune in tomorrow for my first show!"

Bang, instant promo on the competing radio station! Perry walked out of the hotel lobby and into a waiting getaway car.

Over the next several months, Perry and Trish took the market by storm. Perry had worked at Boston's V66 video music TV station in the late 1970s with Bob Rivers, another future famous radio morning man and parody song producer. After the rough road of small market radio, Stone found himself on the west coast working at the underdog rock station KSJO. My role would be organizing and cleaning up their playlist and tweaking their music scheduling to be more competitive.

One of the best on-air bits Stone pulled off was a continuing claim he was in contact with the famous serial killer Charles Manson. The elaborate ruse took the form of a series of phone calls to the supposed warden of San Quentin State Prison. During one of calls to the fake warden, Stone "convinced" him to let Manson out of jail for one day. The warden commented that Manson had a burning passion to see a baseball game, and Perry Stone quickly said he would make that happen. Perry and the guy playing the role of the warden agreed Manson would attend a game during the final week of the San Francisco Giants 1988 season. The ongoing phone calls were outrageous and created a major buzz in both San Jose and San Francisco.

Well, baseball fans calling into the Giants ticket office were not impressed. Many ticket holders were asking if they could exchange their tickets for a game where Manson would not be present. Riding in my cab on the way to the airport to catch my flight back to Seattle, I wasn't at all surprised to hear this, "Good morning! This is KGO Radio, the home of the San Francisco Giants. This just in from our newsroom, the rumor that Charles Manson will be attending Tuesday night's game is just that… a rumor."

The next thing I heard was an actuality, the recorded voice of the real warden of San Quentin saying Manson is not permitted to leave the prison for the rest of his life. I'm sure it had nothing to do with the radio stunt, but shortly after that broadcast Manson was moved to the Protective Housing Unit at a different jail, California State Prison in Corcoran.

You might think his stunt would have gotten Perry Stone fired, but something else would trigger that event. KSJO went through a crisis when their GM, who shall remain nameless, fell deeply into a state of paranoia brought on by excessive cocaine use. He believed he was being followed around the clock and his stalker should be apprehended. The station owner didn't have time for this. He was focused on pumping up the value of the property for future sale, so he fired the manager and replaced him with a know-it-all kind of guy we'll call Brandon. The station probably had to widen the door of Brandon's office so his oversized ego could pass through it. For some reason Brandon didn't like Stone and waited for an opportunity to get rid of him. Brandon also thought I was an unnecessary fixture and fired me, which is a badge of honor for a radio person.

Then came the day when Stone aired a crazy phone call with two Brownie Scouts, during which he told one of the nine-year-old girls she should keep all the Girl Scout cookie money collected from her customers rather than handing it over to the scouts. Of course, an angry parent wrote a letter to the station and copied the FCC. Brandon now had his opening and fired Perry Stone from KSJO on the ides of March in 1989.

It's funny, you see. A DJ can concoct a farce about taking a serial killer to a baseball game but must never attempt to convince a child to enter a life of crime within earshot of the public. My short-lived consultancy was fun, but it occurred to me I would rather be spending my weekends at home.

There was something a little off with Brenda when I got back from San Jose. She was certainly happy and engaged with her work, but there was an odd twist to our conversations. She had met a lady named Deborah at a Seattle coffee shop, and Brenda's dialogue was now peppered with stories about her new friend. It seemed almost obsessive.

Of course, Brenda was an extremely sexual person, but I never pegged her as bisexual. Rather than over-probe the matter, I chalked it up to nothing more than a friendship and told Brenda I was looking forward to meeting Deborah.

Love makes people do stupid things and buying a cake to repair a wonderful relationship that's coming to an end won't set things right.

There's a proper moment to turn inward and ask that one painful question, "Was it something I did?"

I didn't know then that moment was on its way to me.

40. Technology and Science

Curiosity and excitement always follow new, innovative technology introduced to the public. Yes, some had to fight it out in the marketplace like Betamax versus VHS video tapes. The vinyl phonograph record waved its white flag and ran away when the compact disc invaded the market. Those CDs sounded wonderful, and we all bought into the myth they were indestructible.

For decades, radio introduced its listeners to new songs. Before radio, a human had to go to the park and listen to a marching band play the latest John Philip Sousa tune or hear a streetcorner barbershop quartet sing a new composition. From its earliest days, radio played music for free and attracted loyal audiences, but technology doesn't step lightly. It generally stomps on what currently exists and demands to be heard.

Karlheinz Brandenburg is an electrical engineer, and in 1991 he was part of the group that developed digital audio data reduction for use in MP3 music files. The Moving Picture Experts Group (MPEG) is an alliance that sets standards for audio, video, graphics and genomic data. That group lent its name to the process of digital audio and video encoding to reduce file sizes, allowing them to be more quickly and easily transferred. The technical specification of the process is named MPEG Audio Layer III. So, should you ever hear a geek engineer speak of an MPEG-3 file rather than an MP3, you now know why. MP3 files are ubiquitous and have had a profound effect on both music and radio.

I won't overwhelm you with the technical details of how a series of ones and zeroes can store and reproduce sound, but after the CD was invented, smart technicians figured out a way to "rip" or extract the code from any CD into a file that could be played elsewhere. Consumers played MP3 files, which were smaller in size but had reduced audio quality, while radio stations relied on WAV files, which were full fidelity but much larger.

Around this time the internet was becoming so big that most authors gave it a capital I. Still, there were disbelievers. One tech guy bluntly told me, "The internet is just a fad." I wasn't at all sure he was correct, because even in those early days I was scouring bulletin boards and some early World Wide Web sites to get information about the latest song releases, artists and concert tours. In less than nine years from now, a young kid named Sean Fanning would develop a web-based music sharing program named Napster, which grabbed the attention of record companies and legal experts all around the world.

When Brenda asked me to attend the Consumer Electronics Show (CES) with her in Los Angeles, I almost jumped out of my shoes. That series of conventions began in 1967 and had become the yearly January showcase of the latest technological products with potential to change the world. Those gatherings featured more science in one location than anywhere else.

Our trip would have an interesting twist. Brenda had invited a third wheel along for our adventure, her new friend Deborah Hubbard. She planned a dinner at our home before travel, saying it would allow me to get to know and understand Deborah. I was curious about what that meant but kept an open mind.

The moment Deborah entered our apartment, I noticed her perfectly coiffed long blonde hair and striking blue eyes. Her jeans were as tight as could be and she had opened her white blouse one button lower than most women might, displaying over three inches of cleavage. Soon I noticed Deborah had what I later learned was "concomitant strabismus," a misalignment of the eye muscles in which one or both eyes point in different directions. It's commonly known as crossed or wandering eyes. When Deborah turned my way, both her eyes were aimed in different directions, and neither was pointed directly at me.

We shook hands and took seats on the sofa. Brenda had laid out some crackers and cheese and poured two glasses of wine. Deborah asked for a grasshopper, which is not a drink I would suggest for snacking. I asked Deborah what she did, and thus began our night,

"Well, I moved here to be with my brother. He has become so happy since joining his friends."

I thought that was a curious reply but decided to use my interviewing skills to clear a path for her,

"Are you working or just staying with your brother?"

"Well, staying with him for now, but I will be moving to LA soon. I used to be a bartender in D.C."

I figured her relocation would be bolstered by tagging along on our CES trip, and I honestly had a slight feeling of relief that Brenda's new obsession would be leaving town. Deborah continued,

"I am a free spirit and not concerned with my body or mind."

I looked at Brenda who had a shit-eating grin on her face as if she was listening to the Lord himself. I probed,

"Well, hopefully we will be feeding our bodies tonight, right Brenda?"

"Sonny, please, let Deborah speak."

That took me aback. Never before had I experienced such blowback from Brenda, and I was suddenly concerned this could evolve into a fateful night. I moved my eyes from Deborah's moccasins to her lopsided eyes and offered a retort,

"So, Deborah, who are we as humans if not a body and a mind?"

"We are more than our environment or genes; we are all immortal spirits, and our capabilities are unlimited. Our goal is reaching a clear level of consciousness."

I quickly changed the subject and talked about the LA trip and where we would stay. I was happy to hear Deborah had plans to room with friends, meaning it would be just Brenda and me at the convention hotel.

Both women laughed heartily at some of my radio stories during dinner, and the evening ended on a positive note. We walked Deborah to her car, and she turned to me,

"I'll show you something in LA, Sonny, and then you'll understand."

After Deborah drove off, I asked Brenda what her new friend was talking about, but she just shook her head while saying she had no idea. For the very first time in our relationship, I felt like she wasn't being completely honest with me.

The radio headlines were crazy around this time. Howard Stern had been fined thousands of dollars per incident of what the FCC claimed to be a "dwelling on sexual matters." Meanwhile, other morning shows were gaining ratings by dipping their collective toes into the water of shock lake. On the other side of radio, the old Beautiful Music format, once referred to with the claustrophobic nickname "elevator music," had died. One syndicator sold a format branded "Music for the Two of Us," and we used to joke by adding, "…and sometimes three." The listeners and ratings for that one quickly evaporated, so "bye-bye in the car-car."

My brain was distracted by all the radio news and disruption, and I knew it might be time to begin looking toward a new opportunity, but it was complicated because of Brenda. She was making a ton of money working for the software giant, and those stock options given to her years ago were now growing into a colossal pot at the end of the rainbow. It wouldn't be long before she could sell some of them.

As we were making our way to the CES, the battle between two Los Angeles CHR stations was on the front burner. Power 107 and KISS-FM were competing head-to-head. KISS was on top for now, but that battle would continue for decades with no clear winner. I enjoyed listening to the music on KROQ and the morning show on KLOS hosted by Mark & Brian, two guys who leaped from Birmingham, Alabama straight to LA. I was also curious about The Wave and spent some time checking them out in the rental car.

Brenda and Deborah said they wanted me to see something, but the vibe gave me the impression it was some sort of secret between them. I went along for the joke, but as things unfolded it became clear this wasn't a prank. They instructed me to pull into a parking lot off Sunset into what used to be the Hollywood Hospital. I parked the car and the ladies instructed me to be good because this was a church. I flashed back to my college radio days when the student GM reprimanded me even before I did something wrong. As we approached the front door, I couldn't help noticing the three parking spaces closest to the entrance were occupied by brand-new Mercedes 450SLs in candy-apple red, pure-as-snow white and sparkly-metallic blue with California license plates reading Clear 1, Clear 2 and Clear 3. My mind was clicking.

After walking through the doors, we found ourselves in a large atrium. On the right stood a mammoth, golden-brown mural of a sphinx at sunset with a face combining the features of a lion and a man. A label underneath the painting read "L. Ron Hubbard." Jeez, L. Ron shared Deborah's last name. Coincidence? I think not. Suddenly it felt as if I was the subject of a recruitment effort.

The rest was a haze of touring classrooms and small double-seat booths where a human subject held onto a device that showed… what? Deborah explained the cubicles were used for "auditing," a process in which an auditor takes an individual through the times of their life to rid them of negative influences and energies from past events or behaviors. The goal was to advance to "Clear" status and, I guess, win a brand-new Mercedes? "Don't say hello, just give me all your money and you'll win big." Am I being clear?

On the plane back to Seattle, Brenda was reading the book Deborah had given her, *Dianetics: The Modern Science of Mental Health* written by Scientology's so-called prophet L. Ron Hubbard. She and I were on different wavelengths and the tension was palpable.

Now I know a fair amount about technology and science, some of it self-taught, but nowhere have I ever seen any reputable evidence saying your soul or spirit emits waves of data that can be detected by an electro-psychometer, also known as an "E-meter." This was all made-up hooey by a conman science fiction writer who wanted power, money and sex with gullible women. I honestly tried to read Mr. Hubbard's book, but I had to put it down. It was all crazy shit and Ron was a piss-poor writer to boot. I couldn't believe that an intelligent person like Brenda Shaw, the love of my life, was being sucked into this crap.

It was 1991, and President George H. W. Bush decided to send troops into Iraq to teach Saddam Hussein a lesson about his country's invasion of Kuwait over oil pricing and production disputes. I'll say only this. No matter what you hear, every war in the world is based on someone wanting someone else's money. Oh, sure, they'll offer other excuses to get the conflict started and keep it going, but it's really all about money. When they say, "Weapons of mass destruction," think oil. When they ignore human rights violations, it's all about individuals over there cheaply making stuff we buy over here.

I didn't want a war with my Brenda, but I feared this division we faced would sooner or later boil over into an all-out conflict. I don't remember the date, but I recall the events of that day and always will. Brenda had been talking on the phone with Deborah, and our discussion afterward began with this,

"I'm thinking about a change, Sonny."

"What do you mean? What kind of change?"

"I'm going to cash out all my stock, quit my job and move to LA."

"What? Are you nuts? Stop playing around!"

"The church needs our help, dear. I want to use my earnings to help them spread the word, build more centers and grow the ministry. You do know that many famous movie stars in Hollywood are part of this, right?"

Why is it we so often use the famous-people card as justification? I couldn't hold back,

"Brenda, it's a fucking cult! You're being used."

She looked down and I was thinking she was reconciling her intellect and emotions, but I was wrong,

"L. Ron Hubbard was a visionary."

"No, he was a crook, and if he was such a goddamn immortal spirit then why the fuck is he so dead right now?"

Brenda abruptly stood, walked into the bedroom and slammed the door. I skimmed the latest R&R and saw a full-page ad for Rush Limbaugh. His fat, puffy face was speaking into a gold-plated microphone, and I gagged. In my moment of anger and stress, I hated that microphone. I saw it as the golden calf Moses found at the bottom of Mount Sinai. Some listeners followed every word of this man, distracting them from life's important things. Limbaugh was no different than the scam of a phony religion being used as a tax shelter. How could a mediocre science fiction writer be taking my woman from me? How could so many Americans learn to hate others because of what was blown through Limbaugh's golden microphone of exploitation?

I will always remember the good times, the joys, the deep discussions and the belly-hurting, tear-flowing laughs that were fundamental to our relationship. There was something so special about Brenda, but I learned that despite her intelligence and awareness she saw L. Ron Hubbard as a god, whereas I believed any thinking, level-headed person should be able to see right through him. It's like I often said, "Pull the camera back far enough and you might discover it's only an old man pulling the strings of his puppets."

Radio was a bit like this because some fanatical listeners would fall in love with the voice of a person they never saw, never met. They had no comprehension of the person behind the voice.

The pledge of Brenda's new faith was based on a "science" that would produce spiritual enlightenment and freedom, but at this point it was a force pulling my love away from me. I compensated with the realization that many sons, daughters, husbands and wives were drawn into this false prophet's unscientific religion, which had no facts to back up the "ology" part of its name. The golden calf can be hard to resist.

I didn't care about the money, but had Brenda kept her stock options for another ten years she would have been a billionaire. While she never bought a professional sports team or built a museum, I learned later in life her four kids convinced her that goofy Herbie from Dayton was right. She was penniless when she finally escaped Scientology.

When you get right down to it, who has ever achieved spiritual enlightenment without the struggles and challenges of the human condition? For me it was simple. I just wanted to find a new job far away from the pain.

I took some time off, money out of the bank and planned a drive to Nevada to see some radio guys. I had run into Sam "the Man" Richardson at the R&R convention in Dallas, and he said if I was ever in Reno to look him up. That city is the rancher-cowboy version of Las Vegas, and a railroad runs right through the town. More than a few drunken locals and out-of-towners have been torpedoed by a freight train when crossing the street. I checked into a Reno hotel and some dark thoughts creeped into my mind. Was I thinking about offing myself?

Several radio guys I once knew checked into hotel rooms and blew their brains out, separate incidents of course. I flashed on another sad story of an old friend who in a fit of deep depression jumped to his death from a San Francisco hotel. I had no gun and no desire to skydive, not yet. Part of my brain played the MP3 file of a positive song about an imminent something that was much bigger and better.

Technically, and perhaps clinically, I was depressed, but the scientific aspect of my brain was so damn curious just as it always has been. I had to keep going because I didn't want to miss that next "monumental thing."

41. Guns and Poses

Surely by now you have figured out I'm a sucker for a delightful or intriguing tale and Sam "the Man" Richardson was chock full of them. After losing the obligatory two hundred bucks on Reno's finest slot machines, I washed that part of the trip off my hands and got together with the Man. True to my belief about broadcasters, it took only a few minutes for Sam and me to feel comfortable opening up about all things radio.

Sam said his gig as PD at KOZZ was going extremely well and he was happy working for Lotus Communications, a group out of LA that also owned stations in Arizona, California, Nevada and Washington state. I was always impressed with their Las Vegas stations. That classic slogan "What happens in Vegas stays in Vegas" was probably all about money, but things can be strange in Sin City. When Lotus proposed changing the call letters of their Las Vegas FM station to KMOB, a few individuals from a certain "organized" group of wise old guys told them to find a new name. Lotus, being reasonable community business partners, snatched the call sign KOMP, which in Las Vegas means getting free stuff, typically hotel rooms and drinks for high-stakes gamblers. It was a brilliant choice that raised a positive emotion and went well with their AM call sign, KENO. While that was true, I often thought those call letters would have been better as a station name in Reno, you know, KENO in Reno.

The Lotus stations in Reno were KOZZ-FM and KHIT-AM. When I asked Sam about the general manager in Reno, he smiled and told me the back story. The name Tommy Lee "Hound Dog" LeDeau, sounded like a cast member of that old TV show *Hee-Haw*. I always figured a station general manager with a nickname had been a disc jockey previously in their career, but this wasn't the case with Tommy. Back in his home state of Louisiana, he was a famed hound dog breeder and trainer. LeDeau had a contract with the state police to deliver skilled detection dogs, and those canines made him a ton of money.

His ability to sniff out a good deal brought Tommy Lee to Reno, where he purchased a chain of gas stations, an electric grid transfer station and, to keep the theme going, a small, suburban AM radio station. While being an owner during the age of deregulation, Tommy saw an opportunity to sell his station for a huge profit when the radio buying frenzy was underway. Knowing LeDeau was now available, Lotus hired him at KOZZ because he was wired into the local advertising community and could deliver healthy monthly profits. Tommy had also hooked up with a beautiful young blackjack dealer with three kids and had no intention of leaving Nevada, a perfect situation for both manager and radio station.

When we mwt in the restaurant parking lot before dinner, Sam the Man was telling me about his time in Vietnam flying helicopters. He opened his trunk to show me a large case. I turned to him and asked,

"Oh, you play guitar?"

He chuckled and undid the container to reveal an M4A1 modified Delta HBAR, a hefty automatic weapon. Sam claimed the army released only a few dozen of them to the marketplace. I was a little surprised, but I also knew that some people just love guns. After getting seated at the restaurant, he told me about the time he was driving from Dallas to California and got pulled over by a Texas Ranger,

"I'm going ninety-one miles an hour in my 1991 Camaro RS and this ranger pulls me over and asks to see my license and registration. Then he asks that stupid question, 'Do you know how fast you were going?' and I answer, 'Yes, officer, I believe I was doing ninety-one and maybe hit ninety-nine before you saw me.'"

I assumed this story would include a ride in the back seat of the police cruiser, but I was wrong,

"So, he asks me to get out of the car and open the trunk, probably thought I was a drug dealer, so I pop the trunk lid. Then the cop asks the same question you did, 'Do you play guitar?' and I say, 'No it's an M4A1.' He looks at me, nods and asks, '…Nam?' and I say, 'Yep,' and his eyes open wide as he asks, 'Can I see that thing?'"

Sam the Man proceeded to tell me that after twenty minutes talking about the army and guns, which ended with the cop asking to hold Sam's prized weapon, the officer told the program director to slow down and take care. No ticket.

But the cop story wasn't the most amazing tale Sam shared that night. The next one should surely make it into a book about crazy radio stories. Sam asked the waiter to bring us six shots of his finest tequila, with salt and limes of course, and started his story,

"My 7 p.m. to 12 midnight jock's air name is "The Thing" and, while he is a total whack job, he is also a great broadcaster. He has an unusual voice, sounds somewhat like Darth Vader, and he uses it to communicate effectively. So, I am driving over to my lady friend's house one night, and I hear that son of a bitch play a song that's not on the log."

At this point, most stations scheduled their music on the *Selector* software program and jocks had to play the songs listed on the printed schedule in exact order. The program did an amazing job with music flow and timing. After his MD generated a music log and before printing it, Sam would look through every hour to make sure the stream of songs had his stamp of approval. If need be, Sam would edit the computerized schedule, and he had an uncanny knack of remembering exactly which songs should play where.

"So, I figure, okay he cheated on one song, I'll let it pass. Just as I got on the freeway, he plays another song that wasn't scheduled, but worse, wasn't even on the station's playlist. He must have brought in a CD from home. I look for the next opening on the four-lane highway, you know, where the cops usually park, downshift my Rally Sport Camaro to pull a Starsky and Hutch skid, make it through the gap then into a U-turn. Heading back to the station doing ninety, I was in no mood to deal with any cops."

The shots arrived. I salted my hand, took a gulp and bit the lime. The fire went from my tongue to my belly. Now I could truly focus on Sam's story,

"I get to the station and park. As I walk into the building I hear *The Pusher*, which is also not on the playlist. I open the thick, wooden studio door. The Thing takes his headphones off, turns to me and I see he's holding a Luger P08 in his right hand. I close the door and walk directly to my car. I reach into the glove box, pull out my Glock 19 and march back to the studio."

I gulped a second shot of tequila,

"Sam, this is crazy shit. Was the jock off his meds? Where is this going?"

"Well, The Thing sees me on the black and white security monitor in the studio. He stands up, props open the door, and gets into a ranger shooting position at the threshold. I come through the station's front entrance and yell, 'Put the gun down, asshole!' and he yells back, 'Don't you come any closer, Charlie, or I'll blow your fucking head off.'"

"Charlie? Wait, who the fuck is Charlie?"

Sam slammed down his three tequila shots in a row — one, two, three — and then bit a lime. After shaking off the thrill of a massive alcohol infusion, he continued,

"Oh boy, don't you remember we called the Vietcong Charlie? So, The Thing fires a couple shots down the hall and then ducks back into the studio. I crouch behind the copy machine, he discharges another round, and the copier takes a direct hit. I fire maybe three or four more shots, then The Thing shoots a few more rounds, followed by a loud crash of shattering glass. Next, I hear the click, click, click of his empty gun and I'm hoping he doesn't have another clip. I fire once more and then yell, 'I'm coming in. Stand down soldier and that's an order!' After that, silence. When I get to the studio, he's in a fetal position on the floor crying like a baby. I start the next song, one that's on the log, and then grab him a Coke from the vending machine."

"That is a wild story, Sam. What happened to The Thing?"

"He's on the air right now."

"Wait, you didn't fire him?"

"Nah, he gets great ratings, and when he gets into a little funk being in the studio means he's off the streets. But that wasn't the end of it."

I took my third shot and listened to, as us radio folk say, the rest of the story,

"So, I go home, get a lousy night of sleep, and drive over to the station the next morning. I pull into the parking lot and see workmen putting up plywood over one of the front windows of the building. I get this bad feeling that maybe our little shootout did more damage than I thought, so I wasn't at all surprised when Beverly the receptionist said,

"Sam, Mr. LeDeau wants to see you in his office as soon as possible."

The tequila had landed in my brain, and I was feeling no pain, but had to prompt him,

"Well, what happened?"

Sam lost focus as a beautiful lady walked by our table, and he made a lewd comment, typical. He continued,

"So, I walk into Tommy Lee's office and there he is, feet up on the desk and wearing his camo outfit, swamp boots and all. The only thing missing is a shotgun across his lap. He politely asks me to sit down and I'm thinking this is it, but then, in his rich, thick-as-a-roux accent, he declares, 'Now Sammy, I know y'all got into a bit of a rhubarb last night and you and The Thing shot up the place. Now, I don't mind paying for the front window and fixing the holes in the walls, but you son a bitches did in the Xerox machine.' I don't know what to say, but he goes on, 'We don't own that machine; it's a lease and we have a two-hundred-dollar deductible on the insurance. You boys are going to have to pay for that.' I humbly answer, 'Yes, sir,' and he says, 'Now, you go have a good day,' and that was that."

I'm sure Sam the Man shared other stories during dinner, but those three tequila shots make it impossible for me to remember.

The following day I was driving into Sacramento and next to me on the passenger seat was my new Motorola DynaTAC 8800X. Descendants of this G.I. Joe-looking communications device would eventually be in the hands of just about everyone in the world. My unit was ten inches tall, and I had to carry extra batteries to stay connected to a call on this early cell phone. Signals were sketchy back then, and many times I'd get a call but then have to find a landline when it dropped.

So, my cell phone rang and on the line was Randy Michaels, the program director of Q102 in Cincinnati. He had been successfully running that station since 1975 and I knew his name but not much else. Some said his station was the model for the TV show WKRP in Cincinnati, but Hugh Wilson, the creator of that sitcom, said it was modeled on his experiences at WQXI in Atlanta. In fact, the character Arthur Carlson, played by actor Gordon Jump, had a remarkable resemblance to WQXI's Jerry Blum, the station's actual general manager, and that's the truth.

I was extremely curious about Randy's call and considering possible reasons in my head, but none of them matched his intentions. He was asking me about Lady Glenda, who gave my name as a reference. She was a potential hire for Randy, and I had worked with her when she did the overnight show on KDKB. In today's world, radio stations have corporate policies and H.R. guidelines, which need to be considered when asked for a reference, but back in those simpler times we were open, honest and simply trusted one another. You never thought a PD would tell a potential hire they didn't get the job because so-and-so trash-talked them.

The damn cell call disconnected, and I had to pull off the road to find a pay phone to return a long-distance call to Randy on my Pacific Bell credit card. I was pissed off. Based on some things I shared, Randy didn't hire Glenda and perhaps that was a good thing. I'm not sure Lady Glenda would have fit into his college boy surroundings. Randy became one of the most famous, and infamous, radio programmers in the business. He went from Taft Broadcasting to Jacor Communications to Clear Channel Media then on to Tribune Broadcasting, and he reigned supreme at each one of those major media companies.

About this time, several investigative TV shows were digging into charges of hostile, sexually charged working environments in both the radio and record industries. Wherever Michaels was in charge, a culture of winning at all costs, fraternity house pranks and not-so-practical jokes was mostly overlooked because of his massive ratings and bottom-line success. But incidents of naked strippers in the studios and on-air sexual innuendos with female announcers set the stage for legal issues. One of Randy's borderline-criminal stunts was killing a live pig on the air at a remote broadcast in Tampa. Oh yes, Benjamin Homel, Randy's legal name, was part bully, part P.T. Barnum and part Buzzy Bennett, *regrediens ad vitam*.

Deregulation inspired large radio group owners to gobble up the marquee stations, those we all wanted to work at, making it harder and harder to find a wonderful job. If you pissed off Randy, you wouldn't be able to work at any of the Clear Channel stations. If you had a negative experience with Mel Karmazin, you would be persona non grata at any Infinity/CBS/Viacom station. NBC left the radio business to focus on their television and cable properties. ABC was slowly plotting an exit from radio as well. Perhaps the most perfect punctuation to signify the end of excellent American radio as we knew it came in 1998 when Robert W. Morgan, famed Los Angeles disc jockey and one of Top 40's best, left this place for that swanky studio in the sky. There aren't too many of those kinds of radio personalities. As for the east coast, the good old days of FM rock faded further from our memories in 2004 when New York's legendary WNEW-FM jock, Scott Muni, made his earthly exit.

Between the politics, the purchases and the stockholders, the language of the radio craft changed profoundly. If you were to overhear two folks talking at a radio convention, you might have thought they were bankers or stock traders. In 1997 alone, CBS Radio shelled out two point six billion dollars to acquire stations. That's "billion" with a capital B.

It was a period of rapid change in the radio trade. Joel Denver, who served as Radio & Record's CHR editor for fifteen years, left that magazine in late November of 1994 to create All Access Music Group. In October of 1995, Joel launched AllAccess.com with free song charts and content. One year later, R&R attempted to thwart his effort through RadioAndRecords.com, with a ten dollar per month paywall. It's likely that the monthly charge contributed to Radio & Records demise, proving the old adage that free is better than fee. The final nail in the R&R coffin came in July of 2006 when VNU, the parent company of Billboard magazine, bought R&R and poached their staff. In thirty days, Radio & Records ceased to exist. Printed news about the radio biz was on the way out.

A couple of knucklehead radio and record guys, Steve Resnik and Kevin Carter, started a daily email service named RAMP, which stands for Radio and Music Pros. It's a wildly popular news service similar to the historical Vox Jox and Street Talk columns. RAMP's clever positioning statement is, "Before news breaks, it must bend... and that's where we come in." Great line! Of course, no trees were sacrificed by these electronic radio news distributors.

I received a call back from a resume I had sent to San Antonio's KTFM, which in 1991 launched as a Texas Music Station, whatever the hell that meant. Weirdly enough, the station didn't want me as a DJ but rather an in-house consultant, and it was clear they really needed help with their music. As the saying goes, too many chefs in the kitchen were pulling their playlist all over the road, and I'm not talking about an AOR format. KTFM played a strange mix of country, rock and reggae. The station said they wanted to compete with KFAN-FM, which was running an authentic Country format.

I wasn't sure if I wanted to make the journey halfway across the country, but I needed a change. I met a programming consultant named Gary Burns at a radio convention, and he not only drank me under the table but also talked my ear off about a new concept in broadcasting called a local marketing agreement or LMA. It was a legal loophole where one party agreed to operate a radio or television station licensed to another. Think of it as a sort of lease or time-sharing arrangement. The original owner still held the license, but the management of the LMA completely took over operation of the station. It was essentially an end-run around the FCC, while they spent more than five years trying to figure out how to deregulate broadcasting.

Even though we have drastically different political viewpoints, Gary and I have been friends ever since we met. I later found out that he had suggested me for the gig at KTFM, where station owner John Barger was totally into the LMA arrangement, given that he was a typical Texan not wanting the Federal Government to mess with him.

I decided to buy a cowboy hat and boots, a wide, tooled belt sporting an oversized, metal buckle and a colorful, embroidered shirt to become "Hopalong Herbie" for a few years. I looked at myself in the mirror all decked out in my new country and western getup and mouthed, "You're such a fucking poser."

42. Free Man in Paris

There are only a handful of people in the music business who have profoundly changed that industry's trajectory. If you look over the past sixty years, you'll see certain names were there at every turn. One is Phil Ramone, the musician turned recording engineer and pioneer producer. The Beatles certainly would not have been as productive without the parenting and prodding of Sir George Martin. Quincy Jones was the American version of Martin, and his legacy is full of fine musical works. Two others must also be mentioned in this paragraph, Berry Gordy of Motown and Tom Dowd of Atlantic Records. Gordy was once a professional boxer and Dowd was a smart kid from New York City who had worked on the Manhattan Project. We were the beneficiaries when these guys turned their attention to making records. In addition to those named here, the minds and hands of many other women and men behind the microphones and mixing consoles helped capture and master those fantastic hits, and they put up with countless prima donnas, divas and drug addicts along the way.

Independent productions popped up to show the big boys that no one owns the atmosphere that births creativity. When Def Jam and other startup record labels began to make loud noises, the bankers coughed up the coins to finance those operations. One doesn't start out small with a desire to stay small. The idea is to become significantly successful, and that means growing large.

People learn things when they are young and then use those gifts to excel in special ways. One record executive I have followed and admired over the years is David Geffen. He grew up in Brooklyn, New York, and just as many other successful people in the industry seem to be, he's a college drop out. In fact, David left three colleges and blamed his academic misfortune on dyslexia. Several biographies mention Geffen skipped high school classes on Wednesdays to sneak into Broadway matinees. His love of music led to a career initially on the artist management side of the business.

David Geffen is the one person who can honestly say he started in the mailroom, the one at the William Morris Agency. There's a great tale of him intercepting a letter from UCLA that stated he was not a graduate of that university, as he had claimed. Knowing such evidence could have stopped his vertical movement, Geffen replaced the letter with another he fabricated saying he graduated; then he was promoted.

In 1971, Geffen teamed up with fellow artist agent Elliot Roberts to form Asylum Records. The name was an inside joke about signing artists no other record company wanted. The partners were so crazy and possessed by work that being institutionalized might have helped them. Asylum leaned toward folk-rock artists like Jackson Browne, Linda Ronstadt, John David Souther, Joni Mitchell and Glenn Frey, whom Geffen and Roberts encouraged to form the Eagles. Jo Jo Gunne, a band mentioned earlier, was also signed to Asylum.

Things were going so swimmingly sound at Asylum that Elektra Records acquired them. Later, Warner Communication bought a bunch of other record companies and merged them all into Elektra/Asylum.

In 1976, Geffen was targeting the movie industry as his next mountain to climb when he was diagnosed with bladder cancer. He retired from the music business, and it's said the Joni Mitchell song *Free Man in Paris* is a tribute to him. About four years into his retreat David learned he was not ailing and made a strong comeback.

Shortly after his return, Geffen formed a custom label for Warner Brothers named Geffen Records. I saw him at an R&R convention being interviewed by my previous boss Bob Wilson. It occurred to me that Geffen would be the only person on the planet who could ever convince me to leave radio for work in the record business.

Geffen was from New York and understood how money drove politics. He clearly grasped the reality that converting movies and music into small, shareable files could end the massive profits of selling songs and stories. Geffen was a major Democratic Party donor and extremely close to Bill Clinton. Rumors, then newspaper articles, revealed Bill and Hillary stayed at David Geffen's mansion when visiting the west coast. Of course, while David was twisting Clinton's arm to propel legislation to protect the record and film businesses from Napster and those nefarious movie download web sites, he slept in the Lincoln bedroom at the White House. Cozy!

In 1998, the Digital Millennium Copyright Act was passed in the United States, which made it a crime to disseminate content that circumvented Digital Rights Management, commonly known as DRM, a copyright protection mechanism for digital media. Not long after, the Recording Industry Association of America, the RIAA, was out suing grandmothers for downloading their favorite songs, which made complete sense to me. After all, I would hate people stealing my intellectual property, setting aside any discussion about what my intelligence might be worth or if it even exists.

Around 1992, Arbitron, the dominant ratings company for radio, began developing new audience measurement technology in the hope of improving listening estimates gathered by their paper diaries. The company had developed a small electronic device named the Portable People Meter, or PPM, which looked somewhat like an old-school pager. Arbitron launched the results of their innovative PPM technology in eight radio markets with their September 2008 survey.

The PPM was worn all day by radio listeners participating in the ratings measurement. Each station embedded a unique but inaudible audio signature in their programming which the device detected and logged. Much like the unseen signal of radar that allows a cop to know how fast you are driving, this smart gadget could hear those embedded sonic patterns, which you could not. The PPM silently tracked each station and duration of listening the wearer encountered. When the user plugged the unit into a charger at night, it would upload the day's listening data to Arbitron.

There were issues, of course, like a station not knowing its ratings signal had not been working for days. Some argued that just because the PPM detected a station's signature didn't mean the wearer was actually listening to the broadcast. Worse, crazy-cheater radio stations would arrange remote broadcast promotions at shopping malls and other large public areas. They played their station's audio over loudspeakers with the intent to inflate ratings when casual passers-by wearing PPMs were measured as listeners. Those were dubious attempts, at best, but the ratings police did find a few successful tricksters and delisted them.

Of course, Arbitron charged stations and advertisers a premium for PPM-based ratings, and it took them more than a decade and a half to extend the service to smaller markets. Unlike diary measurement which sampled listeners for one week, PPM participants would be on the payroll for nine months or even longer, forming a class of people who determined which radio stations won or lost. Years later, Arbitron would be eaten by the larger Nielson ratings company, but they retained the PPM technology.

Meanwhile, I was hard at work in San Antonio, trying to figure out which stations to buy and what to do with them once we purchased or LMA'd them. Yes, that awkward term was extensively used. In the middle of working on a dozen station acquisitions, in 1996, I attended the Texas Broadcasters Association meeting in Houston.

During a break for coffee, I shared a high-top table with a guy whose name tag was filled with eight capital letters, which puzzled me. I asked if he worked in the automobile industry. He laughed and said,

"No, that's my name, Bob Chrysler."

We got to chatting and Bob asked me if we could get together later, explaining he wanted to discuss an initiative he'd been working on. I wondered if there could be some consulting work for me in this and we booked a dinner.

I eventually discovered Bob was an excellent programming, marketing and engineering radio guy who was always on the "cutting edge." At dinner, he opened a manilla folder and spread out several technical documents in front of me. They were drafted by a well-known radio engineering firm and outlined a process of placing transmitter pods in satellites to transmit radio signals to listeners on Earth. Bob explained some of the technical details in the papers and it became clear he was speaking about radio programming for mass consumption beaming down to our planet from space. I asked,

"Wouldn't a radio transmitter's weight make it impractical for use in a satellite?"

He laughed and rifled through the paperwork to locate the drawings and specs of a transmitter prototype,

"You see, a geo stationary satellite is about twenty-three thousand miles above the Earth, meaning a transmitter would need a lot of power to reach our planet and would necessarily be heavy. However, satellites in lower orbits are only twelve hundred miles above us, so the signal of this tiny, one-hundred-watt, solar powered transmitter could easily reach Earth, and using an advanced compression algorithm a dozen audio feeds could be broadcast by just one unit."

I took a big gulp of single malt scotch,

"Bob, this could put radio out of business."

He took his drink in hand, and then smiled,

"That's why we have to introduce HD, high-definition radio, as soon as possible."

At this point in radio history, American broadcasters were being sold a bill of goods beyond anything seen in the past. Let's remember that music radio had new competitors with innovative music distribution technologies, and some broadcasters were saying the industry needed its own kind of digital infrastructure. Those pitching HD radio claimed this new means of transmission would better "serve the public interest," which was pure poppycock.

While David Geffen was having tea in the Lincoln bedroom, lobbyists were twisting the arms of legislators to fast-track policies and rulemaking to bring HD radio to the public. There were competing systems and patents for the technology, and for a while the FCC said they would let the market determine which system would win. What a dumb idea!

On October 11, 2002, the FCC endorsed the technology of a company named iBiquity as the digital solution for AM and FM radio in the US and authorized them to broadcast HD signals full time.

The public never asked for digital radio, they felt FM sounded perfectly fine. As for those with tape players, then CD players, then digital audio receivers in their hands and cars, they didn't give a fiddle-fuck about HD radio signals because they carried their personal collection of music with them.

To my way of thinking HD radio had no reason to exist, but some foolish corporate broadcasters immediately jumped onboard. They convinced a few Detroit automobile manufacturers to place HD radios in their vehicles, but the car makers imposed an up-charge. They weren't about to sacrifice profits to help radio with its latest fad. As for the public at large, consumers had to buy a specialized radio to receive HD broadcasts. Bob Chrysler eventually came to believe HD Radio failed because of the implementation, not the concept.

I remember walking into a Radio Shack and asking the salesguy how many HD radios were being sold. He laughed and said, "No one cares. We don't sell many of them." Gee, I wonder whatever happened to Radio Shack.

To this day, debates about HD radio quality, signal strength and even the reason for its existence continue. When I listen to a football game on the HD receiver in my car, the signal continuously fades from stereophonic to monophonic and back again. Who needs this?

By the way, we weren't the only country plunging into HD radio. Europe and Canada were far ahead of the US, but despite all effort, radio listeners just didn't see a need for HD radio. Besides, who would pay for all the extra content? Advertisers were already buying more spots on cable TV and that new internet thing.

Meanwhile, my career focus had become less radio and more research into leveraging technology to stretch budgets. One goal was automating three Texas radio stations with the exact same music programming but different local commercials on each. We also ran sporting events on many of our stations, high school football is huge in Texas, and that presented a tremendous technical challenge to get the automated music and commercials of each station back in sync as each game ended at a different time. No one wanted to lose a dime.

I was home in my San Antonio apartment and thinking about heading out for a drink when the phone rang. I grabbed the handset and yelled,

"I listen to the new sound of 13Q!"

"Hey, dickhead, it's me, Billy!"

I couldn't believe it and almost fell backwards off the couch,

"Brewster Billy, what's going on man?"

"I'm in town, Herbie. What the fuck are you doing?"

"What? What are you doing in Texas? Isn't there a warrant out for your arrest in the Lone Star State?"

"That went away; I paid your mom to drop the charges."

"Fuck you, Kalpolski. Let's meet at Dick's Last Resort, the one on the Riverwalk. I can be there in twenty-minutes."

"So can I, see you there!"

Finally, a chance to get together with someone who knows me so well. I had to laugh, and while grabbing my car keys I said out loud,

"I don't even know myself."

43. Know When to Fold 'Em

Radio work entails dealing with mountains of egos, misguided corporate whims, and, oh yeah, ever-changing audience desires. The term disco became toxic, but rhythmic dance music never died, it morphed from Donna Summer to Whitney Houston, to Beyoncé to today's EDM, electronic dance music. It's all rhythmic, but artist personalities often overshadow the songs and the beats. We also have the talentless ones using television and the internet hoping to become famous without any significant contribution to art, science or business. To understand my meaning, just spend an hour with TikTok.

As artists became smarter and more cunning, they figured out ways to pull more money from the corporate music machine. Groups and singers fought hard for performance rights, which meant they could own their publishing, likenesses and recordings to reap financial rewards forever. Musical performers eventually secured royalties for streaming music online when the RIAA created SoundExchange, an agency that collects performance royalties from the digital streaming services. Without a license purchased from SoundExchange an internet streaming service cannot legally play music. Each streamer is required to report how many times they play each song, and SoundExchange uses that data to set its rates. This new agency was a different source of income for gifted musical artists, and it leveled the playing field with radio. Major market radio stations were paying as much as a million dollars each year for the rights to broadcast music, and now the internet services had to pony up.

I was eager to see Billy and find out what he was up to, but first I made a concerted effort to pin down and memorize the exact location of my parked car. You see, with Brewster Billy many brewskis would be involved and I wanted to avoid searching for my vehicle later in a liquor smog. I found Billy sitting by himself in the restaurant with an Arnold Palmer before him. I slapped a high five, we exchanged a tight hug and then I said,

"Boy, am I glad to see you!"

"Likewise, my brother from another mother."

"Would you please leave my mother out of this? By the way, she says hi."

The conversation began with that Arnold Palmer and Billy's revelation that he had stopped drinking alcohol. He explained that not only was he having trouble with his liver, but he was becoming unfocused and depressed about his place in life and decided a change was needed. My friend was upbeat as he talked me through the markets and stations he worked at since we last spoke. I was so happy to hear he was no longer struggling with financial debt, thanks to the Illinois State Lottery,

"Man, Billy, that's so great. Your luck has changed."

"Yes, and now I am out of radio."

My jaw just about hit the shiny, thick polyurethane-coated table,

"What the hell, Billy; that can't be true."

It seems Billy had moved to Cleveland and was now working at a start-up tech company preparing the launch of a unique internet music service. He explained it will play songs which have been tailored to a listener's musical taste. My great radio programmer friend was helping the computer math guys who knew nothing about how to measure the appeal of songs and sequence them accordingly. He moved in closer to tell me this new service would track and analyze how a listener responds to each song using terms like Love it, Like it, Just Okay, Dislike it, Hate it, then couple those responses with the attributes of each song such as Artist Name, Tempo, Mood, Energy, and so on. The software team was developing an algorithm to analyze the data and establish a musical profile, which would be saved, modified and improved over time and used to select and arrange a chain of songs the listener would like. One goal was blending into the mix new songs the listener never heard before but would probably like.

I pondered every word and had to ask,

"This program has a name?"

"Well, our code name is Bongo."

We both cracked up and I ordered another beer and a large plate of Macho Nachos as we continued to trade radio stories. Out of nowhere, Billy asked,

"You remember Charlie Minor?"

"Of course, why do you ask?"

"He's dead."

Billy was a great storyteller and there were times people couldn't tell if he was pulling their leg or laying out a true tale. I knew he wasn't joking by his brutally direct statement, and I was shocked,

"Dead? How?"

Billy sipped his tricked up iced tea and said,

"He was murdered, shot to death!"

Recall that Charlie Minor was one of the most powerful music promoters in the record business. He was extremely well-paid and had an upbeat, outgoing personality. He also was a workhorse and at a point in his life where he was concerned about becoming an alcoholic. He swore off booze and spent his on-the-wagon moments drinking countless cappuccinos. He used to take a brewing machine to his beloved University of Georgia Bulldogs games, and he would use it to brew fresh cups of cappuccino at various bars between Atlanta and Athens.

Charlie worked the phones eighteen hours a day, and he bought suits, got haircuts, ate lunch and had his shoes shined while making calls pitching songs to radio folk. He was a handsome, jet setting man in his late forties with tailored clothing and a gigantic expense account. And, as we have already seen, Charlie had an eye for women. Even though the record industry was chock full of nuts with one addiction or another, Charlie didn't do drugs. Well, maybe a little cocaine every now and then just for fun, but he was laser focused on getting PDs and radio group programmers to add his records. He was a straight shooter and didn't have to waste Mr. Alpert's or Mr. Moss's money on buying favors. Herb Alpert nicknamed Charlie "Jaws" because of his P.R. prowess.

Charlie had no commitments to the women he dated, but when an up-and-coming actress named Danitza came into his life, he took the plunge and got married. Their union produced a beautiful redheaded baby girl they named Austin. Like so many other marriages in Hollywood, this one ended as well. Once Charlie was back on the street and holding court at Le Dome on Sunset, the bevy of beautiful babes became an endless stream of fanciful distractions without obligations.

After finishing my beer, I ordered a cappuccino to set my mind straight and perhaps pay fitting homage to a major radio legend. I also wanted to remember every detail of the story Billy was about to unfold,

"So, Charlie goes out to this strip club in LA, I think it was Bailey's 20/20 Gentlemen's Club, and sees this lady up there showing her stuff. He tells the owner of the club he'd like to meet her."

The woman was twenty-seven years old and an unemployed aviation worker who took on an adult entertainment gig to pay bills. The LA Times described her as a petite brunette with dark, sad eyes. Charlie was mostly into blondes, and I just about spit out my cappuccino when Billy described the memorial service he attended in Charlie's hometown,

"In the Marietta, Georgia church there were more blonde heads and silicone breasts than any other location on Earth. The Guinness people should have been there."

In Charlie's mind, the few dates with stripper Suzette McClure were nothing more than booty calls and casual hook ups, but the newspaper stories revealed Ms. McClure had described Charlie to her friends as "the one." She claimed to be deeply in love and planned to marry him. All her troubles would then go away.

Meanwhile, Charlie had recently met a lady named Dorothy and entered into what he described to his good friends as a very meaningful relationship. He was excited about taking it to the next level. He left A&M records and was now an executive at the music industry publication Hits magazine.

One Sunday morning, Suzette McClure surreptitiously entered Minor's Malibu home, where many famous Hollywood and Malibu folks had hung out and partied in happier times. She found Charlie in the bedroom with his new girlfriend, but what neither of them knew was Suzette had a .25-caliber automatic pistol in her purse. Charlie told McClure to leave, which she did, but she was intensely angry and hid in a closet downstairs. Not long after, Dorothy came down the stairs and passed by the crazy stripper who was on her way back up. McClure told Dorothy she wanted to have a one-on-one with Charlie. Not long after, six shots rang out and Charlie was dead.

Billy looked at me,

"You know that Kenny Rogers' song, *The Gambler?*"

"Sure, we play it on all our stations. It's a huge hit in Texas."

"Well, there is a life lesson in that song about the need to contemplate before making a momentous change in life. Is it the right time? Is it time to hold 'em or fold 'em?"

"I'm not quite following you."

"You see, it's happening to a lot of people in our business. One radio consultant who lived a dual life went out and picked up a gay lover for a night, but it all ended tragically with the scumbag killing the radio guy and setting his house on fire."

"Okay, I know that story, but how does it relate to Charlie Minor?"

"Well, our famous record promoter friend finally decided it was time to beat his addictions to drink and sex and settle down, but a past mistake created a fatal encounter. Maybe Charlie folded too late, but who can really know what would have otherwise happened."

"But wasn't that just bad luck?"

"Herbie, you are so naïve sometimes. We make our own luck. We decide when to go all in or when to call it quits. We have the power to make those decisions, and it's time for you to make one yourself."

"What do you mean, Billy?"

"Well, I have a proposal. I spoke with the owners of my company about you, and they are highly interested. I would love you to move to Cleveland and join me in this song streaming project. You'll probably make a little less money than what you're making here, but we'll be working together again, and you know how well our minds mesh. Let's join up to make something better than radio."

"Better than radio, are you high?"

He snickered and then asked for the bill,

"I got this Sonny Joe. Please think about it. The landscape is changing and if we pull this off, which I believe we will, we'll still be standing when technology finally gobbles up music radio. We won't be working in broadcasting, but something damn close and way more exciting. Think of it as future radio."

When walking to my car that night, a deep feeling of despair and heartbreak crept over me. I wasn't at all close to Charlie Minor, but there was something magical about him. I admired his professionalism and work ethic. He loved sports and was full of creative ideas that made him far more than a record pusher. Time after time his over-the-top energy level had swept up so many, but now he was soundless. Silence in the radio or record business is never good. I flashed on the Billy Joel song *Only the Good Die Young*. Yeah, that seems to be true.

Billy and I had breakfast the next morning, then he left town. I started some deep thinking about where radio was going and if I still wanted a place in the business. My mind replayed that ugly final scene of the Charlie Minor murder movie, and my thoughts planted a fear of some kind of fatal attraction. I found myself asking, "Where can I find happiness but still remain safe?"

I kept plugging away at running too many radio stations, having more work and less fun. I knew that for the past three or four years I had been drifting, falling asleep on airplanes as soon as my big, white ass hit the seat. I could no longer listen to the radio for entertainment. The corporate broadcasting machine kept adding more voice-tracked disc jockeys and even more commercials. Those damn sales departments would sell anything, "And now here's your TK101 Hershey Kiss-My-Ass 10K Run for Jesus, brought to you by the Fairlawn Baptist Church and Dishlicker Chevrolet!" Yes, tongue in cheek.

I thought about all the radio people I had met, thousands across the country, and found myself wondering where I could go next. Looking for greener pastures has always been part of the business, but once you get there it's just another radio station that's always on the air. Green grass never stops growing, bringing endless mowing.

Know When to Fold 'Em

Most of us have experienced moments the famous, best-selling book by Malcolm Gladwell calls *Tipping Points*. The trick is being aware enough to realize when the exact moment arrives and say, "This is it, bubba, time to make a move!"

We received the memo from the boss at the radio group's home office. It started out complimenting the staff on such a profitable year, but then came this, "As you know, much has been written about the profound change coming at midnight on January 1, 2000, a moment now known as Y2K. We don't know if this event will cause any disruption to our operations, so I am asking every program director and chief engineer to be on duty at their station from 10 p.m. until 2 a.m. the night of the year change, fully prepared to manage any situation or event that could take us off the air."

I was pissed off but understood the order. I'd have to cancel my plan to ring in the New Year together with that beautiful Asian woman I recently met. The lunar new year in 2000 was the Year of the Dragon, and it was time to see if the beast had breathed fire on all the computers.

I brought some snacks and a bottle of champagne to share with Director of Engineering Dick Crane. He was a goofy southerner with a wicked sense of humor, but never one to forcefully push a boss. He had used Y2K to gently petition the GM for cash to make improvements and replace old computers. I was sitting in my office thinking about how a technological oversight had ruined my celebration of a new year. Software developers hadn't thought to make room for a year greater than 1999 and that screwed all of us. Very soon we would know if the fixes they've been coding the past few years actually work.

I switched on the TV in the breakroom as the countdown to midnight was underway. We made a list of all the computers and digital devices we needed to check, and when the ball dropped, Dick tore the page in half. He would do the front of the building and I would take care of the back.

We went through dozens of machines and were just about finished. To our mutual delight, all the computers and digital broadcast gear we tested were fine, except for that piece of shit fax machine which refused to boot. I pictured us throwing it out the window or smashing it with a sledgehammer. Dick was in the lobby investigating the final machine, the receptionist's computer, when I heard him call out,

"Oh my God, the date on this machine is 1344!"

Just before he was about to reboot the device to see if it had any life after Y2K, I joked,

"Wait a minute, let me go into AOL and see if I've got mail."

"Are you expecting a message from Edward the Third?"

I walked back to my office and sat down. Then, it hit me like a ton of bricks. What the hell am I doing? Here I was with decades of radio experience behind me, rebooting computers for a small broadcasting group on New Year's Eve. I picked up the phone and called Billy in Cleveland,

"Hey, Brewster Billy, happy fucking New Year, dickwad!"

I could hear he was at a party, and he asked me to hold while he moved to a quieter place, then I asked,

"You still have that job for me in Cleveland?"

He laughed and yelled,

"Fuck yes, brother; call me on Monday. Oh, by the way, that whole Y2K thing was a hoax, a myth, a fabrication…"

"Yeah, no shit!"

Then he said something that really made my night,

"I can't wait until you get here. It's going to be just like the old days. Love you, man."

Our call ended but I held the phone for a few minutes longer with only one thought rolling through my mind. It really was time for me to fold 'em.

44. The Final Reckoning

The rules about storytelling are timeless, steadfast and eminent. Perhaps the most important rule is a tale must have a beginning, a middle and an end. With respect to my radio journey of some fifty years, I will say my middle has become significantly bigger than when I started.

So, I began working at the Big Bongo in a Box software company, that catchy code name had stuck, and it was fantastic collaborating with Billy again. We kept those software engineers busy with our ongoing requests for new Bongo features. One day, I asked one of the principals,

"Why headquarter in Cleveland when most of the software in the world is being developed on America's west coast?"

He explained that he and his partner wanted to be near music heritage, so they chose the home city of the Rock and Roll Hall of Fame. That venue opened its doors on the first day of 1995 and it houses an amazing collection of all things rock 'n roll. My first tour of those hallowed halls gave me a renewed understanding and appreciation of the music that has always been central in my life. The beautiful pyramid shaped building was designed by I.M. Pei, the same architect who gave us the new entryway to the Grand Louvre in Paris.

In addition to all the garments, guitars and gear in the museum, I have always been weirdly attracted to the two pieces of Otis Redding's plane that hang on a wall there. I get goosebumps seeing the double shades of green on the white fuselage which spell out his name. I have no idea what a shrink might say about that, but I take it as a sobering reminder that we all have a final reckoning; we just don't know when or where.

For those who have made this journey with me, please don't ever feel sorry for little Herbie Klotenfelder from Dayton, Ohio. You see, Billy and I helped create a successful internet service to play, or as we say now, stream your favorite music on computers, televisions, cell phones and smart devices scattered around your home. All you have to do is bark out the order, "Bongo, play Sonny Joe's playlist" or "Bongo, play some new music I might like," and the songs begin.

I also took a few years away from the software business to consult radio stations in every state of the union and a half dozen countries around the world. After reaching a few million miles in the frequent flyer programs, I returned to Cleveland and again worked with Billy until we both retired in December of 2016.

My love life and the fate of my former partners should have scared off any smart woman, but a great lady walked into my life shortly after my mother passed away. She wasn't at all fearful of my past and the more time we spent together the less we wanted to ever be apart. We became the loves of each other's lives, and we married. She's a scientist for a chemical company, and we have two wonderful, smart twin girls, Polly and Ester. Okay, if you're laughing, I must still have it.

My wife of twenty years has always been a schoolteacher. Her bravery of volunteering during a global pandemic really made me proud. Sorry, but I am not going to reveal her name or the names of our girls. By working in software and on the internet, I have learned it's all too easy to lose various aspects of privacy. Protecting my family from cruel or malicious internet trolls is my goal. Sure, the girls have Facebook, Twitter and TikTok, but they have been schooled, maybe brainwashed, by their mother and father not to overdo it. They are secure in their own minds and bodies to know only idiots misuse the online presence of others. Our girls have been taught how to avoid the blue meanies.

The remarkable thing about working for a startup is your early paychecks are small, but boy oh boy once those stock options kick in a much different story unfolds. Billy and I got huge payouts every time our company was bought and sold, and I'll also mention those quarterly royalties from design patents and licensing agreements are easy to digest.

Billy and his wife, yes, he too finally settled down and moved to Arizona, while us Klotenfelder empty nesters landed in Florida. He and I still talk, just about every day, and we have a plan to memorialize all our experiences in a book with the working title *Crazy Radio Stories*, but only time will tell if that ever happens. Why, just yesterday we reminisced about that outrageous DJ Joey Reynolds, who told the tale of what he did after being fired from a radio station, "On my way out, I took off my shoes and nailed them to the station manager's door with a note that demanded, 'Fill these!'" Now there's one that should definitely make it into the book.

It's bittersweet reflecting on the magic of what radio once was to us and our millions of listeners, and the voice-tracked, predictable, robotic product it's become today. It's like that hardworking parking lot attendant who buys a lottery ticket and wins four million dollars. The next thing you know, he's dead. The police say his wife didn't poison him, but we knew that's exactly what happened when she got married a week later and left the country. Or how about that hard-working PD who builds an amazing radio station for an owner who suddenly sells out, poisons the dreams of his staff and jets off to the south of France leaving only disruption and a new temperamental owner in his wake.

There were so many moments that made me want to leave radio. Like the time I witnessed a station owner throw a chair through the conference room plate glass window because his sales staff didn't meet their monthly goals. I wasn't about to walk on glass for that bastard, but I never let him or any other radio nutjob get me down. My love of broadcasting persisted.

There has been some justice, of sorts, in the business of radio and records. After that radio consultant was murdered, the state of Missouri jailed the wrong person, but a prison priest believed the wrongfully condemned man and the real killer was eventually found and convicted. That insane woman who shot and murdered industry titan Charlie Minor got fifteen years to life for murder and another four years because she used a gun. Those additional years were due to a well-defined law in the State of California. As I write, McClure is still in prison and has been denied parole four times. Her next hearing will take place late in 2022.

It started out so divinely innocent, but radio eventually disowned, then devoured, its lifeblood. When college students realized all the action was on the internet and TV, they stopped wanting to work at college radio stations. In fact, dozens of university stations have been sold to public radio corporations. Young people today want to be social media influencers, not DJs.

I am not an old, disgruntled radio guy complaining about how things turned out. My life in the industry hasn't been a tale of renewal, redemption or retribution. Don't think of me as an aging disc jockey getting fired after many years of work. You won't find me down at the dock screaming, "I could have been a contender!" Sonny Joe the radio guy was one lucky son of a bitch, and just like a person in any other job he had the ups and the downs, the sorrows and the parades.

I have but one regret; I never got a full, four-year college diploma. But then again, no one ever needed a degree to work in radio. Oh, back in the day a First, Second or Third-Class Radiotelephone Operator License was required, but that was just to power the transmitter up and down, adjust its power settings and log meter readings to verify the station wasn't creating illegal interference to others.

People ask me, "Why radio?" and my response is always the same, "Because it's so damn much fun." It was like the first time your neighborhood buddy took you downstairs to his game room and played the Beatle's *Sgt. Pepper's Lonely Hearts Club Band* album for you. That very first listen made you feel something special inside, and that very same reaction returned every time you heard one of those songs again.

I loved music and wanted to turn on the folks "out there" to great songs. It was so cool and rewarding to finally achieve that opportunity. I remember after making love to a past girlfriend we put on Led Zeppelin's *Stairway to Heaven.* It was a spanking brand-new song then, and when it ended, we questioned whether what we just heard was better than our experience between the sheets. Well, it was seven minutes and fifty-five seconds long, but who counted?

For those of you who aren't radio insiders, I understand your lack of enthusiasm. I vividly remember coming home from college with one of my first airchecks from the university radio station. I played my high school girlfriend the telescoped, ten-minute cassette tape of my Herbie da K routine. When it was over, I stopped the tape and looked up seeking her approval. She said,

"That's great, but why is the music cut out? That's the best part."

I died a thousand deaths with that comment, and soon after she was no longer my girlfriend. We both survived, me on the radio and she in the Peace Corps.

It's difficult to describe an experience to a person whose frame of reference is so far removed from yours, but here, right now, I'm about to take my best shot at doing exactly that. I want you to understand and feel the excitement of working on the air at a radio station.

It's nearly time for your shift as you pull open the heavy studio door, walk inside and have a brief chit chat with the DJ you are following. Sometimes that disc jockey had courteously gathered and stacked your commercial carts and would say, "Hey, I pulled your first hour." As her last song plays, the changing of the guard takes place. The first thing you do after sitting down behind the control board is adjusting the height of the "air chair," and if you're lucky the damn thing wasn't destroyed by Dynamite Dickie, the fat-ass all-night guy. You raise the chair to a height that gives you complete and comfortable command over the audio console.

In earlier days, the volume controls were rotary knobs but today they're vertical faders. There's one pot for each audio source, including the studio microphones, turntables, cart machines, reel-to-reel tape decks, telephone audio, feeds from other studios and, in many cases, network newscasts. Below each fader are buttons that turn the audio on and off or start and stop the turntables, tape recorders and cart machines. Fancy consoles have lighted buttons to indicate the state of each device. For example, when a turntable is playing its start button glows green. If you have a thoughtful engineer, he has marked each fader with his Dymo label maker. Hung on the wall above you and aimed downward are two high quality speaker systems you can play as loud as you can stand. They will make your ears bleed long before they distort. The console has rotary volume controls for those speakers and your headphones.

As one record is playing you must cue the next. A switch on the console routes the audio from the turntable about to be cued to a separate speaker, usually located under the control board. You cue a vinyl record by using your finger to spin it forward on the felt turntable until the opening sound is heard, then spin it backward to the point just before the audio begins. The scratching sound coming from the cue speaker is the same heard today from rapper DJs. Cueing requires precision, too close to the audio and you'll get a horrid whirl-up sound during the beginning of the song as the turntable motor comes up to speed, a novice mistake. If you cue too far from the start of audio your show becomes loose, and it goes without saying that only tight is right.

After having your next song cued and ready to go, you check the commercial log to see which spots and promos need to air in the upcoming break, then you grab those carts and load them into the playback machines. That's when you start thinking about what you will say and how you will fire off all the carts to get from the ending of one song to the beginning of the next. So, while the listeners are enjoying the previous DJ's last song, you are busy behind the scenes and may even have the monitors turned down low so you can concentrate. You're not there to relish the music. Yes, it's fun, but the bottom line is you're on the job and there are things to do.

There are numerous processing devices between the console and the transmitter collectively known as the "audio chain." An engineer carefully tunes these components, and a gifted technician can make a radio station sound amazing. One such device is an audio compressor. It "squeezes" the minute differences in the sound level of a voice, giving punch and presence to every spoken word. If reverberation is active somewhere in the audio chain, your voice in the headphones sounds as if you are on stage with a sustaining echo rushing at you from the back of the theater. That powerful feeling of using your voice and your hands to produce an audio dance for the listeners is electrifying and never gets old. It's empowering to be the maestro, totally in control behind the board, and the ladies and men come 'round and want to be with you, delivering an added benefit of this occupation, which is, but never feels like, work.

As the previous jock's last song is ending, you slip on your headphones, then pick that perfect place in the fade or cold ending to open your mic and begin your "outro." When you speak, your voice travels instantly through all the audio chain gear, and if the engineer has done his or her job properly, the voice you hear in your headphones is like that of a god or goddess. That instant feedback of your powerfully processed voice bursting into those loud headphones vibrates all the joy synapses of your brain.

DJs made millions for radio station owners, but only the crème de la crème made big bucks themselves. There were franchise talents who could bring an audience from one station to another in the same market, but when they left the nest for the greener pastures of another city sometimes the magic didn't make the move. As the Portable People Meters were rolled out, a stale morning show that once did well in the diary ratings might now be a case of, "Houston we have a problem." With electronic devices now capturing actual listening, the ratings of some outdated morning shows dropped severely.

As time wore on, radio stations launched sophisticated research projects such as perceptual studies, focus groups and music tests to uncover listener opinions about radio personalities, programming content and positioning statements. Most of this research data was valuable, but some amateurs made mistakes and implemented changes based on small samples or poor methodologies. Even with a solid and well-designed study, there were times a PD found it difficult to stop playing a song they liked because it didn't test well. Favoring science over feelings, however, made a positive impact on ratings, and formal research became part of the radio game.

Labor unions were once powerful agents of change in terms of working conditions and policies, but they faded with industry deregulation and loopholes owners found in contracts. We came a long way from the International Alliance of Theatrical Stage Employees (IATSE) and the International Brotherhood of Electrical Workers (IBEW) throwing bricks at DJs who crossed the striking engineers' picket line. The organized labor unions held on to theatres, stadiums and motion pictures, but they weren't successful at stopping automation from taking their jobs in radio.

Competition has always made radio better. When a station got fat and lazy, a new upstart would pop up in the market to prove the king had no pants. Radio programmer John Sebastian, no relation to the singer, put Boston's WCOZ on the air, and I am sure WBCN felt no worry because they held the throne, but it took only a couple of rating periods before they were defeated. No one in radio is ever safe from an attack, and many bodies have been thrown to the roadside as proof of that statement's truth.

There are times when a station throws caution to the wind to be competitive. Consider the case of the Sacramento radio station that devised a contest with the prize being a Nintendo Wii (pronounced "wee") video game console. This was in 2007 when the Wii was fresh, immensely popular and scarce in stores. The station named the contest

"Hold your wee for a Wii." Contestants were given many bottles of water to drink, and whoever lasted the longest without a bathroom break would win the prize. The woman who came in second died a few hours after the contest due to "water intoxication," a known and true medical condition. That station not only lost a listener, but they were sued and ended up paying sixteen and a half million dollars for wrongful death. So, you see, there are times radio shoots itself in the foot with overzealous sales and promotion departments.

People change and radio had to change, but I have some thoughts on what would have kept our industry from the lions, tigers, and bears of deregulation. First, let's all acknowledge that Ronald Reagan, Bill Clinton, and a bunch of rich investors pushed broadcasting laws and rules to accommodate banks and large corporations at the expense of radio's art and audience. Those large networks and broadcast corporations produced the nightly news, and if the politicians kept them happy, they might catch a break on how the media reported their latest scandals.

Broadcast deregulation was designed by those who emphatically believed that fewer rules and fewer people in charge was a grand idea. Now we know this incontrovertible force of deregulation didn't serve the public, it just put more money into fewer people's pockets.

Perhaps you're wondering why deregulation was damaging to radio. In and of itself, technology was not injurious, but what it eliminated is distressing. There is nothing inherently wrong with voice tracks. Some broadcasters used the technique on all of their seven FM stations well before deregulation, but that was mostly for special programming or artist spotlights. Nowadays, most of the people talking to you through the radio have no understanding of or feelings for the place where you live, and a vital element of local broadcasting has gone missing. Should something terrible happen in your town and you need to know what to do or where to go, you can no longer depend on the radio for information.

The Final Reckoning

I confess that I may have helped move radio into this phase, but I'm proud of the things we once did to serve our audience. Deregulation forced owners to concentrate on one question. How do we do this with fewer people so we can make more money? When an industry forces job cuts in America, it's just as ruinous as outsourcing.

There was one major financial assumption embedded in the rush to own radio properties; things would always get better. The financial fat cats took out huge mortgages, far beyond the values of the radio stations they bought, then drastically stripped expenses and added tons of commercials to stay in the game, all to the detriment of the product.

Some heritage broadcasters willed their stations to their kids, and those offspring survived for as long as they could, but eventually the lure of a tremendous payout seduced them into selling. It was all too tempting, and greed was a major ingredient in the poison that finally ended the era of individual radio owners. The cost of entry and competing was now too great for a little guy to own a radio property in a major market. Perhaps you are asking, "Why does it matter?"

Radio should be a source of diverse opinions, presentations, points of view, music and other content. When homogenization takes over the airwaves, it's next to impossible for a new format to be discovered or created. It's been said that was the purpose of all those HD channels, but to this date no one has created a highly rated, breakout format on an HD signal.

Broadcasting has grown up much too quickly but giving up our youth was somewhat of a blessing. DJs used to make off color jokes, poke fun at homosexuals and disrespect women. In the early 1970s, a major Boston talk show host said, "Women have no place on the radio." It did take women a seriously long time to get on-air radio jobs, and even longer to become music directors, programming heads, general managers and, finally, presidents and CEOs, but they did it. Radio was slow on the uptake but not deaf to the marching beat of progress and liberation.

True Radio Confessions

As much as I disdain those right-winged talk show hosts, I know it would be wrong to censor, cancel or castrate them, although there are times… The best way to effect changes on a media platform is to take away its income. A sponsor boycott is the most powerful radio and television programmer in the land, because the stockholders of large public companies absolutely despise reduced revenue and demeaning publicity. One thing I will say with certainty, goofballs like Alex Jones spouting their lies are useless, hurtful, mendacious bastards who make radio ugly, not diverse. They should not be allowed to reproduce.

On the other hand, those gifted radio performers will forever have my respect. I was always in awe when WABC's Dan Ingram would do a perfectly funny and relatable talk-up over a song intro and then fire off that substitute rim shot, his acapella name jingle, precisely before the song's vocal began. Let me tell you, that was goosebump radio magic!

Then there was the entertaining schtick of disc jockey Ron Britain working in the Windy City on WCFL, owned and operated by the Chicago Federation of Labor. His nighttime antics captivated this young radio boy when that large signal skipped its way into Dayton. I should also mention WCFL's Barney Pip. His thin, high-pitched patter gave me inspiration and understanding that content was vastly more important than a deep, resonant voice.

Sometimes a radio personality must quickly respond to tragedy. Here's the story that unfolded one particular night in 1977, when my on-air disc jockey called me at home to share the news bulletin about Lynyrd Skynyrd's plane crash,

"Boss, what should I do?"

I told him to read the news report verbatim in a calm and serious voice, then play nothing but the band's music for the rest of his show. I also told him to take phone calls from listeners and play the best of them on the air between the songs. He asked more than once if it would be okay to break the format. I explained that sometimes radio must stop the format to tell the truth, show its feelings and become the heart of the audience. When radio fails to be live, it might as well be dead. That young broadcaster went on to do one of the most sensitive, awe inspiring and heartfelt tributes imaginable. I don't think I've ever heard better.

Then there was that night in Abilene, Texas when four twisters hit the ground and tore through the town. Local radio station KRBC opened its phone lines, and the listeners gave up-to-the-second eyewitness reports over the air so the audience could track the demons coming to get them. That's exactly what local radio always did best... past tense.

I love music radio, always have, always will, but the radio I love most is that of the past. I hate this manufactured, voice-tracked, rancid pablum that oozes out of radio speakers across the nation these days. We cannot hope for a return to the past, but we can certainly take pride in knowing we were effective. We played the song that encouraged a first kiss, we rotated the tunes that ended an unjust war, we shared a joke that either got a laugh, got us scolded or got us fired. It all unfolded so quickly and ended so suddenly. The quagmire of ratings, corporations, stockholders and endless commercial breaks sucked the breath out of everything radio once was. I fear that's here to stay.

When I got back to the Cincinnati airport that cold and cloudy December morning, I was eager to board the plane, fly home to Florida and ask my wife the most important question, "What's for dinner?"

I watched out the window to the east as the airplane climbed through the cloud cover, when suddenly the sky became drenched with golden sunlight. As I gazed at the horizon, all the thoughts and feelings of my life rushed into my mind, leaving a warm and comforting peace in my heart.

I thought about Billy and all the rest of us college kids back in the day, naïve yet nurtured by each other. It was pure, innocent and real. We were making radio and playing music while hanging out in our private electronic clubhouse. We were little radio freaks, free and unmotivated by money, ratings, bosses or lawyers. We had our run, and then it was done. Despite all I did since those youthful days, somehow those early memories persist and touch me the most.

Last night's party was nothing less than a wake-up call for radio itself. As for me, I don't want to hear one more "tall tale" about how great it all was. I don't need any crazy radio stories because I was actually there. I lived them, I loved them, I know exactly how all of it felt, and no one can ever take that away from me.

Glossary

7-7-7 Rule   A 1953 FCC rule that stipulated no company could own more than seven AM radio stations, seven FM radio stations and seven television stations.

AC   Adult Contemporary: A radio format featuring pop songs from soft to upbeat but no rock.

Actuality   Recorded voice of a newsmaker typically played during a newscast.

Add   A new song added to the playlist of a radio station is known as an add.

Ads   Commercials, advertisements, spots.

Aircheck   A recording of a radio show, with all elements other than the disc jockey removed, a process known as "telescoping."

Air Name   The name a disc jockey uses on the air, which is typically not his or her legal name.

Air Studio   An acoustically treated room where broadcasts originate.

Airplay   An audio entity that plays over the air is said to have airplay.

Airs / Aired / Airing   Is broadcast / Was broadcast / Is being broadcast

AM

Amplitude Modulation: A radio transmission process in which audio information modulates (varies) the amplitude (height) of the carrier wave, which is then detected in the receiver and reconverted to sound.

AOR

Album Oriented Rock: An evolution of the Progressive FM format featuring selected tracks from extraordinarily successful rock record albums with more sophisticated song rotation controls.

Arbitron

A company that measured radio listening in the United States from 1949 until its acquisition by the Nielsen company in 2013.

Average Quarter Hour

The average number of persons listening to a particular station for at least five minutes during a fifteen-minute period. Often abbreviated as AQH.

Block Programming

Different formats or musical genres broadcast on a radio station throughout a day or week.

Board

Audio console, control board, console, desk, mixer: A control surface with buttons, switches and faders used by a DJ to start and stop audio events, open and close microphones and other audio sources and control the volume levels of all.

Break

The elements between the ending of one song and the beginning of another which typically consists of disc jockey patter, commercials, promos, jingles and sometimes news.

Call Letters / Calls / Call Sign

The legal name of a radio station. In the US, each station name consists of three or four capital letters unique to each station, such as WABC.

Glossary

Cart   A tape cartridge, used for decades in broadcasting to record and play back commercials, promos, songs, news actualities and other audio elements.

CHR   Contemporary Hit Radio: a radio format featuring the most popular current songs across diverse musical genres. Originally called Top 40.

Clock   Also known as a format clock, specifies which music category to play at various positions within an hour. A clock may be a graphical pie chart or instructions in a computerized music scheduling system.

Cold End   A song that doesn't fade-out but ends abruptly or with a sustained chord.

Cold Start   A song with no instrumental intro that immediately begins with a vocal

Console   See Board

Copy   A script written or typed on paper and read by a DJ either live on the air or recorded for repeated playback. The word typically refers to the text of a commercial but can refer to other content such as dialogue for a comedy sketch.

Cue   The process of readying an audio element for instant airplay at the push of a button.

Daypart   A ratings construct that defines a part of a day or days, such as 3 p.m. to 7 p.m. Monday through Friday or 6 a.m. to midnight Monday through Sunday.

Daytimer   An AM radio station licensed to broadcast only between sunup and sundown.

Dead Air   Silence on a radio station, typically caused by a technical problem or flustered disc jockey.

Delisted   The status of a radio station after disciplinary action by a ratings company for the station's fraudulent activity to influence ratings. The station's rating results aren't published causing a damaging economic impact.

Disco   A rhythmic, dance oriented musical style, a radio format based on that style or a discothèque nightclub.

DJ/Jock   Disc Jockey, jock: A radio presenter who plays recorded music.

The Dream   A recurring nightmare that just about every DJ experience, in which they are behind the control board, the song is ending, and they have nothing ready to play and no idea what to say or do next.

FCC   Federal Communications Commission: United States governing body which regulates radio and television broadcasting.

Format   The programming structure of a music radio station usually named after the genre of the music played.

FM   Frequency Modulation: A radio transmission process in which audio information modulates (varies) the frequency (width) of the carrier wave, which is then detected in the receiver and reconverted to sound.

Glossary

Free Form An early rock non-format with no structure. The on-air DJ selected all the music, typically wrapped around a theme.

Full-Service An older radio format, typically aired on an AM station, which featured a heavy emphasis on local news, civic events, traffic and weather, with music being a second-class entity.

GM General Manager: the highest-level manager of a local radio station who oversees the programming, engineering and sales departments.

Intro The instrumental opening of a song before the vocal begins.

License A legal document awarded by the FCC permitting a radio or TV station owner to broadcast a signal over the air.

Liner A positioning statement for a radio station typically typed on an index card and read live by disc jockeys.

Market The service area of a radio station which typically extends beyond its city of license.

MD Music Director: Maintains the station's music library, takes calls and visits from record promoters, schedules and prints music logs and assists the PD in selecting songs for airplay.

Mic Pronounced "mike," abbreviation of microphone.

Music Log A list of prescheduled songs for every hour of a radio station's music programming.

PD	Program Director: Manages the programming department of a radio station. Primary job duties are hiring, firing and scheduling DJs, constructing the station playlist and being responsible for every sound broadcast by their station.
Playlist	A list of all the songs played on a given radio station.
Portable People Meter	PPM: An electronic device worn by a participant in a radio ratings survey that collects data about station listening by the participant.
Post	A musical accent during the instrumental beginning of a song. Some songs have multiple posts.
Pot	Shortened form of potentiometer. A sliding or rotating electronic mechanism that adjusts volume level.
Production Director	The person who oversees all production at the radio station. Typically, he or she voices a good many of the station's recorded commercials and works with station disc jockeys to produce others.
Progressive FM Radio	An early rock format that brought some structure into the Free Form/Underground formats. Playlists were instituted and systems were developed to control song rotations.
Promo	A live or recorded promotional announcement describing a station's name, features, contests, upcoming concerts and the like.
Rating	A ratings term that expresses listenership as a percentage of population.

Glossary

Record Promoter An individual working for a record company or independently who visits radio station programmers urging them to play newly released songs.

RIAA Recording Industry Association of America: A trade organization that supports and promotes the creative and financial vitality of the major music companies.

Segue Blending the end of one audio element into the beginning of the next.

Selector A computer program that schedules a radio station's music log according to clocks and rules the PD specifies.

Seven Second Delay The process of broadcasting content seven seconds after it occurs, typically used for radio talk shows. A device between the studio and transmitter delays the signal and a "dump button" immediately stops the playback to prevent objectionable content from being broadcast.

Share A ratings term that expresses listenership as a percentage of total listeners.

Shift The time period of a radio show. "Sonny Joe will work the 10 p.m. to 2 a.m. shift tonight."

Simulcast Simultaneously broadcasting the same programming on two or more radio stations, a frequent practice in the 1960s.

Spots Commercials, advertisements, ads.

Sweeper   A short, prerecorded positioning statement or promotional announcement for a radio station usually played between two songs.

Stopset   A cluster of commercials played back-to-back.

Talk-Up   Disc jockey patter spoken over the intro of a song which ends exactly when the vocal begins.

Top 40   A radio format featuring the most popular current songs across diverse musical genres. This was the original name for the format known today as CHR, Contemporary Hit Radio.

Traffic   The process of gathering and readying commercials for broadcast and then scheduling them according to specifics in the sales agreement between the station and advertiser.

Underground   Nickname for an early rock non-format with no structure. The on-air DJ selected all the music, typically wrapped around a theme. The proper name for this un-format was Free Form.

Urban   A radio format consisting of all Black artists in various musical styles such as rhythm & blues, hip hop, disco and rap.

Voice Tracking   A technique in which a single disc jockey records breaks for multiple radio stations This saved station owners money but at the sacrifice of local content on the voice tracked stations.

Resume of Herbert A. Klotenfelder

A life-long radio guy whose career spans more than fifty years
AKA Sonny Joe McPherson
467 Maple Street
Dayton, Ohio
937-555-1212 / sjmp@SJMP.com

Skills

Entertaining musicologist, concise presentation, tight board, plays well with others

Experience

JAN 1969 to APR 1970

On-Air Talent / WBAT-FM, Ashtabula, Ohio

JUL 1970 to SEPT 1970

On-Air Talent / WNCR-FM, Cleveland, Ohio

JAN 1971 to SEPT 1972

On-Air Talent / KSFR, Santa Fe, New Mexico

SEPT 1972 to AUG. 1974

On-Air Talent - Production Director / KDKB, Phoenix, Arizona

SEPT 1974 to JUN 1978

D.C. Correspondent / R&R Magazine, Washington, D.C.

Jun 1978 to Oct 1979

Program Director / Disco99-FM, Indianapolis, Indiana

JAN 1982 to JAN 1984

On-Air Talent / KROY-FM, Sacramento, California

JAN 1985 to DEC 1986

On-Air Talent / KSJO, San Jose, California

JAN 1987 to JAN 1991

On-Air Talent / KZOK, Seattle, Washington

FEB 1992 to JAN 2000

Programming Strategist / KTFM Group, San Antonio, Texas

Education

SEPT 1968 to DEC 1969

University of Dayton

DJ and studio construction at campus radio station WVUD

JAN 1980 to SEPT 1981

University of Michigan, Dearborn

Associates Degree in Communication and Marketing

Thanks for the Help

Authoring a book isn't a simple task, but should you have the urge I suggest you take the plunge, even with the knowledge of how difficult it will be. Before you start, however, make sure you harvest the right words to tell your story and then get yourself a crack editor, just make sure he or she isn't *on* crack!

I could not even think of publishing a book without the editorial assistance of Kenny Lee Karpinski. This book is as much his as it is mine. We grew up together in radio, and during our fifty-year careers we worked together at three different companies. People freak out when I tell them that, and it's one of the key reasons we collaborate so well. If my English teacher at Brentwood High School, Mrs. Apple, or the great Vinny LaBarbera at Point Park University, were ever to read a first draft of my writing, they would gasp in shock. Kenny translates my gobbledygook into paragraphs that tell a story, and I offer him tremendous thanks for guiding me. You may have already guessed he appears in these pages. Kenny and first I met in college, and that should serve as a clue regarding the character he plays in my book.

I'm sure you realize that people do judge a book by its cover, and this one is no exception. The artwork is an homage to all those radio gypsies who traveled the country, sometimes the world, in search of an innovative station, a larger market, potential stardom or just more money. Ginger Sinton, an author in her own right, grew up in a radio and records family and was gracious to pause her university teaching career to render this book's cover. Radio broadcasters will get its theme immediately, and readers who don't work in the industry will understand the cover after perusing the pages it wraps.

My life partner for more than twenty years has been very flexible, patient and understanding with my routine of knocking out a book every year. I love J. Roxy Myzal and really appreciate her giving me the space and time to turn words into stories and books.

Thanks for the Memories

Shotgun Tom Kelly, Kent Burkhart, Lee Abrams, Austin Minor, Batt Johnson, Bill Tanner, Bob Wilson, Bobby Applegate, Dave Crowl, Howard Stern, Buddy Rich, Jeff Roteman, John Gorman, Mark Driscoll, Ed Weigle, Todd Storz, John Tyler, John Grinnan, Peggy Armstrong, Tom Yates, Ted Ferguson, Brian Gregory, Fred Fiske, Allen Shaw, Chris Hood, Paul Drew, Bob Henabery, Rosemary Winter, J.B. Stricklett, Wanda Ramos, Gary Burns, Buzzy Bennett, Chuck Brinkman, Bob Chrysler, Sandi Banister, Bo Wood, Bob Pittman, Randy Michaels, Tom Birch, Vic Cianca, Patsy Peters, E. Alvin Davis, Jessie, Billy Bass, Jon Wolfert, Robert W. Walker, Jim Schulke, Jon Sinton, Dennis Waters, Jack Armstrong, Don Davis, Ross Simpson, Tom Donohue, Denise Oliver, Scott Shannon, Malcolm Gladwell, Mike O'Harro, Brady Miller, Buzz Brindle, Walter Sabo, Robin Quivers, Steve Dahl, Dave Logan, Tom Daniels, Dick Byrd, John Sebastian, Rick Carroll, Kevin Metheny, Perry Stone, Kenny Reeth, Bob Rivers, Denny Sanders, Mara Davis, Ron Chavis, Simon Mayo, Louise Sahene, Fred Jacobs, Jackie Jenkins, Howard Page, Cecil Heftel, Jay Davis, Steve Conti, Humble Harv Miller, Bill Drake, Val Garris, Bob Elliot (consultant), Lee Michaels, Ed Siegel, Little Jimmy Roach, Trish Bell, Mitch Fuchs, Dennis McBroom, Carolyn Smith, Skip Finley, Dan Vallie, Carl Wagner, Hugh Wilson, Bob Reich, Richard Cohn, Morty Bender, Gary McKee, Howard Kalmenson, Charlie Minor, Ken Anthony, Joel Denver, Bob & Tom, Mark & Brian, Jim Quinn, Dick "Wilde Childe" Kemp, Erica Farber, Ken Nixon, Ralph Guild, Bob Elliott (Ft. Wayne), Bill Meeks, Ted Turner, Traci Douglas, Eric Hauenstein, John Landecker, Frank Cody, Richie Balsbaugh, Charlie Van Dyke, Sonny Joe White, [Your name here], and all the folks at the three-hundred-plus radio stations I consulted over twenty-five years on the road.

Should you not see your name listed, please don't think it's a lack of appreciation. My aging brain isn't quite what it used to be, and recollecting names and events is definitely a young man's game. [cheap microphone drop]

Other Books by Dwight C. Douglas

If God Could Talk: The Diary of a TV Journalist
Cable TV talk show host Jonas Bronck is approached by a friend who offers a guest who has never before appeared on television.

Donald Trump: Repeal, Replace, Impeach
A collection of daily diatribes from a delusional blogger covering the first two hundred days of America's 45th President in office.

If God Could Cry: The True Meaning of Mercy
Jonas Bronck, famous cable TV talk show host, leaves New York on a quest to find truth.

Gold, God, Guns & Goofballs: A Collection of Essays on America
This book is an accelerant to move the middle off their collective asses to do something positive for America.

How to Hire Great People: Tips, Tricks and Templates for Success
This short, easy-to-read book will help you recruit, review and refocus your new workers into the style and culture of your company.

MASHED POTATOES: Cancer, Covid & Comfort Food
A work of survival to motivate those who desire to get beyond Covid-19, beat cancer and defend our precious democracy.

Facebook Group
www.facebook.com/groups/1129845394493883

My Home Away from Home
www.dwightdouglas.com